SARAH HEGGER

Cover: Deranged Doctor Design
First Electronic Edition: October 2022

ISBN: 978-1-990731-12-9
ISBN: 978-1-990731-13-6

✿ Created with Vellum

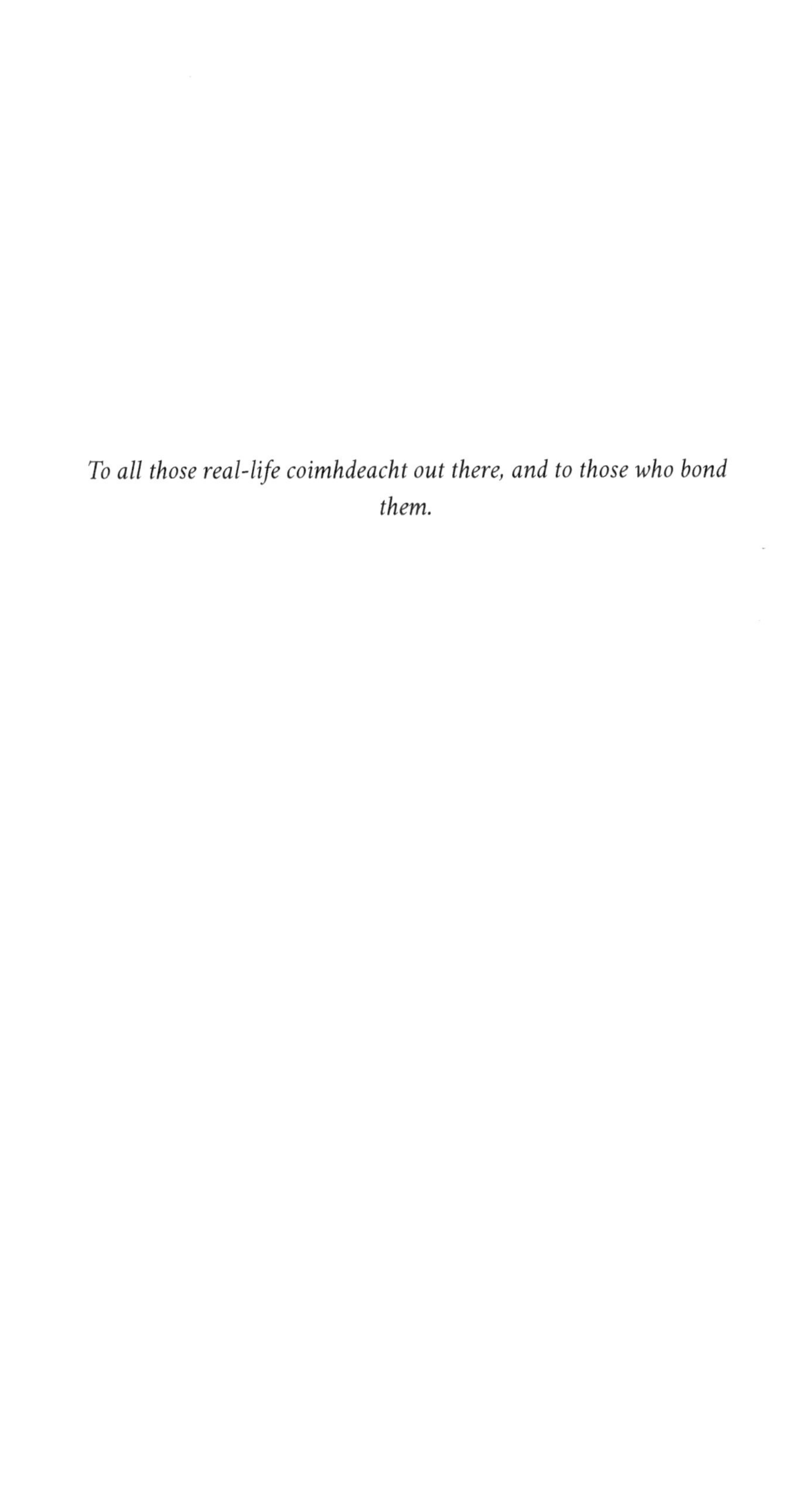

To all those real-life coimhdeacht out there, and to those who bond them.

CHAPTER ONE

Two weeks in Canada, and nary a sight or sound of the bloody earth point. Needing to get away from the stifling atmosphere in their room, Sinead paced the lobby of their Montreal hotel. It was too dangerous to go out on her own, so she stuck to the communal area in front of the check-in desk and pretended to study a stack of tourist brochures.

Cirque de Soleil looked amazing, but they were not here on a jolly.

Alannah had stayed upstairs tapping away at a laptop she'd brought with her from Baile. Alannah didn't have enough internet friends to be spending that amount of time online, so she was probably doing more research. Or avoiding talking to her. Things had been strained between them since their fight over Thomas.

Goddess, but Sinead wished Roderick was here. Tussling with his medieval mentality was just the outlet for her frustration she needed right now.

The Bonsecours Market brochure advertised everything from wind chimes to windbreakers. Alannah loved to shop. It was just her kind of place.

A warm touch at her nape startled her, and she jerked around.

A good ten feet away, a family of three teens, a Mom, and a Dad stood arguing. The mother looked up and offered her a tentative smile.

Sinead smiled back. No way one of them could have touched her and gotten over there again. Not the Asian couple waiting for the elevators either.

The touch came again, and Sinead leaped to her feet. There wasn't a soul within arm's reach, but that had felt exactly like a hand on the back of her neck. "Bloody hell," she whispered and shivered. The combined danger and uncertainty must be scrambling her brain.

Warmth stroked from her nape down her spine.

Sinead whirled.

The family were all staring at her, their argument momentarily forgotten.

"Allergies," Sinead muttered, and took her seat again.

She debated returning to the room, but there wasn't anything threatening about the feeling, and not one whiff of blood magic. Just to be sure, she took a stronger sniff of the air.

A smartly dressed woman in the hotel uniform approached her. "Can I help you?"

"No." Her spine tingled, and her skin flushed with warmth. "Thank you." Dammit, the sensation was sexual. She was losing her bloody mind, and her ovaries were coming along for the party.

The hotel employee was still looking at her.

"I'm...er...just having a look." She held up her handful of brochures. "Planning our itinerary and all."

"Lovely." The woman flashed her a professional smile. "Be sure to let the concierge know if we can help you make bookings or arrange transportation."

Transportation straight to the nearest vat of ice-cold water would be a good start. Sinead smiled, and the woman moved on.

Edging closer to a potted palm, she dangled her fingers over the edge and touched the soil in the container. Rose and cloves floated lightly through the air as she drew earth.

There!

Her magic zeroed in on the source of the sensation. Her head swung as if on a swivel and her gaze went straight to the open-plan restaurant at the far side of the lobby.

The soft bustle of the hotel disappeared. The people around her vanished.

All she saw was him.

Hair so dark it swallowed the light spilling from the soaring street-facing windows. Rich, olive skin over defined, bladed features. Eyes that almost seemed to glow. Not classically handsome, but a compelling face, beautiful in its uncompromising lines. And he was looking right at her.

Sinead's mouth dried, and the flush covered her entire body, peaking her nipples and rolling through her lower belly.

A white T-shirt stretched taut over his shoulders and chest.

And she was now officially ogling him.

But he was doing the same right back.

Their gazes locked, and she forgot to breathe.

Who are you? Her lips formed the words without her brain having a say.

He smiled, a flash of brilliantly white teeth in his darker face.

The man sitting opposite him turned and stared at her. She formed a vague impression of big, tall, dark, and handsome, but not much registered beyond the man she was caught in a leer-off with.

Panic swept through her. He was too much. Barraging sensations overwhelmed her, and she had to get away. The quiet *ping* of the lift sounded, and she scurried toward escape.

Sinead had no idea if the lift was going up or down, but it was getting away from him, and that was good enough for her.

Only after the lift doors swished closed did she draw a full breath again. She'd almost been expecting him to chase her, and a tiny part of her was bitterly disappointed he hadn't.

She pressed the button for their floor and tried to get a grip on herself. Dammit! He could have been one of Rhiannon's people. She needed to be more careful, and she probably needed to get bloody laid as well.

Her hands were still shaking as she swiped their room card and let herself in.

Alannah glanced up from the desk near the window. "Hi."

"Hi." Sinead grabbed a bottle of water off a bedside table and drained it.

Cocking her head, Alannah studied her. "You all right?"

"Uh-huh." She nodded. No sodding way she could explain what had just happened. Not that she had the right words anyway. Didn't really want to either. Instead, she pointed to the laptop. "Any luck?"

Their search had brought them to Montreal. Instead of the earth point, however, they'd found a construction site. A multi-storied office block, to be precise, exactly where they'd expected to find the earth point.

"Nothing." Alannah grimaced. "I have found a whole laundry list of strange stuff and woo-woo crap happening in and around Montreal." She scraped her hair back and tied it into a ponytail. "The best I can come up with is we work through them one by one and see if anything turns up."

It beat hanging out next to a construction site getting leered at by the supervisor. They'd tried that yesterday and been propositioned for a threesome. What the hell was it with people? She and Alannah were sisters. *Sisters, people!* They did not want to get hot and sweaty with a man sandwiched between them.

It was stress. The incident with the man in the lobby had to be some kind of panic attack. Sinead went with the best response she had. "Okay."

"None of the strange happenings seem to tie up." Alannah walked to the television unit and picked up the room service menu. "I couldn't find any kind of link."

"Hmm." Maybe her magic had gone on the blink. She hadn't caught even a whisper of the earth point near the construction site, and she had drawn earth moments before she'd spotted lobby hottie. Mags's magic was all twisted out of shape and not working properly. Same thing could have happened to her. "I could take a look. Two sets of eyes and all that."

Alannah glanced up from her menu. "You sure you're all right?"

"Perfect." She slapped a grin on her mug. "Cracking."

"Right." Alannah shook her head. "I'm hungry. I was going to order something."

"Splendid." Sinead motioned the menu. "I'll have a look after you."

"Do." Alannah studied her through narrowed eyes. "You're behaving oddly."

"Am not."

"Are too."

Being a twin was too bloody inconvenient sometimes. "It's nothing." She took the menu Alannah handed her. "Just my head playing tricks on me."

"What's nothing?" Alannah's undivided attention made her want to squirm. Keeping secrets, however, had never worked out well.

"I saw a man. In the lobby." She shrugged and tried to keep it light. "He kind of gave me the wig." In a manner of speaking. No need to go into salacious detail. "It's got me a bit stirred up."

"Don't do that," Alannah snapped. "Don't dismiss your

instincts. If he gave you the wig, then that's enough for me. We move hotels."

"Now?" Over the last two weeks, they'd been through a dizzying array of hotels and motels.

Alannah paused and frowned. "Well…no. But in the morning, definitely. And neither of us move from this room or each other's sight."

Sinead agreed wholeheartedly and nodded. "And thanks."

"For?"

"Not thinking I'm overreacting." The distance between them made it hard to talk to the one person who'd always been her go-to, and she felt adrift.

Alannah sighed. "Choose something to eat, and I'll order." She perched on the end of the bed, her head lowered. "I might be angry with you, Sinead, but I still love you, and we still have to work together."

"Right." Tears burned her eyes, and she hid them behind the menu. "I could go for a pint."

"Make that two," Alannah said. She ordered for them.

Television provided a welcome distraction as they lounged side by side on the bed and waited for room service.

Alannah turned to her. "What did he do?"

"Not much." The whole incident was probably an overreaction on her part. She was halfway to convincing herself she'd made the whole thing up. "He stared at me."

"He stared at you?" Alannah chuckled. "Men stare at you all the time."

Sinead struggled to find the right way to put the experience into words. "Not as intensely as this one did."

"Oh." Alannah went back to watching *MasterChef*. "He scared you."

"He did." Admitting any man scared her was like swallowing curdled milk.

"We'll change hotels tomorrow."

She took a deep breath and shoved the man from her mind. "Yup."

Their dinner arrived shortly thereafter, and Sinead committed her attention to an excellent club sandwich and fries. She couldn't call them chips here in Canada. Her beer took the edge off, and they settled in to watch a movie.

Alannah shifted beside her and yawned. "I thought I was over the jetlag."

"Yeah, me too." Sinead's eyelids felt heavy and her head fuzzy. The television swam in front of her gaze. Voices seemed to come from a long way off. "Alannah?" She didn't feel right. Tired was one thing, but this was different.

"I don't feel well." Alannah pressed a hand to her head. "I feel strange."

"Strange how?" Sinead didn't like how pale Alannah had gotten, and she shook her head to clear it.

The fog in her brain thickened.

Alannah slumped on the bed. Her eyes rolled back in her head.

Alarm shot through Sinead. "Alannah?" She shook her twin. "Alannah?"

"Sinead." Alannah grabbed for her hand. "Something's not right."

Black swarmed the edges of her vision, and Sinead fought against it, but it was like wading through thick wood glue. Darkness tugged at her limbs and her mind, inexorably dragging her in.

"Stay awake." She pulled at Alannah's hand to get her to her feet, but her grip lacked strength, and Alannah couldn't coordinate her limbs.

They'd been drugged. The thought sluggishly rose in her consciousness.

Alannah went limp.

Panic sounded dimly inside her, and she checked Alannah's

pulse. A steady, slow beat reassured her. Sinead tried to move, get off the bed. She needed to pull them both out of this room.

Her legs wouldn't move. Her hand slipped from Alannah's neck. She rolled and tumbled off the bed. The floor lurched and swayed. She tried to get her hands beneath her shoulders to push herself up. Her head wouldn't lift.

The door opened.

Wavy figures stood against the light from the hallway, moving toward them.

"She's still awake," a man said.

Another man answered, "Not for long."

Booted feet and jeans approached.

Sinead desperately tried to keep them in focus, but her vision blurred. The dark closed in.

"Get the other one," the first man said. "I'll take her."

She felt weightless, floating, and then nothing.

CHAPTER TWO

The conversation Warren had been dreading was upon him. He was surprised Debra had waited this long for answers. She'd moved into the room Baile had readied for her the day of her arrival and had spent most of her time with Taylor. He hadn't wanted to stir things up and had kept the truth about Baile to himself. Last night, Niamh had made it clear he needed to tell Debra before she found out some other way.

This morning, Debra had woken too late to join the rest of the coven for breakfast. Taylor sat beside Debra at the kitchen table while Warren made his ex-wife a late breakfast of eggs on toast and coffee. Debra was never her best when she was hungry. And he was going to need all the help eggs, toast, and great coffee could buy him.

Niamh had made herself scarce, but he could feel her lurking in his mind, there and waiting if he needed her. Despite Debra now being in the castle, Taylor had slept in the suite with him and Niamh for the last two weeks. She was still having bad dreams.

Not that Warren was feeling amorous with his ex sleeping a few doors down.

The she-wolf had expedited matters by trotting into the kitchen this morning with her litter behind her. The pups had more than doubled in size and were looking more wolfish every day. The she-wolf was weaning them, and a soft growl warned even the most adventurous of pups away.

"Gosh." Debra eyed the forty-kilogram animal with trepidation. "She really does look rather vicious."

Since her blessing let her know stuff before it happened, Taylor had made sure to be in the kitchen with him and Debra for this conversation. She slipped from her seat and went over to the wolf. She held her hand out for permission to touch, and after getting a nudge from the wolf, smoothed the fur over her head. "She's really gentle, Mum. You just have to be polite."

"Hmm." Debra looked at him for confirmation.

Warren nodded. "She's not very cuddly, but she's good with people." At least people she decided to be good with.

Debra tucked her hands under her thighs. "What's her name?"

"She doesn't really have one." Taylor plopped down beside the range. Pups swarmed all over her. "Niamh doesn't name any of the animals around here."

"Animals?" Debra nodded her thanks for the coffee and added cream and sugar. "I noticed there's quite the collection hanging around."

"It changes from day to day." Warren dropped her eggs on the toast and put the plate in front of her. "But yes. There are all sorts living at Baile." And more arriving every day. Just this morning, a hamster had scurried into their bedroom and made itself at home in his boots.

Debra frowned but tucked into her breakfast. "Isn't that unhygienic?"

"Not at all." Warren had to smile. House training with

Niamh translating meant no accidents inside. Not that all the animals really understood the why, but they did as Niamh asked. "Look around you."

Niamh nudged his mind. She wanted him to get things settled with Debra, so they didn't all have to guard their tongues around her. Besides, Niamh had reasoned, Taylor was her daughter, and she deserved to know the truth. The full truth.

He took a seat opposite Debra at the table and fiddled with his own mug as he hunted for the right words. There weren't really any. "Deb, we need to talk."

Debra stilled and went on high alert. "Oh-ka-a-a-y"

He didn't blame her. He couldn't think of a time in his life when someone telling him they needed to talk had ended in a conversation he'd enjoyed.

Niamh gave him another mental nudge.

Yup, he was stalling.

Taylor glanced at him and gave him an encouraging nod.

"There are some things you need to know." He cleared his throat. His palms were sweating, so he wiped them on his jeans. "About Baile. And Taylor."

"What's wrong with Taylor?" Debra stopped mid chew and stared at him. Her gaze flicked to Taylor. "Are you all right?"

Taylor smiled back. "I'm fine, Mum, but Dad and I really need to tell you some stuff."

"Yes, we do." His voice came out too eager.

Debra narrowed her eyes at him. "You're doing that thing."

"What thing?"

She pointed at his face. "That thing you do with your eyes when you're about to tell me something I don't want to hear."

Warren nearly asked her to tell him what he did with his eyes, but Niamh gave him a stronger push to get on with it. She then sent him a mental image of him being squinty-eyed. Apparently, he did do an eye thing when he was getting ready to drop a bomb. So much for a poker face. And he was still not getting on with it.

Where to start? Where to start?

Julie Andrews chirruped in his head. *Let's start at the very beginning. A very good place to start.*

"Well, Deb, you know how you had to go to Hermione because you couldn't get into the castle?"

"Strangest thing." Debra finished her breakfast and pushed the plate away. "I kept driving, and I could see the castle, but it always seemed to be around the next bend."

"Right." He sipped his coffee to ease a case of cottonmouth. Debra was going to lose her shit—spectacularly—when he told her the truth about Baile, Taylor, the coven, and magic. And he'd been married to her and had a front-row seat to plenty of Debra losing her shit. "And you must have heard some rumors about Baile around the village."

She snorted. "Bloody nonsense."

"The thing is, Deb, that it's not. Not all of it anyway."

"Not what?"

"Nonsense."

"Which part?"

"What did you hear?"

"Warren." Debra leaned back in her chair. "You're not making any sense."

Niamh heartily agreed. He sent her the thought to get her ass in here if she wanted to be part of the conversation so badly.

Her amusement rippled through him like a gentle, balmy breeze.

"The rumors around the castle speak of witches, a coven." He took another desperate sip of his now lukewarm coffee. "They attribute strange happenings to the people of Baile."

Debra laughed and flapped a hand. "Some crazy woman stopped me and bent my ear about some woman who heals cancer. She wanted to get her son up here. Apparently, he has diabetes." She shook her head. "People are so gullible." Her expression softened into sympathy. "Still, I suppose if your kid is sick…"

"It's Bronwyn." Warren took the plunge.

Debra blinked at him. "The Bronwyn I met? Are her babies sick?"

"No." He needed to get them back on track. "Bronwyn is the one who healed the child with cancer. She's a healer."

Debra laughed. "Oh, go on now. Pull the other one."

From behind her, Taylor grimaced.

Yeah, he got it. So far, not a good beginning. He pushed his coffee cup aside and leaned on the table. "It's not a joke, Deb. Bronwyn is a healer, and she did cure that girl of cancer."

She stopped laughing and blinked at him. "But…" Debra pushed a hand through her hair and sat back. "I don't under-stand. That's impossible."

"Actually, I think you'll find a lot of what you'd think was impossible, is—in fact—quite possible. The girl was Gemma, and she's Hermione's daughter. She had a brain tumor and Bronwyn healed it."

Eyes wide, Debra opened her mouth and shut it again. "This is not funny, Warren."

"I know that, and I'm not joking." Debra wouldn't stay quiet for long, so Warren forged forward. "And it's not just Bronwyn who has special abilities. All the women here have gifts. Unique gifts that are all magical." He winced at the last word, but what else could he call it?

"Magical?" Debra's eyes widened. "That can't be…" Her confusion cleared into a frown. "I don't know what you're trying to do here, Warren, but it's cruel and stupid, and I'm not going to fall for it."

"He's telling you the truth." Niamh strolled into the kitchen and put a hand on his shoulder. "Bronwyn is a healer, and she healed Gemma. I am a guardian, which means I have an affinity with animals." She motioned the pups playing with Taylor. "And those really are wolves."

There was a long silence in which Debra gaped at Niamh. And then she exploded into action.

"What!" Debra shot to her feet. "Taylor! Get away from them."

"Mum—" Taylor tried to cut in.

Debra lurched for Taylor, grabbed her, and put herself bodily between her and the wolves. "Get back." She shooed the pups. "Get back."

The black male pounced on her ballet flat.

Debra shook her foot and looked like she might kick him.

"No." Niamh got there before Debra could carry through and picked up the pup. "I understand you're upset, but I cannot allow you to hurt them."

"They're wolves," Debra shrieked. "Wild animals. I'm not letting my child get eaten." She scowled at Warren. "You lied to me. You said they were dogs." She gaped and clutched Taylor close to her. "You let my daughter near wild, savage killers."

"Stop, Deb." Warren spoke firmly, hoping to cut through the building tirade. "Those are babies too." He pointed at the pups. "And yes, I lied. Because I had a lot to tell you and I couldn't do that over the phone."

"Take a seat." Niamh used the tone she sometimes used when soothing a hurt animal. "We'll explain everything, and then you can ask whatever you like."

Amazingly, Debra did take a seat, but she kept Taylor tucked to her side.

"There are seven witches in the coven," Niamh took the seat beside her. "Besides Bronwyn, Maeve, and me, there is Mags who is a seer, and the twins Alannah and Sinead who aren't here right now, but they are wardens."

"Wardens?" Debra's arm tightened around Taylor. "What does that mean?"

"It means they take care of the earth and the things in it and growing on it." Niamh glanced at Taylor.

Warren read her concern for Taylor through the bond.

"You said seven." Debra stared at him as if she could incinerate him.

"Warren is not really a caretaker here," Niamh said. "He's mine."

"Well, I know that—"

"He's my guardian and protector. I am not able to use my magic to harm people in any way, even if my life is in danger. Warren is here to make sure I'm not harmed." Niamh kept her tone neutral but firm, like she was training Debra. "Roderick is the same, but his witch is Maeve."

Debra glanced at him. "That sounds dangerous."

"It can be." Warren pushed up his shirtsleeve. "These markings appeared on my skin when I arrived here. They're not tattoos. They are the markings that tell my story as Niamh's coimhdeacht, or warrior guardian."

Shaking her head, Debra glanced from one to the other of them. "You can't be serious."

"Mum." Taylor took her hand. "You really need to keep an open mind here and listen. I know this is a lot, but you need to try."

Debra snapped her mouth shut, but hostility built in her eyes.

"We're here to restore balance to the world," Niamh said. "Each of our gifts draws its strength from one of the four elements." She ticked them off on her fingers. "Earth, fire, water, and air."

Warren took over the explanation. "Look around you, Deb, at the shit going on in the world right now. Things are so skewed and out of whack. So much happens that doesn't seem to make sense. Crazy politicians doing whatever they want to serve themselves. Disease. War. Unadulterated greed in some places, while millions starve in others."

"But isn't that the way things have always been?" Debra kept her gaze locked on him. A muscle twitched near her eyes. She was seconds away from losing it completely.

"Right." He wished he was better with words. "But it seems to be getting worse. Despite thousands of years of evolution, we seem to be right back where we started. We"—he gestured to Niamh, himself, the castle, and Taylor—"believe the reason behind all of this is a lack of balance. Restoring that balance is the first step to going forward into something better."

"Maeve is a…witch?" The eye muscle jerked and spasmed. "Sweet, little Maeve?"

"She is." Warren decided to skip the part about Maeve being hundreds of years old and having reanimated from a statue. There was only so much ground they could cover in one conversation. "She's a spirit walker."

"A what now?" Debra frowned.

"She can commune with the souls of witches past," Niamh said. "I understand she can see and contact all spirits, but she's mostly here for the dead witches."

"That's six. Not that I believe a bloody word of this drivel, but that's six." Debra glanced at Taylor, stopped, and cocked her head. "You said seven witches."

"We did." Niamh smiled at Taylor. "We recently discovered a new witch."

Comprehension dawned, and Debra shook her head and gripped Taylor even tighter. "No."

"Yes, Mum." Taylor wriggled free enough to meet Debra's gaze. "You remember when I was little, and I said I was magic." She shrugged. "Turns out it wasn't just my imagination."

This time, Debra sounded like a wounded animal as she moaned, "No."

"My element is water." Taylor raised her chin. "And I'm a seer."

"This is not possible," Debra whispered.

"It's not only possible," Niamh said, "it's true." She held one hand out placatingly. "We didn't expect it. Warren had no idea. None of us did."

Taylor held her mother's gaze. "Neither did I until I walked into the caverns and bond...found out I had the gift."

"Warren?" Debra looked at him like a drowning woman, her expression warring between desperation and fury.

"I was bloody clueless," he said. "To tell you the truth, I was angry as hell about it when I found out."

Taylor nodded. "He really was."

Debra rubbed her temples. "I don't understand why you're all saying these things. I don't understand what any of this means."

"It means I belong here," Taylor said. "And now you do too."

"I can't stay here." Debra jerked upright. "And I'm not going to stay here." She stood and tugged Taylor to her feet. "And neither are you." Her face flushed, and she glowered at Warren. "You bastard! I knew I should never have left her here with you. I knew you'd do something ridiculous, but this is a new low. Even for you, Warren." She gathered steam, her chest rising and falling as she panted. "Well, you've done it now. You'll be lucky if I let you see her this side of her eighteenth birthday. I can't believe you would do this. You...you..."

"Mum." Taylor's eyes filled with tears. "He didn't do anything."

Debra glared at him. "You'll be hearing from my lawyers, and I hope your magic bloody friends can help you find your daughter again, because when I'm done with you, she'll be sodding invisible."

He had to try to reason with her. Whatever she did and did not think of him, she couldn't leave Baile, and neither could

Taylor. They both had a great big X on their backs for Rhiannon to follow. "Deb—"

"And to think I was stupid enough to believe you'd changed." Debra gave a wrathful laugh. "You've gotten worse. Making up stupid stories and pulling Taylor into your lies. You're despicable. You're…you're—"

Niamh stood and approached Debra cautiously. "Please, Debra. If you'd let—"

"I bet you're behind this." Debra's hand shook as she jabbed her finger at Niamh. "Look at you." She sneered. "I bet all you have to do is smile and jiggle and men do exactly what you want them to."

Her criticism of Niamh pissed him off, but he wasn't going to add fuel to Debra's fire. "You're in shock, Deb."

"Too bloody right I'm in shock," Debra yelled. "You're fucking delusional, and dangerous."

"Madam." Andy's smooth voice cut through the tension in the kitchen.

Warren groaned. That was all they needed now.

"I understand your perturbation." Andy walked into the kitchen and straight up to Debra. "You have received a nasty shock."

Debra stared at him, face red and eyes snapping wrath.

"Dad!" Taylor went rigid, her eyes turned opaque, and the sharp tang of apples and the earthy aroma of coriander filled the kitchen. "Dad, it's happening."

Niamh sprang for Taylor and guided her into a chair. "Just breathe, sweetie, breathe and reach for your element. It will stabilize your blessing."

"What is it? What's wrong with her?" Debra gripped Warren's arm, her nails almost drawing blood.

"She's scrying," Niamh whispered, soothing Taylor with long strokes down her spine. "She's okay."

"She looks terrified." Debra lunged for Taylor.

Andy stepped into her path and laid a hand on his chest. "All will be well. You can trust me." He took Debra by the shoulders. "I'm an accountant by trade. A normal man who was living his life with no knowledge that any of this existed." He arced his hand through the air, gesturing Baile and her inhabitants. "But what is occurring now is best left to the blessed."

Christ. Debra would eat Andy alive.

"Why is she terrified?" Debra's voice rose. She tried to get around Andy. "That's it. I'm putting a stop to this."

"Don't!" Taylor held up one hand to deflect her mother as she closed her eyes. "I need to concentrate."

Debra threw him a dirty look but stood quiescent beside Andy.

Andy must have some major juju to keep Warren's ex in place when she was this upset.

Debra peered around Andy at Niamh. "What's happening?"

"Give us a minute." Niamh glanced at her. "I'm not going to let anything happen to Taylor, but we have to let her do her thing."

"She's my daughter," Debra hissed.

"I understand." Andy put his arm around her shoulders and patted Debra. "And this is all very shocking, but your daughter is special. She has a unique and wonderful gift."

"The twins are in trouble, Dad." Taylor frowned. "But it's weird because it's a different kind of trouble." She sat back suddenly and blinked. "They're gone." She clicked her fingers. "Just like that."

"What did you see?" Warren crouched beside Taylor.

Niamh grabbed a glass and filled it from a pitcher in the fridge. She opened Taylor's hand and closed it around the glass. "You did well, sweetie. Drink this."

Debra leaped to intercept. "What is that?"

"Chill, Mum." Taylor took a sip. "It's apple juice."

"She's young," Niamh said. "We want to make sure she doesn't get physically exhausted."

"They were in a hotel." Taylor wiped the condensation off her glass with her free hand. "At least, it looked like a hotel. These men came, then things went all fuzzy, and then I saw them being put into a van." She frowned and sipped. "Then I heard a wolf."

"Wolf?" Niamh's gaze sharpened. "Not one of ours?"

"More wolves." Debra threw Andy a desperate look. "Wolves are dangerous."

"Not one of ours." Taylor handed her empty juice glass back to Niamh. "It's hunting them, but it doesn't seem to be..." She shook her head. "It wasn't hunting them like they were prey."

Debra's eyes filled with tears as she stuck her chin out. "Wolves are predators."

"Yes," Niamh said, and held Debra's glare. "But wolves are not mindless hunting machines." She looked back at Taylor. "Could you tell why it was hunting?"

Taylor shook her head. "Not really...but he felt...different." She threw her hands up. "I can't explain how."

Niamh touched Taylor's shoulder. "Never mind, sweet girl. You did very well."

"Can you get them back?" Warren kept his tone gentle. Despite what Debra might think, he was still not comfortable with the burden her blessing placed on Taylor.

She grimaced. "I tried, I really did, but they vanished."

Debra evaded Andy and bustled forward. "Stop it. It's upsetting and hurting her."

"Mum." Taylor looked at Debra and sighed. "It's my blessing. It's what I do. Of course I have to do it."

"But—"

"Listen to me, Mum, please." Taylor stood and went to Debra. "If I was a runner or could play a sport really well, wouldn't you encourage me to do it?"

Debra frowned. "Well, yes, but this is not the same. This is dangerous."

"Sport is dangerous." Taylor shrugged. "Last term Libby Watson broke an ankle playing netball."

Andy produced a bottle of white wine from the fridge, filled a glass and pressed it into Debra's hand. "I myself have received some nasty injuries from the odd game of rugby."

Andy played rugby? Warren tried not to stare

"I just had breakfast." Debra blinked at the glass of wine.

"Nasty shock." Andy lifted her hand closer to her mouth. "Seems the right thing to do."

Gaze on Andy, Debra took a small sip, and then a larger one.

Andy beamed encouragement at her.

"Wolves doesn't sound like Rhiannon." Niamh looked at Warren. "Remember that leopard and the lions when we were in South Africa? Animals sense the nasty in her and avoid her."

"Wise creatures," Andy drawled. "But Taylor said the wolves felt different. I shall ask Roderick if he has ever encountered wolves in any other form."

Warren suppressed an eyeroll. Andy lived for following Roderick around and questioning him. "Good idea."

"Unless they're connected to guardians, I've never heard of wolves, or any other creatures, doing Rhiannon's bidding." Niamh chewed on her pillowy bottom lip.

Oh, the plans Warren had for that lip. *Focus!* "We should let the coven know. This is the first time Taylor has been able to get anything on the twins."

"They could be warded in some way." Niamh indicated Taylor. "A seer can't get through wards."

Warren didn't want to consider the far more sinister possibility. The dead moved beyond a seer's abilities too. Even though Taylor couldn't locate Mags, she knew she was alive.

"They're not dead." Taylor tossed the elephant out of the room. She touched her chest. "I would feel it if they were."

"So would Maeve," Niamh said. "She would sense their spirits moving into the nether realms. And they would probably pop up here to be released."

"Oh my God." Debra leaned against Andy. "What has my daughter been exposed to?"

Andy patted her shoulder. "She has a gift. Trying to deny her that gift would be crueler."

"Do you really think so?" Debra blinked at him.

"Indubitably." He smiled. "Here she is with the best people to teach her how to use her gift and keep her safe."

Debra blinked at him and sipped her wine.

"And, quite frankly, my dear"—Andy gave Debra a crooked smile—"the horse has already bolted."

After a pause, all the fight bled out of Debra and her shoulders slumped. "You're right." She nodded. "I know you're right. It's just that…"

"You're her mother." Andy smiled tenderly at Debra. "She is yours to protect and succor."

If Warren had said any of what Andy had, Debra might have carved his liver out with her fingernails. They were getting on much better, and she was calmer, but Debra's gaze still accused him of doing this to Taylor. It would take time for her to get her head around all of it.

Niamh slid her hand into his and squeezed.

"What do you say to a walk?" Andy's tone brimmed with enthusiasm as he gazed at Debra.

"A walk?" Debra looked confused. "I don't want to go for a bloody walk."

"You'll find the forest is lovely, and beyond it is the most spectacular view of the sea." He put his hand on Taylor's shoulder. "If you prefer, the young one can accompany us."

A long, laden silence stretched across the kitchen.

"Please." Andy held out a hand. "I understand your feelings on this matter. But there's much you need to understand and perhaps"—he placed a hand on his chest—"as someone who understands and has experienced your skepticism, I can make it more palatable for you."

Warren could have been knocked down with a feather when Debra nodded. "Okay. A walk. But I'm taking Taylor."

"Lovely." Andy smiled and motioned her toward the door. "The day is crisp but clear and rather bracing."

Niamh slid her arm around Warren's waist, and they stood and watched Andy lead Debra and Taylor into the bailey.

What a fucking mess. "Well," he said. "I never thought I'd say it but thank God for Andy."

CHAPTER THREE

Training and habit kept Emma still and patient as she and Jack lurked in the alley beside a busy cafe. The stench of garbage on the warm night made her want to gag. A rat investigated the scraps.

A huge shadow in the muggy night, Jack paced and muttered beside her. The big guy might not keep it together for much longer. Tourists enjoying the sights and sounds of Montmartre, oblivious to anything but overpriced food and trashy curios, wandered past the alley entrance in couples and groups. Bustle and chatter drifted down the alley.

Jack stopped and glared toward the main street. "Are they coming?"

"They said they would." Emma hid her doubts and tried to infuse confidence in her tone. This morning, as she and Jack had woken in their Air BnB in Paris, she'd received the coded message indicating this alley in Montmartre.

A burst of noise and laughter from the cafe startled Jack. "It's been too long." He went back to pacing.

Any length of time was too long with Mags in the hands of that homicidal bitch with world domination delusions.

Summer was drawing to a close, and the changing season made the clock in Emma's mind tick louder. She didn't know where Mags was or what was happening to her, but Rhiannon kept moving her.

After she and Jack had left Baile, it had taken a few days to find out Mags was no longer in England. Another week to discover Rhiannon had left England on a private jet the same day Mags had been abducted. Another couple of hours to get the jet fueled and the flight plan for Paris filed. And here they were. And had been for the last week, waiting for Sasha to turn something up.

"They know where she is?" Jack shoved his hands in his pockets.

"I don't know." Emma kept her shrug light. She didn't want to get Jack's hopes up. Hell! She didn't want to get her hopes up. This wasn't her first time trying to track Rhiannon. The bitch could globe hop like a demented genie and had contacts and safe houses everywhere. Sasha had been trying to compile comprehensive lists for years, but with Rhiannon's resources she always managed to stay one step ahead. "They have information, and that's all I know."

Jack snorted. "We have to find her."

They absolutely did, but rushing around blindly helped nobody. Rhiannon knew how to cover her tracks, and with Mags in tow, would be doubly cautious.

Emma checked her watch. Her contact was twenty minutes late. Another five minutes, and they would need to get moving. No doubt Rhiannon had eyes on her and Jack. Making themselves sitting targets wouldn't help Mags.

"Look sharp," Jack whispered.

A figure stood at the alley entrance, paused, lit a cigarette, and slid into the alley.

The acrid smell of cigarette smoke hung in the heavy humidity.

Emma palmed her knife. They couldn't risk gunfire in such a crowded area.

"Looks like rain." The man drew on his cigarette. Orange light revealed the fine-boned features of a man in his early thirties or late twenties. He wore jeans and a windbreaker with a ball cap pulled low over his face.

Emma responded, "My app said it was going to stay fine."

He stopped about eight feet away, still and tense. "You can't trust those things."

Emma gave him the answer he needed. "Hasn't led me wrong so far."

Nodding, the man dropped his cigarette and ground it out. He took a step closer to them.

Still and alert, Jack was a good man to have at her back.

Emma stepped in close and dropped her voice low. "What have you got?"

"Not much." Her contact sighed. "Her plane arrived in Paris on the same day it left England. A car picked up the passengers. Three women and a handful of muscle followed in another car."

"Where'd they go?" It was more than she'd had two minutes ago.

He shook his head. "We lost them just outside Paris."

"Fuck." Jack growled.

The contact glanced at him and then turned his attention to Emma. "Who's that?"

"A friend." Nothing like spending two weeks tied at the hip to get the measure of a person, and she now considered Jack very much a friend.

"We've got some whispers though." The contact shoved his hands in his pockets.

He needed to spill it fast, or she was afraid Jack would lose it. "What?"

"Luberon region." He shrugged. "A rental villa." He reached inside his jacket and withdrew a scrap of paper. "Address is on there. We haven't been able to confirm anything. But the place is a known location, and security recently got tighter than a duck's ass."

Added security generally meant something worth protecting. Emma pocketed the scrap. She'd read it and destroy it when they got back to their Air BnB. "We'll check it out."

"There's more." The contact adjusted his cap. "We've picked up some chatter around Canada."

"Canada?" Jack stepped closer.

Emma filled him in. "The earth point is there."

Jack glanced at her, his expression grim, but he didn't say aloud what they were both thinking. The twins were in Canada looking for that earth point. "What chatter?"

"Lots of hostile activity." The contact gave Jack a loaded stare. "Lots of questions being asked.'"

Emma didn't like the sound of that, and a lifetime of tracking Rhiannon had trained her to obey her instincts. "Make sure Sasha filled Baile in on the Canada chatter."

"Already done." The contact pulled out a cigarette and lit it.

Emma nodded. She was glad Sasha was working with Baile.

"We'll check out the Luberon information." She motioned to Jack. "Let's go."

"Go well," the contact murmured.

They were all in danger. She clapped him on the shoulder. "Stay well."

Emma and Jack left the alley and slipped arm in arm into the steady flow of tourists. Just another couple amongst myriad like them, spending a romantic couple of days in Paris. They kept their conversation to mundane nothings as they traversed the street. Weren't the lights lovely? Did Jack enjoy Sacre Coeur? Did Emma want another one of those chocolate croissants from the bistro near their apartment?

Back in their apartment, Jack bolted the door while Emma swept for electronic surveillance.

"We're clean," she said, and toed off her boots by the door.

Jack entered the kitchenette and flipped the kettle on. "Where's Luberon?"

"Provence." Emma opened a travel app on her phone. "Looks like we can take the train to Aix En Provence and drive from there."

Jack nodded. "Tea?"

"Please." Her Sig dug into her back, so she removed it, checked the safety, and placed it on the table.

Jack wanted nothing to do with firearms and had refused her offer of one. He reckoned he could do more damage with his fists and a knife. As the man was built like a rugby forward, and she'd seen him palm that knife faster than she could blink, she'd left the discussion there.

She pulled a small caliber pistol from her ankle, checked it, and put it beside her Sig. Her dad had always said guns in untrained hands could do more harm to the user, and she was inclined to believe him.

Rhiannon could have stashed Mags anywhere. They were clinging to the hope that she was too valuable to Rhiannon for the bitch to have killed her. Rhiannon had gone to a lot of trouble to get her hands on Mags. For about the millionth time, Emma wished she'd bucked the fuck up and got on that flight from Moscow with Mags and Jack. What had she been thinking? She'd been shocked rigid to find out she was coimhdeacht, reeling from the sudden about-face her life had taken. Her Moscow people had needed her, her work at the university had needed to carry on, the organization had placed her in Moscow for a reason—an entire smorgasbord of justifications for why she was too shit scared to take her rightful place.

Her dad would be furious with her for not doing her duty. She thanked God her grandparents were no longer alive to see how she'd failed.

"You're doing it again." Jack put a mug of tea next to her weapons.

Looking at Jack with his tough-guy handsome face and powerful build, you'd never guess at the incisive, perceptive mind behind those russet eyes. "You're right."

"Do I need to let Roderick sort you out again?" He sank into the armchair facing the couch and stretched his long legs in front of him.

Emma snorted. She'd handed Roderick his ass the last time that medieval son of a bitch had tried. The bigger they were, the harder they fell. "As if."

Outside their accommodation, Paris kept the night party going. Voices rose and fell from the small bistro beneath them. Scents of garlic, herbs, fresh bread, cheese, and strong cigarettes somehow permeated the closed windows. If she shut her eyes, she could almost pretend she wasn't on the most important mission of her life.

"I understand." Jack blew on his tea before taking a careful sip. "Regret."

She knew he did. When he was barely an adult, Jack had killed Martin, a shifty little fucker who probably would have ended up dead anyway. Involuntary manslaughter had been the official charge. After she'd first encountered him, Emma had gotten Sasha to research Jack Langham from ass-crack to gullet. If there was anything raising red flags close to Mags, Emma had made it her business to know.

The results had been initially concerning, but someone's history didn't always tell the full story. Working with him, sharing her mission with him, had filled in the important blanks, and she trusted him with her life, and with Mags's.

Since his release from prison, Jack had kept his nose clean, gone to his weekly anger-management classes and worked construction. Jack had come to Baile to check up on his friend Warren. He'd met Mags, and here they were. With him as

Mags's man and her as Mags's coimhdeacht, they were destined to spend a large portion of their future together. "I know about Martin," she said.

"Thought you might." He sipped his tea and dropped his head back on his chair.

"Why's that?"

"You seem like the sort." He chuckled. "Not likely to go into anything blindly."

He had her to rights there.

"You can't go back," he said, gaze still on the ceiling, mug cradled in his massive paws.

Emma didn't feel like platitudes, so she grunted.

"What I mean is, even if you could go back, there were always factors that led to what you did." He lifted his head and locked gazes with her. "If I hadn't gone after Helen, Martin might still be alive. But if I hadn't gone after Martin, Helen might also be dead."

Helen was his younger sister, the reason he'd gotten into a fistfight with the tough he'd killed. The police report stated that Jack had intervened before the fucker could rape his sister. Emma would have cut Martin's balls off and left him to bleed out.

"Maybe I could have stopped Helen from going that night." Jack shrugged. "But nobody ever stopped Helen from doing what the hell she wanted. She'd only lie to your face and do it anyway."

Emma didn't like delving into her feelings. She'd failed Mags. End of story. "Yeah, I know."

"No, you don't." Jack put his mug on the table. "We all walk around thinking if we'd done one thing different, it would have changed only that one moment we want to get back."

For want of something to do with her hands, other than shoot Jack before he got to the point, she drank her tea. "And?"

"And it doesn't work like that." Jack leaned his elbows on his knees and stared at his interlocked fingers. "One thing changes, and everything around it changes as well. Maybe Helen wouldn't have gone to that club, and everything would have been fine. But then I wouldn't have met Warren, and through him, Mags. Or maybe she would have met Martin somewhere and he'd have done worse, and I wouldn't have been there to stop it."

Emma got where he was going. "If you'd have known better, you'd have done better." She'd heard that somewhere.

"Exactly." Jack picked up his tea and sat back again.

But she had known better. She'd been raised in the war against Rhiannon. She knew exactly how high the stakes were. She'd even known what coimhdeacht were, and in theory, how they worked. "I freaked out," she admitted the truth aloud for the first time.

"I get that." Jack chuckled. "Like I freaked out when Mags kept telling me we were having four children together."

Emma choked on a sip of tea. She'd not heard that detail before. "Four?"

"Two boys and two girls." Jack grinned and shook his head. "And I just thought she was hotter than hell and wanted to get my leg over."

She had to laugh. "Sounds like you definitely will get your leg over then."

"When we find her." Jack's face went stony, and the iron determination gave her reassurance.

"Yup." She breathed in and tried to take some of his resolve deep inside. "When we find her."

Jack nodded at her phone. "You booked those train tickets yet?"

Of course she had, and her glare told him as much.

"Do you think she's there?" Jack's gaze probed her mind.

"I don't know, but we'll chase down all leads."

He grunted and dropped his head back. "If Warren and

Roderick are to be believed, you'll sense her when you get close enough."

"So they say." Interesting times ahead. As Mags's coimhdeacht, Emma would share her every thought, feeling, and experience. Looks like they were about to be the world's weirdest thrupple. And they would be together again, because neither she nor Jack would stop until they were.

CHAPTER FOUR

Noah checked over his shoulder at the two inert bodies in the back of the van. He'd tried to make them as comfortable as he could but bundling two women into the back of a van parked behind a popular Montreal hotel—and not getting spotted—had its limitations.

Abe tapped his forefinger on the steering wheel as he drove. He loved Shania Twain, and Noah had heard more Shania on the jaunt to Montreal than he'd ever hoped to.

Go to Montreal, Zach had said. *Find the earth witch, watch her, and report back.*

Earth witch, singular.

Zach had attached another instruction. Along with the reporting and watching, they needed to do as circumstances dictated. So they had.

Glancing over his shoulder again, Noah took in the two identical women asleep on pallets behind them.

"There are two of them," Abe said as he checked the rearview and changed lanes. "Two."

Zach had insisted Noah bring Abe with him. As the

strongest fighter, Abe was a good man to have on your team. Noah liked Abe, he was a good man, but all that muscle had squeezed the guy's brainpower into a poppyseed.

Their mission had doubled.

Two witches, both reeking of earth magic, were definitely the reason he and Abe had been dispatched. Long reddish hair spilled around their heads, their pale faces were slack and vulnerable, and he couldn't see the color of their eyes.

Noah had to laugh. Goddess had a sense of humor sometimes. One of the knock-out redheads they'd just kidnapped would have been enough for anyone to handle. Two sent the risk factor off the charts.

"What's so funny." Abe frowned and then whistled through his teeth. "Do you think they're twins?"

"Seriously?" Noah turned back to staring out the window. There were days when Noah didn't understand how Zach managed to lead this bunch without throwing throat and nut punches. Guess that's why Zach was their leader and not him. He couldn't wait to tell the big cheese about this little wrinkle.

The road stretched in front of them, only a few cars breaking the monotony of the late hour. People in those cars went about their business with no idea an abduction was taking place. Noah had officially rung a new low on his sins bell.

Abe grunted and narrowed his eyes in thought. "They could be…those things…I watched a TikTok about them. You know, double bangers."

It took Noah a hot minute to work that one out. "Doppelgängers?"

"Yeah." Abe nodded and scrunched his face as he chewed it over. "You know like people who don't know each other and look the same." He glanced over, his face deadly serious. "Did you know everyone has a secret twin?"

Noah didn't have the strength.

A tantalizing scent filled the van's cab. Earth magic, for

certain, but mixed with cloves and roses, and something else. It was that something else that made Noah almost forget about the dumbass driving the van. It made his mouth water, his skin prickle, and his cock harden in his jeans.

He turned and studied the twin in fatigues and combats. It was coming from her.

Abe sniffed and frowned. "What is that?"

"Nothing." Motherfucker! Now? Goddess must be pissing herself at him. Thirty-three years on this planet, and it struck now. Apparently, the unplanned wrinkles kept coming.

Chin up, nose working the air, Abe's frown deepened. "I know that smell."

"No, you don't." Abe never could let something go either. Another of his charm school attributes. "Tell me more about the doppelgängers."

"Really?" Abe's face lit up. Residual streetlight played across his features. Objectively speaking, the guy was good looking in a Jon Hamm way: tall, broad shoulders, dark hair, jaw you could chisel rock on. It was amazing how many women would over-look Abe's peanut brain in favor of his hefty pecs and pretty face. No mental giant, but he had the best batting average in their pack. "Okay, so you know…"

Noah stopped listening. Dhara had sensed the earth witches touch down in Montreal, and Zach had sent him and Abe a-sniffing. This far from their pack land, their senses, although still sharper than the average person, were not as keen as they were when they were connected to their birth soil.

"Nope." Abe shook his head. "I can still smell it."

So much for not as keen. Super sniffer at his side just had to buck the trend. Noah hadn't even worked out what he felt about the new development. He didn't want to hear Abe's thoughts on the matter. Not that hearing Abe's thoughts would take long.

"I don't smell anything." Noah mentally scrambled for

another distraction. Meat always worked. "Are you hungry? I'm hungry. Wanna grab a burger?"

"I had a burger for lunch." Abe grimaced.

And breakfast, but what the hell, Abe was as compelled by his nature as they all were. "So?"

"Excellent point." Abe chuckled and bopped his head along to Shania warbling on about what didn't impress her much.

Noah needed rest. He and Abe hadn't gotten much shut-eye since they'd been tailing the twins, and he wanted to be fresh for his turn at the wheel. They had precious cargo onboard.

Abe stopped his fingers. "I know what that smell is! It's the bonding scent."

Fuck!

Turning to him, Abe gaped. "And it's coming off her...and it's not mine."

Wait for it. Let the gears churn.

Abe gaped. "It's yours."

Nausea woke Sinead, and she lay there battling it down. Her head hurt like a motherfucker, her brain was in a fog, and her mouth was dry. The ground beneath her shifted.

A fresh wave of nausea hit her, and she breathed deep.

A low hum vibrated through her spine.

Shit! Alannah.

She opened her eyes and saw the back of Alannah's head.

It took a few more moments for reality to fully assert itself, and she remembered the hotel, eating room service, and then feeling drugged. The room service had been drugged.

Evidence pointed strongly toward that being the truth. And Sinead could come up with only one being who would drug her and Alannah. Calling Rhiannon a woman or a person stretched credulity way too far.

And if all of that tallied, then they were in trouble. Big, big, fucking trouble.

Alannah groaned and stirred.

A man spoke. "They're waking up."

"Really?" a second man responded. "What gave you that idea?"

"She groaned," said the first man. "I mean, unless you groaned—"

"Forget it," snapped his companion. "I'll get the stuff."

There were some shuffling noises, and then a figure blocked the light, dark hair and blurry features. Or was her eyesight blurry? A tingle shot through her, and she shuddered as the figure crouched beside her.

As near as she could tell, they were in a van of some kind. She and Alannah were lying beside each other.

"Sorry, sweet thing." His face surged closer.

Sinead tried to blink his features into focus. She knew him from somewhere, but her fuzzy head wouldn't get with the program and spit up the memory.

A syringe in his hand caught the light.

"No," she croaked. "Please, you don't need that."

He grimaced. "Like I said, sweet thing, sorrier than I can say."

He lowered the syringe, her arm stung, and she winced.

"Here." He held a water bottle nozzle to her mouth. "You probably want to puke, so take it easy."

Sinead would love to have refused, but her head was already swimming, and her tongue stuck to the roof of her mouth.

Cool liquid washed through her mouth, and she swallowed.

He took the bottle away and moved to Alannah.

"No." Sinead tried to stop him, but her hand dropped short.

She watched as if from down a long, dark tunnel as he jabbed Alannah and gave her a small sip of water.

Sinead's eyelids drooped, and she tried to force them open again.

"Don't fight it." He was back with her, leaning over her. Something brushed her hair, and he murmured, "You're going to be fine. Just sleep."

The man from the hotel lobby. Her mind coughed up the answer before her lights blinked out.

CHAPTER FIVE

Standing at the kitchen window, Alexander cradled his coffee mug between his palms. Outside in the bailey, a pack of dogs sniffed around the edges near the healer's hall. The number of stray animals wandering into Baile had grown since Niamh had started working her blessing more.

A goat trotted after the dogs and bleated. She must be new. Daily, a new four-legged or feathered—sometimes scaled—friend swelled their growing menagerie. The old, the sick, the stray, and the abandoned, he had no idea where they came from, but they all ended up here . He rather liked it, and Niamh kept the zoo under control. This morning, he was drinking his coffee under the watchful eye of a bearded dragon.

"G'day." According to Niamh, someone must have tired of their exotic pet and left this Australian native to fend for himself. "Found yourself a nice patch of sun, I see."

The lizard blinked at him.

Alexander had left Bronwyn asleep in their bed and come down to the kitchen for some quiet time before the rest of the coven woke. His current companion had staying silent down to a fine art.

"I don't mind telling you, we're in a spot of bother." Alexander inhaled the rich cherry, dark chocolate, nutty aroma of his unique coffee blend and sighed. "Not bad," he said. "But not quite there." He missed the great coffee he'd been able to blend when he lived on his estate.

The bearded dragon bobbed its head.

Not everyone was a coffee connoisseur.

Goddess alone knew what had happened to Alannah and Sinead. Taylor's vision yesterday had created more doubts and worry than before. Rhiannon had Mags. Fourteen days and counting. He yanked his head back from the black hole of what might be happening to Mags and the twins.

Hundreds of years circling the sun, and he was useless. All their contacts had turned up nothing. Taylor couldn't scry Mags and had lost Sinead and Alannah. Even Andy had found no trace of any of their missing witches. Emma's contact, Sasha, kept turning up one dead end after another. Out there, somewhere, Jack and Emma kept hunting. Nothing so far. Also out there somewhere, presumably Canada, Alannah and Sinead had disappeared in the back of a van.

"Good morning." Andy spoke from behind him.

The bearded dragon skittered away and disappeared into an open cupboard.

Alexander nodded a greeting. "I made coffee."

"Lovely." Andy bustled about then came to stand beside Alexander at the window. "Actually, we have a situation."

Lovely! Just what they needed, another situation. "What?"

"The police." Andy sipped his coffee and sighed. "This is marvelous coffee."

"It's good coffee. Marvelous coffee requires a subtle bean blend that I no longer have access to," Alexander said. "What about the police?"

"Ah." Frowning, Andy stared into his mug. "Right, well, they're on their way here."

Alexander must have heard that wrong. "Eh?"

"Yup." Andy grimaced and sipped his coffee. "They've been attempting to enter Baile for the past forty minutes. I judged it prudent to ask our lady to allow them ingress."

"Why?" Baile's wards were nifty at keeping unwanted visitors out. Anybody trying to reach the castle would keep driving around in circles until they gave up.

"It's the police." Andy blinked at him. "I thought it better to allow them access rather than raise their suspicions. They clearly have a reason for coming here."

A troublesome thought entered Alexander's mind. "Where's Roderick?"

"Asleep." Andy met his gaze and nodded. "Better not to wake him."

"Good idea." Roderick would not react well to modern police poking about, especially if they had an axe to grind. He was still battling with this century. The notion of paying property taxes had nearly driven Roderick out of his tiny mind. His large, former foe did not play nicely with modern authority.

Good old Dad. Emphasis on the old.

Alexander didn't think he'd ever get used to the idea that Roderick was his father. Bloody hell! They'd been trying to kill each other for most of their extended lives. "Do you know what they want? The police."

"No." Andy shook his head. "Only that they are intent on speaking with us. The order to come here descended from higher up the chain and is marked urgent." Andy had a way of noodling things out via his laptop and his savvy. He nodded to the window. "It looks like we're about to find out."

"Damn!" Police paying a house call couldn't mean anything good.

The police car stopped in the bailey outside the kitchen. A uniformed copper stepped out from the driver's side, and a heavyset man in a suit heaved his bulk out of the passenger seat.

He took a moment to look about him before nodding to the uniformed copper.

Best meet them head on. Alexander opened the kitchen door before they reached it. "Good morning."

"Morning." The suited copper nodded. "I'm DCI Lennox, and this is Constable Acharya." He heaved his waistband over his belly. "We wondered if you had a moment to chat."

It wasn't really a question, and DCI Lennox's gaze moved constantly, taking everything in.

Alexander discreetly sniffed the air. No sign of blood magic.

A wolf slunk out the kitchen door and trotted across the bailey.

Both coppers turned to stare after her.

Constable Acharya pointed. "Is that a—"

"Dog." Alexander smiled.

"Wolf dog," Andy chirruped cheerfully. "We run a sort of shelter for them here. Very misunderstood breed."

Constable Acharya glared after the wolf. "Shouldn't it be on a lead or restrained? Aren't they dangerous?"

"Private property." Andy beamed at him. "And as I said, very misunderstood breed."

"Well…" Constable Acharya glanced at Lennox for support.

Lennox glowered at him.

"Just make sure it stays on your property and doesn't create any mischief with other village residents." Acharya deflated and dropped his head.

"Of course." Alexander stepped to the side and motioned them in. "Won't you come in? I'm—"

"Lord Donn." Lennox stared at Alexander. "Alexander Donn."

So, the man had done some homework and wanted him to know it. "I see my reputation precedes me."

Hand out, Andy stepped forward. "Andy Braithwaite."

Lennox shook his hand and turned back to Alexander.

"We're here about a disturbance on the road up from the village."

Constable Acharya slunk into the kitchen and made himself inconspicuous near the sink.

Lennox sniffed and peered around the kitchen. "We understand the road from the village leads to the castle. Solely leads to the castle."

"As far as we know." The only disturbance Alexander could think of was Mags's abduction. Andy had assured him he'd spoken to Sasha of Emma's organization, and the matter had been tidied away. The driver of Mags and Jack's car had been badly injured, but Sasha apparently had him in excellent medical hands. "What kind of disturbance?"

"We were hoping you could tell us." Digging in his pocket, Lennox brought out an evidence bag. "A couple of weeks ago, Constable Acharya responded to a report of a traffic accident. When he reached the reported scene, however, he found no cars. Only a lot of broken glass and this." He jiggled the evidence bag.

A lone bullet casing lay in the bag.

"Is that a bullet?"

"It appears so." Lennox studied the casing as if seeing it for the first time. "At least, it's what remains of a bullet that was fired. However, handguns are illegal in this country, and a bullet casing does raise red flags."

"Oh my." Andy shook his head and frowned. "Someone was firing a gun in the road?"

"So it seems." Lennox peeled his lips off his teeth in a parody of a smile. "The question as to firing at what or whom remains a mystery."

"Two weeks ago, you say?" Alexander put on his mulling face. "Is it customary to investigate a traffic accident two weeks after it occurred?"

Lennox scowled. "We have a very busy caseload, Lord Donn. Budget cuts, you understand. We need to prioritize."

"Quite so." Apparently, Sasha's people had missed a rather pertinent little detail. "But still, two weeks ago. Are you sure the…er"—he peered at the casing in the bag—"bullet is linked to the accident? Is it possible it was dropped there?"

"Quite possible." Lennox rocked on his heels. "But that wouldn't explain the three separate reports of sounds of gunfire received on the same day from Greater Littleton." He shrugged. "Or the glass, and of course, the traces of human blood found on the road."

Alexander gave him a benign smile. "No, indeed, it would not. Gunfire?"

"Gunfire." Lennox nodded.

Acharya spoke up from his post by the sink. "Three separate reports."

"Oh my." Andy looked genuinely shaken. "Forgive me, could we offer you a cup of tea, coffee?"

"Glass of water?" Andy bustled over to the Welsh dresser and picked up two glasses. "Fresh strawberry lemonade? I made it just yesterday from our own fruit."

Constable Acharya opened his mouth.

"No. Thank you," Lennox said.

Acharya's mouth snapped shut.

"Normally, this is not the sort of thing we would pay much attention to. And as you pointed out, it did happen two weeks ago." Lennox shoved the evidence bag back in his pocket. "But when combining the casing and the reports of gunfire with the fact that one Conrad Lester also appears to have gone missing, then we do start having a look about."

"Conrad Lester?" Alexander didn't need to fake his confusion. The name rang no bells.

"Chauffeur." Lennox nodded. "Works for Elite Transport." Leaning in, Lennox got all chummy and good cop. "One of those highbrow driving services. Picks VIPs up from the airport and gets them where they need to go, safely and discreetly."

Alexander hadn't thought much beyond getting a badly injured Jack back to Baile that day, and then going after Mags. Andy hadn't given him the name of the driver, and he hadn't asked. He hoped the poor sod was going to be all right.

Andy frowned and mulled it over. "I don't think we have ever used them."

"Really?" Lennox's dark eyes brightened. "It's funny you should say that, because airport security footage shows Mr. Lester leaving Heathrow with a Miss Magdalene Cray." He raised one bushy brow. "Resident of Baile Castle, and a Mr. Jack Langham." He pursed his lips. "Mr. Langham is known to us."

"Jack." Alexander nodded and shoved his hands in his pockets to keep them still. "As he currently resides here, I guess that would make him known to us as well."

"Here? Seems Jack has stepped up in the world." Lennox whistled and glanced around the kitchen. "We have an entirely different address for him. At least, the one on record with his former probation officer."

Lennox was rattling cage bars to see what he could shake free. He'd have to try harder. "Resides might be a little premature." Alexander kept his drawl smooth and easy. "He and Mags. Magdalene," he confirmed for Lennox, "are a recent item."

"As in…"

"Romantic item." He forced his mouth into a smile. "Seems Jack is rather smitten with our Mags."

Nodding, Lennox studied the copper pots hanging near the range. "How recent?"

"Maybe a month. A month and a half." Alexander looked to Andy for confirmation.

Andy nodded. "About that."

Enough of the chatty interrogation. "May we ask why you're here?" He wasn't really asking either.

"Just getting the facts straight." Lennox grinned like a hunting hyena. "And idle curiosity." He stepped deeper into the kitchen. "People say a lot about Baile Castle. Most of that is speculation, as they've never been here. Now that the tours are stopped."

"Right." Alexander waited him out.

"Surprisingly, none of the reports of gunfire came from here." Lennox flinched first. "As the incident happened closer to the castle than it did to the village, I find that interesting."

"Right," Alexander said.

Lennox had bugger all, or he wouldn't be tap dancing around the kitchen like this. He was on a hunting expedition.

"I can't speak for the other castle residents, but I've not heard anything out of the ordinary." He stopped and slapped on his best thinking face. "Then again, this did happen two weeks ago. And you believe the car accident and all the other stuff are connected to Mags being picked up from the airport?"

"You tell me." Lennox smirked.

The cars had been cleared away within hours of the accident. Andy had assured him of that, and Alexander was learning to trust Andy.

"If Mags was at Heathrow," Andy chipped in, "it must have happened on the fifteenth. That's the day she and Jack got back from Moscow."

Andy was signaling him to stay close to the truth.

Alexander snapped his fingers. "Right! The fifteenth."

"Two weeks ago." Acharya waved his phone with a calendar app open. "That's a lot of coincidences."

Andy looked struck. "Yes, indeed it is."

"As a matter of idle curiosity, what were you doing on the fifteenth?" Lennox asked.

Idle curiosity his ass, and Alexander suppressed a snort. "I couldn't say offhand." He shrugged. "But if we are talking about the day Mags and Jack got back, I would have been here waiting to welcome them home."

Lennox nodded a few times and then stared at him. "Moscow?"

"Yep."

"Not your usual travel destination."

Alexander chuckled. "Mags is not your usual girl."

"Woman," Andy said.

"Eh?" Alexander turned with Lennox and Acharya to stare at him.

"Woman." Andy shrugged. "It's demeaning to refer to a grown woman as a girl."

This time, Alexander's laugh came naturally. "You're quite correct, Andy. Bad habit of mine." He turned back to Lennox. "Mags is not your usual woman."

"What were they doing in Moscow?" Lennox's eyes went cold. Clearly not appreciating the levity.

Alexander raised his palms. "Why does anyone travel? Curiosity? Wanderlust? The desire to broaden one's horizons?"

Grunting, Lennox studied Andy. "You reside here too, Mr. Braithwaite?"

Andy beamed. "I do."

"And yourself, Lord Donn?"

"Guilty." Alexander couldn't resist the smirk. "And nobody calls me Lord Donn anymore. It's more of an honorific than anything else."

Lennox looked as if he'd like to take Alexander's honorific and shove it somewhere unspeakable. "Quite the little community you have going here."

"Is that a problem?" Alexander raised an eyebrow.

"Not unless someone is being held here against their will." Lennox gave a jovial chuckle which ended rather abruptly. "Are they?"

"You're welcome to ask." Alexander spread his arms wide. "Although, I caution you that most of the castle is still in bed."

"Would it be possible to talk to Miss Cray? Ask her a couple of questions." Again, with the request that was more like a demand. "As we believe she and Mr. Langham to be the last people to have seen Mr. Lester."

"Ah." Alexander pulled a face. "Regrettably, not."

Puffing out his chest, Lennox stepped closer. "Now, look—"

"She's not here." Alexander tired of toying with the DCI. "And before you ask, neither is Mr. Langham."

"Really?" Lennox glowered, not believing him for a second. "Do you know where they are?"

"Again." Alexander smirked. "Regrettably, we do not."

Lennox sneered. "How convenient."

"Not really." Alexander pulled his hauteur around him like an invisibility cloak. "Because the fact that they're not means you lot will be back."

"You can count on that, Lord Donn."

"The truth is, they had a bit of a falling out." If you could call Mags being abducted and Jack racing to find her a falling out. Probably not. "They had a falling out. Mags hared off to God knows where, and Jack went after her."

"Just like that?" Lennox scowled.

Alexander shrugged. "You are more than welcome to look about. Andy would happily take you around the old pile of stones." Baile could keep her secrets from anyone. Including a couple of oddly persistent and curious coppers.

Lennox cogitated, clearly dying to verify the truth of his statement and then shook his head. "That won't be necessary. After all, we have no evidence to suggest a crime has been committed."

"No, you don't," Alexander said, driving the point home.

"It would be no trouble to show you about." Andy rubbed his hands together. "Baile is a fascinating place. Fascinating."

Lennox kept his attention on Alexander. "No evidence of a crime." He held up one finger. "Other than the bullet casing."

"And the broken glass." Alexander helped the lumbering sod out.

"And the human blood," Acharya said, leaning forward.

"And a missing person." Lennox narrowed his eyes.

"Three missing people, in fact." Alexander was done playing, and if the copper had nothing more than a gut load of suspicions, then he needed to come back when he had more.

Lennox nodded and whirled. "I will be back, Lord Donn. Hopefully, you'll have found your missing two when I do."

Alexander didn't have to fake his fervent response. "Yes, indeed."

As they stood and watched the coppers leave, Andy murmured, "That's not good."

Alexander didn't like coincidences. Finding a stray bullet casing in the middle of the road two weeks after the fact seemed an awful lot like a coincidence to him. As they were coming to learn, most coincidences lately led straight back to Rhiannon. "Find out what you can," he said to Andy. "And check on Conrad Lester."

"Right you are." Andy whipped out his phone and started tapping.

Alexander nearly thumped him while he waited.

"Sasha's people have him." Andy grimaced. "They are providing him the best medical care they can. He was rather badly injured, I'm afraid. He might not pull through."

"Fuck!" Before Rhiannon was done, people far and wide were going to get dragged into her deadly web. "Get him here."

"But—"

They could and would help who they could, and he knew just the witch for the job. "Get. Him. Here."

CHAPTER SIX

Beside Mags's bed, Rhiannon crouched, her long black velvet gown pooled behind her. Waist length black hair lay in a gleaming sheet down her back. Fiona had grown immune to Rhiannon's ridiculous wardrobe, but today she was giving them Morticia Addams or Maleficent.

"Magdalene," Rhiannon murmured. "It's Jack."

Fiona didn't know what magic Rhiannon wielded to convince Mags she was Jack, but it worked every time. Increasingly, Rhiannon was keeping secrets from her. She didn't know Fiona had let that doctor and her kid go, or Fiona would be six feet under by now, her blood feeding Rhiannon's magic, but Rhiannon definitely had lost trust in her.

As soon as Mags outlived her usefulness, so would Fiona.

Mags turned cloudy green eyes toward Rhiannon and tried to focus. "Jack?"

"Yes, Magdalene. It's Jack, and I'm with you. We're at Baile, and all your coven sisters are waiting for you to have breakfast."

"We should go." Mags tried to sit up, but with all the narcotics Rhiannon kept in Mags's system, she wouldn't be able to move.

"Relax, sweetheart." Rhiannon gently pushed Mags back on the bed.

Mags frowned and silently tried to form words before she found her voice. "Alannah doesn't like it when I'm late."

"She's fine." Rhiannon clenched her hands into fists. Being patient and careful with Mags went against everything inside her. "We'll go to breakfast in a minute."

Sitting on the hard wooden chair near the door, Fiona stayed as quiet as she could.

"Tell me what you dreamed," Rhiannon said.

Mags blinked rapidly, and her gaze shifted to Fiona and around the room. She went even paler than her sickly white. "Where am I?"

"Magdalene." Rhiannon kept the edge from her voice, but her knuckles protruded as she gripped the bedclothes. "It's Jack, Jack Langham. Remember? You're at Baile. Everything's okay. You get confused sometimes."

Mags sighed and turned her head away. "I don't know about time." She raised her shaking hand and rubbed her forehead. "It all gets tangled up inside my head."

"I know, sweetheart." Rhiannon smoothed Mags's matted hair back from her face. "But it's Jack, and you can tell me. I'll help you get it straight."

"I'm making new bed curtains," Mags said. "They have feathers and flowers on them. I want to feel like I'm waking up in summer. Summer is my favorite season. Do you know that?"

"That'll be beautiful," Rhiannon said. "Tell me about your dreams."

Mags turned suddenly. "I need my book. My journal. I lost it."

"We'll find it," Rhiannon snapped, and then took a deep breath. She softened her tone. "Tell me about your dreams."

Sighing, Mags turned her head away. "They're not nice

dreams." She shifted to her side, turning her back on Rhiannon, and stared out the window. "I dream of Alexander a lot."

Rhiannon went still as a hunting cat. "Alexander?"

"The threads." Mags tucked a hand under her chin. "They make him and then unmake him. And there's the blood. It rises around him until he disappears beneath it." Her eyes drifted closed as she murmured, "I must warn Alexander. I think he's going to die."

"Sodding hell." Rhiannon surged to her feet and paced. Between the bed and door could barely be eight feet, and it didn't give her much room to move. The ceilings sloped in the eaves of the old French farmhouse, and Rhiannon had to duck every time her trajectory took her that way.

The thread dream about Alexander was old news. As much as Rhiannon didn't want to admit it, she still felt something for her son. She wasn't capable of love, but what she felt for Alexander was as close as the centuries-old witch could get. Still, impatience was building in Rhiannon. Fiona hoped like hell, for both their sakes, that Mags gave her something useful soon.

"Alannah isn't making breakfast." Mags's eyes popped open, and she turned back to Rhiannon.

Rhiannon paused and went back to the bed. She crouched and took Mags's hand. "Of course she is, sweetheart. Just like always."

"No." Mags looked childlike and fragile. "She's in a forest. She can't make breakfast in a forest." Mags grew agitated, her hands fluttering to her throat. "Why is she in a forest? She's in danger. She needs to leave the forest. The wolves are coming."

"Wolves?" Rhiannon's gaze bored into Mags. "Tell me about the forest."

"It's very thick. The trees are tall, and their trunks are so thick I can't wrap my arms around them." Mags licked her chapped, dry lips.

Fiona got up from her chair and took the glass of water to her. She edged past Rhiannon and raised Mags's mouth to the glass.

Mags blinked at her. "Who are you?"

"It's me, Magsie." The words burned her throat. "Bronwyn. You're feeling a bit under the weather, so I brought you some water."

"Thank you." Mags drank thirstily, water spilling down her chin on her filthy blouse and the blood necklace circling her throat. The thing stank of the blood magic that had wrought it. Fiona didn't know how it worked, but between the blood necklace and the drugs, Rhiannon had absolute control of Mags. Rhiannon hadn't made her privy to the creation of the necklace either. A clock ticked in her head, counting down her numbered days.

Just like Edana. When she no longer served a purpose, she would die. Not that she cared as much as she used to. The ruthless way Rhiannon had disposed of Edana, the awful blood draining that had resulted in her eventual death, had broken something fundamental in Fiona.

They'd devoted their lives to Rhiannon, she and Edana. They'd betrayed their coven for her, even murdered their coven sisters because they had believed in Rhiannon and her cause. Or at least they'd believed that when Rhiannon's star rose, theirs would rise along with her. For women like them, it was motivation enough. Over the long years, she and Edana had killed and stolen, bribed and manipulated, taken and hurt, even whored body and soul for Rhiannon. Now Fiona was exhausted. It didn't even matter that it finally looked like Rhiannon would win this war of hers. Fiona wanted it to end. She didn't want to die, but she'd lived more than her fair share of years, and death felt like the only form of relief she'd get.

"Tell me about the trees," Rhiannon urged Mags. "What kind are they?"

Mags giggled. "I don't know trees, Jack. You'd have to ask Sinead what kind they are." Her eyes lost focus, like cloudy jade. "The wolf howls for Sinead."

They'd heard that one before as well. Despite the danger it posed, Fiona took a kind of smug satisfaction from how little that was useful Rhiannon was actually getting out of Mags.

"The sea." Mags blinked, and her eyes grew sharp again. "The sea is close to the trees. And there are mountains."

"That's good, Magdalene." Rhiannon stood and took a deep, calming breath. Her black eyes skewered Fiona.

Mags closed her eyes, and her breathing deepened and slowed.

"Has she said anything else?" Rhiannon stared down at Mags, her expression shuttered.

"Not much more than you just heard." Fiona produced a small notebook from under her chair. "I write down everything she says."

Rhiannon glared at her. "Are you sure? Everything?"

"Yes, Mistress." Fiona lowered her gaze to the floor. "When I'm not sitting right here, I make sure to go over the camera footage." She pointed to a small CCTV camera on the ceiling.

Brushing dust from her skirt, Rhiannon said, "See that you do."

"Of course, Mistress."

"She stinks." Rhiannon waved at Mags. "Do something about that."

"Yes, Mistress."

"And find her something else to wear." She plucked at the soiled blouse. "I can't bear to look at that thing anymore."

"Yes, Mistress." Fiona hadn't dared do the barest minimum for Mags until she got permission. "I will see it done."

Rhiannon pushed her face closer until they were almost nose to nose. Her gaze searched Fiona's, as if hunting for some truth only she could see.

Fiona held her ground. Like a predator, if Rhiannon smelled fear, she would attack.

"Do not remove that blood necklace."

"I understand, Mistress."

"Jack?" Mags lurched into a sitting position. Her eyes widened and darted around the room in panic. "Jack?"

Rhiannon hurried back to the bed. "What is it, sweetheart? Another dream?"

"No." Mags shook her head. A soft, sweet smile spread over her face. "Tell me about our three children."

Three children? Fiona could have sworn Mags had said four children before. Confusion, maybe, and not surprising given the magic and the drugs. Fiona, however, spent all day, every day with her, and there were times when Rhiannon wasn't around that Mags had a gleam of something close to awareness in her eyes.

"Later." Rhiannon's jaw clenched. "We'll talk about it later." She pressed Mags back against the pillow. "Why don't you rest for a while."

Mags smiled and closed her arms. "Okay, Jack. I'm very tired."

"Rest." Rhiannon stroked her hair. "And when you wake up, we'll talk about our three children."

Mags nodded and closed her eyes.

"God's balls." Rhiannon clenched her fist. "If I have to hear about those fucking children again, I'll scream." She turned for the door and opened it. "Let me know if she says anything useful." Lip curling in disgust, she glanced over her shoulder at Mags. "She needs another dose. Bathe her, change her, and see to it."

Fiona bowed her head. "Yes, Mistress."

Rhiannon swept out of the room and floated down the stairs, the train of her gown slithering along the floor in her wake.

In the small bathroom across the hallway from the bedroom, Fiona ran a bath for Mags. She went downstairs and found her a new set of clothing from the stash in the kitchen.

A car pulled up, and Rhiannon climbed inside. The car eased down the long, olive-tree-lined lane toward the road, kicking up dust as it went. Fields of lavender stretched out on either side of the lane. The harvest was over now, and only the bushy green plants remained. It must have been something when it was blooming.

Upstairs again, she checked the temperature of the bath before going back to Mags. First, she disabled the camera feed, before gently shaking Mags awake.

Mags blinked at her. "What is it?"

"Bath time." Fiona helped her to her feet.

She checked outside the window. The car was long gone. Fiona unclipped the blood necklace. She had no great claim to humanitarianism, but if she could give Mags a stolen moment of reprieve every now and again, she would do it. Fiona dropped the blood necklace on the bed.

CHAPTER SEVEN

Thomas lingered unseen at the library's periphery as Taylor scried again for the twins.

After a long moment, Taylor looked up at the coven members around her and shook her head. "Nothing."

"Shit!" Alexander spun away and stalked to the window.

Bronwyn pressed a hand on Taylor's shoulder. "Thank you for trying, sweetie." She threw a dark glance at Alexander. "Alexander is just worried about the twins."

"I understand that." Debra glared at Alexander's back. "But none of this is Taylor's fault, and he needs to watch his language around my daughter."

Thomas had heard enough. He scattered his molecules and reformed on Baile's ancient battlements.

Like a slowly suppurating wound, Alannah's absence nagged at him. He missed her more than he would have thought possible.

If he'd had substance, he would have punched something. People very rarely came up to the battlements anymore. From here, he could see past Greater Littleton, way out to sea. A ship hovered on the very edge of the horizon.

He could not see far enough to see his love, however.

Canada. A place he'd never been and would never. His essence was tied to Goddess and Baile, along with the other spectral coimhdeacht. The other ghosts chose not to appear before the castle folk and became corporeal only for special occasions or for a new coimhdeacht. Many of them sought to pass on and waited patiently for when they could.

The pain in his chest was like a physical sensation. He didn't know what Alannah smelled like, couldn't touch her creamy skin, or hold her to him. Since her departure for Canada, he spent a lot of time in her chamber, trying to find the essence of her and draw it into himself.

"You always came up here when you were alive." Roderick stepped onto the battlements and walked to the edge.

Thomas moved closer to him. "Aye."

"You miss her."

They both knew it for the truth, and there was no point to his answering.

Roderick glanced at him. "And Lavina?"

His former witch was now trapped on the village green because of her final and desperate act of heroism. She and twelve other witches, along with a novice, had performed a forbidden blood magic rite that had trapped Roderick and Maeve in a statue. Those fourteen souls had paid the ultimate price and were cut off from the cycle of death and rebirth forever.

"She is a constant awareness." Her torment and confusion played through him over and over again, until some days he wanted to scream with it. When Alannah had been about, she had provided a welcome distraction. That's how his friendship with her had begun.

Friendship. The word made him want to curse. He wanted so much more than that from her.

"We will free her." Roderick spoke of Lavina. "Once the earth point is active, we will attempt to free them all."

Thomas's love for Lavina was the purest thing in his existence. They had never crossed the line into being lovers, but their bond had been beautiful and complete. For Thomas, who had never had a relationship with a woman without sex, it had been a revelation. He had learned to see women as more than objects to be desired, pursued, and conquered. Lavina had been the woman he held closest to his heart.

Until he had become aware of Alannah, he would have said Lavina was the most important woman of his existence. Alannah was beautiful, no denying the fact, and her beauty had drawn him to her. He had stayed near her, however, for her warm, lovely heart and the gentle strength running through her very being. She was a lot like Lavina in that way.

Roderick leaned his back against the crenelations and folded his arm. "You heard what Taylor said?"

"Aye." Thomas nodded. "We still know nothing."

"We know they're alive," Roderick said. "And that is worth knowing."

"Is it?" Anger burst from Thomas. "She is still not mine."

Roderick nodded and dropped his chin to his chest. "I am sorrier for that than I can say, brother."

"Of course, I'm glad she's alive." Thomas knew that he sounded bitter and ungrateful, but he wanted things he could never have. For a man who had always gotten the girl, it was a humbling experience. "I never thought this would be me."

With a wry laugh, Roderick smiled. "Nor I. After Tahra passed on, I never thought I would find anyone who would fill the hole within me."

Roderick had loved his first witch, Tahra, and they'd been bonded for many years. It had all happened before Thomas's time, but coimhdeacht gossiped like washerwomen, and he'd heard the story of how Roderick had stepped back and allowed

Tahra to travel beyond the veil. He'd never understood, at the time, what could make a man release the woman he loved. All too late, he got it. He had walked away from Alannah to ensure her happiness. "And now you have Maeve."

"And now I have Maeve." Roderick turned and faced the view. "I would not abandon hope."

Hope! Goddess, hope hurt more than anything. "For what?" He balled his fist. "I am technically dead, and she is alive."

Roderick sighed. He had no answer.

Because there was no answer. At least, not one Thomas could stomach.

NIAMH OBEYED her instinct as she approached Debra in the library. After a tense exchange that had somehow dragged the entire coven into taking sides, the others had left, and it was only her and Andy with Debra.

Debra looked up at her.

"I'd like to show you something," Niamh said. "I think it might help."

With a wary look, Debra glanced at Andy, before saying, "What?"

After a quick mental debate, she went with the truth. "The wolves."

"No." Debra recoiled and took a big sip of wine.

"You can trust me." Niamh opened her senses and reached for Debra's awareness. Her mistrust and fear were prickly and sour. Nudging them gently, Niamh tried to convey trust and safety.

Andy popped to his feet. His eyes sparkled behind his glasses. "Could you show me?"

"You want to meet them?" She'd never thought to make the

offer to Andy. Pack was not a sideshow amusement, but Andy was part of Baile now, and she should have taken him earlier.

Debra's hackles rose again. "You want to see wild animals?"

"Indeed." Andy rubbed his hands together. "How many people can say they have interacted with a wild wolf pack?"

Chewing her lip, Debra wavered. She looked from Andy to Niamh and back again. "I'll be safe?"

"Safe as houses." Andy got there before Niamh could answer. "Niamh will control them."

Niamh opened her mouth to correct him, and then shut it again. She didn't control animals or master them. She wasn't their leader or their owner. She was their guardian, both part of and responsible for them. She was their voice in a world that had forgotten how to hear. But Debra's mistrust was receding, so she kept that to herself.

Sending her awareness out, she touched Alpha. He took from her mind what she wanted and agreed. As one, Pack rose and moved closer to Baile. It would be better if she didn't have to take Debra out into their domain for this meet and greet. A cornered creature always felt safer on familiar turf.

"Come." Niamh gestured for Debra and Andy to follow her.

"This is terribly exciting," Andy said. "I hope I shall not embarrass myself before them."

"You won't." Niamh smiled her reassurance. Pack would read his excitement and pure motives and have no problem with Andy. With Debra's fear a strong smell, she would have to remind them the woman wasn't prey. Pack perceiving Debra as a snack was all they bloody needed to finish the day.

Warren's questioning thought brushed her mind.

Niamh opened her senses to let him know what she planned.

He didn't love the idea, but he trusted her. And she melted that he trusted her that much.

When they opened the bailey door, Pack was already waiting.

Debra drew back.

"It's all right, Mum." Taylor appeared beside her. "Take Niamh's hand, and you'll be fine."

"You saw this?" She looked at Taylor.

Taylor shook her head. "No. But Pack would never hurt anyone connected to Niamh."

Cheeks flushed with excitement, Andy shifted from foot to foot. He gestured the wolves. "Might we?"

Pack stood behind Alpha, arrayed in their order of dominance, ears pricked and eyes alert.

Niamh soothed the spiking edges of Debra's fear, and they moved forward.

Alpha lowered into a sit as they stepped outside. Pack lay down around him and lowered their heads, signaling their nonaggression.

Alpha picked up Taylor's scent markers on Debra and grew more interested in her. Pack liked Taylor and saw her as a kind of puppy.

The wolf pups streamed from the kitchen with them, yipping and prancing in their excitement. A little like furry versions of Andy.

"This is their alpha." Niamh moved closer to the large gray and white wolf. "Alpha is a bit of a misunderstood concept. He's not necessarily the strongest wolf, but he will be the most intelligent. He will hold the best memory of where to hunt."

"Oh." Debra almost trod on her heels as she tucked herself behind Niamh. "Do I put out my hand for him to sniff?"

Niamh almost laughed. "No. His sense of smell is so finely tuned he doesn't need your hand to know what you smell like already."

Alpha lay down and made himself even more nonthreatening.

"What's he doing?" Debra hissed in her ear.

"He's letting you know that you're not in danger," Niamh said. "Would you like to go closer?"

"Yes."

"No."

Andy and Debra had spoken at the same time.

"Crouch." Niamh motioned Andy. "Show them that you mean no harm."

Crouching, Andy waddled forward. "They're so beautiful."

Alpha smelled Andy's admiration and appreciated it.

"He's glad you think so." Niamh translated as well as she could. Animals didn't have fully expressed thoughts. It was more like a sense memory and vague images.

Andy toddled within reach of Alpha. "May I touch him?"

Niamh checked with Alpha first. "Yes." Then as Alpha sent the desire to her, she added, "He likes to be scratched under the ears. He can't reach that spot."

"Are you sure they're wild." Debra inched out from behind her.

"Quite wild." Niamh nodded. "If you were a threat to Baile or anyone in it, they wouldn't be sitting there so patiently."

Already Pack was restless and wanted to move.

"Oh my." Andy's face was rapt as he scratched behind Alpha's ear. "Oh my, oh my, oh my."

"Will they let me…" Debra indicated Andy in a jerky wave.

Niamh made sure first before she nodded. "If you like."

Alpha sent a prey thought to Niamh and she rejected the idea. She withheld from Debra that Alpha considered her to be a particularly ungainly deer.

Debra dropped to her knees in front of the wolf and extended her hand.

Alpha nudged her fingers.

She drew back with a gasp. "It's magic."

Yes, it absolutely was. Niamh smiled and conveyed the feeling to Alpha. It was the best kind of magic.

CHAPTER EIGHT

Alannah came to with light spearing into her eyes. She shut them again quickly. Oh Goddess, she wanted to be sick. She breathed deep and the nausea subsided. The floor wasn't moving beneath her anymore, and she wanted to weep with gratitude. Moving her head seemed like a spectacularly stupid idea, and sure to make her vomit.

She lay on something soft and warm.

A bed.

Big round wooden beams supported the roof. The ceiling was made of wood planking, and the resinous scent threatened the precarious situation in her tummy. Dull pain throbbed through her head, and she really needed a drink of water. And she needed the toilet. She risked moving her gaze to the left and right. Even her eyeballs ached.

The walls were also made of a rich, amber wood. She seemed to be in a cabin of some sort. Cottage-paned windows on the walls on either side of her admitted clear, bright light, and a glimpse of green foliage. Against the opposite wall, a door stood open, and from what she could see, it might be a bathroom.

Bloody hell, she hoped it was a bathroom, because her stomach lurched, and she ran.

Alannah made it to the loo as her system rebelled and tossed up the contents of her stomach, wave after wave until she felt like it came up from her toes. Finally, when she had nothing left, the vomiting stopped.

Wrung out and shaking, she slid to her butt and rested her head on her arms on the closed toilet seat. The bathroom floor was cool beneath her jeans and bare feet.

Smelling of lavender and mint, the bathroom looked clean and functional. Toilet—she was now on good terms with that—double vanity with wood cabinets beneath it. Claw-foot tub and a stall shower. Soft green towels hung from a towel rack, and a matching bathmat broke the tiny white octagonal pattern of the floor tiles.

She staggered to her feet. Her head swum, and she clung to the vanity. Her last moment of clarity was feeling woozy before everything went black. Now she had no idea where she was or how she'd gotten here. Vague images flit through her mind of a moving vehicle, and the murmur of men talking.

Things were not looking good.

And neither was she. A large rectangular mirror reflected her pathetic appearance back at her. She was pale enough to have been raised from the dead. Dark circles bruised the skin beneath her eyes. And her hair—ugh! Nasty clumps of what she strongly suspected were dried vomit glued it together in patches. The rest snarled around her head like a bird's nest.

Her hair would have to wait. First, she needed to find Sinead. On shaking legs, she staggered back into the bedroom.

Sinead was on the other bed. Her sister looked about as bad as she did, but still fast asleep.

Alannah staggered over, touched her cheek, and found it warm but not too hot. Sinead's chest lifted and fell in a quiet and steady rhythm.

"Sinead." Alannah shook her shoulder lightly. "Wake up."

"Argh!" Sinead rolled to her back, and her lips pinched.

Yup, she was likely feeling the same aftereffects.

"It's Alannah." She perched on the side of the bed furthest from the bathroom.

Sinead blinked her eyes open, winced, and then closed them again. She swallowed convulsively.

"It's Alannah," she whispered. "I'm okay, and so are you."

Slowly and carefully, Sinead opened her mouth.

"Where ar—" Sinead paled and heaved.

Alannah stood and pointed. "Over there."

Sinead lurched for the bathroom.

The sound of her upchucking almost got Alannah going again. She distracted herself by taking in the rest of the cabin.

It was small and neat, with an open fireplace to the right of the bathroom door. Two comfy looking, worn armchairs in a cheerful red plaid faced the stacked hearth.

A large wooden stable door led outside. She'd check it when her tummy settled.

Sinead heaved, coughed, and retched from the bathroom.

Now that her senses were coming back to her, she was aware that she stank of sick. On the two bedside tables sat bottles of water. She was desperate enough to reach for one. The seal looked still intact, and she cracked it.

The twin beds she and Sinead had been lying on were made with white sheets. Patchwork quilts, now tangled with the sheets, must have been tucked around them.

The entire place looked homey and *Little House on the Prairie*.

Where the fuck were they?

In the bathroom, Sinead stayed silent, and then the toilet flushed. She stumbled into view and leaned against the doorjamb. "You look like crap."

"Have you seen yourself?" Alannah had to laugh.

"Ugh." Sinead tripped over a rug and snatched a bottle of

water. "I haven't the stomach to face it." She cracked open the bottle and took a swig.

"Easy," Alannah said as she sipped her own water. If it was drugged, it wouldn't be much different from how last night had gone. Still, she'd rather not.

From the light pouring in, it must be daylight again.

Alannah got to her feet. The water tasted sweeter and better than any drink of water she'd ever had. Probably had something to do with the Sahara situation in her mouth and throat. She tried the door. Not surprising, it didn't budge and looked strong enough to need a tank to get through without the key. Alannah tried the window. It didn't budge, and she couldn't find any sort of latch. Outside the window was a bright, green forest. Mottled gray and white tree trunks soared farther than she could see even craning her neck. A thick blanket of fallen leaves covered the forest floor—yellow, orange, and bright red. It was beautiful. "Oh."

Sinead joined her at the window. "Wow."

"Yep." She nodded. "Look like maples to me."

"Yep." Sinead nodded. "As prisons go…"

But still a prison.

There didn't seem to be anyone else about and no sign of other buildings.

"Have we been left in the middle of a forest?" Sinead moved to the other window and peered out.

Birdsong came from the forest, and a pair of fat squirrels chased each other up one of the trunks. Maybe they had been left here to slowly starve to death. That didn't seem like something Rhiannon would do, but then again, she was no expert.

Alannah approached the bathroom. At the basin, she turned the tap. The pipes creaked and clanked, but water gushed out. She tried the warm and was pathetically glad when it responded.

Fluffy facecloths made fat sausages in a small basket on the vanity. Almost like the way they rolled linens in a hotel. She took one, wet it, and wiped her face. Goddess, that felt good.

Two toothbrushes in unopened wrappers and a tube of toothpaste nestled beside the facecloths. Alannah bent and opened the cabinets. Bars of wrapped soap, a couple glass bottles labeled face wash and bodywash and few other odds and sods occupied the shelves. It looked like they had been expected.

Alannah eyed the shower. Did she dare?

"Go ahead." Sinead appeared in the doorway. "I'll keep watch."

She didn't need asking twice, and she turned on the water in the shower. More bottles with neatly penned labels—bodywash, shampoo, and conditioner—inside the shower confirmed her suspicions about them being expected.

As gross as she felt, she didn't take long in the shower. Still, she felt better with clean hair and the smell of vomit off her. She found a brush beneath the vanity and attacked her snarls.

"Hey!" Sinead called from the bedroom. "Our stuff is here."

Alannah moved to the bedroom. "What stuff?"

Sinead stood in front of a built-in wardrobe. She gestured. "Our clothes. And somebody unpacked them."

Sure enough. The clothes hanging on hangers, or neatly folded on the shelves certainly looked like theirs. They'd even been divided on separate shelves for her and Sinead.

They were dealing with the most considerate kidnappers ever. Or the creepiest. She felt odd about somebody else handling her knickers.

"Take a shower." Alannah dropped her towel and found clean underwear. She pulled on jeans and a T-shirt and her runners. She needed to be ready for anything. Chilly after her shower, she added her most comforting wooly jumper.

Feeling a lot better, she examined every inch of the cabin. The door was still locked, and the windows still didn't have a latch. A small coffeemaker with some mugs and whatever else they might need nestled on the wardrobe's top shelf. Her system was not ready for coffee yet, so she left it there. A large geometric rug covered the floor in front of the fireplace. Wood had been laid in the fire, and she wished for a match.

Sinead was quick in the shower and even quicker to get dressed. Of course, she pulled on one of her Arcane Activist T-shirts. Sinead had started Arcane Activists a few years back, and the AA—membership of one and a half, Alannah being a supportive half vote—stood for bringing an end to discrimination against the supernaturally endowed, the dilution of magical lore through juvenile literature, the commercialization of pagan sacred sites, and fracking. It gave Alannah a small moment of normal to cling to.

They went through the cabin again, together, just to be sure. Throwing herself on her bed, Sinead huffed. "What now?"

Alannah reached for earth. It bounded back at her like a wave of power, and she reeled.

"What is it?" Sinead sat up.

"Earth." Alannah joined Sinead on the bed. "It's really strong."

"What?" Sinead took her hand.

They sent their awareness into the wooden floor beneath them.

Earth unfurled in a brilliant green shockwave that dug into the ground beneath them and fanned out. The ancient maples surrounding the cabin had the sonorous awareness of trees about to go dormant for the winter. The rose and clove scent combo of their magic was overpowering.

Sinead dropped her hand and looked around her. "I've never felt it that strong before."

Excitement fluttered in Alannah's belly. "Do you think that means we're close to the point?"

"I think we're about to find out." Sinead tensed. "Listen."

Footsteps scuffed outside, and a key turned in the latch.

A tall, muscular man stood in the doorway and grinned at them. "Oh hey, you're awake." He carried a tray in one beefy hand as he stepped into the cabin. He wrinkled his nose and winced. "Damn, it smells funky in here."

Alannah suppressed the desire to apologize. It certainly wasn't their fault they'd been sick.

"Yeah." Sinead eyed the stranger like he was shit on her shoe. "That's what happens when you kidnap people."

The man blinked at her and frowned. "Really?"

He was classically handsome, with a strong jawline, high cheekbones, and dark hair. Muscle strained at the seams of his pale blue T-shirt. He tapered to a slim waist and long legs encased in worn jeans. His booted feet clumped on the floor as he moved closer. "I've never kidnapped anyone before," he said, as he put his tray on the coffee table in front of the hearth. "So, I really wouldn't know."

Sinead shifted closer and jerked her head at him.

This was their chance. Alannah grabbed the nearest object, one of her boots, and closed from the other side.

"Uh-uh." Another man entered the cabin. "Don't be like that, ladies."

He wasn't as tall or broad as the first man, but he moved with a sort of animal grace that made Alannah take notice. Roderick and Alexander moved like that, with an economy of movement and the balance of a fighter.

Sinead had certainly taken notice and stared wide-eyed at the newcomer. "You?"

"Hey, sweet thing." He winked at her. His compelling eyes were a yellow-brown and brimmed with mischief. And something else as he ogled Sinead.

"Who are you?" Sinead bristled. "And what are we doing here?"

Both very fair questions that Alannah would also like the answer to.

"Noah." He jabbed at his chest with a thumb. "The big guy you were about to brain is Abe."

Abe straightened and blinked at them with a wounded expression. "You were going to brain me?"

"Pretty small target." Noah grinned.

Abe looked hurt and glanced from her to Sinead. "Why would you do that?"

Noah chuckled. "We kidnapped them, Abe. They're feeling a bit hostile."

"Well, yes." Abe frowned at them. "But the cabin's nice, and we stocked it just right." He pointed to the tray. "And I brought them food."

"What about any of that makes the kidnapping thing okay?" Sinead stared at Abe as if he'd lost his last brain cell.

Despite everything, Alannah felt the insane urge to laugh. Maybe it was stress getting to her.

Abe pointed to Sinead as she said to Noah, "And she's your ma—"

"Let's leave them to get settled." Noah grabbed Abe by the arm and shoved him out the door. He turned and looked at them. "Look, you're not going to believe me now, but you're in no danger. Eat." He pointed to the tray. "And rest. We'll come and get you soon, and then you can yell all you want."

Alannah drew her dignity around her. "I don't shout."

"Yeah." Noah chuckled and jerked his head at Sinead. "But I bet the sweet thing does."

CHAPTER NINE

"Assholes!" Sinead yelled at the locked door. Noah was too bloody right that she yelled, and he best get used to it, because she'd built a thunderhead of shouting inside her. The door didn't seem bothered by the insult, and she swore she could hear Noah chuckling from the other side.

Footsteps clomped away again.

Alannah inspected the food tray. "Is that him?"

"Him who?" How the hell did those prats think she and Alannah would, firstly, stomach food after the morning's heave-a-thon, and secondly, trust a bloody thing they gave them. Given how they'd broken into her and Alannah's hotel room conveniently on the tail end of the food being drugged, she'd rather starve than risk it again.

Her stomach growled its emptiness, but it would just have to cope.

Lifting a basket of bread rolls, Alannah took a sniff. "They're still warm. Freshly baked."

"Baked with arsenic probably." Sinead gave the door one more glare just in case anyone could see her and hadn't gotten the message yet. She was well pissed off.

"Was that the man from the hotel?" Alannah moved to the window and peered out. "The one who gave you the wig."

"That's him alright." And she hadn't seen his companion's face in the hotel lobby, but those shoulders matched.

"Hmm." Alannah started making her bed.

Sinead gaped at her. She was being a polite captive now? "Why are you making your bed?"

"Because I have to sleep in it." Alannah straightened the fitted sheet and shook out the comforter.

She had a point, so Sinead got busy on hers. She had nothing better to do anyway.

"You didn't mention he was fit." Alannah smoothed down her comforter.

The conversation had veered right off track. "So what?"

"I just think it's interesting." Alannah shrugged and plumped up her pillows.

"Rhiannon is a looker." Sinead needed to point her sister back in the right direction, namely, getting out of this place. "And so was Edana. Looks are hardly indicative of good character."

"Hmm." Alannah picked up her damp towel and shook it, then took it into the bathroom.

"What does that mean?" That humming was getting annoying.

Alannah bustled around, tidying up in the bathroom. "It doesn't mean anything. I just find it interesting. And you never did say how he gave you the wig."

"Do you have Stockholm syndrome or something?" For two women who were adept at guessing each other's thoughts, she was well and truly baffled by what Alannah was on about.

Coming back into the bedroom, Alannah sighed and took a look around them. She went back to the tray. "It doesn't look poisoned."

"Neither did the last meal." Okay, technically drugged and

not poisoned, because otherwise they were in the sacred grove with a cocky, mouthy spirit captor. Although, that maple forest was really lovely, and if she had to imagine her version of the sacred grove it would look a lot like what was happening outside the window—minus the snarky men in it.

Alannah took the top off the teapot and sniffed. "I don't smell anything."

"You didn't last—"

"Point taken." Alannah threw herself into one of the armchairs. "We could start a fire."

"With what?" Sinead searched for matches or a lighter on the mantel, and then went through all the drawers. "I can't find anything to light one."

Alannah pulled a face. "That would make sense." She gestured around them. "With all this wood, we could set the place on fire."

"Right." She'd been thinking along those lines. Sinead took the other armchair and stared at the stacked wood.

Outside, a woodpecker rattled, and the wind sighed through the maples. As prisons went, this one wasn't the worst. Not that she had any experience to go by. She couldn't sit here and stare at the unlit fire. She'd go mental. "Let's review what we know."

"Good." Alannah nodded, looking relieved to have something to occupy her mind. "The man from the lobby?"

"Yep."

"At the hotel, was that the first time you'd seen him?"

Sinead scoured her memory to be sure and then nodded. "Absolutely. I don't remember him at the airport, or from the plane. He hasn't been anywhere else we've been, and I definitely do not remember him at that construction site."

Alannah straightened and blinked at her. "I do."

"What?"

"I do." Alannah spoke slowly as if piecing it together. "At

least, I saw someone there. It was from a distance, but it could have been those two. I mean." She winced. "They do stand out."

Sinead suppressed her irritation. "You never said anything."

"No, I didn't," Alannah snapped. "I didn't think it was relevant to mention two blokes staring at us on a public street. Because that never happens, right?"

Alannah had a point, but the snapping was just another example of how torn things were between them. "That makes sense. I wouldn't have said anything either." Their roles had been reversed. It was normally her being bolshie and Alannah smoothing the waters.

Sinead bit back a sigh. Five hours from Greater Littleton to London, an eight-hour delay before they had found a flight to Montreal, seven and a half hours in the air, and the two weeks they'd been scouring Canada, Alannah had been this angry, icy version of herself. Sinead hated it. It felt like she'd lopped off her right leg, and the stump still ached for its missing part.

"So." Alannah tapped her fingers on her armrest. "I think we can safely rule out coincidence and say they were following us."

Sinead agreed. "Waiting for the chance to snatch us."

"Right."

Alannah shrugged. "And nobody has hurt us, so maybe we can assume they need us alive?"

"Probably." Sinead really hoped so, in any case. Then something else occurred to her. "I haven't smelled blood magic. Have you?"

"No." A tiny glimmer of hope lit Alannah's eyes. "Maybe they're not with Rhiannon?"

As much as Sinead would love to believe that, it didn't add up. "Then, who else?"

"I guess we'll find out." Alannah sighed.

"Right." Fear tightened her belly. "Just in case." Unable to voice the full extent of her fear, she cleared her throat. "You know. If things go bad. I'm sorry." She didn't want her last memory of Alannah to be of them fighting. "I'm sorry about the Thomas thing. I never meant to hurt you."

Alannah looked at her, then nodded. She looked so sad it almost broke Sinead. "I know you are. And I know why you did it. I just wish—"

Footsteps crunched outside the cabin. Sinead tensed and stared at the door. The key turned in the latch and the door opened.

Noah strolled in and grinned. "There you are."

Sinead and Alannah stood.

A man and a woman strolled in with Noah. The woman was tall and willowy with dark hair cropped close to her head. She had stunning pale blue eyes and cheekbones to die for. If these were Rhiannon's minions, she certainly chose them for their looks.

The new man was an inch or so shorter than Noah, but with the same athletic build and easy way of moving. He smiled and nodded. "I'm Josh."

"Rachel." The woman jerked a thumb at her chest.

All three were dressed in jeans and hoodies and wore thick boots.

Rachel cocked her head and sniffed. She threw a pointed glance at Noah. "She's your—"

"Yup." Noah looked away and frowned at the tray. "You didn't eat." He turned that frown on Sinead. "You need to eat."

"No, thank you." Sinead considered flipping the tray, or throwing it at him, but maybe saving her fight for what came next would be the best option. She didn't like their chances. Rachel looked fast, and Noah and Josh were both bigger than her and Alannah.

"You should come with us." Josh approached Sinead.

Noah growled and pulled one side of his lip up.

Alannah glanced at her and raised an eyebrow.

It was a strange thing to do, for certain, but even stranger was the effect it had on her. That same tingly sensation shot through her that she'd had back in the hotel lobby. Never mind bloody Stockholm syndrome, had she developed a kink?

With a chuckle, Josh put his hands up and backed away. He threw a wicked look at Noah. "Just testing."

"Don't." Noah scowled at him.

Rachel rolled her eyes. "Knock it off, you assholes." She motioned to Alannah. "Come on."

"Where?" Sinead took Alannah's hand and kept her beside her. Like sodding hell they were trotting along like good little girls.

"To get some answers to your questions." Rachel tilted her head. "Are you going to make this difficult?"

Damn fucking right they were.

"Understandable, I suppose." Rachel sighed. "Would you believe me if I told you nothing bad is going to happen to you?"

The neck on the woman. Sinead had to laugh. "You mean other than being drugged and kidnapped."

"You wouldn't have come if I'd asked." Noah shrugged and grinned.

"Ignore him." Rachel waved a dismissive hand at Noah. "He's only trying to get under your skin. Look." She spread her hands out in front of her. "You need to come with us, and it would be better for everyone if you did it without a fight."

Sinead snorted. She'd take them all on if she had to. She'd probably lose, but that didn't mean she wasn't going to try.

"Oh, sweet thing." Noah strolled closer to her. "Just so you know, I like a little feisty."

Sinead got between him and Alannah. "Don't touch her!"

"I won't." He kept coming. "But I am going to touch you."

Before she'd worked up the intention to kick or punch, he was behind her, both her wrists locked in one of his hands.

Alannah lunged for him, but Rachel got between them.

Sinead took no satisfaction from being right. These people were lightning fast.

"I really don't want to hurt you." Josh approached Alannah. "But we are going to take you to meet the reason you're here."

"Willing or not," Rachel added.

Sinead tried to wrench her hands free.

Noah tightened his hold, not actually hurting her, but not giving her an inch. "Let go of me."

"Will you behave?" His voice rumbled in her ear, and goose-bumps sprang up over her skin. He smelled bloody heavenly, and she shivered.

Cut that out.

Pressing his nose close to her neck, Noah took a breath of her.

His body was warm against her back, and Sinead was shaken. "Are you sniffing me?"

"Just be grateful he's not pissing on your leg." Josh chuckled and motioned Alannah to precede him. "Your choice."

Alannah looked at Rachel, then Josh, and finally, Noah. Her eyes met Sinead's. Now was not the time to fight.

Sinead nodded, message received and understood.

Their captors' boots clomped across the wooden floor as they left the cabin. A deep porch guarded the front of their cabin, and they stepped off to a well-trodden path scattered with falling leaves. Outside, crisp fresh air was filled with the scents of autumn. With the colder climate, winter was approaching fast, and the earth felt slow and sleepy as it readied itself for a long rest. The connection to earth thrummed up through the soles of her feet. Sinead had never felt it this strong or this present.

She gave her hands another tug. "You can let go of me."

"Maybe I don't want to." Noah chuckled, but he did release her hands.

Sinead gave her wrists an experimental twist.

"Did I hurt you?" Noah frowned down at her wrists.

"Not bloody likely." Even if he had, Sinead wouldn't give him the victory.

He nodded. "Good."

They rounded the cabin, and Sinead stopped.

They were in a sort of village, with cabins nestled between the trees and paths connecting them. People, men and women, and even children, moved between the cabins.

Noah prodded her to move. "I can carry you if you like."

"Do it, and I'll rip your hands off," she snarled over her shoulder.

Rachel laughed. "She's got some fire, your ma—"

"Yup." Noah motioned her forward.

People stopped and stared as Sinead and Alannah were marched past.

A woman frowned and then gave an odd sort of bob and nod. "Blessed."

"Blessed." Another man bowed.

What the actual fuck?

Noah murmured in her ear. "Don't let it go to your head. We don't get many visitors."

"Fuck you," she said.

"Promise?" He chuckled.

Alannah openly stared around them. "What is this place?"

Smoke rose from chimneys and filled the air with the bite of woodsmoke. Behind a couple of the cabins, neat gardens wound between the trees. People were working in those gardens, preparing the plants for the frost. Sinead couldn't help but approve. The cold would come early this year, and it would be a hard freeze.

Nothing around them looked threatening or dangerous.

They trudged past a small knot of four or five women, who stopped chatting and turned and stared at them.

"Two of them?" An older woman spoke.

Her friend nodded, and said, "Twins."

The women all nodded, as if that explained everything.

Sinead wanted answers, and she wanted them more with each step she took. She went for a not-so-wild stab in the dark. "You're not with Rhiannon, are you?"

"Now, sweet thing," Noah said, "no bad words in front of the children."

CHAPTER TEN

"I'm not your sweet thing," Sinead hissed at Noah.

Alannah nearly rolled her eyes. Sinead was right about that; she wasn't anyone's sweet thing. Feisty, snarky, opinionated, and ballsy, but very rarely sweet; that was her twin.

Alannah wasn't vocal like her twin, or incisive like her coven sister, Bronwyn. She didn't have Niamh's innate practicality, or even Mags's wonderful weird. Unlike Maeve, she wasn't sweet and charming. She cooked, and she nurtured. And she tended the earth with Sinead. She was Alannah, the meh cré-witch. Had she mentioned the cooking?

Their march through the settlement headed toward a larger log home atop a slight rise. The cabin backed into the forest, and the gentle murmur of water suggested a stream tucked somewhere in the trees.

Earth pulsed through her, prickling beneath her skin and centering in her solar plexus. Sinead would be feeling it too, if she dragged her attention away from the snack smirking at her and looking like he was loving every minute of it.

Thomas used to smirk like that, like he reveled in every part of her. She missed him like the final puzzle piece to her happiness. Reflexively, she pressed her palm to the constant ache in her chest. What a bloody mess. How the hell had she fallen in love with a ghost? It wasn't fair, and it sodding well didn't make any sense.

Flanked by their escort, they climbed four wide wooden stairs to a deeply shaded porch. Large rocking chairs with brightly embroidered pillows decorated the space. It would be a lovely place to sit and appreciate the beauty surrounding them.

Rachel knocked before opening the bright red cottage-paned door. "Kate," she called. "We've got them."

"Great." A short, curvy woman with long wavy chestnut hair bustled toward them. Over her leggings and hoodie, she wore a large floral apron with *Get Your Fat Pants On* emblazoned across the top. She wiped her hands on a dishtowel as she walked toward them.

She had keen gray eyes that fastened on Sinead and then Alannah. Her face was arresting rather than pretty. The sort of face that would grow on you and owed its attractiveness to the intelligence in her eyes. "Hi." She held out her hand. "I'm Kate."

"I don't care," Sinead snapped. "What the fuck are we doing here?"

Kate blinked and then grinned at Noah. "This is your one?"

"Yup." Noah winked at Sinead. "She's my sweet—"

"I will deball you if you call me that again." Sinead turned her hostility on Noah.

They needed answers, not a fight, so Alannah stepped forward and took Kate's hand. "I'm Alannah, and that's Sinead." She pointed to her sister. "And we would like to know why we're here."

"A valid question." Kate crinkled her nose. "And I'll answer all your questions, but first an apology." She grimaced. "The way we brought you here was—"

"Abduction," Sinead snapped. "Kidnapping. Held to ransom. Hijacked. Seized." Her smile was more of a snarl. "Take your pick."

"Right." Kate smoothed her apron and then her hair. "All of those. And I don't know if it helps, but we're really sorry."

Sinead folded her arms and scowled at her.

"Are you hungry?" Kate turned and fluttered deeper into the home. "You must be hungry if the drugs made you sick." She stopped and winced, as if she'd just realized she wasn't helping her cause. "We have to wait for a couple people, and this lot could always eat." She waved a hand to encompass Noah, Rachel, and Josh.

"It's true." Rachel laughed and peeled off to sit at a large wooden table.

Sinead looked about ready to explode, and Alannah sidled up beside her and put a hand on her arm. She wanted answers as much as her sister, but Kate hardly looked like a hardened criminal. She looked like the sort of woman Alannah might have been friends with—minus the drugging and abduction part of their introduction.

Kate's cabin was homely, with a gleaming, bright kitchen that made Alannah itch to rattle pots and pans. Stainless steel appliances were surrounded by gleaming white granite marble top. Cream cabinets and open shelving adorned the walls, while the lower cabinets were painted sage green.

Beside the kitchen was a rough-hewn table with ladder-back chairs. Josh took a seat beside Rachel and looked at Kate expectantly.

"See what I mean?" She smiled and bustled back into the kitchen.

The rich, nutty aroma of freshly brewed coffee lured Alannah closer. And now that her tummy had settled, she was hungry. The aroma of fresh baking and bacon hung in the air.

Kate scooped fluffy yellow eggs on a platter, a mound large enough to feed twenty Rodericks. Goddess, she missed Baile almost as much as she missed Thomas.

"Sit, sit." Kate waved them toward the table. "Coffee?"

"Yes, please." Alannah would risk another drugging for a cup of coffee.

Sinead threw her a dark look. "No, thanks."

"Tea?" Kate looked at Sinead hopefully.

"Answers." Sinead folded her arms.

"Soon. I promise." Kate opened the fridge and pulled out a jug of orange juice and placed it on the table.

Josh and Rachel helped themselves from the grouping of mismatched glasses in the center of the table.

"Food is important around here." Josh winked at Sinead.

Despite the situation, Alannah nearly laughed.

Kate poured Alannah a mug of coffee and handed it to her. "Cream and sugar on the table."

To the left of the table was a comfy sitting room filled with robust squishy furniture in front of a large burning fire. It looked happy and welcoming and not the lair of some evil minion.

The door opened again, and another tall, dark man walked in. He was undeniably handsome, taller and broader than both Noah and Josh, but his aura of authority drew her to him.

Rachel and Josh stood and nodded to him before taking a seat again.

"There you are." Kate brushed past him and put a basket of pastries on the table. She jerked her head at the newcomer and pointed. "Sit!"

Rachel laughed while the newcomer raised an eyebrow at Kate.

With a smirk, Kate went back to the kitchen.

The newest addition approached Sinead first. "I'm Zach." He

held out a large, broad hand. "And I'm the one you should be mad at." He gestured to Noah. "I sent Noah and Abe to find you and do what was necessary."

"Why?" Sinead bristled and glared at Zach.

"Won't you sit?" Zach said it politely enough, but it had the unmistakable ring of a command.

Alannah could have told him not to try that with Sinead.

Spine snapping straight, Sinead raised her chin at him. "I'll stand."

Zach stared at her, and then took a long sniff. He looked at Noah. "Well, that's unexpected."

"Tell me about it," Noah grumbled and moved around Sinead to take a seat at the table.

The food Kate spread on the table looked delicious, and Alannah approached cautiously. The stack of golden, fluffy pancakes made her mouth water.

"It's safe," Kate said and smiled. "I made them this morning, and there's nothing in them that shouldn't be there."

Sinead snorted.

Taking a different tack, Alannah pulled out a chair and sat. She added cream and sugar to her coffee and took a sip. It was delicious, and she took another. "Lovely coffee."

"Thank you," Kate said. "I'm fussy about my beans."

"Do you grow them yourself?" Alannah recognized a fellow foodie.

"Yes." Kate grinned. "Of course, in this climate, we have to make certain adaptations, but I'm very happy with the result."

Alannah was dying to ask more, but the look on Sinead's face promised imminent war.

Handing a platter to Rachel, Noah looked at Sinead. "You can sit over here and be comfortable while you glare."

"Go fu—"

"She's still upset," Noah said to Zach.

Zach glanced at Sinead and then Alannah. "She has every reason to be. Now stop being a dick."

Noah chuckled but got down to eating.

The next few minutes passed in a flurry of food being put on the table, and people helping themselves. Kate took a seat opposite Alannah.

Zach stayed beside Sinead near the door.

"Bacon?" Kate held up a perfectly crisped rasher and waved it at Zach. "Treat?"

Zach looked at her, but what a look it was, loaded with all sorts of unspoken messages, and Alannah was glad she wasn't Kate in that moment.

She could risk a pancake. With the way Josh tucked into them, there didn't appear to be anything wrong with them. She salivated as Josh poured an amber stream of maple syrup over his stack. It dribbled over the side and pooled with melted butter.

Alannah put a pancake on her plate and Josh passed her the maple syrup. She added a small dollop.

"You'll need more than that." Rachel grinned and dug into her eggs. "We tap that ourselves, and it's the best you'll taste."

Josh grunted his agreement and went to town on a pile of bacon.

With a nod of encouragement, Kate motioned Alannah's plate. "Eat. Or it'll be gone before you know it."

"We'd like those answers now." Alannah cut into her pancake as she spoke. She nearly groaned her appreciation out loud. "These are delicious. I must get your recipe."

"Alannah!" Sinead scowled at her.

Bugger! She shouldn't be getting chummy with her captors. She threw Sinead an apologetic glance. "They really are very good. You should try one."

"You really should." Noah stared at Sinead. "You haven't eaten since yesterday."

Sinead glared.

"Right." Zach nodded. "I wouldn't trust us either after what you've been through."

Alannah's pancake bite jammed in her throat. She was eating with the enemy. Oh, well. Too late now. She grabbed the egg platter and helped herself. And as it was already too late, she wasn't going to miss that bacon either.

Zach strolled into the kitchen and poured himself a mug of coffee. "Why don't we start with what we know about you."

Sinead watched him like a hawk.

"We know who you are." He sipped his coffee. "We know that you're cré-witches and that you came here from Baile Castle. We also know you're looking for the earth point." He shrugged like he hadn't just blown their minds. "We weren't expecting two earth witches."

"They're twins," Josh said.

Zach took a breath. "Yeah, got that."

Sinead glanced at her and shook her head. Not that Alannah had any intention of volunteering any more information.

"We're like you," Kate said, and then flushed. "Well, not exactly like you. We don't have your…er…level of gifts, but we also serve Goddess."

"As do we," Zach motioned himself, Noah, Josh, and Rachel.

The way Zach spoke suggested the four of them were different from Kate and her *we*. Alannah had assumed they were all part of the same group. When Niamh had gone to South Africa, she'd found a group of hidden witches guarding the fire point. It was entirely possible that a similar group existed here around the earth point. Maybe Mags had even found her own hidden witches in Moscow. Goddess, she hoped Mags was well and safe. Since they'd discovered Rhiannon's ability to spy on Baile via Warren, they were all operating in secret.

"This settlement," Kate said, "was established back in the fifties, by a group of hippies really. But they were more than hippies." She rested her elbows on the table and cradled her mug in her palms. "They were people who had special abilities, abilities that were not…mainstream."

"Or accepted," Zach added.

"From the outside, we're a band of misfits who keep to ourselves." Kate jerked her chin toward Alannah. "Much like you were at Baile. We hide what we're really doing here."

"Which is what?" Sinead asked.

"Serving Goddess." Kate glanced at Sinead. "Practicing our limited gifts." She looked at Zach before she continued. "And guarding the earth point."

"It's here?" Excitement won over Alannah's suspicion. She had felt earth strongly since their arrival, and so had Sinead.

Sinead was looking a little less bellicose, but still suspicious.

Kate nodded, but her expression grew wary. "It is."

"It's the real reason this settlement was established." Zach leaned his hips against the kitchen counter. "There was mounting pressure on it being discovered. So much so that the folks who established this place brought it here to hide it." He folded his arms and looked grim. "We have a mutual enemy, and she's not playing around."

Alannah couldn't help but gape at him. The Rhiannon commonality was one thing, but Alannah didn't want to risk the Voldemort effect by saying her name, so she took another route. "Cardinal power points don't move."

"Not easily, they don't." Kate sighed and looked sad. Then she plastered a smile on her face. "Anyway. We're here to help, and you're safe here."

"Really?" Sinead scoffed. "And we're supposed to believe all this just because you tell us."

"No." Zach shrugged. "You're free to go anytime. But if you do"—he stared at Sinead—"you need to consider two things. One." He counted points off on his finger. "The earth point is here, and you're going to need Kate and her people to activate it. And two, Rhiannon knows you're in Canada, and she's looking for you."

Noah pushed back his chair and folded his arms. "She almost had you in Montreal. We had to move fast."

CHAPTER ELEVEN

As they left Kate's cabin, Sinead sort of wished she'd eaten some of the breakfast on offer. Her stomach growled and reminded her she hadn't eaten properly since yesterday lunch. "What the hell was that?"

Alannah strolled beside her, taking everything in. "What?"

"Swapping recipes, eating their food." Alannah was just too trusting sometimes. It always made Sinead need to play bad cop. "Must I remind you what happened last time we ate anything from these people?"

Shrugging, Alannah took a deep draft of fresh forest air. "I went with my instinct, and I don't think they're dangerous. But I do have more questions."

"That makes two of us." Sinead's head hurt with all it was trying to process. Nobody seemed to pose any threat, and Kate had invited them to walk around and talk to people freely, but the way they'd been brought here still pissed her off. They'd been drugged, for fuck's sake. And however charming everyone appeared to be, she wasn't ready to let that go yet.

"Earth is strong here." Alannah changed direction toward the forest. "It's everywhere."

"Right." Sinead had felt that too. "Want to check in with it?"

A big smile broke over Alannah's face but didn't quite dispel the sadness in her eyes. "My thought exactly."

As they drew closer to the forest, Sinead half expected someone to leap out and stop them.

Her nape prickled and she turned.

Noah stood on Kate's porch, one muscular shoulder propped against a support post. Coffee mug in hand, he jerked his chin at her.

She didn't have time for him and his crap. In a perfect world, however, she would definitely take a big old bite out of him.

"He's fit," Alannah said.

He certainly was. "He's not my type."

"Oh, please." Alannah snorted. "He is exactly your type."

No point in arguing that because Alannah knew her too well.

"We both know if Maeve hadn't—"

"No." Sinead didn't want to hear the rest of that sentence. There were some things she wouldn't even admit to her twin. She'd take her attraction to Roderick to the grave. But there had been times… Roderick adored Maeve. End of a story that hadn't started and never would.

Zach left Kate's house and Noah dropped into step beside him. They had their heads together, and their conversation looked intense. They took a path going in the opposite direction and disappeared amongst the trees.

Sinead toyed with following them, but she'd had enough Noah for the day, and she would much rather check in with earth. Despite their situation, the strength of their cardinal point excited her. It raised endless possibilities, not the least of which was finally being able to heal Baile's wards.

"What's with the sniffing?" Alannah was staring at the forest where Zach and Noah had gone.

Sinead had noticed the same thing. "It's odd."

"It really is." Alannah stopped at the edge of the forest. "Will this do?"

Sinead sensed eyes on them and motioned Alannah deeper between the trees. "Let's go a little farther."

Wind sighed through the towering maples around them. Colored leaves fluttered down in a bright aerial ballet. It was a lovely spot, and Sinead stopped and took a deep breath. It felt like the first proper breath she'd taken since they'd left Baile. "I don't sense any danger."

"That doesn't mean much." Alannah crouched and pushed her fingers through the leaf carpet into the earth beneath. "You coming?"

"Right." Alannah was right. If Rhiannon walked around with a great big banner and a marching band playing creepy music, it would be a lot easier to spot her coming.

Sinead twined her fingers with Alannah's in the rich, damp soil. Earth rose like a gleeful puppy in a green nimbus around their joined fingers and in the smells of rose and cloves that perfumed the forest.

Joined, they sent their guardian gift into the earth.

The land was rich and healthy. The great tree's root systems stretched deep down into the cool dark of the soil. The magic of growing things all around them swept through and over them in a peaceful, calm blanket.

A shimmer caught their magic, and they approached it slowly.

"Wards?" Alannah whispered.

Sinead narrowed their magic focus on the shimmer. "Definitely." Earth reacted in a surge to her surprise. "They're similar to the ones at Baile."

"Not as...strong." Alannah frowned and glanced at her. "But they definitely have a familiar feel."

"Which means..."

"They were probably set by a cré-witch."

Considering who had set the Baile wards, that wasn't necessarily a good thing. "Rhiannon?"

"I don't think so." Alannah drew their magic merge closer to the shimmering, opalescent wards. "They're definitely cré-magic, but the signature is different. Not as ancient."

"Huh." Sinead let her warden senses roam and pick up what they could. Kate had mentioned the commune being similar to Baile in magic.

"There's also a strange, different something here." Alannah frowned and closed her eyes. "Oh!" She opened her eyes.

"What?"

Alannah shook her head. "No, it's nothing. You'll think I'm mad."

"I already know you're mad." It was so close to their normal banter it made Sinead's heart hurt. "Tell me. No more keeping stuff to ourselves, we agreed."

"Well." Alannah shrugged. "It feels a bit like Niamh's pack."

"What?" That couldn't be right. There was certainly overlap with guardian and warden blessings, but they were two different branches of blessing. Sinead concentrated on their merge and let it touch the wards. That's exactly what it felt like. She didn't bother keeping the amazement out of her tone. "You're right."

"So." Alannah dropped earth and took her hand back. "We know they're warded, and they know all about us. We also can make an accurate guess that one of those original founders was a cré-witch."

"Or descended from one." Sinead dropped to her bum. "I also don't think we're getting the full story here."

Alannah glanced at her. "Meaning?"

"I don't know." And she hadn't had time to sort through her impressions enough to fully develop her instinct. "I sense they aren't telling us the whole truth. There's a lot of loaded looks and pauses when they speak."

"Hmm." Alannah nodded. "We should keep our eye on that."

Earth magic surged beneath Sinead's skin.

Alannah gasped as she felt it too.

By tacit agreement, they plunged their joined hands into the earth. Their blessing shot out in a series of ever-growing tendrils, stronger and more vibrant than either of them had ever felt it. The green glow around their hands flared emerald and eye-searingly bright.

"You're doing it, aren't you?" Two young girls stood to their left. In leggings and sweatshirts, they looked like typical teenagers. One dark, the other with nutty brown hair similar to Kate's.

Sinead studied the girl with hair like Kate's. The similarities went further. She had the same eye color, and although her face was rounder, it had the same delicate bone structure. She'd never believed in beating around the bush. "You look like Kate."

"Sister." The girl sniffed and pointed to herself. "Younger sister."

Earth magic sparked and tingled beneath Alannah's skin. She rubbed the pebbled skin on her forearm.

The darker girl stepped forward and stared at the spot their hands were still connected in the earth. "Is that how you do it?"

"Do what?" Sinead wasn't going to toss information about until she knew more about this place.

"Earth magic." The girl rolled her eyes. "You're the earth witch." She grimaced. "Well, earth witches. We weren't expecting two of you."

Kate's sister nodded at her friend. "They're twins."

"Cool." Her friend shrugged and stuck her hands in the front pouch of her sweatshirt. "I'm Sara, and this is Dhara."

"Nice to meet you." Ever the friendlier of the two of them, Alannah got to her feet and dusted the seat of her jeans. "I'm Alannah, and this is Sinead. And you've already noticed we're twins."

Sara studied them with gleaming amber eyes. "You're like, identical."

"Yup." Feeling at a disadvantage, Sinead stood as well. She jerked her head at Alannah. "She's the nice one."

Dhara laughed, while Sara studied her like a smear on a microscope slide. "Noah is my uncle."

Clearly, weird ran up the family tree.

"And you live here?" Alannah gave the girls a disarming smile.

Like Alannah's smile did with just about everybody, it relaxed the teens. "Yeah." Dhara shrugged. "Kate and I were born here." She crossed her arms. "Our mom died when I was born."

"I'm so sorry," Alannah said. "Ours died when we were three."

"But we looked after her," Sara said and nudged Dhara. "All of us."

Dhara smiled at her. "Yeah, you did."

"Our aunts took care of us," Alannah said. "We were raised in a castle, but it was a group of people, a bit like this."

"Baile Castle." Dhara nodded. "That's in England."

"Huh." Sara cocked her head. "Is it cool like the forest?"

"It doesn't suck." Sinead had never felt this old. Thank Goddess she'd gotten some practice speaking to children with Taylor. Not that these two were children, and at their age, she would have set anyone straight who suggested as much. "But your forest is lovely." Then she went information diving. "And it's warded."

"Why wouldn't it be?" Sara looked at her as if she had a screw loose. "We need to protect the people here."

Alannah took over, and her nonthreatening manner was a definite improvement on Sinead's attempt. "From what?"

"Lots of stuff. People." Sara's gaze narrowed on Alannah. "You ask a lot of questions."

Dhara touched Sara's arm like she was comforting her. "It's okay," she said. "We can trust them. We've been waiting for them."

"But—" Sara shook her head. "Want us to show you around?"

"Yes, please," Alannah said before Sinead had decided if she wanted that.

Sara nodded. "Well, this is the forest." She rolled her eyes. "Obviously, and it's all around us." She jerked her thumb over her shoulder. "You've seen that part of the village. That's the main part, and Kate lives there because she's kind of the head around here."

Sinead had definitely gotten that vibe from Kate, and she tucked the useful nugget away.

Sara pointed to their left and behind them. "I live down there with my family."

"Your Uncle Noah?" Alannah turned and looked in that direction.

"No." Sara shook her head. "Noah lives with the other wo —guys."

"We should take them to see the craft cabins," Dhara said and tugged at Sara's elbows. Her smile seemed a little too bright as she looked at them. "Everybody here has a job, and that's where those happen."

Alannah motioned them onward. "Sounds lovely."

Sara led the way as Dhara walked alongside them. "Will you tell me about Baile?" Her gray eyes were almost pleading. "And the rest of the coven."

Sinead let Alannah handle the chatting as she looked around her. The settlement appeared to be more or less self-sufficient. It was also divided into sections within the forest. There could be many more segments, so she was glad Alannah had accepted the offer of a tour.

"We have a lot fewer people than you do," Alannah said. "There were only four of us: Sinead and me, Mags and Niamh."

Dhara nodded. "And then Bronwyn came."

"Right." Alannah threw Sinead a lightning-fast glance. Apparently, what Kate had said about the settlement knowing all about them hadn't been an exaggeration.

"And then Maeve and Roderick." Dhara looked at Alannah for confirmation.

"Right." Alannah hesitated as if choosing what to say next.

Dhara leaned closer. "We know about them too. That they were part of the statue."

"Okay." Alannah kept it impressively cool. "Why don't you tell us what you know, so I don't bore you going over what you already know."

Sara scowled over her shoulder at Dhara.

Dhara shook her head. "The witches who started this place came from Baile." She waved a hand through the air. "A long time ago. They were descendants of the witches from there."

That cleared up the wards.

"There were three of them," Dhara said.

Sara sighed and growled something under her breath.

Sinead thought it sounded a bit like TMI.

"They escaped from Baile the night of the coven massacre," Dhara said. "A guy helped them, but nobody knows who that was." She shrugged. "Or if they did, they never said."

"Down there"—Sara raised her voice and pointed to their right—"is the river. It's fine now, but you don't want to go there in spring. The snow melt swells it, and the current can sweep you away."

The possibility of witches escaping that night had been theorized at Baile, but this confirmed it. Sinead had her suspicions about who that helping hand had been, but until she could ask him, she didn't want to go spreading rumors. Alexander would hate it if she ruined his bad boy persona. "How did the witches get here from Baile?"

"That's another long story," Dhara said. "They didn't come

straight here. They hid in England for a while, then went to Europe, and finally traveled to the States." She shrugged. "Then when things got difficult in the States, they came north."

Alannah made a sympathetic face. "Witches are never really welcome anywhere, not even now."

"Right." Dhara shook her head. "Ignorance."

"And you?" Alannah asked. "What do you do here?"

"Oh!" Dhara bit her lip and stared into the trees. "Well, actually I'm the—"

"You also don't want to walk in the forest alone at night." Sara was near enough yelling. "We don't get a lot of wild animals, but there are bears and coyotes."

"Sara!" Dhara snapped. "Stop, it's okay."

"You don't know that." Sara whirled and pinned Sinead with a hostile stare. "And…"

Sinead wasn't going to let it go there. "And what?"

"Some of the trees are first growth." Sara locked on her with a fierce gaze. "They grow older here because of the wards."

"I see what you're doing." Sinead wasn't going to let some teen with an attitude get away with that load of bollocks.

Sara snorted. "Duh!"

CHAPTER TWELVE

Andy wanted to thank Baile anew every time he sat in his office. He ran a palm over the supple green leather of his chair. It helped him to think.

The view helped as well. The sea was choppy today, white horses riding the waves and the water a stormy gray. It echoed the laden, pewter clouds blocking any sun.

"They're a clever one." He often spoke aloud to Baile. He liked to think she enjoyed their chats. "I almost didn't catch them worming their way about."

Earlier this afternoon, he'd discovered another IP address lurking around all the areas of cyber space that most interested Andy. Tricky little perisher too, and Andy had almost not picked them up. Almost. He chuckled. "But not that clever."

Trouble had been coming at Baile and the coven for weeks now, and from multiple directions. A man with a keen eye for a touch of skullduggery would consider that to be too many coincidences for his peace of mind. So, he'd started his own mini witch hunt.

"Witch hunt," he said. "Get it?"

The fire gave a soft *pop*.

When he'd still been part of the Valuation Office Agency, the order to evaluate Baile for rates and taxes had come down the line, and at the time, he hadn't thought any more about it. At the VOA, you received an instruction and acted on it. It wasn't the sort of place that encouraged free or creative thinking, but they'd paid his salary, and the benefits had been marvelous. The job itself was like watching paint dry, but it had given him plenty of free time for the Malden Marauders and his internet explorations. So, he'd hopped in his car and headed this way to do his job.

At first, he'd been distracted, and quite frankly, frustrated, by his inability to physically reach Baile, or he might have caught the irregularity sooner. The instruction had originated out of nowhere, and now another one had popped into the system with someone else from the VOA on the job. His attempts to trace the source of the instruction had dead ended. Not that he'd give up, but he didn't want to raise suspicions by blundering around.

Next, he'd wanted to understand why the local constabulary was so very interested in a stray bullet casing. Again, one of those mystery orders that originated from the ether and turned the screws. Another dead end. Another item on his to-do list.

Stealth and subtlety were the key. Like a phantom, he ghosted his way through cyber space. *"They seek him here, they seek him there. Those Frenchies seek him everywhere. Is he in heaven, or is he in hell? That damned elusive Pimpernel."* When a quote fit, a quote fit. "Literal reference, my lady."

He'd been shadowing his way along one of those cyber trails when their mutual friend had appeared. So subtle, and so sly, he could almost admire the bugger.

Andy's logical first step had been to reinforce Baile's cyber security. They didn't want Nosy poking around his system and gaining access to their information. It took him about forty minutes to lock Baile up tighter than a drum.

And wouldn't you know it. Look who had just dropped by for a visit. "Ah! Well, my lady, they are a persistent blighter." Andy watched the activity on his screen as Nosy tried to code around his newly applied measures. "Well, I spiked your guns." Andy snickered. "Hoist on your own petard."

A floorboard creaked, and he smiled up at Baile. "Liked that did you?"

A bookcase groaned and a book dropped on its side.

Time to take the game to them. Andy got back to his paperwork for having Baile declared a religious site. As a religious site, they would be tax exempt. Of course, Roderick would bluster and blow about playing their cards close to their chest, but until Roderick could produce a way to finance their tax shortfall, Andy would have to get creative.

"Our Roderick won't like this," he said to Baile. "Of course, we'll have to prove that you have a following, and that said following come here for spiritual guidance, but I don't foresee a problem there." He grinned at the room. "You are a truly marvelous place in which the wondrous is possible."

A cushion appeared behind his back.

Mags had told him that he'd been here at Baile before, in a previous lifetime. That he had failed to be accepted as a witch. Andy knew, down to his marrow, that he was now exactly where he should be, when he should be, and doing exactly what Baile needed of him.

Swords and battle-axes had been all very well in days of yore, but this modern world demanded finesse that a man of his talents was uniquely qualified to offer.

He did love a sword though. Roderick had been teaching him how to use one, and a part of him would love to show the Malden Marauders all that he'd learned. Particularly that blowhard, know-it-all Crispin Caruthers. Bloody man thought he knew all there was to know about sword fighting. Andy would love to set him against Roderick, just for five minutes. "He'd be pissing in his braies."

His application for Baile to be declared a religious site would demand a response, and their covert friend would be most interested in this newest development, and as eager to quash it. That's when Andy would spring his trap. A neat little sequence that would track the bugger to their source.

It was like a game of chess. You always needed to be thinking several moves ahead. And if they didn't take the bait, Andy had a couple of other traps to deliver.

He sat back with a satisfied smile. In truth, he'd enjoyed the challenge. It had been quite some time since an opponent had actually forced him to think.

"I'll get the blighter," he said. "And they will never bother you again."

Someone tapped on the door.

"Enter," he called.

Debra popped her head around the jamb. "Are you busy?"

"Never too busy for you." He stood and motioned her in. Debra was a damn attractive woman. With her aggressively blond hair and revealing clothes, she was not his usual type. Women like Debra intimidated him, and never ever gravitated to nerds like himself. In the outside world, they would have passed each other by. Here at Baile, however, he'd had time to get to know her.

Behind her tough exterior, Debra was a hard-working single mum who wanted the best for her child and would do what she must to make that happen. She chose the wrong man over and over again because her relationship with her father had given her a skewed idea of her own value.

"Taylor is scrying." Debra took the chair that faced the view by the hearth. Her tight jeans showcased long, shapely legs. The tight fit of her pink, fluffy sweater conformed to her full breasts.

If Andy had seen her in a pub, he would not have bothered.

Women with asses like Debra's didn't talk to men with faces like his—to paraphrase a popular movie. He poured her a glass of white wine and took it to her. "It is her blessing."

"I know." Debra smiled her thanks and sighed. "It's a lot, you know?"

"I do know." He chose a single malt and joined her by the fire. "But there is something wonderful about it."

She sipped her wine and gave him a small smile. "I suppose."

They sat in silence for a while. Warmth from the fire and the gathering twilight made it feel cozy and intimate.

"Talk to me about something else," Debra said. "Tell me what you've been doing."

"Ah." Women like Debra, in his experience, would glaze over if he went on about his computer stalking. Still, she had asked. "I was working on Baile's taxation issue."

Debra nodded and sipped her wine. She didn't look like she was ready to make her escape.

"And I discovered something." As much as he enjoyed his chinwags with Baile, Debra would speak back with words. "It seems we have a very busy mole making trouble for us."

"Oh?" Debra's hazel eyes widened, and she leaned forward.

He resisted the urge to peek into the intriguing shadows at her neckline. "And they're very good. I almost missed them."

Debra winked. "But not better than you, because you found them."

Well, yes, he had, but he wasn't one to boast. "Indeed."

"Did you smash them?" Debra's eyes glittered.

"I did not." He had to laugh. "I did something better."

Her gaze fixed on his face in a most gratifying manner.

"I laid a trap for them," he said. "Next time they come poking around, I shall follow them back to their lair."

"Oh." Debra bit her bottom lip. "And then you'll smash them."

"To smithereens." He grinned. The single malt slid down his throat in a peaty burn. Roderick had excellent taste in scotch.

"I'm not clever like you." Debra stared at the view, shadows in her pretty eyes.

"But you are clever in other ways." He wanted to banish those doubts from her eyes and her heart. "You are a wonderful mother and have managed to raise a daughter with very little help and make a life for yourself. And"—he held up a finger—"Taylor tells me you are a gifted decorator."

Debra's cheeks went pink. "She would say that. She's my daughter."

"A daughter who you have raised to have a good mind of her own, and to form her own opinions."

Debra bit her lip, and Andy experienced the compelling and visceral need to do the same to that lip.

"Will you tell me about Rhiannon?" Debra's gaze was direct. "All of it."

Andy nodded. She had every right to know the extent of the danger she and Taylor faced. "We'll need another drink for this conversation."

NIAMH DIDN'T GIVE a crap about social media. She'd spent most of her life paying it no attention, but even she was disappointed as she looked at the results of her latest TikTok. A stiff breeze came over the seawall like the harbinger of the coming autumn. Animals all around them were preparing for winter. A newly arrived Scottish wildcat slunk closer to her.

According to her phone, thirty-two people had viewed her TikTok, and only twenty-eight had liked it. It was nice that fourteen people had shared it though. At least those fourteen were enjoying what she put out.

Still, the number of views just made it clear this was a thundering waste of time. She was going to have to find another way to practice her blessing.

"Right." Taylor marched around the bailey like a miniature general. "I like that cat, but today, we're shooting a thing with birds." She jammed her hands on her hips. "What can you do?"

"They're not trained toys." Niamh needed to keep pointing this out. The animals came to her because she was their guardian. They didn't perform for her because she offered them treats or frightened them into it. The wildcat batted at her legs.

Taylor rolled her eyes. "I know that. We've been over it."

Niamh clenched her jaw before she sounded like a twelve-year-old herself.

"We need something impressive." Taylor narrowed her eyes and tipped her chin up as she gave it some thought. "Something that will grab attention."

All animals were worthy of attention in Niamh's mind, but they'd "been over" that too.

Perched on the seawall, Warren shot her an amused glance.

Niamh had a theory he only came along to watch because it made him laugh. She let him know through the bond what she thought about that.

Warren chuckled and winked at her.

That wink went straight to her girl bits. Between Taylor having nightmares, Mags being kidnapped, the twins missing, and now Debra, they never had a moment to themselves. And she dearly wanted a whole bunch of moments alone with her sexy coimhdeacht. She'd start begging if the abstinence went on much longer.

Warren shifted and let her feel his own frustration through the bond. He was right there with her.

In the forest surrounding Baile, stags were coming into rut, and that definitely was not helping matters.

"We need a big bird, a raptor." Taylor clicked her fingers. She put her thumb tips together and made a box with her forefingers. Peering through the square, she closed one eye. "Moody sky. Bird winging in. Lands on your forearm." She swung her hand camera on Niamh. "Perched on your forearm. Intense look. Settles. Maybe you feed it something. Flies off." She nodded and muttered to herself before looking at Niamh. "Got it?"

"Taylor?" Niamh really hated to dent her enthusiasm. "That's easy enough, but how is this helping me use my blessing?"

Warren gave her an encouraging smile. More than anyone, he understood her frustration of being isolated at Baile until it was safe to venture forth and use her blessing. Bronwyn understood as well, but as the healer was pregnant, that gave her an even greater incentive to stay out of harm's way.

"We're building your following," Taylor said as if it were patently obvious. "I'll put a couple of bird facts in the soundtrack, and we're done."

As much as Niamh didn't like doing these things, she loved Taylor's enthusiasm. "But, lovely, that will only work if people watch them."

"Eh?" Taylor gaped at her.

Niamh went gently. For all the attitude, Taylor was only twelve. "Only thirty-two people watched the last TikTok. Maybe we should try something else?"

Taylor blinked and glanced at Warren as if he might shed some light.

"The views." Niamh handed her phone to Taylor. "There are only thirty-two." She voiced as much enthusiasm as she could as she added, "But twenty-eight of those liked it, and we did get some shares."

"K," Taylor said and stared at her.

Niamh put her arm around Taylor's shoulders. "Okay," she said. "Let's think about something else. Maybe there isn't a market for animal TikTok."

"K," Taylor repeated and threw up her hands. "Thirty-two k,

Niamh." She glanced at Warren and raised her eyebrows. "That means thirty-two thousand people."

That couldn't be right. "Eh?"

Taylor shoved her phone toward Niamh. "Look at the little k next to the number. That means thousands."

Warren stood and came over. He looked a little flummoxed. "Thirty-two thousand people watched this thingie?"

"Since this morning," Taylor said. "Yesterday's TikToks have cleared three hundred k, and the day before are even more."

"Oh." Niamh couldn't think of anything to say. That did sound gratifyingly impressive.

Warren smiled at her. "You're an internet sensation."

Her chest warmed with his approval.

"She's getting there." Taylor nodded to her father before turning back to Niamh. "You have over two hundred thousand followers and growing," Taylor said. "And look." She held up her phone. "That thirty-two k is now fifty-eight k."

Warren grinned at Niamh. "I'd watch you."

"Gross, Dad." Taylor made retching noises. "Now." She clapped her hands. "About that bird."

Niamh went with the flow. "How would a white-tailed eagle work for you?"

"How big are they?" Taylor narrowed her eyes.

Niamh had to give that some thought. "About a two-meter wingspan." Then she produced the clincher. "And they've been missing from Britain for two centuries. It's very exciting that they're back."

Taylor beamed at her like a proud parent. "Do it."

CHAPTER THIRTEEN

Sinead woke suddenly. Everything looked, smelled, and felt unfamiliar. Even the bed didn't feel like hers.

It came back to her slowly. She was in Canada, in a settlement outside Ottawa, sleeping in a log cabin, and Alannah was in the second twin bed. She felt vaguely uneasy, as if something had woken her, and she lay still, eyes straining against the dark, and listened. Far from any city or town, it was so much darker here.

A soft whimper broke the night silence. Then the keening of a being in distress. The sound came from Alannah's direction.

"Alannah?"

Silence.

That must have been what woke her.

Alannah thrashed, startling Sinead, and whimpered again.

"Alannah?" She sat up in bed and tried to peer through the dark at Alannah. As her eyes adapted to the night, she could make out the shadowy shape of the bed beside her. "Alannah?"

Alannah sniffed and sobbed. She muttered quietly and shifted in her bed.

Easing out of the covers, Sinead padded over to her twin. "Alannah?"

Alannah was fast asleep, her face twisted in distress.

Snapping on the light, Sinead reached out to wake her, and then stopped. Tears tracked down Alannah's face as she cried in her dreams. The sounds Alannah made were heartbreaking and filled with the pain she concealed during her waking hours.

Goddess, but she had done this to Alannah. She had separated her from Thomas. When she was awake, Alannah covered her pain in a cold and aloof mask, but these were her true emotions.

She almost woke her but stopped. Alannah had a right to grieve in private.

Feeling like an unwelcome voyeur, Sinead turned the light off. The least she could do was leave her sister to dream in peace, even if those dreams hurt her. She didn't have the right to interfere.

Going back to bed wasn't an option. She couldn't lie here and listen to Alannah cry. Kate had said to go where they liked.

After slipping on a pair of rain boots someone had left inside the cabin door, she grabbed a thick sweater and slipped into the night.

The settlement was dark and still. It felt peaceful and serene, and Sinead stepped off the porch. The air smelled of frost, damp earth and leaves, and the only sound came from the soft crunch of her boots on the dirt path. If it had been warmer, she would have gone barefoot and relished the earth beneath her soles. The night was clear and crisp. Overhead, a glittering canopy of stars reigned supreme with no cloud cover.

As much as she thought Sara was ladling on the crap about the dangers of the forest, she was still in a strange place. Finding the comfort of the trees, she stopped at a fallen log and sat. There was virtually no breeze, but still a few leaves drifted down to the waiting carpet on the forest floor. Through the thinning branches, she could just make out a waning moon.

Goddess, she felt like the worst kind of shit. But she honestly didn't know that if presented with the same circumstances, she would have done anything differently. Alannah had fallen in love with a ghost, and he with her, but that couldn't end well. Sinead had reasoned, that given time, Alannah would get over Thomas and find someone breathing to fall in love with. She hadn't realized, or allowed herself to realize, how deep the connection between the two ran.

A twig snapped, and she jumped.

A pair of luminous eyes gleamed in the darkness, and Sinead froze. The eyes were set far enough apart to suggest a large animal.

Perhaps Sara had not been entirely full of shit.

Her heart hammered, and sweat broke out over her skin as a large black wolf slid out of the trees and stopped. The animal looked at her.

Her first instinct was to scream and run, and she'd half risen before a memory of Niamh stopped her. Niamh had always said never to run from a predator; it made you prey. But that was one fucking enormous wolf, easily twice the size of the pack members they had at Baile.

It must be able to smell her fear.

The wolf sat. Its fur was almost entirely black; only the eyes had any color.

Sinead couldn't take her gaze off it. She didn't dare move, and her breath rasped in the still night. "Nice wolf," she whispered, weirdly comforted by the sound of her own voice. "I'm not running. No need to see me as prey, but I am going to take myself back to the cabin." Slowly, so perishingly slowly it hurt, she started to stand. "Leave you here to do your thing."

The wolf whined and dropped to its belly.

Well, that didn't look like it had dinner on its mind. The wolf reminded her of the she-wolf back at Baile. She'd come into the castle to birth and raise her pups. Sinead had even cuddled with several of those. Still, this one was full grown, not even remotely cuddly, and unknown to her.

She stood.

So did the wolf.

She sat again.

The wolf lay down.

She didn't need Niamh's abilities to read that message. Stay where you are. Kate said the settlement was guarded. One of the guards might be along shortly. Maybe even Alannah would sense she wasn't there and come and find her. Most likely, the wolf was tired and would rest a bit and grow bored. Maybe it was tired from a gut load of a fresh kill.

Her heart thumped, and her mouth dried. Best not to think fresh kill while sitting so close to a wild predator.

Those eyes still on her, the wolf laid its head on its front paws.

"I'll just sit here," Sinead said. Talking kept her from panicking. "It's a lovely night." Really? *Really!* She was discussing the weather with a wild animal.

The wolf chuffed.

It beat the crap out of the thing growling. "I only came out here for some peace," she said, unable to control her word spew.

The wolf raised its head and cocked it. It looked like it was asking her a question.

"Why?" She'd officially lost her marbles.

Head still cocked, the wolf stared at her.

"Ummm…I couldn't sleep, and I find the forest peaceful."

It laid its head back down. Leaves scattered as it stirred its tail.

Perhaps this was all a dream. If it was, the dream tree stump was digging into her ass, and the night chill making her shiver.

The wolf belly-clawed closer.

Fuck, fuck, fuck. She should have run for it when she had the chance.

It reached her, sat up and pressed its flank against her thighs. Sinead didn't dare twitch.

The wolf lay its head on her knee.

Like it was being friendly. Even comforting. And the animal was warm against her chilled legs.

"Hello." She tried to sound friendly and non-terrified. "I guess you want to make friends?" Or maybe it was warming its dinner.

The wolf sighed and closed its eyes.

"Right." Sinead nodded. Up close—disturbingly pissing close —it really was the most magnificent animal. Muscles rippled beneath its gleaming coat, and its strength radiated through their contact. "Friends it is."

She risked a pat on its shoulder.

The wolf made a rumbly contented noise and leaned against her. It must weigh close to what she did.

They sat. Sinead had no idea for how long. A light breeze chased the fallen leaves and sighed through the trees. She pulled earth, and it responded on a warm, gentle hum beneath her skin. Breathing deep, she calmed her clamoring pulse and let the night wash over her.

The wolf's nostrils flared as it tested the air. Then it sighed and grumbled and there was nothing threatening about either of those.

Gradually, she relaxed. The animal's warmth seeped into her, and its presence became oddly comforting.

With a start, she realized she had sunk her hands into the thick fur at its ruff.

"I don't know what to do," she said.

The wolf opened its eyes.

"About Alannah." She couldn't swear to it, would deny it if

anyone asked, but the animal appeared to be listening to her. "She's heartbroken."

The wolf whined.

"She's in love with someone—not really a someone at all—and she can't have him."

The wolf looked at her.

"I wouldn't say this to a person, but you're a wolf, so you wouldn't think I was daft anyway." The weirdness of the situation snuck up on her. "Mainly because you can't understand a bloody word I'm saying, and for some Goddess-alone reason are sitting with me in the middle of the night."

It chuffed.

Was it laughing?

Whatever. She wasn't going anywhere until forest prince here said she could. Well, he'd asked for it.

"She's in love with a bloody ghost."

It whined.

"No really, a ghost." Even a wild animal deserved more of an explanation, and she could talk to it like she wouldn't be able to with another human. Niamh had always said animals made the best listeners. Apparently, they really did, because she wanted to tell the wolf everything. "Back at Baile—that's where I come from—there are a few ghosts." The wolf had the silkiest ears, and she threaded them through her fingers. "They're the old coimhdeacht—that means warrior guardian. They are linked to the place somehow and hang around. Not in a scary way."

The wolf sighed and pressed its head closer to her hand. So, it liked the ear thing. Who could have known? Niamh might have.

"Anyway, there's this one called Thomas. And he really is a great guy, or was a great guy." Being technically dead. "It's hard to get the tense right with the walking dead. Ghosts, not zombies."

Again with that chuffing noise that did sound remarkably like a chuckle.

Maybe because she was a witch and had seen stuff in the last few months that would blow the average brain explained why she wasn't running screaming for the hills. That, and she was one hundred percent sure he'd catch her if she did. *He?* It fit. And she had bugger-all intention of asking him to roll over so she could check.

"Thomas is charming and funny, and quite frankly, hot as hell."

The wolf growled, low and deep, but it didn't sound much like an I'm-going-to-eat-you sort of growl. Not that she'd know the difference, and he was so close that he could pretty much gobble her up anyway.

"Well, he is!" She decided to go with her gut, which said he'd disliked her statement about Thomas. "But I'm not the one in love with him, so it's more of an observation than an ogle."

He sighed and closed his eyes.

"Thomas and Alannah started spending time together, got friendlier, and fell in love." Maybe if she'd put a stop to it sooner, it wouldn't have come to this. "I could have said something sooner, but Alannah's not generally like that," she said.

He opened one eye and looked at her.

"She's not. I've never known her to take any man's attention seriously before. And men look at her all the time, I mean, why would they not? She's gorgeous."

He cracked open the other eye.

"Yes, I know we're twins and look the same, but men don't look at me as much."

He raised his head and stared.

"They don't. Alannah is..." How to put this into words? "She's warm and kind and draws people to her. She's a nurturer." Then she considered herself. "I'm more of a ball breaker."

The wolf chuckled. *Chuffed!*

"I tend to scare them off, while she draws them closer. And sometimes she'll let a man close enough for a bit of fun." She raised an eyebrow at him. "You're an animal. You know what I mean."

He nodded. Now, she had the wolf nodding. She'd heard about anthropomorphizing before, but she was taking it to new heights…or lows.

"Anyway." Best to steer away from animal instincts, all things considered. "She didn't take men seriously. Until Thomas."

He kept that intent gaze on her as if he wanted to hear more.

So, she gave him more. "I broke them up."

He cocked his head.

"I did." She nodded. Because humans nod. Wolves don't. "I was worried about what would happen. There's no future in it. I wanted to save Alannah from getting her heart broken." She'd waited too long apparently. "I spoke to him and told him if he really loved her, he'd back off and step aside. Give a living man a chance."

The wolf laid its head on her knee.

"And he did." The weight of what she'd done pressed against her breastbone, and she wanted to cry. "But it broke her heart anyway." The picture of Alannah tonight rose up again. "She was crying in her sleep. That's why I came out here."

The wolf pressed against her hands, and she sank them into his fur.

"I caused that, and I hate myself for it."

The wolf nuzzled her cheek and licked a stray tear off her skin.

The tenderness of the action broke her, and Sinead buried her face in his neck and cried. She cried for Alannah, and Thomas. She cried for the shitty situation. She cried for the rift between her and Alannah, and she cried because her world had become a strange and terrifying place, and she didn't know if she was strong enough to get through this.

The wolf sat still while she sobbed. Eventually her tears dried up, and she rested a moment more in his soft, silky fur. "Thank you," she whispered. "I needed that." Sitting up, she disentangled her hands from his fur.

She felt foolish now.

"I'm sorry. I got your fur all wet."

He nuzzled her hand as if it didn't matter, then stood and nudged her leg.

"What?"

He repeated the motion, more of a prod this time.

"Must I go back to bed?"

He nodded.

She didn't care what anyone said, that wolf bloody nodded.

"Okay then." She stood. "Enjoy the rest of your night. And thank you again."

He padded beside her until she reached the edge of the forest.

Sinead looked behind her as she walked back toward her cabin.

The wolf stood at the edge of the forest and watched her until she turned the corner to her cabin and went inside.

"Well," she whispered to the silent cabin. "That was one for the fucking books."

CHAPTER FOURTEEN

Alannah was already awake by the time Sinead surfaced the next morning. It took her sluggish mind a few minutes to catch her up on the events of the night before, and then she shook her head. She'd had a chat with a wild wolf and liked it. She didn't think there was a Katy Perry ditty for that contingency.

Her normal serene self, Alannah left the bathroom and selected a sweater and a maxi skirt from the closet. "You're awake," she said, without turning around.

"Yes." Sinead hauled herself up to sitting and propped her back against the cast iron bedstead. It wasn't the most comfortable position, and she fidgeted. "I didn't sleep well last night."

Alannah glanced over her shoulder. "No?"

She disappeared back into the bathroom, and Sinead got out of bed. They couldn't go on avoiding the subject much longer. More important shit was at play. And next time Alannah woke her up crying in her sleep, Sinead wanted to be there to comfort her.

Beneath her bare feet, the floorboards were cold. They really needed to get into the habit of lighting the fire. Some kind soul always set it for them, ready to light. With her stomach growling, though, Sinead didn't think they'd be in the cabin long enough to benefit from its warmth. They needed to get the earth point active and get home, not settle in and get comfy.

In the bathroom, Alannah had gotten dressed and was brushing her hair. She never wore much makeup, neither of them did, and out here in the woods, going natural felt right.

"So, last night." Sinead fished around her tired brain for the right words. Then again, subtlety had never been her thing. "You were crying last night. In your sleep."

Alannah stopped mid stroke and her eyes met Sinead's in the mirror. "Oh?"

"Look, about Thomas." No time like the present.

Alannah stilled, and her eyes went cold.

Sinead forged on. "I'm sorry."

Alannah blinked at her.

"I should never have interfered; it was none of my business."

With a sigh, Alannah carefully placed her brush on the vanity and turned. "You did it because you were worried about me."

"I was." Sinead ventured closer, wanting to hug her sister and make the defeated look go away. "I am worried about you, but that doesn't give me the right to interfere in your life."

"No, it doesn't."

"And I'm sorry." Sinead didn't know what else to say. "If I had it to do over again, I wouldn't have said a word. I would work on accepting your choice and let you and Thomas live your lives."

Alannah turned and picked up the brush again.

Okay, well now Sinead really didn't know what else she could say. She turned to get her clothes for the day. There had to be a way to heal the gap with Alannah. If she had to go the rest of her life estranged from her twin, it would kill her.

"You weren't wrong," Alannah said.

Sinead stopped and waited.

"You weren't wrong." Alannah brushed her hair, her reflection in the mirror sad but resolved. "There was no future for Thomas and me." She gave a rueful chuckle. "There is no future for Thomas and me, but that doesn't stop me from wanting one."

"I know." Sinead ventured closer.

"I never meant for it to happen." Alannah's arms fell to her sides. "I know everything you said and felt was the bloody truth, but it didn't stop me. I just wanted so much for things to be different. Maybe deep inside, I kept hoping that somehow Goddess would intervene, and I'd get a happy ending like Alexander and Bronwyn, or Maeve and Roderick. Niamh and Warren seem to be finding a way forward." Tears glittered in her eyes. "Even Mags found someone, and she's insanely shy."

Sinead took the brush from Alannah's limp fingers and took over brushing. "I wanted that for you too." She admitted a truth she had not really acknowledged before. "I want that for both of us. I never really thought about it before Roderick came, and then Alexander. The way they were, the way they loved and were loved, I found myself wanting things I never had before." She met Alannah's gaze in the mirror. "Don't get me wrong, though, there definitely is a part of me that will always resent any man in your life."

Alannah gave her a sad smile in the mirror. "Same with me. We've always been part of the coven, but even more than that, we've always had each other. Whichever one of us fell in love first, it was never going to be easy."

"No." Sinead could see the truth in that. "But you and Thomas walking away from whatever you have is wrong."

"He's a ghost," Alannah said.

"He certainly is." Sinead put the brush down and put her arms around her sister. She rested her chin on Alannah's shoulder. There they were, peas in a pod, so identical it was like looking at her own face. "But neither of us know how any of this is going to play out. We may not have tomorrow. Take whatever happiness you can find."

"You mean that?" Alannah's gaze softened.

"I do." Sinead gave her a final squeeze and stepped away. "I'm going to back off."

Alannah laughed. "You're not really known for your backing off ability."

"This is true." All guns blazing and damn the torpedoes were much more her style. "But you're the most important person in my life, and knowing I've made you unhappy is not something I can live with."

"You didn't make me unhappy," Alannah said. "You just made me face something I didn't want to see."

"But I could have handled it differently." Maybe shut her mouth and listened more before she spoke.

Alannah pressed her head against Sinead's. "Yes, you could have."

Goddess, but she'd missed Alannah. "Are we okay?"

"We're okay." Alannah nodded. "Now get dressed, and let's go find something to eat."

"Alannah?" Sinead stopped in the bathroom doorway.

"Yes."

"Next time you're feeling sad, tell me?"

"I promise."

It didn't take Sinead long to pull on a pair of pants and a jumper. Alannah hated her cargo pants, and the look her sister gave them told her as much. Sinead liked all the pockets, and she got busy filling them with stuff she might need. Hate the pants as she did, it didn't stop Alannah from handing her a tube of lip balm to carry for her.

Noah was leaning against a porch upright and straightened as they opened the cabin door and stepped out. His grin was all dancing eyes and white teeth. "Morning."

"Morning." Alannah smiled at him.

No man had the right to look that good before her first coffee, and Sinead scowled. "Are you stalking us?"

"Do you want me to?" He raised one dark eyebrow.

It hit her right in the knees and sent a warm thrill coursing through her middle. It must be caffeine deficiency setting in.

"I came to take you to breakfast," he said and held an arm out for Alannah.

Alannah tucked her hand into the crook of his elbow, all besties now.

The smile Noah gave Alannah was sweet and nothing like the smolders he reserved for her. "Did you sleep okay?"

"I did." Alannah glanced at her. "But Sinead didn't. She's a bit grumpier than normal this morning."

Noah smirked. "Really? I hadn't noticed."

Alannah giggled, and Sinead wanted to smack the pair of them.

Noah led them back through the center of the village and down a winding path through the trees. "There is a communal area where most of us eat."

"We saw it yesterday." Alannah looked around her with interest. "Sara and Dhara showed it to us."

"Ah." Noah nodded. "Then I really am stalking you by showing up at your door this morning."

Sinead snorted her response. She wasn't as easily won over as Alannah.

"You're stalking one of us." Alannah threw him a mischievous look.

Unabashed, Noah threw back his head and laughed. "So obvious?"

"Yes." Alannah giggled.

"I have zero game." Noah shrugged. "I'm more of a straight-up kinda guy. If I like you, you know it."

He'd come right out and admitted it, and it did weird shit to her insides, so he better give that a rest. Sinead searched for a subject change.

Around them, the woods were quiet and peaceful, leaves muffling their footsteps. Her encounter the night before had taken place not far from where they were walking. Sara had mentioned wild animals, but nothing about tame wolves. Last night's animal had to be someone's companion. Wild wolves did not sit while someone chatted to them. And they certainly did not let women cry into their fur. This community was keeping secrets, and secrets got people hurt, or worse.

Noah looked over his shoulder at her as if checking she was still there.

"I went for a walk last night." She plunged right in.

Alannah stopped and looked at her. "You did?"

"Yup, when I couldn't sleep."

Noah's face gave nothing away, but the gleam in his eyes made her more suspicious than ever. Time to push for answers. "I had an interesting encounter last night."

He raised that annoying brow.

Alannah blinked at her. "What sort of encounter?"

"A wolf," Sinead said.

Alannah blinked at her and looked concerned. "You came across a wolf? A wild one?"

"Seemed wild to me." Sinead kept her eyes on Smirky McSmirkerson. "Unless someone around here keeps pet wolves."

He smirked—of course he did. "No tame wolves around here."

"Were you frightened?" Alannah stepped closer to her.

"No." Sinead glanced at her before returning her attention to Noah. She got the definite feeling he knew more about the wolf than he was saying. "That was the strange thing. It came right up to me and sat beside me."

"Are you serious?" Alannah gaped at her. "I can't believe you didn't wake me up and tell me."

"Nah." She gave Noah the stink eye. He needn't think she didn't know he was full of bollocks. "It wasn't that big of a deal."

His strange golden eyes glinted a silent dare. "Are you sure you weren't just a tiny bit scared?"

"Not at all." She met his stare. No bloody way she was telling him how frightened she'd been when the wolf had first appeared. Or did he know? Had he been spying on her?

Noah grinned and walked on.

This conversation was not over. Not until she got some answers, it wasn't.

Sinead followed him and Alannah to a large, low-slung wooden hall. The double doors were open, and people drifted in and out. As they drew closer, the sound of people chatting and the smell of breakfast surrounded them.

A large dining hall, with long tables, it looked like it might seat a couple hundred people at capacity. The settlement was clearly bigger than they'd seen so far.

Noah took them to a table and motioned a buffet setup at the far end. "Help yourselves."

"You're not staying?" Alannah motioned him to join them.

"I'll catch you later," he said. "I need to talk to Zach."

Three tables in front of theirs, Zach sat with Abe and Rachel. All three nodded a greeting and got right back to whatever kept their heads together.

Sinead waited until she and Alannah had filled their plates and grabbed cups of coffee before she got to it. "This place is strange."

"But in a nice way." Alannah looked around them as she buttered her toast. "Everyone is very friendly."

"They are." Sinead nodded and smiled at the people who met her eye. "But they're hiding stuff."

"Yes." Alannah looked thoughtful and frowned. "I don't feel threatened at all, but getting the full story is imperative."

As if drawn that way, her gaze snagged on Noah and stuck. It had been months since a man had made her sit up and take notice—months of watching Roderick love Maeve—and for all her grouchiness with Noah, he definitely made her pay attention.

His topaz eyes met hers, and for a moment, it was like being back in the hotel reception again. All the breath left her lungs, and her pulse kicked up its rhythm.

"You going to do anything about that?" Alannah's eyes brimmed with mischief.

Sinead wasn't ready to admit to shit. "About what?"

Alannah's eyebrow called her lie.

"We're here to find the earth point." Sinead avoided the subject by concentrating on her breakfast. Crispy bacon exploded with flavor in her mouth and made her want to moan. She should have taken more. "Nothing is more important than that."

"Have you noticed that they've told us the earth point is here," Alannah said as she drowned her pancakes in maple syrup. "But nobody's told us where it is."

"That's our first order of business then." Sinead took her sister's example. The maple syrup was to die for, and the pancakes light and pillowy. "We find that Kate woman and ask her where the point is."

"Agreed." Alannah braced her elbows on the table and cradled her coffee mug. "And maybe a certain hot Canadian would like to help us with that?"

"You're stuck on repeat with that." Sinead glared at her sister. "We don't have time for buggering around here."

Alannah laughed at her. "I'm sure if you ask him nicely, he'll fit himself in around your schedule."

"You know—" The injustice of it made Sinead want to smack things. "People think you're the sweet one, but you really are a bloody pain in the ass."

CHAPTER FIFTEEN

Rhiannon stroked Mags's slim, pale arm as it lay on the blankets. Such beautiful skin, so fine and delicate, almost like an eggshell, and as easily broken. "Hello, Magdalene. You look well." No need to change her voice. The brokenness in Mags's brain would do what she needed it to do. "Did you sleep well?"

Mags turned toward the sound of her voice, her green eyes a dull, opaque jade. "Yes, Jack."

"That's good, sweetheart, very good."

Fiona stood by the door, hands obediently clasped in front of her, head lowered. That one had been different since Edana's death. Such a pity. She was like a bird with a broken wing now, but she still had her uses. "Is she eating?"

"Yes, Mistress." Fiona nodded. "I make sure of it. She does not have much appetite."

Rhiannon's sweet, sought-after seer's chest rose and fell beneath her thin pajama shirt, her clavicles harsh lines against pale skin. She had fought hard to get Mags, and she would not release her until she had what she needed. Not back to Baile, never that. Mags couldn't be allowed to return, couldn't be allowed to live once she had served her use.

"Tell me, sweetheart." She touched Mags's gaunt, cold cheek. "Tell me what you've seen."

"The blood. In the cave." Mags shuddered. "It rises and rises, it swallows everything."

Rhiannon had heard about the blood vision before. It gave her a visceral thrill. She would spill the blood that would drown Baile. That Mags saw it so often and so clearly augured well for her. Not that she needed auguries anymore. Plans within plans, wheels within wheels, all turning and churning her way forward. She had built her network slowly, year by year, and it now spanned the globe.

"Alexander," Mags whispered. "He is disappearing."

Rhiannon suppressed the twinge of regret that shot through her chest. Alexander was already dead to her. The vision of his death shouldn't bother her. And yet, it did. She hadn't anticipated her attachment when she had become a mother. Perhaps naively, she had believed she was beyond any sort of maternal emotion.

Did Roderick know now? She had used Edana and stolen his seed to get what she wanted—the perfect male child to fulfil the prophecy. Except, he had not fulfilled his promise. His father's blood had done things to him—changed him—in ways she had not accounted for.

"Jack?" Mags's eyes widened. "Can you hear the wolves?"

Her nape prickled. "Wolves, sweetheart?"

"The wolves. Can you hear the wolves calling for Sinead?"

Mags spoke of one of the twins now. A thrill rippled through Rhiannon. Finally, closer to the answer she sought.

Alannah and Sinead were in Canada, searching for the earth point. They'd left Baile in secret, thinking she wouldn't know. It was almost laughable. Of course, she had eyes on Baile constantly. The twins had been followed from the moment they deplaned in Canada. Infuriatingly, her people had lost track of them in Montreal. They'd disappeared in the middle of the night. Rhiannon suspected a nemesis she hadn't caught sight or sound of for seventy years.

And she'd hunted for them, but nothing thus far.

Beyond galling. In the fifties, a group of Canadian witches had managed the impossible and moved the earth point and kept it hidden for all this time.

Despite her fury, however, she'd known all she had to do was wait. Goddess would need to rise to defend her witches, and that would mean activating the cardinal points. It had only been a matter of time before they went to activate earth, and she had been ready when they'd made their move.

Sinead and Alannah, like Niamh before them, would find the point, and she would be waiting. Spider meets fly. Checkmate.

Even with limited powers, those Canadian witches had still managed to move the earth point and conceal it from her. And more. They hid the ultimate prize, and they had no idea. Only she and Goddess knew what else the Canadians hid, and again, she would wait. But for now, she needed to find those bloody Canadians. "What's happening with Sinead?"

"She feels the earth power." Mags smiled. "It feels...warm and safe. Constant."

"Where does she feel it, Mags?"

Fiona shifted, no doubt listening and tucking away information.

"I'm not sure..." Mags frowned. "I see trees. Big trees and lots of them. They stretch as far as I can see."

Fucking Canada was full of fucking trees. "We need to find them, sweetheart. They're in danger. Can you see what kind of trees?"

"Tall." Mags winced. "Rising high and blocking out the light." She laughed suddenly. "I don't know much about trees, Jack."

Rhiannon gritted her teeth. "Describe them to me."

"Like Christmas trees," Mags said. "But only much bigger."

Fir and spruce trees in all likelihood. Again, not specific enough.

"There are ferns beneath them and moss," Mags said. "It's cool there, and there is water everywhere."

Now they were getting somewhere. "Is there anything nearby that you can see?"

"It doesn't work like that, Jack." Mags chuckled. Then she gasped. "Mountains, there are tall mountains all around." She wrinkled her nose. "They have snow on the top, and it's so pretty."

"That's so good, Magdalene." Rhiannon dug her nails into her thighs. She needed more. Mountains, trees, rivers, lakes—in short, Canada. An immense space to try to narrow down.

"Oh!" Mags's smile grew beatific. "I know where they are."

Rhiannon left ten minutes later, smiling. Mags had been worth all the effort she had put into getting her. She could kill Mags now and be done with it, but a seer was not a gift to be squandered.

She took her mobile phone out of her pocket. She detested these things, along with most modern technology. In this time, people were slaves to them, and Rhiannon refused to be a slave to anyone. Had she not left Baile because of being enslaved to Goddess? A being with her power had no need for limits on her abilities. She could almost taste the return of earth magic—her magic—and she had missed it more than she could ever miss her spawn. Pressing a button on her phone, she tapped her thigh to contain her impatience.

"My lady?" A man answered.

"I have the place. Gather your people." Then she risked a little joke. "We're going on a good, old-fashioned witch hunt."

"This is the place." Emma crept closer to the square farmhouse, its light stonework gleaming in the moonlight. Heavy vines clambered over a pergola and up the walls. Tall, ghostly cypress trees rose over the tiled roof.

Jack crouched in the shrubs to the side of the door. "It looks empty."

The shutters were open, but the windows remained dark. A moped sat in the driveway with a helmet balanced on the handlebars.

Emma motioned for them to creep closer. She agreed with Jack; it didn't look like anyone was here. Even more disheartening, she couldn't feel the bond with Mags. Fuck it!

Only the sound of their boots crunching on the gravel drive broke the natural night symphony. Emma palmed her firearm and gestured Jack to do the same.

Stubborn prick shook his head and pulled a knife from the small of his back. Despite their differences, they made a good team. Spending these days with Jack had reassured her about him being in Mags's life. Not that Jack would give a flying crap anyway. Jack loved her witch with the kind of here-for-all-of-it love.

She ducked beneath a window ledge and sensed him drop into place beside her. Moving slowly, she inched up to see over the ledge. A kitchen, as she'd suspected. No smell of anything cooking, no lights, and not a single soul about.

They crept to the door, and Emma held her breath as she turned the handle.

Locked.

Jack nudged her and handed her a lock pick.

That's what she meant—a good team. She inserted the pick and listened for the click of the tumblers. Fortunately, whoever had owned the house hadn't been suspicious enough to put in better locks. The door swung open on a soft squeak, and the warmer brush of air from the interior swept over her.

She signaled Jack to wait, and he nodded.

Alert for any nasty surprises, she eased into the kitchen and across it to the dark doorway at the far end.

She crouched and listened.

The house remained silent. The soft buzz of night insects came from the open door.

Emma motioned Jack the all clear.

He crept into the kitchen, able to make very little sound for the size of the bastard.

She risked a torch, the gentle blue light barely penetrating the dark, but also not visible to any curious eyes outside.

The ground floor unfolded into a lounge and dining room, a small study, and a bathroom.

All empty.

"She's not here," Jack growled.

Emma felt every bit of his frustration but kept her voice level. "Let's check upstairs."

Upstairs was a small landing space with narrow corridors to the left and right.

By tacit agreement they went left first. Two bedrooms and a bathroom. Again, nobody at home.

To the right was a single bedroom, built low in the eaves with a large, low window. A bed rested beside the window. The bedding was rumpled, and a glass and a plate sat on a small table beside the bed.

"Somebody was here." Emma examined the contents of the plate. The remains of a sandwich, and by the feel of the bread and the state of the cheese, not too old. "And not too long ago."

Jack shone his torch over the bed. He grunted and leaned down and snagged a long, red hair from the pillow. "She was here."

"Certainly looks like that." Not many people had hair that red or that long.

"Fuck." Jack shook his head and kept searching. At this stage, anything might help them to know where next. "We missed her."

"But she was here." Emma suppressed her own disappointment and frustration. The idea of Mags in Rhiannon's power beat like a toxic pulse through her. "By the look of that sandwich, no more than a day ago."

Jack grunted and knelt to look below the bed. He stilled and then reached beneath the bed and picked something up.

"What is it?" Emma shone her light on his palm.

A small, sparkly bead rested in his huge hand. "Mags," he said.

"She might have left it behind for us?" Emma knew she was grasping at straws, but they both needed something.

Jack shrugged. "Let's see if we find any more."

They found a second bead at the bottom of the stairs, and a third in the driveway outside the front door. A tiny sparkle of hope for them to cling to. Mags was aware enough to have left them a breadcrumb.

They searched the rest of the house thoroughly but found nothing else of use.

Jack turned to her. "Where to now?"

"Back to my contacts," she said. "And we squeeze them until something comes out."

CHAPTER SIXTEEN

In an effort to alleviate her growing frustration, Bronwyn ground herbs for her jars. Preparing and storing herbal remedies seemed like a waste of time if she was never going to even use this part of her gift.

"Morning." Hannah appeared in the door to the healer's hall, Charlie on her hip. "You busy?"

Bronwyn didn't bother concealing her sour expression. "Busy doing busy work."

"Right." Hannah nodded and walked into the room. Two wolf pups trotted in after them and Charlie wriggled to be put down. "I've been watching TikTok."

"Niamh?" Bronwyn couldn't help but resent that Niamh, at least, had some outlet for her blessing. "I hear she's trending."

"Oh, yes." Hannah gave a rueful smile and pushed her glasses up her nose. "She's quite the sensation."

Bronwyn's sigh came from her toes up. She understood; she really did. Every time a witch left the wards, they were in danger. Using her blessing amongst people who needed her help meant leaving the wards. Along with the little matter of her being pregnant with twins, a pair of babies Rhiannon would move heaven and earth to get her hands on. "Want to give me a hand?"

"Might as well." Hannah joined her at the table. "What are we doing?"

"Grinding valerian root."

Hannah grabbed a mortar and pestle. "Sedative, right? Even I've heard of that one."

"Yup, works like Valium but nonaddictive."

They worked in silence for a minute.

Charlie and the pups played some sort of rolling and tussling game near the window. Puppy growls and child laughter warmed Bronwyn's insides. A minute snippet of normal in their increasingly difficult reality. Charlie looked to have recovered from the ordeal of Rhiannon kidnapping and using him as leverage over Hannah.

Hannah pushed a strand of hair behind her ear. "Did you learn about all the herbal remedies here?"

"No." Bronwyn scooped valerian extract into capsules. With all the tension surrounding Baile, you never knew when someone was going to need to calm the hell down. "Not all of it." She gestured the huge bookshelves on the far wall. "Those are full of all kinds of information about herbs, but my grandmother taught me most of it."

"Your grandmother? Was she a...witch." Hannah was still having trouble with the witch concept.

"She raised me," Bronwyn said. She still missed Deidre, but knowing her soul had passed through the veil to the sacred grove gave her a lot of comfort. After a lifetime of being viewed as an oddity, Deidre was finally amongst her tribe. "My mother died when I was very young. And my aunt." Her family legacy of the women dying young was the reason she'd come to England in the first place. Her search for answers had brought her a whole lot more than she'd bargained for.

Hannah gave her a sympathetic smile. "I'm sorry. I lost my mother in my teens."

They shared a silent moment of understanding.

"I did one of those ancestry tests after Deidre—that's my grandmother—died and ended up here."

"Where you met Alexander?"

"Yup."

"And activated the water point?"

Hannah must have been asking around. "The very same."

"Huh." Hannah watched Charlie for a while, her face tender.

Bronwyn touched her growing belly. The twins responded with a warm flush of love. They were hers to protect and love, and as they grew, to guide and nurture.

"How are you feeling?" Hannah turned back to her.

Bronwyn thought about her answer before giving it. "I'm well. The nausea has passed, and I'm not quite so tired anymore. Otherwise, perfectly healthy."

"Good." Hannah smiled. "You're in the blooming stage."

Bronwyn felt it as well.

"I've been thinking," Hannah said, and tipped the valerian into the waiting jar.

Bronwyn gave her the silence to fill.

"About where to now, for me and Charlie." Hannah frowned and perched on a stool. "I mean, I came here to check on Gemma. I had no idea how things would play out."

Nobody could have predicted how heinous Rhiannon would get in kidnapping Hannah and forcing her to milk Edana for blood to fuel her magic. As a healer, Bronwyn could appreciate how horrific that must have been for Hannah. Trained as a doctor to respect and preserve life, she had been forced to go against her ethics or lose her son.

"I appreciate that you've taken us in and protected us." Hannah motioned Baile around them. "And we've certainly felt welcome here, but I'm a doctor. It's more than my job, it's my calling."

Bronwyn nodded because she understood that as well. Being a healer was fused into her very being.

"At some point, I'm going to need to pick up my life again." Hannah sighed. "I've had an email from my hospital. They want to know when I'll be back at work."

"What did you tell them?" Bronwyn took a seat on the stool opposite her. There weren't any easy answers for Hannah. She'd been dragged into this battle and was now stuck in the middle.

"I stalled." Hannah shrugged and chewed on her bottom lip. "I still have some leave banked, and I'm using that, but I can't just stay here and do nothing for the rest of my life." She motioned Bronwyn. "You have a place here, a role. Charlie and I are just collateral damage."

Bronwyn had promised never to lie to her or edit the truth, so she said, "I don't know what to tell you. The danger to you and Charlie is still very much alive and out there. It goes without saying that you're welcome here for as long as you need us, but I get it." She had come here and also been swept away by the tide of events. "I can say that I've been giving Andy's idea some thought."

"About me working with you?" Hannah looked at her and frowned. "A marriage of science and witchcraft?"

"Yes." Just because it had never been done before, didn't mean it couldn't work. "As I see it, even when we come out of hiding, it's going to take a long time for the world to get their heads around all of this." She gestured Baile. "And they will feel more comfortable if it appears to have some basis in science."

"I agree." But Hannah didn't look happy. "But that's you doing what you do. I don't see a place for what I do, other than being a sort of screen for you." She shook her head. "I went to med school to help people, to heal them. If I'm not doing that, I'm not sure who I am anymore."

"I understand." And Bronwyn did. Hannah was too intelligent and driven to spend her life as a figurehead. "And I don't know where the balance lies. I remember when we were working with Jack, we found a kind of rhythm. Not all injuries or diseases need magic. But I've also been thinking about how my magic works. I find the problem and transmute it, but often, I have no idea what I'm looking for or how it works. But the process of doing that is reactive."

Interest sparked in Hannah's gaze. "You've got an idea?"

"I do." Bronwyn hadn't fully thought this through, but sharing it with Hannah might help. "Even at full strength, we are speaking about a handful of healers working on millions of sick people. I wondered about the potential of us getting out in front of the problem."

"You mean working toward a cure instead of healing?" Hannah was sharp as a tack and right with her.

"Like Gemma, for instance." Bronwyn tried to verbalize what she had been teasing out in her mind. "If we could have stopped her tumor at its source, before it developed."

"Like working with the problem in her DNA?"

"Exactly." Bronwyn hoped it didn't sound as foolish or far-fetched as it felt. "I can spend my life curing the Gemmas of the world, or I could look for a way to eradicate her disease before it even manifested."

"Shit!" Hannah looked struck by the idea.

"My magic can't find a problem that isn't there." Bronwyn was happy to see Hannah wasn't looking at her like she was an idiot. "But science can point me in the right direction. Show me where I need to tweak and adjust." She threw her hands up. "I don't know if that will even work, or if my magic can even do that. But based on what we did for Warren, which I'd never even thought was possible, there are iterations of my blessing that I haven't explored yet."

Hannah grew thoughtful and chewed on her lip. "I could

certainly help with that. As an oncologist, cancer is my specialty, but I'm thinking conditions like diabetes. What if you could address the problem in the pancreas?"

"Right!" Bronwyn's mind suddenly started cycling through other chronic conditions that they could work at eradicating. "I don't have the scientific background to know where to start looking. But you do."

Hannah chuckled and shook her head. "I mean, the possibilities are endless."

"They are."

"Let me give this some thought." Hannah shook her head. "I can't do much more until you get rid of that cow anyway."

Rhiannon always brought a downer to any conversation. "And we're working on that."

"What are we working on?" Alexander sauntered into the healer's hall.

Tall, dark, and delicious, he always caused a hitch in her breathing. Some part of her would always struggle to believe he loved her and only her.

"Bronwyn and I are talking about ridding the world of disease," Hannah said.

Alexander raised an eyebrow. "Before lunch?"

Hannah laughed. "It might take a bit longer than that. But speaking of lunch," she motioned Charlie. "Someone needs to eat and go down for their nap." She scooped Charlie up and turned to leave. Stopping in the doorway, she looked at Bronwyn. "You've given me a lot to think about. We'll chat again?"

"Count on it."

Alexander waited for Hannah and Charlie to leave before he pounced on Bronwyn and pulled her into his arms. His kiss was soft and sweet with a touch of heat. "Hey, little witch," he murmured.

"Hey yourself." She looped her arms around his neck. He was hers, and she'd no idea how she'd gotten so lucky. The prophecy had never said she would fall so much in love with her fated mate. "Hannah is getting restless."

He kissed her nose and stepped back. "I can't blame her. She's an intelligent, educated woman whose life has suddenly ground to a halt."

"Any news from Jack and Emma?" She got busy cleaning up from the morning's work. Her belly growled as the twins let her know they'd like their lunch, followed by a nap. With Alexander. That last part Bronwyn added to the agenda.

Alexander shook his head. "They tracked her down to a farmhouse in the south of France, but she was gone when they got there."

"Ugh!" Bronwyn's frustration and worry soured her mood. They all wanted Mags back home, safe and sound. "That bitch is always one step ahead."

"She's spent hundreds of years perfecting the art," Alexander said as he took the jars out of her hands and placed them on the shelf. "Nothing from Sinead and Alannah either, but Taylor insists they're not in any danger."

"At least we still have her to give us some relief." Speaking about the twins always brought her thoughts around to Thomas, and she turned to Alexander. "How is he?"

"Not good." Alexander's face grew somber. "He barely goes corporeal anymore, and when he does it's like he's a…well… ghost. The strain of Lavina being trapped on the green isn't helping." He folded her tight against his chest. "I can't imagine how shit this is for him. He can't be with the woman he loves. If I couldn't be with you…" He released a long breath.

Bronwyn's heart twisted for Thomas. She didn't know what she'd do if she'd found Alexander and lost him again. He was her everything.

Andy appeared in the doorway. "Alexander?"

"Yup." Alexander moved her to his side.

"That other matter." Andy made a portentous face. "The one you asked me to take care of the other morning?"

Alexander frowned, before light dawned. "Conrad?"

"He's on his way. ETA tonight." Andy nodded. "Sasha took care of it."

"Well, little witch." Alexander kissed her forehead. "You and Hannah have a job to do."

Bronwyn was there for it, and she marched for the door. "Who is it? What's the problem?"

"Andy will brief you." Alexander pulled her back. "After you eat."

Maeve stepped into the sacred grove. Her senses lurched and hurried to catch up with her as they accustomed themselves to the magical plane. The grove had changed again, and not for the better.

"Shit." She borrowed one of Sinead's favorite swear words.

All color had bled from the grove into a shifting, swirling silvery gray. Barren trees stretched bare branches into the leaden fog, and the earth beneath her feet shifted pale and ephemeral. Mist clung in small pockets between the trees, and the silence was the sort of absolute that almost hurt to hear.

Three figures appeared in front of her, the first three witches: Deidre, Tahra, and Brenna. They clasped their hands prayerlike and bowed. "Blessed be, Spirit Walker."

"Blessed be," Maeve said. The barren, lifeless feel of the grove worried her more than she wanted to admit. Last time she'd walked the grove, it had shown signs of recovery. "What happened here?"

Brenna stepped forward, her green eyes clear and direct. "The grove is a reflection of the magic that is." She waved a hand around them. "It is in flux."

"What does that mean?" It came out plaintive, but Maeve didn't care. She would scream if they gave her one of their cryptic non-answers. The grove was a constant, the heart of cré-magic.

"All that was will alter," Brenna said. "All that is known will become unknown, and all that is will cease to be."

They'd summoned her here, but Maeve felt like she was running through quicksand. "Is the grove dying?"

"The grove is becoming," Brenna said. "And what it becomes is not known, even to us."

Tahra stepped forward. "What you see now is our manifestation of what you are accustomed to. It no longer exists in this form."

Maeve didn't know what that meant, and her head went fuzzy, unable to grasp the repercussions. If the grove died, did cré-magic die?

Tahra stepped closer to her, and Maeve saw the grove through her, like she was growing increasingly transparent. "We summoned you to take our leave," Tahra said. "Like the grove, we are becoming."

"Becoming what? Take your leave? Where are you going?" Maeve was panicking, but she couldn't stop herself. Spirit walkers entered the grove to commune with witches past. The very reason she had been put into stasis had been so she could travel forward in time and have access to all the wisdom of the dead witches.

"We don't know that either," Tahra said. "We only know that all that is must end before all that should be can come to pass."

"This is goodbye." Brenna stood beside Tahra, no more substantial. "We will miss you, Maeve spirit walker." She smiled. "You were always one of our favorite walkers."

"You're leaving me?" Maeve felt as if her heart was being ripped open. The first three were another constant, a thing that always was and always would be.

Deidre nodded. "We are moving on." She motioned the grove, which had suddenly filled with the spirits of the thousands of cré-witches who had come before. "Some of our sisters will reincarnate on the earthly plane once more before, they too, will move on. We three will move on now, and the souls who do not reincarnate to the earthly plane will move with us."

Standing around the first three, Maeve could pick out faces of witches she had guided into the grove, both in this time and in the time before. She knew them all. Their life stories had played through her before they could move on. They couldn't be going. Where were they going? "I don't understand."

"Your work nears its completion," Brenna said.

Of the hundreds of souls who'd been unable to enter the grove with her in stasis, Maeve had only a few left to release. She'd worked day and night, to the point of exhaustion to give them that. For them to cease to be any longer. Goddess could not be that cruel.

"Not cease to be." Tahra smiled. "Ascending this plane."

She must be asleep, and this was a nightmare.

"Release the fourteen." Deidre said, her voice filled with authority. "Finish what you have started and release the fourteen. Remember, the spell was cast in four and can only be released in four."

Tahra touched her cheek, a cold brush of nothing that made her shudder. "Say farewell to Roderick for me. Tell him that there are no endings, merely spirals that join and grow. The end of one is the beginning of the next."

"But—"

Maeve was tossed into darkness, her senses dead.

"Maeve!" Roderick shook her shoulder.

The cold press of the cavern floor beneath her cheek asserted itself on her awareness. The slightly damp smell of the caves. The familiar sound of the sea outside.

Roderick shook her again. "Maeve, wake up." Concern roughened his voice as he gathered her into his arms.

Safely pressed against his warm bulk, Maeve opened her eyes.

His pale blue gaze bored into her. "What happened?"

"It's gone." A sob tightened in her throat and broke free. Wave after wave of desolation swept through her. "It's all gone."

CHAPTER SEVENTEEN

It sounded like Roderick had just told him the sacred grove was gone, but Alexander must have misheard. "What did you say?"

Roderick looked devastated, forlorn, adrift. "The sacred grove is gone."

"Gone, what do you mean gone?" Roderick had to be pulling his leg. The sacred grove was the cornerstone of cré-magic. It was the resting place of witches past, the seat of Goddess's power. It would be like telling a Christian that heaven had just gone bye-bye, or a Buddhist that Nirvana was no longer attainable.

Roderick scowled at him and growled. "Gone!" he yelled. "As in not fucking there anymore."

"Well, shit." Alexander's legs wobbled, and he had to sit down. "Now, don't crap all over me, but is Maeve sure?"

"Yes, she's fucking sure," Roderick bellowed. "She was called to the grove, met with the first three, and they said goodbye."

Around them, the barracks were silent as they sat in the central gathering place. Roderick had left Maeve resting and come straight here to find him. They'd had a sparring session scheduled for today, but that seemed rather trivial at this point. "And all the souls of the witches past?"

"Some are ascending to the next plane—whatever the hell that is—with them." Roderick took the seat opposite him, his anger drained. "Some will stay and reincarnate."

"Well, shit."

"Right." Roderick leaned his elbows on the table. "Goddess is still around. At least I assume she is since magic is still around."

Alexander mirrored his pose and stopped himself. They had so many identical mannerisms, it was incredible neither of them had guessed the truth of their relationship before. "What does this mean in the broader battle?"

On a huff, Roderick said, "Not a bloody clue." He shook his head. "I miss the old days when things were the way they were and stayed that way."

At times like this, so did Alexander.

A bedchamber door opened, and Andy came out. Right after him came Debra.

Normally, Alexander would have questions—quite a few—but that would have to wait.

Andy approached them with a concerned expression. "Is something wrong?"

Alexander glanced at Roderick and got a subtle nod in return, before he said, "No. Just thinking through a couple of things."

He didn't know how or what to do with this new information. For certain, they didn't want to spread panic through the coven, but this was not the sort of thing they could keep to themselves.

Gone? It didn't compute. By tacit agreement, he and Roderick needed to think this through before they announced it.

"Right." Seeming unconvinced, Andy looked between them.

"Debra needs to take a trip into the village to get some things. I was wondering if I could take her?'

"Right." Roderick stood and motioned Alexander. "We'll come with you?"

They would?

"Yep." Roderick answered his unvoiced question. "Let's take Warren with us, just to be sure."

Alexander got it. Roderick wanted to look around a bit, see what was happening outside the walls. Alexander checked the time. He could go to the village and be back before Conrad Lester's arrival. No way he would not be by Bronwyn's side when she worked her blessing. "I'll round up Warren."

Roderick nodded. "And—"

"Agreed." They'd keep this between them as much as possible. The witches were itching to get outside the wards, and they didn't want to open that argument up again.

Roderick turned to Debra and Andy. "We'll meet you at the Landy."

"Right you are." Andy gave him a jaunty nod and trotted off with Debra.

They ran Warren to ground in the new sitting room. He was sitting with Taylor while she practiced scrying. Niamh, along with three wolf pups, a badger, two squirrels, and an assortment of castle cats kept an eye on the proceedings.

Alexander motioned Warren to join him in the corridor.

With a questioning glance, Warren got to his feet and followed him out. "What is it?"

"We're taking a run down to the village with Andy and Debra."

Warren nodded and stuck his head into the room again. "I won't be long," he said to Niamh and Taylor.

Taylor waved and continued staring into her scrying bowl.

"Where are you going?" Niamh narrowed her gaze at them.

Alexander stepped into the doorway and forced a grin. "We

thought we'd line up some hookers and blow, go on a pub crawl, that sort of thing."

"You lying sod." Niamh laughed and waved them off. "But run along and do your secret boy stuff, and we'll see you later."

Warren shut the sitting room door and turned more fully to him. "What's the other thing?"

"What other thing?" Alexander tried for nonchalance.

Warren gave him a don't-bullshit-me look. "The thing you're not saying that has Roderick's knickers in a twist."

Roderick puffed up. "My knickers are not…" He grimaced. "Actually, that's a reasonable description of what I feel right now."

"You can sense that?" Alexander wasn't coimhdeacht, and he still didn't know how deep the bond between the guardians ran.

Warren made a face. "Not like I could if it was Niamh, but the spirit coimhdeacht are all…tense and expectant. It's closer to like a weird gut feel."

"Right." Alexander led the way through the great hall. "Well, we really do need to go to the village with Debra and Andy, but Roderick had some news this morning."

"What?"

There wasn't any way to put this gently. "Maeve walked the sacred grove this morning. Apparently, for the last time, because it's gone now."

"Gone?" Warren stopped dead. "What do you mean gone?"

Now Alexander felt like Roderick must have felt. "Like not there. Missing. Absent. Unavailable. Away. Gone."

Frowning, Warren got walking again. "Is that even possible?"

"I would have said no." They both fell silent as they took the stairs to the kitchen and walked through. Fortunately, nobody was about.

Andy was waiting for them beside the Landy with Debra.

"All right?" Warren greeted Debra with a chin lift.

She nodded. "Yes, I just need to get a couple of things. I wasn't expecting to be staying here indefinitely."

Warren nodded and got behind the wheel.

At least the trip to the village boded well for Debra accepting her and Taylor's new reality.

The village was busier than normal, and they wove through traffic around the green. People had gathered on the green, and more people crowded the pavement. Alexander tried to recognize as many faces as he could, but most were new to him. "There are a lot of newcomers."

"Hermione said the same." Debra leaned over from the back. "Her tour business is booked solid."

Roderick glared out the window. "I don't like it."

"Neither do I." Alexander's nape prickled a warning. "Not with everything else going on."

"It's like Baile is being corralled," Andy said. "And it's coming from all directions. The pressure about property taxes, people in the village, the police."

"The police?" Roderick shot him a glare. "What about the police?"

Alexander groaned and met Roderick's gaze. "They just had some questions about when Mags was taken."

"It's a bit more than that." Andy kept shoveling the hole deeper. "I did some nosing around, and there's a lot of pressure coming from higher up."

"What questions?" Roderick kept his scowl locked on Alexander.

"They wanted to know about a bullet casing on the road," Andy said as Warren drove them down the main street and took the turn to the large supermarket on the edge of Greater Littleton. "Police take a dim view of guns being fired amongst the general populace."

"Nobody told me about this." Roderick folded his beefy arms.

"Probably because you do that." Debra pointed at his posture. "That's very aggressive body language." She smoothed her hair. "If you want people to open up to you, you should try being more approachable."

Roderick gaped at her.

Alexander breathed a sigh of relief as they entered the supermarket parking lot.

The next half hour was spent following Debra from aisle to aisle as she loaded up her shopping trolley. She seemed to be buying enough hair dye to withstand a protracted siege. They were halfway down the personal hygiene aisle when a woman's voice stopped them. "I'm telling you, Gresby, it's them."

"I've told you before, Cressida, I prefer to be called Ovate Treebrother."

"I'm not calling you that. It's stupid." Cressida broke free from their brief scuffle at the far end of the aisle and trotted their way.

Roderick glanced around desperately for escape.

"Alexander." She stopped right in front of him and batted her lashes. "I knew it was you I spotted."

"Cressida." Alexander managed an affable smile. "Nice to see you."

Roderick gaped at him.

Cressida grabbed his arm. "It's actually fortuitous we ran into you today. I have so much to tell—"

"Don't you dare." Gresby Carmichael, aka Ovate Treebrother, shouldered her aside. "I'm the one with the information. I'll do the telling."

"Somebody had best start talking." Warren glowered down at the pair of them. "Because we're on a tight schedule here."

"Right." Gresby straightened his hemp tunic. "We have heard whispers." He made a great show of looking around them. "Dark whispers."

Cressida nodded and simpered at Alexander. "Dark whispers."

"Of?" Warren cut through the crap.

"There are a lot of people in town." Gresby leaned in. "A lot of imposters claiming to practice the craft."

"Liars," Cressida hissed. "And they're not nice people either."

Roderick stepped closer to her. He gentled his tone and gave her a terrific eye smolder. "Tell me more."

Watching his father turn on the charm turned Alexander's stomach, but then again, he hadn't exactly inherited his winning ways from his mother.

"They say they practice the craft." Mesmerized, Cressida blinked at Roderick. "But they feel wrong. Evil." She wrinkled her nose. "And there's this funny smell."

Now Cressida had their full attention.

"What are they doing?" Roderick asked.

"It's all very secretive." Gresby got in on the action again. "They gather at that big estate on the edge of town. You know the one." He nodded at Alexander. "The one with the Georgian house."

Alexander knew that estate only too well. Before his escape to Baile, that had been his estate.

"We can feel the"—Gresby went nose to nose with Roderick and whispered—"magic."

"There are a lot of them," Cressida said. "And more coming every day. We think they're practitioners of the dark arts."

"And we thought we should tell you—"

"—because you can do something about it." Cressida's cheeks went pink.

"Smite them!" Gresby smashed one fist into his palm.

"We're not really in the smiting business," Alexander pointed out. "But thank you for the information."

Cressida and Gresby looked crestfallen. Cressida recovered first. "But you are planning to do something about it?"

"We are." Roderick took her hand and pressed it. "Thank you for the information. It will prove most useful."

Her mouth dropped open, and she stared.

"Perhaps next time you have information, you could contact Hermione Andover," Andy said. "She knows how to contact us."

Cressida looked at him with suspicion. "Hermione Andover. Is she…"

"A friend." Andy winked at her. "A good friend."

"Ah!" Gresby nodded and looked smug. He returned Andy's wink. "Understood."

Alexander spared a thought for Hermione, who Andy had just chucked under the bus. "We really must get going." He wanted to be done with their shopping trip and see what had happened to his old estate.

"Come along, Cressida." Gresby took her arm.

Cressida yanked her arm free. "Goodbye," she breathed at Roderick, before turning and scurrying after Gresby.

Warren looked at him. "Your old estate next?"

"Yup." Alexander wanted to see what those assholes had done to his fucking house.

Twenty minutes later, as the Landy idled at the end of the driveway, he wished he hadn't. Cars choked the driveway and had even parked on the lawn it had taken him literal centuries to perfect. Fast-food debris littered the grounds. Fine antique furniture had been carried outside and left to the elements.

Debra covered her nose with her hand. "What is that smell?"

"Blood magic." Roderick's jaw was set in a grim line. "Lots and lots of blood magic."

"What a fucking shame." Warren shook his head and threw him a sympathetic glance.

Alexander suppressed the urge to leap from the Landy and throw the fuckers off his property. When he'd walked away from Rhiannon, he'd walked away from this as well.

Niamh waited with Maeve, Bronwyn, and Taylor for the men to return from the village. It was all very well to tell them to stay tucked up at Baile, but another thing entirely to make that demand and then go gallivanting.

Bronwyn sat at the kitchen table and glared through the open door into the bailey. "Not one of them said a word."

"Which means they knew we wouldn't like it." Maeve, who'd taken to baking bread in Alannah's absence, pounded her frustration into a ball of dough.

Taylor vacillated between being irritated at her exclusion and a desire to keep the peace. "Maybe they had a good reason."

Niamh barely suppressed her snort. Good reason or not, all those sneaky buggers would be up in arms if any of the witches attempted to sneak off to the village. "They're safe," she said. "I've had animals tracking them the whole time."

"Good." Bronwyn huffed and crossed her arms. "Then they'll be in great shape for the ass kicking I'm going to hand out when they get back."

"It's not like Andy to be sneaky." Taylor sat on the counter beside the window and peered out. "And my Mum is with them."

"Then at least they have one working brain." Maeve thwacked the dough against the table.

Bronwyn jumped and looked pained. "Must you?"

"Yup." Maeve hauled back and slapped the dough ball against the wood.

The men weren't the only ones being sneaky. Maeve was more upset than this village side trip warranted, and Niamh would lay money she was hiding something. She glanced at Bronwyn, who raised a brow. Yeah, she'd caught it too.

Niamh focused on Maeve. "What aren't you telling us?"

"Me?" Maeve flushed.

Thwap!

"Stop that." Bronwyn leaned over and snagged her arm. "You're terrible at hiding secrets."

Maeve opened her mouth to argue, grimaced, and then deflated. "I know, but I also don't know what my secret means."

"But there is a secret?" Niamh pressed.

"Not so much a secret." Maeve patted the abused dough into loaf tins. "It's more like I don't understand, and I don't want to say anything before I do."

"Tell us." Bronwyn leaned forward, her gaze sharp on Maeve. "You know you want to."

Maeve giggled and tucked the loaves into a proving drawer beneath the range. She straightened and sighed. "Okay, but you have to promise you won't freak out."

"Uh-oh." Taylor rolled her eyes. "I hate it when people start with that."

Niamh did too, and she braced for it.

"Well." Maeve fiddled with the kettle and then brought it to the sink and filled it. "You know the sacred grove?"

"Yes." All gazes fastened on her.

She lit the range under the kettle, as if anyone was going to want tea before she got to the good stuff. Judging by the look on Maeve's face, a good stiff drink might be more in order.

"W-e-ll." Maeve tinkered about setting up teacups.

Bronwyn growled. "Just tell us already."

"Okay." Maeve dropped a cup on the counter, straightened it, and then took a deep breath. "It's gone."

"Say what now?" Bronwyn cocked her head.

The she-wolf imitated her and sat up with a whine.

"It's gone." Maeve threw her hands up and leaned her back against the counter. "Or it will be soon."

Taylor scrunched her face. "Gone where?"

"They didn't really say. The first three." Maeve tugged her blouse. "I got a summons to walk with them, and they said a lot about things changing and the known becoming unknown. That the spirits could finally move on, and the grove was disappearing." She bit her lip. "They are only waiting for me to release the souls trapped on the village green and then…poof."

"Poof?" Niamh held her breath, waiting for Maeve to laugh and yell surprise.

Instead, Maeve nodded. "Poof."

None of that made any sense, and Niamh knew one male who hadn't gone to the village and was plugged into the spiritual realm. "Thomas," she yelled into the air.

"Oh no." Maeve made soothing motions with her hands. "Don't bother him he—"

"You bellowed?" Thomas appeared behind Bronwyn.

"Jesus." Bronwyn started and turned on him. "Can't you hang a bell around your neck or something?"

Thomas folded his arms and gave her a sardonic look.

"Maeve says—"

Thomas cut Niamh off. "The sacred grove will cease to be."

"Why?" It was hard to say who yelled that first, but they were all staring at Thomas now.

"Not sure." He shrugged. "But the tethers binding the souls to this plane are fading, and the grove has served its purpose and will now move on."

"Move on?" Bronwyn frowned at him. "To where?"

"Don't know." Thomas shrugged again. "Lavina holds me here, but the other coimhdeacht—the not alive ones—are starting to fade away."

Taylor squeaked. "Well, that can't be good."

"Not sure."

If he said that again, Niamh might get the she-wolf to nip him. From the way the animal glared at him, she might not be averse to the notion.

"Look." Thomas spread his arms out palms up. "I don't get

the feeling it's good or bad. It's certainly nothing to do with Rhiannon. It just is. Like a next phase kind of thing."

"Evolution," Taylor whispered.

"What?" Bronwyn stared at her.

"Evolution." Taylor looked thoughtful. "He said the next phase, and it's like evolution." She shrugged. "When something adapts to fit the changing environment."

Niamh saw her point, but the grove was their constant. "Into what?"

Thomas pulled a face. "Not—"

"And what replaces it, if anything?" Bronwyn had probably had enough of his lack of knowledge too. "And if the grove disappears, what happens to the spirits of the passed witches?"

"That's what I wanted to know." Maeve shook her head. "And all I got was a bunch of cryptic crap about them moving on."

"Well, shit!" Bronwyn summed it up for the lot of them.

Taylor turned to the window and peered out. The coriander and apple scent of her magic won out against the yeasty aroma of Maeve's bread. "Your patient is here." She leaned closer to the window. "Or will be in…about…ten minutes."

"Right." Bronwyn got to her feet and dusted down her jeans. "Let's focus on what we do understand." She looked at Thomas. "Could you get Hannah for me?"

Thomas crossed his arms. "I—"

"I'll do it." Taylor hopped down from the counter and glared at Thomas before looking at Bronwyn and rolling her eyes. "Men! Am I right?"

CHAPTER EIGHTEEN

Trudging through the compound in search of the earth point, Alannah dropped into place behind her twin. As nice as the members of the Canadian community where, she and Sinead had a purpose to fulfill, and time outside of Baile meant time in danger. She missed her coven sisters, she missed her life at Baile, and she missed *him*. She couldn't think in terms of a future, not when that future wasn't guaranteed for any of them. And definitely wouldn't happen until they activated the earth point.

They followed the sound of voices around the dining hall and into the forest. In a small clearing, most of the women of the commune had gathered in an open-sided pavillion as large as the dining hall.

As they approached, conversation dimmed to low murmurs with sidelong glances.

Kate rose from a tight cluster near the middle and waved. "Hi!"

"Hello." Sinead walked under the thatched shelter, equipped with low tables, chairs and sofas, and throw pillows. Nearly every seat was taken.

All eyes were definitely on them, and most of those gazes were wary as hell. All except for Dhara who gave them a sunny smile and a finger waggle.

Alannah tried to look nonthreatening. What was that saying? *You catch more flies with honey.* "What is everyone doing?"

"Weaving." Kate smiled, but her expression remained tight. "We sell our weaving at local craft fairs and online."

"Lovely," Alannah said.

The woman next to her had woven beautiful autumnal colors into a flowing, organic pattern, and the fabric was soft as cashmere.

Earth washed over her in a prickle of heat and power.

Beside her, Sinead stumbled and caught herself. "Whoa!"

The earth point was so close Alannah could almost taste it, and it rioted through her senses, demanding a response.

"It's here," Sinead whispered and turned wide eyes to her. "You feel it too."

"Yes." The pull was inescapable and potent and delicious, like rich, dark chocolate running through her veins. "It's wonderful."

"Right." A beatific smile lit Sinead's features. "It's perfect."

Kate cleared her throat and put fabric on the table in front of her. "You can feel it?"

"It's our cardinal point." Sinead's expression hardened. "Of course we feel it. Activating it is what we're here to do."

"Right." Kate nodded and looked away. "Of course you are."

A woman beside Alannah moaned and covered her eyes. "You can't. You don't know—"

Kate shot the woman a loaded glance.

"What?" Sinead folded her arms and thrust a hip out. "Why can't we, and what don't we know?"

Dhara tried to stand but Sara grabbed her arm and pulled her down again.

"It's...there is something we need to tell you." Kate looked like she might burst into tears.

"You can tell us anything." Alannah kept her tone gentle.

An older woman beside Kate took her hand and squeezed it. "We all knew this is what it would come to."

"I know." Kate drew a deep breath and looked at Alannah. "There is something you don't understand."

"Then tell us." Alannah read grief and heartbreak in the faces around her. Whatever it was they were missing was a tragedy to this community.

"I know you're here for a reason." Kate wiped away a tear. "And we fully support that in theory. Our founding members hid the earth point so an earth witch could activate it. But there is…I know I'm not making sense, but I'm not ready. I'm asking you, begging you really, to give us a day or two." She shuddered. "Please?"

Sinead softened slightly. "But we need to do this and get back to Baile. The longer we stay here, the more danger we're in." She looked around the women. "And by association, the more danger you're in."

"I know." Another tear dribbled down Kate's cheek. "And we won't stop you. Our entire reason for existing is to make sure you activate earth, but please…just today, then?"

"I think you should explain." Alannah got the horrible sense whatever these women were hiding was awful. "Can you do that?"

"I will." Kate dashed away her tears and squared her shoulders. "I promise. But please? Today is all I ask."

Dhara pulled free of Sara and stood. "Kate, it's—"

"No," Kate sobbed. "It's not okay, Dhara. Don't try to say that it is."

"But I'm ready."

Kate imploded and sunk to her knees on the floor. "You can't be. You don't know what you're saying."

"Kate." Dhara ran to her sister and crouched beside her.

Folding her older sister in a hug, she whispered, "I always knew this had to happen. And I am ready. It's my destiny."

Kate shook her head and looked at Dhara. The pain in her eyes made Alannah hurt for her. "But I'm not, Dhara." Kate sobbed. "I'm not."

"A day." Alannah couldn't not agree. Her heart ached for Kate without understanding why. She did understand the love of a sister, however, and she could honor that.

Kate's emotion was reflected on the faces all around her.

"And then, whatever it is that you're hiding, we have to go forward," Sinead said.

"I understand. Tomorrow." Kate nodded and took a deep, pained breath. "We'll do it tomorrow."

As one, the women turned and looked at Dhara, and more than one of them was crying.

"I'M GOING FOR A WALK," Sinead said and turned on her heel. She felt like a fucking monster, and she had no idea why. The women saw her and Alannah as the reason for all their grief, and it slammed into her like a landslide. If Alannah hadn't agreed to the extra day, she would have done it for her. "Want to come with me?"

Face reflecting her own sadness and confusion, Alannah shook her head. "No, I'll stay here for a while. Then go back to the cabin."

Leaving her twin behind with the other women, she stormed into the forest. If she walked fast enough, she might be able to outrun the feeling of dread in her middle.

The emotion amongst the women was too raw to be faked. Whatever they were hiding, it was going to cost them so much more than either she or Alannah knew.

Needing the comfort of her birth element, she sank to her

knees in the concealment of the trees and speared her fingers into the soil. Earth rose around her, strong and compelling, dizzying in its power and potential. She reached for the security and calm of growing things.

The trees heard her magic call and responded. Their sadness seeped into her soul and brought tears to her eyes. The trees whispered of sacrifice and grief, of heartbreak and loss.

"Hey," Noah said and cupped her shoulder.

Sinead turned to him.

Crouching beside her, he enfolded her against his chest, and she wept. She had no idea why, but she cried for the women, and the trees, and the secret they all kept. For someone who rarely cried, she was making a habit of it here.

Noah murmured soft words to her, words that she didn't comprehend, but brought comfort anyway. His earthy, woodsy scent wove around her, and she wrapped her arms around his waist, dug her fingers into the soft fabric of his shirt, and clung.

He held her through the storm, a steady presence that she'd had no awareness of needing as much as she did. When she'd calmed to a few small sobs, he drew back enough to gaze into her eyes. "I'm sorry."

"I'm not normally a crier." Now that the tempest had passed, she felt stupid. "I don't even know why I'm crying. It just feels so fucking sad."

"I know." Noah's fathomless eyes held her in their soft thrall. He brushed the dampness from her cheeks. "But you will understand tomorrow, and it's going to suck."

It sounded so silly that she gave a half sob, half chuckle. "Tell me."

"It's not mine to tell." He cupped her cheek. "But I'll be here when the telling happens."

Her inner fuck-you stirred. Secrets and half truths pissed her off. "But you know?"

"I know." He nodded.

"Then bloody well tell me."

He looked genuinely regretful. "I really can't."

"Can't or won't?" She wriggled out of his hold. All the petting and hugging was fine—more than fine, if she was truthful—but it didn't explain why she was kneeling on the forest floor crying like her heart had been shattered.

Noah shrugged. "It amounts to the same thing in this case."

"This is bullshit." Anger rose in her defense. The entire situation was giving her the shits, and she didn't even know these people. Nudging him away, she rose and pulled herself together. "And that's all you have to say for yourself?"

Noah dropped his head, and when he looked up at her again, the twinkle was back in his eyes. "Well." He pursed his lips. "We could talk about how zombies aren't real."

CHAPTER NINETEEN

The next morning, Sinead was up earlier than Alannah and trying to convince herself she was admiring the nonhuman view outside their cabin window. To be fair, the trees were lovely, but the stripped off men chopping and felling branches had her disturbingly rapt attention.

One man in particular.

A freak storm in the night had brought large limbs down, and Noah was working with Abe to chop the fallen limbs into smaller pieces. A handful of other tall and well-formed men were hauling and chopping beside them. There must be something in the Canadian water to make men that fine.

Noah's worn jeans clung tenaciously to his slim hips. He looked like a makeup artist had body painted his abs and pecs beneath his square, powerful shoulders. He moved with a sort of animal grace that kept her ping-ponging between ogling and disgust at her own lack of restraint. She never objectified men. Jesus Christ, if Roderick were here, he'd be giving her a lecture on her behavior.

"Mmm-hmm." Alannah popped up beside her. "You can't teach that."

Sinead let her self-flagellation show. "And I don't have time for that, or energy."

"I don't know." Alannah winked at her. "You're standing here."

"Right." Sinead turned her back on the pretty and faced the bathroom. "We have an earth point to activate."

Before she could persuade herself to look out the window again, she marched for the shower. "Did you find out anything else yesterday?"

"No." Alannah grimaced. "It seemed insensitive to push them."

Sinead got that. She'd run away rather than dig for answers. Something Noah had said to her yesterday nagged at her as she turned on the shower and waited for it to heat. For the most part, he'd been really lovely and kind. What had he said? Soaping her hair, she let her mind pick through yesterday's conversation. It was the bloody zombie thing. He'd said that zombies didn't exist.

Weird, and completely random.

Or was it?

The last time she'd spoken, or even thought about zombies—because, as a rule, she didn't think or speak about zombies at all—had been to that wild wolf.

"Bloody hell!"

She didn't realize she'd yelled until Alannah popped her head around the bathroom doorjamb. "What?"

"Creepy fucking stalkery men, that's what." Sinead rinsed her hair. Bloody Noah had been spying on her, which meant that maybe that wolf hadn't been wild at all, because surely a wild animal would have smelled or sensed him there and done something about it.

Alannah propped a shoulder on the doorjamb and crossed her arms. "Are we back to talking about pretty men?"

"You know we're failing the Bechdel test right here?" Sinead got to work with the shower gel.

Alannah laughed. "Only you would worry about that."

"Not true." Sinead gave the honey-scented bodywash an appreciative whiff. It came in glass bottles with clearly printed labels, and she had the feeling they made it in the community. "We should all care about the representation of women in literature."

"Indeed we should." Alannah smiled. "So, let's do our part and talk about something else."

Sinead motioned for her to take it away.

"Have you noticed something odd about some of the people here?"

They were in a community of oddballs as far as Sinead could see. Nice people, but odd and definitely marching to their own drummer. "Want to narrow that down to just one thing?"

"Well." Alannah frowned as she put her thoughts in order. "Mainly Zach, Noah—"

"You're doing it again." Sinead snapped off the water and snagged a towel from beside the shower.

"And Rachel and Sara." Alannah rolled her eyes. "They all have the same sort of…strange."

She had noticed a thing or two. "We've talked about the sniffing thing."

"Right!" Alannah nodded. "And they move…" She pulled a face. "It's oddly graceful and not entirely…well…human."

"What are you suggesting?" Now that Alannah brought it up, she had noticed that. With Noah, she put it down to ogling, but Rachel and Sara did it too, and Zach had this odd effect on her. If she didn't know herself better, she might even say she wanted to obey him.

"I don't know." Alannah handed her a toothbrush and the paste. "It's like with Thomas," she said. "He looks real, and he moves like a man, but there's just something…not the same."

"Rachel is fast." Sinead replayed her limited interactions with the woman.

"Yes." Alannah went back to the bedroom and rummaged in the wardrobe for her clothes. "And they growl. Have you noticed that?"

She had noticed that, without really registering it. "And their eyes kind of flash."

Alannah nodded and stripped out of her pajamas.

"Anyway." Sinead wrapped her wet hair in a towel and went to the bedroom to get dressed. "It's not really relevant. Let's get that earth point activated and get our asss home."

"Indeed." Alannah turned on the water and stepped into the shower.

Despite her big words to her twin, Sinead dressed in jeans and a sweater and went back to the window to study the men outside some more. At least, that was her excuse, and she was sticking to it.

Noah hefted half a fallen trunk and placed it on an ATV trailer. She added abnormally strong to the odd tally. That eye flashing thing reminded her of something, and she couldn't put her finger on it.

As if sensing her there, Noah looked over and grinned. He jerked his chin at her and went back to log hauling.

Rachel strolled across to the working men. Dressed in combats and boots, she shouldn't have been graceful, but there was a fluidity to her movements that was decidedly other. She prowled more than walked.

Sinead kept watching, and even did a fairly good job of convincing herself she wasn't keeping her gaze on Noah ninety percent of the time. The men finished, and Rachel hopped on the ATV and chugged away.

Noah and Abe turned and trotted after her.

Abe said something to Noah, then threw back his head and howled.

Noah punched him and kept moving.

Abe's howl had been eerily like the wolves at Baile. That was it! The puzzle piece dropped into place. Their eyes flashed like Baile's she-wolf's did.

Alannah came out of the bathroom dressed and finishing tying up her hair. "Ready?"

"More than ready." Sinead tucked away her wayward thoughts and followed her twin from the cabin.

Kate had asked for a day, and they'd given her one. Time to get to the bottom of the mystery and out of Canada. Noah had told her that learning the secret would suck, and she braced for that. Still, earth needed to be active. Nobody would be safe until Goddess had her power points active again. Baile certainly wouldn't be safe until she and Alannah could strengthen the wards.

"One more thing." Alannah stopped and met her gaze. "Don't hold back because of me." She gave Sinead a hug. "Don't think you can't be happy because of my situation with Thomas."

She turned and marched away before Sinead could respond. But they were a pair, her and Alannah. Being happy when her twin was miserable wasn't possible.

Kate was waiting for them in her cabin, seated at her kitchen table with Dhara and Sara. She looked as if she hadn't slept a wink, and her eyes were puffy and red.

Zach hovered over her shoulder with his arms crossed and his expression severe. The atmosphere was tense, and it felt like they'd interrupted something.

"Blessed." Zach greeted them with a nod.

"You're hovering," Kate snapped at him over her shoulder. "Sit."

Zach gave her an impassive stare. "I'll stand."

"Urgh!" Kate turned in her chair and poked his thigh with her index and middle fingers. "Tsst!"

Dhara laughed. "Did you just Cesar Milan him?"

"Maybe." Kate blushed and glanced at Zach.

He raised a dark eyebrow at her and shook his head. "You're stressed."

"Of course I'm fucking stressed." Kate looked back at them and grimaced. "Sorry. I'm having a difficult morning."

Zach snorted.

"I swear to God." Kate turned on him. "I'll put you outside."

He smirked. "You could try."

"Please, have a seat." Dhara stood and motioned the twins to take a chair at the table. "We need to tell you something."

Sinead was ready for whatever they had to tell her. "We need to get the earth point activated."

"You don't—"

Zach put his hand on Kate's shoulder as she tried to leap out of her chair. "It's not their fault. They're here to do what has to happen. It's *their* purpose."

Looking like she might be on the verge of tears, Kate took her seat again and sighed. "I know that. It's just so fucking shit."

"It is, Katy." Zach squeezed her shoulder. He touched his index finger to her neck. "It's an unmitigated fuck-fest."

"Would you like some coffee?" Dhara seemed unaffected by the interplay.

Alannah smiled at her. "That would be lovely."

"Put a shot of whisky in it," Kate murmured. "We're all going to need it."

The door opened, and Noah's presence prickled up her nape, and her skin warmed. She wanted to turn and fling herself into his arms, and she had no idea why.

Zach nodded to him.

Noah cupped her elbow. "Come." He led her to the table. "Have a seat, and Dhara will make you a cup of coffee."

Sinead allowed herself to be gently pressed into a chair.

Taking hold of her hand, Noah threaded his fingers through hers.

She drew comfort from the contact, like whatever happened next would be okay as long as he kept hold of her hand.

"Katy?" Zach moved closer and rested both hands on her shoulders. "This isn't going to get any easier, and it has to be done."

Kate dragged in a deep breath. Tears shone in her eyes as she nodded. "I know that. It's just she's…"

"I know, Katy." Zach's deep voice reached through the room and soothed them all. "Want me to do it?"

Kate opened her mouth and shut it again. Like her neck didn't work properly, she gave a jerky nod.

"No." Dhara brought the coffee pot and a handful of mugs to the table. "I'm the one who should do it. It's going to affect me the most."

Kate dropped her head. Wet splotches hit the wood table in front of her. The misery in the room was palpable.

"Tell us," Sinead said.

"We already told you that the earth point was moved." Dhara took her seat again.

Noah's grip tightened on Sinead's hand.

She nodded. "Yes."

Alannah's gaze flit between Kate and Dhara. "We didn't even know that was possible."

"It's amazing what you can do when you're desperate," Kate whispered. "Our ancestors were desperate. That's the only way I can even attempt to understand why they did what they did."

"Well, what you don't know is where the earth point moved to." Dhara put her hands on the table and clenched her fingers together. "Or rather who it moved to."

"I beg your pardon," Sinead said.

"Let me." Kate covered Dhara's hands and took another breath. "In the fifties, when our community was formed, it was formed to hide the earth point," she said. "The community at the time became aware of someone—I think we can all guess as to who—trying to destroy it. So, they moved it here and created the community around it to keep it safe."

"I can feel it here," Alannah said. She looked around the table. "Maybe it's because we said we'd activate it this morning, but it feels particularly strong this morning."

In all her ogling, Sinead had failed to notice that, but she felt it now, like an electrical current beneath her skin.

"That's because it's right here," Dhara said and raised her hand.

Sinead looked around the kitchen. "In here?"

"Right here." Noah rested their joined hands on his thigh.

"Why didn't we feel—"

"Give me a minute." Kate took a deep breath. "I'll explain everything, and you'll understand."

Someone had better start explaining, or Sinead would leap out of her skin.

"Our community founders discovered a magical loophole," Kate said. "The point can't be moved to a physical place, but it can be moved to a person."

"What?" Alannah glanced at her, but Sinead had nothing, so she shrugged.

"Inside a person." Kate swallowed. "A person with the right magical qualities or genetics, or whatever the hell it needs." She motioned Dhara and herself. "Our family, in fact. The first witch to carry the earth point was my great-aunt. When she died, it passed on." She looked at Dhara. "To my sister, Dhara."

Sinead must have lost her reasoning because her brain wasn't tracking. "I don't understand."

"I'm the earth point," Dhara said and tapped her chest. "It's inside me, a part of me."

Alannah shook her head, eyes wide. "That's not possible."

"You haven't felt it strongest when you're close to me?" Dhara looked at Sinead and then Alannah.

Had they? Sinead went through each interaction she'd had with Dhara.

"Here." Dhara held her hands out to both Sinead and Alannah. "Touch me."

It took Sinead a long, hard moment to reach back and touch Dhara's hand. It couldn't be true. She didn't want it to be true.

As their hands connected, earth jolted through her like a lightning bolt. It almost drove Sinead out of her chair. Green light glowed from where her hand joined Dhara's, and the ground beneath her feet rumbled.

Alannah made her connection with Dhara and jerked in her seat.

"No." Sinead dropped Dhara's hand and looked at Kate. They had to be making this up.

"Our family was given the honor of holding the earth point." Kate's voice wavered, and she cleared her throat. "It passed to Dhara and not me. We're not sure exactly why, but the point chooses its host."

Dhara's smile was gentle and ancient in her pretty, young face. "I've always known it was inside me, and that it was my destiny."

Alannah voiced the question Sinead didn't have the courage to broach. "What happens when we activate it?" She shook her head, as if trying to clear her mind. "What happens to you?"

"She dies." Kate squeezed her eyes shut. "My little sister dies when you activate the earth point."

CHAPTER TWENTY

Sinead left Alannah with Kate and stormed into the forest. Goddess, stomping into the forest was getting to be a habit here. Still, she needed the peace and tranquility more than ever. What she'd heard left her outraged, confused. The goddess she knew would never have placed a burden like that on a living being. Goddess was life, life was sacred.

She'd known Noah would follow her, and she didn't turn as she said, "It's not possible."

"Lots of stuff isn't possible," Noah said. "And yet, it is."

"How?" She turned and looked at him. "Why?"

He shrugged and shoved his hands in his front pockets. His strange golden eyes compelled her and tugged at her.

"What are you?" she whispered.

He smiled. "How about we deal with one shock at a time?"

Sinead nodded. She couldn't fault his logic, and the colossal shock of Dhara was enough. "Obviously, we're not activating the earth point." She didn't need to consult Alannah about that.

Noah frowned. "But you must."

"No. Nope. Not. *Nyet. Nein. Non.*" Sinead slashed the air with each new denial. "Not fucking happening."

"Sweet thing, that is your purpose." He took a step closer. "Just as Dhara's purpose is to host the earth point until it is activated."

Sinead knew her anger wasn't directed at him, but she couldn't contain it any longer. "That's a girl you're talking about. No more than a fucking child."

"I know that." Noah softened his tone. "I knew that child when she was born, and I've guarded her for her entire life. But this is larger than her, or you and me, or any of us." He motioned the forest around them. "This is about life itself continuing."

Fuck! Way to put the pressure on. "I'm not killing that girl."

"You have a greater purpose. You are a cré-witch."

Now her anger was directed at him. How dare he even suggest such a heinous act. "I know exactly what I am, and that's not a fucking murderer. I don't care what it takes, but we are not killing that young girl to get this point activated."

He remained impassive under her scowl for a long moment, and then he nodded.

"And that does you justice." Expression softening, he stepped even closer until they were separated by a couple of inches. "I'm sorry, I'm being an asshole. I wanted to see what you would do."

"You thought I'd agree to murder?" She couldn't believe he'd even consider her capable of that.

"You are fighting a battle that is bigger than all of us." He cupped her cheek. "Your sole purpose in coming here was to activate the earth point. I had to see that life weighed heavier with you than that."

Sinead went under the current of quick-flowing emotion. "You were testing me?"

"In a way." Noah grimaced. "Like I said, I was part of raising Dhara. She has always been more than an earth point to me."

Under the gentle understanding in his eyes, Sinead's fight

bled away and left her feeling adrift. "I don't know what we're going to do."

"But you do know what you aren't going to do." He cradled her face in both hands. "And that's a start. Together, we will find an answer."

Purpose strengthened within her as she spoke. "We?"

"We." He nodded.

She took a deep breath and tried to steady herself. His closeness worked like magic on her anger and fear. She wanted to close the distance between them and rest her head against his chest. "I do know this," she said, fighting the urge. "Goddess is about revering life, and if she put the earth point inside Dhara, she would never demand her death to activate it."

Noah rested his forehead against hers. "Your fierceness is so fucking compelling."

The air warmed between them. Sinead swore she could feel his heartbeat, sense him as a stirring beneath her skin. It was as if an invisible tether bound them, and with each interaction, wove them tighter together.

She didn't know what she was doing, what they were doing. Whatever it was, it held Sinead in its thrall. "What's happening?"

"What is right and intended." His lips brushed hers.

Sinead forgot to breathe. Forgot everything but the man in front of her. He smelled incredible, and the heat coming off his strong body could power its own electrical grid. "You're going to kiss me, aren't you?"

"I am kissing you." He pressed his mouth against hers.

"Your timing sucks," she whispered.

He chuckled, a low, raspy sound that tugged at her core. "You're right."

"Then again, I don't see a good time for any of this." She wasn't sure who had moved closer, but their fronts now pressed together.

A cocoon surrounded them. Earth pulsed around her and the rose and clove smell of her magic rose.

Noah sniffed and smiled. "That's incredible too." He nipped at her bottom lip and then soothed it with his tongue. "Let's get back to the kissing."

"Good idea." She barely recognized the breathy whisper as hers.

His palms warmed her face, his breath feathered against her lips, and pressed into his chest, her breasts felt full and achy.

Noah slanted his mouth over hers. His tongue touched her lip seam and asked a silent question.

Sinead opened for him, like it was the most natural thing in the world.

On a soft growl, Noah increased the pressure. His tongue danced with hers, invited her to join.

The rightness of the connection roared through her, and Sinead kissed him back. Desire surged through her, and she grabbed his waist to keep herself upright. She'd never felt anything like Noah's kiss. It was an experience all its own, a beginning and an ending, a completion.

Her limbs softened and melted into him as he explored her mouth.

He kissed her like she was the only item on his agenda for the rest of his life.

Hunger for more soared swift and relentless inside her and she tugged him closer.

His erection pressed against her, and she moved on him, everything in her clamoring to get closer.

Breaking their kiss, he breathed deep, as if trying to inhale the essence of her. His lips moved over her cheek, and down to her neck. Burying his face in her neck, he took a deep breath of her. "From the moment I saw you."

"What?" Sinead couldn't focus on anything but his mouth and his body. She wanted him with a sharp ache that left her

boneless and breathless. She'd been kissed before, had lovers—
even good lovers—but this man made all others seem not
enough.

"In that hotel." His lip branded her collar bones. "Even before
then, at the construction site. I knew."

Some distant part of her brain tried to get her to pay attention. Her memory pinged back to those days in Montreal. "You
were there."

"Yeah." He bit into the flesh of her shoulder. "Following
you."

"What?" Understanding pierced her lust-fogged brain. "You
were stalking me?"

"Uh-uh." He slid his hands down her arms and around her
waist. "We were protecting you."

"Hang on a minute." Getting her arms between them, she
pushed at his chest. "You can't just drop something like that and
then keep doing what you're doing."

He growled and yanked her hips against his. "You're mine."

"And you can back up with all that bullshit." Sinead shoved
harder and finally got enough breathing room for her brain to
kick in. "I'm not about all that *my woman* rubbish."

Noah chuckled and shook his head. "I suppose we need to
get this out of the way."

"Bloody right we have to get this out of the way." She
couldn't think when he was close to her, and she took a step
back. She folded her arms over her sensitive breasts. "Explain."

"Zach sent Abe and me to Montreal." Noah yanked a hand
through his hair. With a grimace he adjusted himself in his
jeans.

It was fucking hot, knowing how she affected him.

Concentrate, Sinead! And not on that!

"He sent us to Montreal to make sure you were safe." He
shrugged. "Of course, we weren't expecting two of you."

"And?" There would be no more kissing until he spat it all

out. And depending on what he said next, maybe no more kissing at all.

"We followed you to the hotel," Noah said. "You saw me in the restaurant."

His story wasn't getting better. "And you thought you'd try your hand at kidnapping?"

"We weren't the only people watching you." His expression grew cold and forbidding.

Only a regular diet of Roderick and his death stare stopped her from taking a reflexive and self-preserving step back. "Rhiannon's people?"

"We didn't want to take the chance."

Okay, that didn't sound like all-out stalking. "It didn't occur to you to talk to us about it?"

"You've been here for days. Zach told you most of this." Noah threw his arms wide. "Why is this coming up now?"

"Because you kissed me."

"You kissed me back."

"Not the point."

With a growl, he shoved his hands back in his pockets. "We made a judgment call."

"You made the wrong one."

"Maybe."

"Maybe?" More kissing was definitely off the table now. "You drugged and kidnapped us."

"Say we had knocked on your door and talked to you. How would you explain this?" He gestured around them. "All of this. Any of this."

He had her there. Would she and Alannah have believed him about the community here and Dhara? Reality flooded in like a blast of arctic air. Still, she wasn't going to roll over that easily. "I guess we'll never know."

Noah yanked at his hair again. "How did we go from kissing to fighting?"

"Oh, that's an easy one." She poked his chest—his very hard and broad chest—to get her point across. "Newsflash. And you're going to want to hold on to your hat for this one. Women don't like being stalked, drugged, and kidnapped."

His mouth twitched as if he were trying not to laugh. "Noted."

"They also don't like the growly, manly man possessive crap." If he laughed at her, she would smack him.

Noah raised his eyebrows. "Really? Because you seemed to like it just fine. Or did I imagine your tongue down my throat?"

"You kissed me," she yelled.

"You kissed me back." He matched her volume.

"It was a momentary aberration."

"Bullshit." He stepped closer to her.

He may well be right about that. Even now she wanted to punch his smug face and then kiss it better. She took a dignity-saving step back. "You're being an asshole."

"I want to kiss you again." His eyes glowed hot and intent at her.

She backed up. Not because she was scared, but more because he didn't scare her. No man scared her. But if he started the kissing again, she wasn't confident she wanted to stop him. "Resist the urge."

"You sure about that?" He kept coming.

She kept retreating. "Yes."

"Liar," he whispered.

Her back hit a tree. "asshole."

"But I'm your asshole." He caged her with a hand on either side of her head. He lowered his mouth to her ear. "And you're mine."

"Do you have a fucking hearing problem?" Her voice had dropped into a low rasp that sounded more like a come-on than a put down. Was this really her? She'd slap any woman silly for liking what he was laying down. She'd slap herself silly if her ovaries didn't fucking stop their rampage.

"What I have is a pain in my ass woman who is driving me crazy." He nipped her earlobe.

Sinead gave his abs a half-hearted shove away. "And stop biting me!"

"Nope." He sucked her earlobe. "There will be more biting, and kissing, and sucking, and licking."

Oh fucking hell! Now he really wasn't playing fair. "No, there won't." But she didn't believe herself either. That all sounded like a super fucking idea. Her knees grew a little iffy on the keeping her standing thing. "You need to back off."

"You're right." He stepped away from her.

Sinead shivered as she felt suddenly cold.

His eyes still blazed at her, but he stayed where he was. "When you're ready, you'll come to me."

"That's never going to happen."

He grinned and turned away. "It's going to happen."

She yelled at his insufferable, retreating back, "Don't bet on it."

And the smug bastard laughed.

That! That right there was why nothing was going to happen again. "You're not sexy."

He strolled out of the forest.

"Bloody hell," Sinead whispered to the silent forest. "He is absolutely, positively fucking sexy."

Noah's voice carried back to her. "I heard that."

CHAPTER TWENTY-ONE

"Excellent." Roderick nodded and folded his arms. Behind him, a moody morning sky descended into a choppy sea. Brisk wind ruffled his T-shirt and his hair, and he looked like any man of this century.

Alexander knew different. Another thing that was different was this odd dynamic that had developed between them. It was awkward, like first date awkward, like sixteen-year-old hormone surges awkward, but he didn't know how to put them on an easier footing. Roderick being polite to him was another tally in the different column.

Conrad Lester had arrived the previous evening, and Bronwyn and Hannah had worked on him for a couple of hours. He was now resting comfortably in the healer's hall, his wounds healed, and well on the way to recovery. Sasha's people would be coming for him later today, and they'd assured Alexander there would be no further repercussions. Only once he was certain of that, and that his little witch was taking a nap, had he agreed to another training session with his magic.

Waiting wore on all their nerves. Knowing Rhiannon had something in the works, and sitting behind Baile's wards while her plan swung into action chafed all of them. He could do with the distraction training with Roderick provided.

"So." Andy consulted the laptop in front of him. "That's yes to inanimate objects of a martial nature, with a more than ninety percent success rate."

Roderick peered over his shoulder at the screen. "And a no to anything non warlike."

"Battle mage." Andy nodded and smiled at Alexander like a proud parent.

Speaking of proud parents, Roderick glanced up and gave him a grimace that was intended to be a smile. "Excellent work."

"Thank you." Try as he might, Alexander could no longer find it in him to snort and sneer at the man who had been his lifelong enemy and more recently had been identified as his father. In his protracted life, Alexander had rarely encountered a mind fuck to equal that one. Roderick had somehow fathered him, and not in the traditional, tried and true either. He couldn't wrap his head around what Rhiannon must have done to have gotten pregnant by Roderick. Goddess, examining the conception options made his breakfast threaten to make a reappearance. "I've been thinking."

"Aye?" Roderick locked eyes with him. Three weeks ago, Roderick would have made a verbal jab about his ability to think.

Alexander would have come out with an upper cut about Roderick's age or meat headedness. "Have we considered trying other life forms?"

"Oh my." Andy's eyes sparkled. "That would be interesting."

Roderick frowned. "Meaning animals?"

Alexander nodded.

Roderick's frown deepened. "Is that safe?"

"I'm not saying I would try to inhabit a living creature. The creatures of Baile are perfectly safe from me and this thing Goddess gave me. I would try to become an animal."

"For you," Roderick growled. "Is it safe for you?"

Alexander would have accused him of not giving a crap, but he had the uncomfortable feeling that Roderick did, in fact, give a shit. "I'm not sure, but it would be worth exploring the extent of this…gift."

"Your blessing." Roderick gave him a stern look. "This is a blessing, and best we call it thus."

The more formal, antiquated speech pattern was a tell that Roderick was feeling the teenlike twitch of discomfort around their new relationship right alongside him.

"I've been given this for a reason." Alexander didn't want to push the limits of their new kumbaya-ness too far so refrained from claiming his ability as a blessing. When had he ever missed an opportunity to drive the knife between Roderick's metaphorical ribs? Come to think on it, when had he missed the opportunity to drive the knife between Roderick's literal ribs either? Short answer—since they'd found out they were related. "I think it would be wise to explore the extent." He held up the hand he had made into a dagger not five minutes ago. "We all need to know what I'm working with."

Roderick dropped his head and considered the toes on his size fourteens. "I agree. But…" Up came his head, and his fierce pale blue gaze locked on Alexander. "Nothing like this has ever been attempted, and I am reluctant to risk you on untried and unknown magic."

Peering over his laptop screen, Andy beamed like a squirrel on the verge of a nut cache to end all nut caches. "We could proceed slowly and cautiously."

"Alexander has value to this coven," Roderick snapped and then flushed. "He is a good fighter. His knowledge of Rhiannon is unsurpassed, and there are…er…people here who value him."

With a grimace, Andy subsided behind his laptop. "Forgive me. I got caught up in the excitement of the possibilities."

"I just found him." Roderick cleared his throat and went

back to examining his boots. "I don't want anything to go wrong."

"I think we should give it a try." Alexander tried to ignore the warm glow Roderick's admission caused. As long-last fathers went, Roderick was moving into the role with heartwarming alacrity. "Goddess wouldn't have bestowed this for no reason."

Roderick narrowed his gaze on him as if trying to read his mind. "You're thinking you have been given this to battle Rhiannon."

Reading each other's thoughts and intentions had always made them the very best of foes. "She is my mother. She is mine to battle."

"Ours." Roderick stepped toward him. "She is ours to battle, and I will not sacrifice you in the fight."

Alexander swallowed the lump of emotion. As a boy, he'd often dreamed of who his father could be. He'd dreamed of a day when said father would appear and rescue him. He wasn't that boy anymore, however, and their reality was going to demand sacrifice from all of them. "We're all going to have to make sacrifices before this is over."

"Should I..." Andy motioned the castle. "Perhaps this is something you need to settle between you?"

"No." Alexander shook his head, his purpose strengthening within him. He'd heard Mags's prophecies, and he knew, when it came right down to it, he was the only one who could defeat his mother. The alternative was risking the other coven members, and he wouldn't do that. He'd earned his need for amends. Under Rhiannon, he'd stained his soul with blood. He owed this to every member of this coven, living and dead. "This is my battle."

"Ours." Roderick thrust his chin out. "You will not do this alone."

"Oh, come on." Alexander's veneer of civility snapped. Between him and Roderick, there had always been honesty in their mutual antipathy. "You know what I've done. You know the depth of the debt I owe."

"I know you were molded by that bitch." Roderick strode toward him and grasped his shoulder. "I know what she is capable of, and I know what she tried to make of you. I know also that my blood runs through your veins, and I know the man you are now."

The plaintive howl of a wolf drifted over the bailey.

Roderick gave a grim smile. "There is our answer." He clapped Alexander's shoulder. "If you are determined to try this, let us take our cue from Baile and try a wolf. Perhaps you are the wolf Taylor heard howling in her visions?"

Alexander liked the idea and gave Roderick a nod. Then he considered the repercussions. "If this goes sideways?"

Roderick nodded. "It will not."

"But if it does." He had more than himself to consider.

"Bronwyn is my kin." Roderick held his gaze. "And those babies are my grandchildren."

That was too much of a mind-fuck to deal with, Roderick as a granddad. Plus side, the fucker had some stories to tell, lots and lots of stories to keep young minds entertained.

Squaring his shoulders, Alexander took a deep breath. Then he thought of something else. "If this does go tits up, tell Bronwyn it was my idea."

"Like that would help." Roderick snorted. "Just make sure it stays on track, for all our sakes."

"Right." Now that he was actually going to do this, nerves fluttered through his belly. It's funny how death didn't bother you when it was only your own miserable existence that you would end. But he had Bronwyn now, who—Goddess help her —loved him, and those twins she was incubating.

"Think of it this way." Roderick's eyes gleamed with amusement. "If it goes wrong, I can legitimately kill a rabid wolf."

There was that, and the moment of normal gave him the fortitude he needed.

Alexander drew fire, then air, then earth and finally water. The magic streams rushed toward him in ribbons of red, green, yellow, and blue. He concentrated on the wolves and wound the powers into a rope. As they twined and joined, the colors bled into a steady silver aimed at his chest. He braced for impact as the magic hit him like a tsunami. Magic arrowed into his chest and spread to his limbs. It rampaged through his cells and expanded them. It was too much. He closed his eyes.

Then everything went still, and he felt like him but not him all at once.

"Motherfucker," Roderick whispered.

Alexander opened his eyes.

Andy and Roderick stared down at him. Down, because they were now so much taller than he was.

And Alexander threw back his head and howled. From the forest surrounding the castle, Pack howled back.

FROM THE VILLAGE GREEN, Thomas interpreted the wolf howls for what they were, a battle cry. Pack knew a battle was coming, and they were ready. It had been hundreds of years since he'd had a physical body, but that part of him ached with a core-level weariness that dragged him from one day to the next.

Whilst Alannah had been with him, he'd been able to distract himself from the exhaustion. He was a being out of his time and out of his element. When he'd been first called as coimhdeacht, he'd taken the opportunity with excitement. As a young, living man, he'd craved adventure and challenge. He'd always known it might cost him his life, but he'd had the kind of fatalistic view only the young and arrogant could indulge. Then, he had died, and it hadn't been his life that flashed before his eyes, but more the opportunities he'd squandered and the experiences he would never have.

The half-life he'd experienced following his physical death had not been something he could ever have been prepared for. When Roderick reincarnated out of the statue, he and the other ghost coimhdeacht had been given the ability to become visible at will. He'd enjoyed being seen and interacting with people again. He'd become useful again, part of the new reality of the coven, yet separated from it at the same time.

He stood on the village green, invisible to the mortals going about their daily lives. The number of people on the green grew daily. Newcomers were flooding Greater Littleton, and an alarming number of them stank of blood magic.

He toed the edge of the wards. There was nothing to be gained from crossing. He'd tried it before. He would merely be yanked back and reform in the barracks. Somehow, his essence was tied to Baile and the dead witches on the green.

Lavina's pain ripped inside him, like a long festering wound. He could feel her desperation to leave this plane, and her frustration that she was unable to do so. When Lavina and the other twelve witches and the acolyte had committed suicide to power the spell to put Maeve and Roderick in stasis, they had known what they were sacrificing.

Blood magic was forbidden to a cré-witch, yet to a woman, they had judged the sacrifice worth the reward. With the coven on the brink of extinction, they had chosen Maeve to go forward. It made sense. As a spirit walker, Maeve could always access the knowledge and lives of witches long dead. She was the only one who had been able to keep the magic alive into this new time.

Now the sacred grove faded with each passing hour. Spirits of dead witches left, either to reincarnate or move on, like lingering participants of a glittering ball—sad to go, but tired and eager for what came next.

In his spirit form, he could see the wraiths populating the green. Lavina drifted into his line of sight, looking like she had when he had last seen her, dressed in breeches and a tunic, long hair bound in a tight braid, her form tall and statuesque.

"Blessed," he whispered.

He liked to think she turned and looked at him, but with her incorporeal form flickering like it did, it could have been merely a trick of the light.

Because he was Lavina's coimhdeacht, his essence was linked to hers. Once again, the rules had changed, and with the sacred grove disintegrating, the spirit witches on the green were more agitated than ever. They could sense their sisters leaving on a permanent basis, and it grieved them.

He watched, as he had a thousand times before, as the witches reenacted their last moments on this physical plane. In a circle, they surrounded the long-gone forms of Maeve and Roderick, cast their spell in four and let their life essence and blood seep into the ground.

As they died, their spirits separated from their physical forms and attempted to leave this plane.

Just as they had a thousand times before, the tethers that bound them here yanked them back and kept them. Each spirit wailed and lamented the discovery of their entrapment. Again and again, and a-fucking-gain. It was a relentless loop that would not release them.

And he was trapped with them. He couldn't go forward or backward. He could only float through this reality in near-constant torment.

***

Piercing pain in her chest ripped Alannah out of sleep. Her cheeks were wet, and she suspected she'd been crying again.

Sinead thought she was crying about the reality of her situation, but it wasn't that, and she didn't have the words to express what she felt. Thomas was suffering, and now that she wasn't around to distract him, that suffering resonated through her.

She wished peace for him and knew that serenity might take him from her.

Nothing was ever bloody simple, was it? And there never seemed to be a bright side without a looming dark coming up right beside it.

Not wanting to wake her sister, she slipped from her bed and grabbed a pair of slippers and a dressing gown. The sharp bite of autumn outside made her tighten the robe around her.

She needed the peace earth would give, so she walked toward the nearest entrance to the surrounding forest.

A large dark animal slid out of the forest and trotted down the central path between the cabins.

Alannah froze where she was. That was either a very large dog, or a wolf.

The animal stopped, sniffed, and turned to look at her.

She held her breath.

It trotted on.

Welcoming any distraction from the persistent ache in her chest that was Thomas, she trailed after it, winding through the settlement and back into the forest on the far side. Down a path they went until they came to another clearing containing nine or ten neat dwellings.

It climbed onto the porch of one of the cabins the guards shared and scratched on the door. The door opened in a spill of light, and the animal slipped inside. Sinead had said she'd seen a wolf in the forest, but a wolf being let into a home was madness.

She braced for screams and carnage. Forest noises continued around her.

A short while later, the door opened, and Noah stepped out.

"Alannah." He strolled her way. "What are you doing up?"

She saw no reason to lie. "I couldn't sleep."

"Understandable." He nodded.

The question was out before she could edit it. "I thought I saw a wolf."

"Really?" Noah rocked on his heels and cocked his head. "I wouldn't be surprised. There are a lot of them around here."

She got the feeling he was hiding something and went with her gut. "It went into your cabin."

"A wolf?" He turned and looked toward his cabin. "That would be surprising."

His non answer frustrated her. "You didn't see anything?"

"I can promise you I did not see a wild wolf enter my cabin." His teeth flashed in the night as he smiled. "You can bet I'd have a very different reaction if I had."

"Hmm." She let it drop. He had glibly danced around giving her a direct answer to any of her questions. "Maybe I just imagined it?"

He shrugged. "Could be."

Liar, liar. Dhara being the earth point was not the only secret Noah and the rest of the Canadians were hiding, and for Sinead's sake, she was going to get to the bottom of this newest mystery.

CHAPTER TWENTY-TWO

Victory surged through Rhiannon's blood, triumph so close she could taste it. She needed to be calm. She'd waited too long to act precipitously now. This was her one chance to kill Goddess before she could grow in power.

Around her massed her followers, their gazes trained on her, waiting for her signal.

Below them, the community slumbered, small cabins littered amongst the trees. So trusting, so innocent, and so vulnerable to those who dared. Well, she dared.

She turned to the leader of the humans. "What about the wolves?"

"No sign of them." He grinned and adjusted the weapon at his hip. Stupid moron. One of those prepper conspiracy theorists who thought the gun at his hip made him some sort of hero. If she didn't need him, she would enjoy demonstrating to him how little power he really held. Tapping his blood would be a pleasure once this was done, but for now, his skills would be useful.

Although, she didn't share his confidence in the lack of wolf shifters. They had been guarding the community for years now, and unlike her sweaty, overweight henchman, she took nothing for granted. The magic that had formed those shifters was powerful earth magic, and it pulsed through their veins and muscles. They were connected to the power like a coimhdeacht. The malodorous human beside her had no idea what he was up against. "Stay alert," she said. "They are deadly."

He nodded and unholstered his weapon.

Stupid fuckwit might get himself killed before this day was out, but she had countless thousands just like him to replace him. All he needed to do was get her close enough to Goddess in her current form and she would do the rest.

"Ma'am?" He cleared his throat. "We're burning our advantage here. Daylight in T-minus ninety."

What the ever-loving fuck did that even mean? Rhiannon stared at him.

"I mean." He shifted, sweat already making runnels in the ridiculous green and black streaking of his camouflage makeup. "The sun will come up in an hour and a half, and we want to be gone by then."

How sweet! He thought she gave a crap whether he survived this encounter or not. Or even gave a crap whether his human authorities would round him up like the sweaty hog he was and herd him into custody for punishment.

She took one more slow look around the tidy little settlement nestled in the valley below them. Something was missing, but she couldn't put her finger on what. Fiona would have been useful, but Fiona was guarding her most valuable asset right now.

"Do it," she said.

The hairy monstrosity beside her went into a laughable parody of hand gestures and whistles. Men and women just like him surged down the hill to the settlement.

Rhiannon kept her position. Soon the blood would flow, and then she would gorge herself.

Three acolytes slid into place beside her.

"You know what to do?"

"Yes, mistress." The first woman bowed her head. "We will collect the powered blood."

"Good." She nodded. "We won't have long. Once the life force fades, it's useless to me."

The first sounds of the attack broke the still predawn air. Rapid blasts of gunfire, screams, strangulated cries, glass breaking.

Lifting the skirts of her velvet gown, she picked her way down the hill, careful to keep the fabric from snagging on the thick undergrowth. She despised nature. It had no order, it refused to bend to her will.

Screams and cries grew louder as they drew closer, interspersed with the guttural grunts of her army.

A man broke free and ran toward them, only to be cut short by a staccato burst of gunfire that contorted him into a dancing puppet before he crumpled face-first to the ground. Her people had been told they could do as they pleased with the male residents.

Where were the wolves? Their enhanced senses should have warned them something was amiss by now.

"Mistress," an acolyte whispered. "Forgive my audacity, but I do not sense earth."

She'd picked up the acolyte in Africa, and her connection to earth was stronger than the normal diluted detritus that was all she had available to her in this time. The strength of her connection was what made Rhiannon stop. "What do you mean?"

"I don't mean to quest—"

"What do you mean?"

The acolyte bowed her head, her hands clasped in front of her so tightly her knuckles had gone white. "I cannot sense the earth point."

Shit! Rhiannon quickened her pace. It had been so long since she'd felt the touch of earth, she'd not thought to quest for an echo. Ferns and vining plants tangled with her hem and clung as she strode forward. That was what was missing. Her connection to earth had dulled since she'd been cut off from cré-magic, but she should have sensed something. Still, these Canadians had managed to hide the point from her for all these years, so they might have warded earth's magical signature.

Gritting her teeth, she pulled air, water, and fire. The pain was exquisite as she held a shield around her.

A careening body crashed into one of the acolytes and sent her spinning to the ground. A second caught a stray bullet and cried out. They were expendable, all of them.

Already her army had managed to herd a small group of residents into a central area. More were being shoved into the captive gaggle as she approached.

Most of them were women, some crying, others looking pale-faced and resolute. Children clung to their mothers, eyes huge in their pale and terrified faces. Sniffles and sobs provided white noise against the mounting background of violence.

Another twenty minutes, and it was done. Fighters went from house to house searching for stragglers, but the furor had died down to the muted soundtrack of misery coming from the shivering human puddle.

Rhiannon waited a few minutes longer before stepping in front of them.

Her leader gave a piercing whistle and shouted for silence.

"Good morning," she greeted the community residents. "I am Rhiannon."

A low-level murmur broke through the crowd. Several looked at each other in confusion. They should have known her. Her name should have caused a ripple of fear to run through them.

That niggling sensation grew stronger, and with it, her rising rage. "Who is your leader?"

Again, they glanced amongst themselves. Nobody wanted to step out from the crowd.

Everyone gave up their secrets in the end. One merely had to find a motive compelling enough. She pointed to a tallish man with a bushy iron-gray beard who was still dressed in sleeping attire. "Him."

Her buffoon strong armed the man out of the crowd.

The woman beside him cried out and tried to pull him back.

Another of her fighters stepped forward and cracked the woman across the back of her head.

The woman crumpled like a bloody rag.

Fury lashed through Rhiannon. "Not the women!"

The fighter bowed his head and pulled the woman to her feet. A thin trickle of blood snaked down from the woman's hairline.

Rhiannon motioned the acolyte to the woman.

The acolyte traced the woman's blood with a finger and sucked it into her mouth. She frowned and turned to Rhiannon. "Nothing."

No power in her blood, no trace of the earth point.

A slow certainty entered Rhiannon's mind and near blinded her with the accompanying anger.

The man her fighter had separated from the crowd stood still and quiet, his gaze locked on her with unconcealed hatred.

"I elect you their leader." She stepped back and pointed to him. "If you will not tell me who leads your coven, I will keep electing a leader and killing them." She motioned the sweaty, excited pig who served her. "Kill him."

"No!" The bleeding woman screamed.

Eyes gleaming feral in his twisted face, the pig stepped closer and shot the man.

Rhiannon waited for the terrified whispers to die down and then asked again, "I wish to speak with your leader."

An older man stepped forward. "I am the headsman here."

"What is your purpose here?" She clung to one last moment of hope.

"We live off the grid," the man said. "We're a group of like-minded people." He swallowed and glanced at his people behind him. "We don't want any trouble."

A man. That was not right. Her rage lashed and writhed inside her like a chained beast. All this effort, all her hopes and excitement and now the bitter taste of defeat.

Mags had lied to her. Duped her. Who would have thought that helpless seer had it in her?

"Kill him," she spat.

A gun fired, more screams, the man dropped with a thud.

She didn't care anymore. Now she studied the gathered people before her. There must be around forty or fifty of them, most of them early fifties and late sixties. A few younger women had children clinging to them. The mothers were too old and the children too young.

Despite her fury, she almost laughed.

Mags had led her up the garden path and down again. Rhiannon had been so sure she had the seer under complete control that she hadn't doubted the information for a second. Like a blind, stupid fool she'd come to British Columbia and found an isolated group that looked likely.

The pig had watched them and reported back. She'd been so certain of herself that she hadn't even bothered to really listen to his reports. And now she would pay for her laxity.

"Well done, Magdalene," she whispered. "It appears you are not quite as incapacitated as expected."

"Ma'am?" The pig glanced at her.

She shook her head and looked over the terrified people one

at a time. Her disappointment nearly made her weep. For that, Mags would pay as well.

"Kill them," she said.

Pig blinked at her. Even his porcine little brain struggled with that notion. "Ma'am?"

"Kill them," she spat. "Every last fucking one of them."

Gunfire erupted into the crowd. It played out before her like one of those stupid films mundane mortals were so fond off. Bodies contorting and dropping, blood spattering, voices crying out and being drowned by the gunfire. People tried to run in a last-ditch effort to survive. She stayed, her shield locked around her, and watched them die. Every. Last. One.

* * *

FIONA TOOK the stairs to the upper level of the small villa two at a time. She stopped at the door to catch her breath and center herself.

Was she really going to defy Rhiannon again? She had already let one person escape Rhiannon's clutches, and the decision this time was easier. Mags was as good as dead if Fiona didn't free her.

Yes, she was going to let Mags escape, because she'd started on this path of defiance after Edana's death, and there was no going back now. She cracked the door open to the dimly lit room beyond. The window was open to a breathtaking view of the bay. Creeping vines clustered around the window aperture like strands of hair and waved in the gentle breeze. The room was warm but not uncomfortably so.

She moved over to the large bed and shook Mags's shoulder. "Mags?"

Bleary eyes struggled to focus on Fiona's face. "Wha—"

Bugger it! The help hired to run the villa had dosed Mags's lunch with more sedative, and Mags was out of it. If Fiona had known how the day would roll out, she would have intercepted the lunch tray. She'd received a furious call from Rhiannon not five minutes ago; that attack in Canada had failed, and Mags was getting blamed. Rhiannon believed Mags had fed them misinformation and now she wanted answers. She also wanted Fiona to watch for signs that Mags was more lucid than she appeared.

Well, Fiona already knew Mags wasn't as insensate as Rhiannon believed her to be, because she was the reason Mags was given moments of reprieve from the blood necklace.

Rhiannon was on her way back to Europe. She had a stop in Italy first, and then she would head their way. It wouldn't take her long to discover Fiona was the reason behind Mags's retention of some part of her awareness. Nobody else was allowed near Mags. Fiona intended to be long gone before Rhiannon even got here, and as a last act of revenge for what Rhiannon had done to Edana, she would get Mags out of here too.

She unclipped the blood necklace and shook Mags harder. "You need to wake up. Now."

Mags shook her head, huffing through dry, chapped lips. Christ! She was a mess.

Fiona wrestled Mags into sitting and cupped a glass of water in her hands. "Drink this."

Mags gulped obediently, her teeth clacking over the glass rim. Water ran down her chin to her thin chest. Despite their best efforts, Mags was losing weight she could ill afford.

Guiding Mags's shaking hands back up to her mouth, Fiona insisted she drink more.

"Stop." Mags coughed and weakly pushed the water away from her mouth.

"You need to listen to me, Mags." Fiona put the glass down and cupped Mags's cheeks. She forced her to look at her and hear her. "Rhiannon is coming, and she knows about Canada."

"Canada?" Mags slow blinked as if struggling to keep her eyes open.

Bloody hell! Fiona gave her a shake firm enough to waggle her head on her neck. "You need to listen to me. You don't have much time."

"Stop." Mags gave a feeble attempt to push her hands away. "You'll make me sick."

At least she was making sense.

Downstairs, the vacuum turned on as the housekeeper got busy cleaning.

Fiona ran quick calculations in her head. Rhiannon still had to reach the plane and then fly here. A stop in Italy would buy them some more time. They had a day or so, at least, but every second counted where that bitch was concerned. And she still had to get Mags past the housekeeper.

"I need to get you to your feet." She'd seen this on television once. Actually, that character had been trying to stop another from succumbing to an overdose, but she was out of ideas.

Mags blinked at her and struggled to help. Her legs got tangled in her pajama bottoms and she nearly fell on her face.

Propping a shoulder under her armpit, Fiona levered her back on her feet.

The vacuum stopped, and so did Fiona's respiration. Then the vacuum started again, and she breathed.

It was a good thing Mags weighed very little, but she was tall, and she was deadweight. Fiona winced with each clunk they made as she tried to get Mags's feet under her. They made it to the window and Fiona propped Mags up for a minute or two and took a breath. The fresh sea air might help. It couldn't hurt, and considering what was coming for Mags, anything was preferable.

"What's happened?" Mags whispered. "Why are you dragging me around?"

Fiona reached for patience. Mags was drugged and couldn't

help herself. "Rhiannon and her people attacked a small community in British Columbia this morning. They found out it wasn't where Alannah and Sinead were."

"Attacked." Mags frowned. "Did they hurt anyone?"

Killed every last soul, but Fiona didn't judge it prudent to let Mags know that detail. She skated as close to the truth as she dared. "Nobody was hurt." More like dead as doornails, the lot of them.

Fiona was slowing herself down by trying to rescue Mags, and she didn't even like the woman. But she wasn't going to leave Mags like a sitting duck for Rhiannon's rage. It probably had more to do with wanting to fuck Rhiannon over again. She wasn't stupid. Her own life expectancy was looking shorter by the day. If she was going out, so be it. But she wasn't going to go gently.

Mags lurched away from the window and Fiona barely got her shoulder in place in time to stop a faceplant. They stumbled a few steps to the door and had to stop and breathe, and then back to the window.

She might not like Mags, but the woman had fight.

"She's coming." Mags worked the words out of her mouth like each syllable was a battle.

Fiona hummed her agreement. "As soon as she gets on a plane, which means we need to get you at least lucid and out of here."

"I can't." Mags stumbled to a stop.

Fiona tried to get her moving again. "You must, or you'll die here."

"No." Mags shook her head laboriously. "I mean…come too."

"What?" Fiona stared at Mags's wan face and tried to decipher her meaning.

"Come…with me." Mags tottered into motion again. "The drugs." She pressed a hand to her temple. "Confused. Also…"

Fiona waited before impatience won the day. "Also what?"

"My head…not right."

Not with the amount of sedative it was currently cramming. "The drugs will wear off."

"No." Mags yanked her to a stop. "Before that. Head…not right. Confused."

Jesus, she was right. Mags had been losing her marbles before Rhiannon got her claws on her.

Mags plucked at her arm. "Need…help. You."

Shit! Shit! Shit! Helping Mags escape was one thing. Escaping with her was a commitment to a path she didn't feel ready to make. "I can't."

The seer looked at her for a long minute with those eerie, penetrating green eyes. "You can. You must." She nodded. "You will."

CHAPTER TWENTY-THREE

Jack ducked behind the corner of a large, stone barn and nearly trampled Emma. "Fucking hell!"

Emma leaped out of the way. "What?"

"Cars?" He motioned the driveway they'd been about to cross to enter the dark house on the far side.

They'd been casing this farmhouse in Umbria on a tipoff from Sasha for a couple of days now, and no activity. Now a long snake of cars turned off the rural road and slowed as they took the driveway.

According to Sasha, Rhiannon had been seen leaving Canada yesterday. They all wanted to know the same thing; what was so important that Rhiannon had left Canada without finding Sinead and Alannah? They were all hoping the answer to that question was Mags.

"Look sharp," Emma whispered.

The lead car pulled to a stop outside the farmhouse, and a man jumped out of the front passenger seat. He walked smartly to the back passenger door and held it open.

Jack had never seen Rhiannon before, but he knew, without Emma's hissed breath informing him, who he was looking at.

Objectively speaking, she was beautiful. Tall and lithe, curves in all the right places with a shining sheet of long dark hair. She was dressed in a red dress that was more suited to a Hollywood premiere than a sleepy hamlet on the outskirts of Cortona. If Alexander loosely resembled Roderick, he was a fucking dead ringer for the woman who had brought him into the world. Although they looked more like the male-female twin version of each other than mother and son.

"That's her," Emma whispered.

Jack nodded as Rhiannon strolled toward the house.

Minions spilled out the door and lined the short walkway to the open front door.

"What's she doing here?" Emma murmured to herself.

Jack didn't bother to answer. They'd find out if they stayed right here.

More cars stopped, and more doors opened.

Jack blinked at the man who stepped out of the second vehicle. That international politician would be important enough to have anyone traveling just about anywhere to meet them. Jack still wasn't entirely sure he was looking at who he was looking at. But his own eyes provided irrefutable evidence and that man had a face just about anyone would recognize. "That's—"

"Yup." With a grim nod, Emma removed any last tendril of doubt. "She has friends in very high places all over the world."

Another man emerged from the second car, and Jack identified that politician too. Technically this politician and the first guy were from opposing countries, but there they were, shaking hands and smiling. "Motherfucker."

Emma nudged him to keep quiet.

Dark suited security personnel peered into the evening around the cars, alert for any sign of trouble, and surrounded the entire farmhouse.

Yet another politician climbed out of another car. Like Emma said, Rhiannon did indeed have powerful allies from all over the globe. A chill snaked down his spine. Her plans appeared to be so much bigger than the conquest of Baile.

More car doors opened, disgorging a movie star, a renowned philanthropist, and dark-complexioned man in garish military dress.

"Looks like a meeting." Emma grimaced. "We can't go any closer with that lot watching."

Emma nudged him. "They'll sweep the area."

Jack didn't need her to draw him a map. If the area was swept, he and Emma had better not be here.

One former president, one incumbent president, a prime minister, a household heartthrob, a tech billionaire, and a man known for his good works—all gathered in attendance around Rhiannon.

He followed Emma as she slipped like a wraith into the evening to their waiting car. They'd been hoping to get inside and discover if Mags had left them another clue. Now that would have to wait.

Emma opened their car and slid into the driver's seat. She started it up and put some distance between themselves and the farmhouse before she spoke.

"She's been lining up allies in useful places for years." She shook her head. "More so in the last five years. Sasha speculates that she's getting ready for something big."

"Do you think Mags is in there?" That's all Jack cared about. He wouldn't have voted for that motherfucker even before today, and that actor was a total hack.

Emma pulled a face. "Doubtful, but you never know with her."

"Shit!" Jack pounded his head back against the rest. They'd been lucky to pick up a trail after France. "Now where?"

One-handing her phone, Emma used her thumb to dial. She waited for a man to answer. "Sasha, it's Emma."

Sasha's voice was an indistinct murmur on the other end.

While Emma briefed Sasha on what they'd seen, idyllic hilly landscapes slid past their car. The sort of places he'd love to bring Mags to with a picnic, a bottle of wine, and all the time in the world. They could sit on one of the low stone walls and eat bread and cheese and talk about whatever the bloody hell his Magdalene wanted. Knowing her, it would be something so barmy he'd be mentally sprinting to keep up. Goddess, he ached for her. The need to count her fingers and toes, to gaze into those incredible eyes throbbed like a constant bass line inside him. At times like this, it didn't feel like he could find one more place Mags wasn't, go down one more dead end.

Emma kept him going, like he did for her at times. Emma and the knowledge that life would be worse without Mags in it. Warren had assured him both Taylor and Maeve said Mags was still alive, and as long as she was, he would find the strength to keep searching.

"Thanks." The surge of energy in Emma's tone brought him back to the car.

"What?"

"Greece." Emma looked at him, her eyes gleaming. "They've had a confirmed visual of Mags."

His heart rate sped up. "Confirmed? How reliable?"

"Sasha saw the photo." Some of the grim resigned quality left Emma, and she looked lighter, more hopeful. "This is the best lead we've had since this shituation got started."

"Shituation?" Emma made him laugh sometimes as well.

She looked sheepish. "I read it in a book. I liked it. It's mine now."

"Fair enough." And he'd always wanted to see more of Europe than a lad's trip to Ibiza. Wish granted. "Let's go to Greece."

CHAPTER TWENTY-FOUR

Roderick liked Andy, he really did, but some days, he'd cut off his sword arm to get the man to the point. Like this moment when Andy was standing in the kitchen gardens gazing at him expectantly. Perhaps not his sword arm. He'd grown fond of it over the years, and it had certainly kept him alive a time or two.

The gardens had a strange, abandoned air to them, as if the earth itself knew Alannah and Sinead were gone, and it depressed him to be here. He hated not knowing where his witches were. And aye! They were all his witches.

"What am I looking at?" He tried to tamp down the irritation in his voice. Andy was a good man who had an odd sort of hero worship of him going. God's balls! The man needed to choose a better hero.

Andy pointed. "There."

"I don't s—" And then he did see. A crack. In Baile's walls.

Roderick crouched to get a better look. The crack was tiny, no more than a hairline. He had no idea how Andy had even noticed it, but there it was. He'd been alive for nigh on nine hundred years, and Roderick had never seen Baile crack. The other day, Niamh had mentioned something about dust, and he hadn't paid it much heed. He traced the crack with a fingertip. In any other home, it would have been unremarkable, but Baile didn't get dusty, and she didn't crack.

"By the rood." He stood and glared at the crack as if his ire could make it disappear.

Andy nodded. "I've given it some thought."

"And?" Andy needed to get to the point, and quickly.

"Alannah and Sinead spoke of the wards being under attack," Andy said. "The anomaly within the wards."

Roderick connected the dots. "And you believe this is related?"

"I don't see how it couldn't be." Andy shoved his hands in his pockets. "The wards protect Baile from not just outsiders, but also from time itself. If they are being dismantled somehow, then it stands to reason that time and age are making inroads into the old girl."

An influx of unwelcome memories threatened to surface. The wards had only ever failed once in Baile's history, the night of the coven massacre. He'd been here to see that night too. "The wards must not fail."

That night when Rhiannon and her followers had broken into Baile, the coven had been ninety witches strong, plus the thirty or so coimhdeacht, and they had not won.

"An attack on all fronts," Andy muttered. He counted off on his fingers. "The wards, the tax office, the police, the cardinal points." He cleared his throat and gave Roderick a sheepish look. "It feels like we're being surrounded by hostile forces."

Roderick had reached much the same conclusion. He didn't expect an answer, but speaking thoughts aloud helped him think. "So, how do we combat that?"

"I can handle the cyber stuff," Andy said. "The police? Let's wait and see. They don't have much to go on, or they'd be far more forceful. And now with Mr. Lester well again, they have even less." He gestured the crack. "As for the wards, that should be sorted when Alannah and Sinead activate earth."

There were far too many shoulds, what-ifs, and maybes in their lives lately.

"Roderick!" Warren strode out of the keep and joined them.

"What is it?"

Warren's expression didn't auger well for the news he bore. "It's Canada. There's been an attack."

Not the twins. Alarm shot up Roderick's spine, but he waited.

"Fifty-eight dead." Warren rubbed his nape. "A small community living off the grid was attacked a couple of days ago. It took the authorities a day and a bit to find them, but somebody killed them all."

Andy dug out his internet rectangle, and his fingers flew across the screen. "No!" He shook his head. "Men, women, and children. They're calling it one of the worst massacres in Canadian history."

Roderick knew not who they were, but he had a strong suspicion he knew who had perpetrated the atrocity. "Maeve." He strode for the caverns where his witch was working. If Alannah and Sinead's souls had moved from this plane, she would know. Might know, he corrected himself. With the sacred grove disappearing, even the rules around life and rebirth had changed. He should never have let the twins go. Not that they'd given him a say in the matter, sneaking off as they had in the dead of night. Which is why they hadn't discussed their leaving with him, he would wager.

He yanked open the door in the bailey wall and descended the cavern stairs at a run.

Sensitive to his feelings, Maeve appeared at the entrance. "What has happened?"

Roderick took the sweet reprieve her presence offered and pulled her into his arms. She was the magical elixir to soothe his soul, and he drew in her scent, reveled in the soft press of her curves against him. She was his everything.

In a moment, he would ask her to check if the twins were still on this plane, but he needed one moment of the serenity his Maeve gave to him.

⸻

Niamh paced the cliff path, Pack slinking around her. Pack sensed her mood and was curious and concerned.

"More bad news," she said.

Alpha ventured closer and cocked his head at her.

"I know." She sighed. "It's always sodding bad news these days."

She got the impression Alpha wanted to deliver some of his wolfy wisdom, and she wasn't in the mood, so she tuned out the connection.

Alpha chuffed at her.

News had filtered through the coven about the dreadful murders in Canada. Maeve didn't think Alannah and Sinead had been affected, but that didn't mitigate the tragic event. Taylor had been upset by her inability to scry the twins, and Warren had remained to comfort her. As he should.

Her own selfishness annoyed her. One witch's needs hardly weighed against the crap ton of trouble facing the coven. But that also didn't make her needs disappear.

The twitch beneath Niamh's skin started up again, and she increased her pace. Goddess, this was so inconvenient it was almost laughable. She should have just ruthlessly overridden any scruples to the contrary and jumped Warren's bones in Johannesburg. But no! She'd backed off and let him process his new reality without the complication of a sexual relationship with her.

In reality though, it wouldn't have made a bollocks worth of difference.

As autumn quieted the creatures around her for the dormant winter, stags went into rut. And ramped up her sex drive as they did.

If it wasn't for the shitty situation they were all in, she'd have taken herself off to a big city like London and scratched the itch that burned constantly through her.

Shitty situation aside, she would never do that to Warren. What they were building together was a beautiful and delicate thing, and it needed nurturing, not a storming of the gates, no-holds-barred sexscapades.

Goddess help her, she wanted the no-holds-barred sexscapade. And she wanted it with Warren. She was running on little to no sleep. Sharing a bed with him, night after night, as the stags all around them got their leg over was not helping.

Alpha gave her a low grumbling growl.

"Oh, stop!" She glared at the wolf. "Like you don't leap on the nearest female when you're randy."

He gave her a superior look.

"You can't lie to me." Bloody wolf needn't think she didn't know how animals operated. He'd be mounting anything that moved when the she-wolves went into heat. "And I know, I'm a selfish cow."

Things had been progressing so well with Warren. And then Taylor had arrived, and shortly after, Deb. Then the twins had disappeared, Mags had been kidnapped, and now people were being slaughtered.

And what was she doing?

Moaning and bitching because she wanted sex.

Through Alpha's senses, she registered Warren's approach.

"Keep this conversation to yourself." She gave the wolf a look to convey she meant business. Warren was worried about his daughter, trying to finesse the new situation with his ex, thinking about where and how Jack was, and trying to adjust to now being emotionally, spiritually, and physically tied to her for the rest of his life.

Alpha peeled his lips off his teeth at her.

"I don't care," she snapped. "And you don't scare me."

"Niamh." Warren waved as he climbed the rise to the cliff path.

And did he have to look so bloody edible? A close-fitting T-shirt reminded her of everything she was missing, and his jeans clung to his thighs in a way she'd pay good money to do. She loved the close-cut scruff on his head and around his jaw line. He looked dangerous and delicious and every kind of her flavor. She kept her response jaunty. "Heya."

"You're in a mither." Typically Warren, he cut to the chase.

How was a woman supposed to maintain her feminine mystique when her man could cut straight into her head, heart, and soul. "It's nothing."

No bloody chance she was going to admit she had an itch that she very much wanted him to scratch. Again, and again, and again—

Sodding stags. They had a super charged sexual appetite that played through her libido like wind through chimes.

Warren frowned and cocked his head. "Tell me."

Not going to happen. "I'm great."

"Right, you are." He shoved his hands in his pockets, biceps and forearms bulging and popping as he did. Denim stretched across his hard, honed thighs. His blue eyes told her clearly he knew she was full of shit.

She shrugged and tried to keep it light. "It's nothing. Stupid really."

"Tell me anyway."

Argh! "It's not important."

"It's you. It's important," he said.

Goddess help her. If he said shit like that, how was she to remain all stoic and selfless?

Then he said, "You're important."

Not to him she wasn't. The thought pinged in her mind a half second before he read it.

Warren closed the distance between them, his expression tender. "Niamh?"

"I'm a silly cow." She ducked her head, not brave enough to meet his stare.

"No, you aren't." His big, calloused hand cupped her chin and forced her gaze up to his.

And Niamh stopped shielding her thoughts.

Warren's eyes widened as he read her mind and body, as he felt her coiled frustration.

Then he grinned. "Well, if that's what's bothering you—"

"It doesn't matter."

"Yes, it fucking does." He lowered his head to hers. A challenge gleamed in his eyes. "Say it."

"It's not the time—"

"Say it."

"There's so much happen—"

"Say it anyway."

Goddess, he smelled of warm skin, sage, and musk. "I need you."

"Be more specific."

"I need your body."

Warren hummed and nibbled at her bottom lip. "I like where this is going. Tell me more."

"I need your body on mine." Niamh's knees weakened, and she swayed against him. Released from her stranglehold on it, her libido did a runner through her veins and nerve endings. "I need you inside me."

He squeezed his eyes shut and groaned. "Jesus! I had to fucking ask, didn't I?"

Niamh slipped her hands under his T-shirt and made contact with hot, silky skin. "Now."

"Now?" He hissed as she ran her hands over his taut, rippled belly. "Here?"

"Right here, right now." He had asked, hadn't he? Niamh leaned closer and nipped the skin over his collar bone.

Warren gripped her hips and dragged her against his erection.

He was so thick and hard it tore a moan from deep down inside her. She gripped his ass and pressed him closer. Her mouth hunted for his and fastened with the ferocity raging through her every cell.

He kissed her like he was as desperate for her as she was for him. He kissed her like she was oxygen, and he was dying for his next breath.

Niamh had the means, and Goddess knew, the will to give him what they both needed. She gripped the bottom of his shirt and ripped it over his head.

He was beautiful and perfect and hers. She pressed her mouth to his pecs, found his nipple and sucked.

"Fuck!" He threw his head back, giving her access to the strong, tanned column of his throat.

Niamh took the invitation with her lips, her tongue, her teeth.

Rip.

There went her shirt.

Warren cupped her breasts in his big, lovely hands.

"This has to go," he growled, sliding his hands around her back and unclasping her bra.

Then it was those same lovely hands of his on her bare breasts, and Niamh sighed. The heat hit every part of her.

"Are we really doing this?" She went for his jeans button and loosened it. She slid his zip down and pushed her hand inside the gap. No underwear. *Thank you, Goddess.*

His hot, needy flesh throbbed in her hand, and she closed her fingers around him.

"We're doing this," he said, pushing his cock into her hand. "We're so fucking doing this."

Goddess, she'd wanted and waited for what felt like forever, and the exultation of it finally happening rippled through her. Niamh laughed and tugged his jeans down. Pack had slunk away at the first hint of where things were going, and it was just her and Warren, the sea breeze, and a waning autumn sun.

Warren hauled her tattered shirt remains off and went for her pants. It took him seconds to unfasten them. The gleam in those beautiful blue eyes made her want to shout her joy to the sky.

"You're a wild one, my Niamh." He grinned. "And I love that about you."

"Words are cheap, Masters." She looped her arms around his neck.

Warren leaned down and scooped her thighs around his waist.

And her laughter dried up as she felt his blunt head against where she needed him the most.

"Protection?" He backed up with her.

"Don't need it." She needed him to finish this so badly it made her want to cry. "Goddess deals with it."

Her spine hit the abrasive surface of a rock, but she didn't give a crap.

Warren bent his knees and thrust, and they were suddenly connected in the most elemental and necessary of ways.

He pulsed inside her and dropped his head to her shoulder. "You're slaying me here."

"Shut up." She grabbed his ass and dug her nails in.

And Warren got serious with the thrusting.

Her back scraped against the rock. She was full to bursting with him. The bond snapped into place, and she could feel what they both felt, experienced their connection through dual senses. It was all she wanted and so much more. They were more together in this than she could have ever imagined, and she was greedy for everything.

Niamh dug her nails into him and clung.

His groans and her moans resounded in the still evening. Until they reached the pinnacle together, and just for a moment, everything stilled and stopped, and they got there together.

Niamh held her breath, pressed her face into his shoulder, and tried to hold on to the moment for as long as she could. It was the most complete she'd felt in her entire life. She wanted to laugh. She wanted to cry. She wanted to scream to the sky above them.

Warren moved back from her and looked at her. "Are you all right?"

"I'm more than all right."

His unfettered smile made her heart swell to bursting. She cupped his face and pressed her forehead to his. "I love you, Warren Masters, and I don't care if that freaks you out."

"Niamh." He smiled. "Everything about you freaks me out. In the very best of ways."

CHAPTER TWENTY-FIVE

I f she had her kitchen around her, Alannah would be baking right now.

Pale and resolute, Dhara stood in front of the rest of her folk in the dining area. Men, women, and even a few children stared back at her.

Goddess, but Dhara looked so young and fragile and heartbreakingly small for the destiny weighing on her slim shoulders. "I have always known this is my destiny," she said

"I don't care." Sinead rose.

Heads snapped Sinead's way.

She gentled her tone, but her jaw stuck out at that angle that made Alannah want to placate people. But Sinead was right, and Alannah stood in total agreement with her. "Your life is not something I'm prepared to even consider sacrificing."

The price of Dhara's life for the earth point was too high.

Her need to bake made Alannah wriggle in her seat. Perhaps a lemon sponge with a raspberry drizzle, or a New York cheesecake.

The gathered commune broke into loud conversations. Emotions ran hot and vehement. Nobody wanted Dhara to die, but the commune's entire reason for being was protecting and activating earth.

A taller man, near the back said, "Your reluctance is a credit to you, Blessed."

"It's more than reluctance," Sinead said and folded her arms. "We're not going to do it."

"But the earth point must get activated." A plump woman with curly chestnut hair popped up somewhere in the middle. "I'm sorry, Dhara. Kate." She nodded to the sisters in turn. "But our ancestors made it clear. The consequences of not activating the earth point are dire."

Dire, indeed. Dire if they didn't and dire if they did.

"She's just a child—"

"Our destiny—"

"We always knew this was coming—"

Nope, something savory. Blue cheese and bacon rolls, or a ciabatta.

Voices rose and fell around Alannah, their emotions dipping and swirling in a dizzying rollercoaster ride.

When things got tense, she baked. It helped clear her head so she could think. Goddess, she wanted to bake.

Kate stood from where she sat beside Sinead at the front of the gathering. "Look." She held out her hands. "This is getting out of hand."

People quieted to the odd murmuring here and there to listen to Kate.

"And we're getting off track." Kate's quiet, authoritative voice carried throughout the gathering in the eating hall. "Today's meeting is not about whether or not we're going to sacrifice Dhara; it's about how we can activate the earth point without doing that."

Now people fell silent. Gazes turned to her and Sinead as if they could provide an answer. Once again, they were in uncharted territory.

Alannah and Sinead had been up with Kate and Dhara for most of the night trying to wrack their brains for a solution. They had nothing. The earth point being inside someone was beyond unprecedented. She wished she could phone Baile and ask Roderick or get Maeve to check in with the dead witches. But they just didn't know how the situation stood back home. She hoped like hell the coven had managed to stop Rhiannon from using Warren to listen in on the castle occupants and their plans, but they couldn't take the chance.

The true hero in all of this was Dhara. With her dark brown, waist-length curls and her sweet face, she was the calmest of the lot of them. She was so achingly young, Alannah wanted to scoop her up and carry her away from all this. How had a girl ended up burdened with this awful responsibility? Alannah didn't want to blame Goddess, but for fuck's sake, she must have known.

A large brown and rust wolf trotted into the eating hall.

Alannah grabbed Sinead's hand, not sure she was actually seeing what she was seeing.

The wolf padded closer.

Other than the obvious—being a large tan and rust wolf in the hall—the next thing that struck Alannah was the lack of reaction from the rest of the commune.

Sinead shrunk closer to her, and Alannah was glad she wasn't the only one feeling nervous.

Light shimmered around the wolf, there were a couple of wet plops and squelches, and a very naked Zach stood there.

Nonchalantly, Kate handed him a blanket from behind her chair, and he wrapped it about his waist.

"Are you see—" Sinead whispered.

"Uh-huh." Yes, they were seeing the same thing, and Alannah couldn't drag her eyes away. Her mind went over the details in excruciatingly slow details. Wolf—in the eating hall—gross noises—Zach.

Nope not savory. Sweet and savory. Sweet, savory and anything else in between. A whole bloody table worth of baked goods, and she still wouldn't be okay with this.

Sinead gaped. "Motherfucker."

"I don't think wolves do that." Alannah clapped her hands over her mouth as a hysterical giggle threatened to come out.

Zach threw them an apologetic glance but turned his attention back to Katy. "We've got a problem."

Other than the wolf-man thing it seemed. The giggle burned the back of her throat.

"Why yes, Zachariah, we most certainly do." Kate threw him a hostile stare. "Thanks for that helpful summation."

He folded his arms over a very toned and muscular chest. "Other than the Dhara thing."

"What?" Kate dropped the snark and paled. "What now?"

"There's a large force heading this way." Zach glanced at their riveted audience. "And they're armed to the teeth. My scouts have been running all through the night to get here ahead of them."

By scouts, did he mean wolves? Maybe coyotes? Could be squirrels. This time, the laugh got away from her.

Sinead pinched her, hard enough to stop her from laughing.

Alannah was grateful, but nobody was looking at her anyway.

"Shit." Kate stood and addressed the gaping community. "Let's table this while I deal with Zach's news."

Glancing at each other and murmuring, nobody seemed to want to move.

"Maybe take this to your cabin?" Zach suggested.

Kate nodded like a puppet. "Okay." She turned to the group. "I'll keep you updated, but for now, nobody panic until I know more."

"With all due respect, Kate." A middle-aged man with a beard shot up from the back. "I don't know how you think we're not going to panic."

"Sit down." Command radiated from Zach and for a second, Alannah nearly sat. Oh right, she was already sitting.

Gaze sweeping over the assembly, Zach said, "Remain calm and wait for further information and instructions."

Heads nodded.

Rachel, Abe, Josh, Sara, and a few other people—all of them young and fit and moving with the same innate grace as Zach— stood and took up positions around the gathering. Almost as if they were some sort of security.

Zach motioned Alannah and Sinead. "You'd better join us."

"You better believe we're joining you." Sinead hauled Alannah to her feet. "I have questions. So many sodding questions."

"You too, Dhara." Zach held his hand out for the teen.

Dhara took it, and they followed Kate.

By the time they reached Kate's cabin, Alannah had the hysteria about eighty percent mastered. Her incredulity was still way up there. At least Kate had a kitchen.

Alannah headed straight into the kitchen and opened and shut cupboards as she gathered ingredients.

Kate stared at her, and Sinead shook her head. "When she's stressed, she bakes."

"Okay." Kate didn't look like she understood, but she also had bigger things on her mind right now.

Zach filled a glass with water and gulped it down.

Running must have made him thirsty.

Alannah took the glass from him and filled it again. He smiled his thanks at her.

"Tell me everything." Kate took a seat at the table beside Dhara and held her hand.

"You remember that massacre in BC on yesterday's news?"

Zach finished his second glass of water and waved Alannah away when she went to refill it.

Sinead stood between the table and Zach looking from one to the other. "What massacre?"

"A community in rural British Columbia was wiped out." Zach looked grim. "Police can't find any apparent reason for it, but the community was not dissimilar in appearance and isolation from us."

"Shit." Sinead dropped into a chair. "You think it might be connected."

Zach shrugged. "I don't believe in coincidences, and I don't like to take any chances with this community's safety."

"And you take care of their safety?" Alannah creamed butter and sugar together by hand. "Because you're..." How to put this politely? "Because of the...er...wolf thing?"

Zach winked at her. "Because of the wolf thing."

It made sense. She grabbed a carton of eggs from the fridge.

"About that..." Sinead stared at Zach.

"We will explain." Kate looked at her beseechingly. "But let's deal with this newest shitshow first."

Sinead nodded and folded her hands on the table like an obedient schoolgirl.

"Shitshow is right." Zach tucked the blanket more firmly around his waist.

They must go through a lot of trousers if they kept shredding them and losing them. Or did they take them off before they shifted? Dear Goddess, shifted! *Shifted*! She folded eggs into her batter. Apparently, she was making something of the cake variety. She snapped the oven on to preheat. Should have thought of preheating before she started mixing, but then...the wolf thing. It was throwing her off her game.

"There are about five hundred armed assholes heading our way," Zach said. "And they don't look friendly."

Sinead raised her hand.

With a lip quirk, Zach raised his eyebrow at her.

Alannah shared his incredulity. Sinead was not, as a rule, one to ask permission. Then again…wolf thing. She had the horrible idea she might need to giggle again.

"How do you know they're coming here?"

"There's nothing else between them and us that explains why they're armed and traveling this way." Zach said. "My scouts have been tracking them,"

"As wolves." Sinead nodded like she was totally on board with what was happening. Alannah knew better. Her sister was within a heartbeat of losing her grip. "Tracking them as wolves?"

"As wolves." Zach nodded. "We're faster and harder to spot like that."

"Right." Sinead nodded rapidly. "Makes absolute sense." She made a circle in the air with her hand. "Forest. Wolves. Perfect sense."

Alannah found the baking powder and some cocoa. Red velvet was nice. Everybody liked red velvet, and she'd seen some cream cheese in the fridge that would make a super icing.

She caught Kate eyeing her askance. Kate had a long way to go before she could start tossing looks like that around. A long way to go and a lot of talking to do.

"And these people stink." Zach wrinkled his nose. "Worse fucking smell on the planet."

"Blood magic." Alannah located the baking tins and greased them. "Even we can smell it and we're not…well, you know."

"Right." Zach chuckled. "You're taking this very well."

"No." Alannah dusted the baking tins and banged them on the counter. "I really am not. I'm about thirty seconds away from a total bloody meltdown."

"Thirty seconds is good," Zach said. "Most people don't manage that long."

"Baking." Alannah added ingredients by rote. "It keeps me calm."

"I told you that." Sinead glared at him. "And you want to leave her to it, because she may look like the nicer twin, but"—Sinead whistled—"you don't want to make her lose her shit."

Zach nodded. "Understood."

"Could we get back to the five hundred armed yahoos heading our way." Kate pressed her hand against her temples. "For now."

Any sign of levity vanished from Zach's expression, and he straightened. "We can't fight that many, Katy. Not with the rest of the commune underfoot. The wolf pack will default to protecting them. It's how we're made."

"The wards." Kate sat up straighter. "They will help."

"The wards are a warning system." Zach shook his head. "They're not defensive."

Unlike the ones they had at Baile.

Sinead put her hand up a second time. "We have wards around Baile. They keep people from finding us."

"Those were created by Rhiannon," Dhara said. "They're stronger and better made than ours." She grimaced. "She was… is…crazy powerful."

"What do you suggest?" Looking at Zach, Kate braced as if she knew what was coming and didn't want to hear it.

"Kate." Dhara patted Kate's hand. "You know what we have to do."

Kate sighed. "Leave?"

"It was always the emergency plan," Dhara said. "Once we're gone, they won't have any reason to attack the others."

"Actually, Dhara, that was the emergency plan," Zach said and took a seat opposite Kate. He took her free hand in his. "But you not being there didn't stop them in BC, and we can't take the chance it will make any difference here."

"No." Kate snatched her hand free. "You're talking about an

impossibility. I can't ask all these people to pack up and leave their homes. Most of them have been here—"

"I don't see any other option." Zach took her hand again and twined his fingers with hers. "It's that or die."

Kate jerked straight and opened her mouth to argue, then she deflated. "And you're sure they're coming this way?"

"I'm sure." Zach raised her hand and kissed it. "You know I wouldn't suggest this unless I was."

She looked at him with broken eyes for a long moment, and then took a deep breath. From somewhere deep inside, Kate found a store of resolve and it spread over her shocked face. "We've gotta do what we've gotta do to keep everyone safe."

"And I should go to Baile," Dhara said. She looked at Sinead as if wanting her support. "I think it's the safest place for me. When Sinead and Alannah and I are behind Baile's wards, nobody can get to us. And we're who they really want."

Zach looked pained. "Dhara is right, Kate. We let the other community members scatter to their safety points, and we use the distraction of all those moving parts to get Dhara and the Blessed out of the country and back to safety."

The oven pinged it was up to temperature, and Alannah looked at her filled baking pans. It didn't look like anybody had time for cake now.

"The scouts ran through the night to buy us some time, but we have a day at most. The forest will slow them down, and the wards might give us a few more hours, but we need to be long gone before they even reach the outer edge of the trees." Zach placed Kate's hand tenderly on the table and stood.

The door crashed open, and Alannah dropped her baking pans. They clattered against the floor, and everybody jumped and stared at her. Chocolatey goop seeped over the kitchen floor.

A black wolf loped into the cabin.

And—

Sparklies, yucky noises, and then—ta da—Noah.

Sinead straightened in her chair. "You!"

"Boss." Noah didn't spare her a glance as his eyes locked on Zach. He also didn't have a blanket handy and it was impossible not to notice how well put together the man was.

Sinead had certainly noticed and was glaring at his taut, muscled body.

"We've got bigger issues." Noah looked exhausted.

Alannah filled Zach's glass and handed it to Noah. This shifting was thirsty work. Or maybe it was the running.

He took it with a smile of thanks. "There's a second force, closing in from the west."

Her chair scraped on the wooden boards as Kate sprang to her feet. "How many?"

"Eight, nine hundred." Noah chugged the water and handed it back to Alannah.

She refilled it and gave it back. Then she grabbed a cleaning sponge and got busy with the mess on the floor. They were definitely not having cake now.

"I'll give the order." Kate's hands shook as she smoothed hair into her ponytail. "We evacuate as per the plan."

"You're doing the right thing, Katy." Zach stepped into her path.

She gave him a sad, worried smile. "I'm doing the only thing I can."

Alannah watched them go as she tossed the contents of the baking pans. "We never did find out about the wolf thing."

Narrowing her eyes, Sinead tracked Noah as he passed the window. "But we will, sister. We most certainly bloody will."

CHAPTER TWENTY-SIX

"*aylor.*"

Taylor looked up from her phone to the door between her room and Mum's. She'd moved out of Niamh and Dad's room a couple of nights ago. There were times when being a seer was just plain gross. Nobody wanted visions like that about their father. Seeing what Niamh and Dad got up to was bad enough in a vision flash, she certainly didn't want to catch the live action.

Someone had called her name. "Mum?"

The muted buzz of a TikTok was the only thing breaking the silence. Taylor nearly went back to her phone and then stopped. A woman had called her. It wasn't her imagination. Rolling off her bed, she approached the door to Mum's room. It was late at night, and most of the castle was asleep. Mum would probably have a shit-fit about her not being asleep already.

Tapping lightly on the door, she whispered, "Mum? Did you call?"

She cracked the door open and peeped in. Mum wasn't in her bed.

"*Taylor?*"

The air smelled like coriander and apples as Taylor's blessing prickled beneath her skin. She suppressed her nervous butterflies. Dad didn't like her using her blessing without a mature witch present.

You're in control. She breathed deep, and repeated what Maeve always told her. *You control your blessing, not the other way around.*

She shut Mum's door, clambered onto her own bed, crossed her legs, and closed her eyes. Coriander and apples grew stronger as she tapped into water. As pressure built inside the old pipes, they responded with a creak.

Taylor opened her mind and quested.

Her blessing went old school *Millennium Falcon* as it zeroed in on the source of the voice. It left her momentarily disoriented, and her tummy lurched before it caught up with her vision.

"Taylor?" The voice was stronger now, and Taylor knew who it was.

"Mags. I'm here." Her heart thumped in her chest. This was big, and she needed to keep her head.

"I need you to see," Mags spoke into her mind, tinny and hollow like a landline.

The vision skewed, and she was looking through Mags's eyes into a dark, stone-walled space. She could smell the damp and hear the annoying drip of water. Wherever Mags was, it was hot and humid.

Together, they crept over to a window and peeped out. There was some dull green, scrubby sort of bush, lots of dry earth but nothing she could place.

"Can you tell me where you are?" Taylor pulled stronger on water to get her message through clearly.

Mags's mind glitched like a faulty upload before coming into focus again. *"I'm in Greece, I think."*

"Greece?" Taylor's geography wasn't the best, but Greece

consisted of a number of islands, and she needed to narrow it down. *"Do you know which island?"*

The link wavered and went silent. For a minute, Taylor thought she might have lost Mags altogether, and then she came back. *"Alonissos."*

"Alonissos, got it. Where on the island?"

Dad, Jack, Maeve, Sinead, Goddess Pool, her, a woman with brown hair—a barrage of images hit Taylor hard and fast, some of them from weeks ago, a few she'd only seen in visions. It almost made Taylor drop the connection to protect her mind, but she forced herself to stay calm and stay with Mags.

Mags was sending the contents of her mind, and Taylor pitied her the constant confusion. If this was what Mags put up with, then Taylor was doubly determined to get her safe again. It also made her grateful Dad was always so protective of her when she used her blessing. What was happening to Mags was enough to make anyone think they were losing it.

"Slow down, Mags." She kept her tone gentle. *"Look out the window again. Let me see."*

Mags's sightline changed slightly, as if she was standing on something. Taylor got an impression of a garden, and then a sharp drop off. Down the hill, a town nestled beside a crescent harbor. A big boat entered the bay and turned in a churn of turquoise water.

"Come quickly," Mags whispered, and then the connection dropped completely.

It took Taylor a minute to calm down and reorient herself in her bedroom at Baile, and then she sprinted for a pen and some paper. She needed to get this down while it was still fresh in her mind. Mags needed her to remember every single detail.

She left her room, yelling as she went, "Dad!"

Maeve and Roderick's door opened. Roderick stepped out in track pants, his hair mussed. "Taylor?"

"Mags," she shouted as she ran past. "She just contacted me. Dad!"

"Taylor?" Dad ran toward her, yanking on a T-shirt as he came. "What is it?"

"Mags." She thrust her notes at him. "She contacted me. She's in Greece. Alonnisos. I could see through her eyes, and this is what I saw."

Her notes crumpled in his hand as Dad took her by the shoulder. "Breathe, Taylor."

She dragged in a needed breath. She was already feeling lightheaded.

"And again." Dad locked pale blue eyes on her.

He waited until she took the second breath before he nodded. "You saw Mags?"

"How?" Roderick asked.

Alexander spoke from behind them. "Taylor saw Mags? Where is she?"

"She's telling me." Warren glared over her head. "If you lot will shut it for five seconds."

Taylor got her breathing under control. "She spoke into my mind. Like we did before when she was on the train."

"Did she tell you she was in Greece?"

Thank Goddess, Dad had understood at least some of her word vomit. "She did. When I ask her which island, she said Alonnisos."

"Alonnisos?" Bronwyn spoke. "I've never heard of it."

"We can look it up." Niamh joined Dad. "Well done for getting the island, lovely."

"I got more." Taylor pointed to the paper in her dad's hand. "She looked around with me in her mind and I wrote it all done."

"Great work." Roderick squeezed her shoulder. "That was quick thinking."

"I was afraid I'd lose her, and she could be anywhere on the island."

Andy came down the passage with Mum right behind him, his phone already in his hand. They were both dressed in pjs.

"Alonnisos," Andy said as he scrolled. "Northern Sporades. Comes after Skiathos and Skopelos." His phone made a whooshing sound. "Just sent that through to Emma's phone." His phone pinged. "She's got it."

Andy's phone rang, and he answered. "Yup. She managed to contact Taylor." He handed the phone to her. "Emma wants a word."

"Taylor?" Emma sounded tired but excited. "Did you get anything else?"

"I did." Everyone was staring at her now, and it was hard not to feel proud of herself. "I got the view through her eyes. I'll send you my notes."

"You did good, sweetheart," Emma said. "Jack wants a word."

The phone was passed over and then Jack said, "Taylor. You spoke to Mags?"

"Yup."

"How was she?" Jack's worry came down the line.

"She was clear for the most part, but she drifts in and out."

"Okay." Jack sounded like he was moving around as he spoke. "Tell everyone there that we're on our way." He cleared his throat, and his voice was gentle as he said, "If you make contact with her again, tell her we're coming."

Tears came to Taylor's eyes. Jack really did love Mags. "She said to hurry, Jack."

"I'm on this," he said, his voice hardening. "Emma and I are going to find her and bring her back."

"Bye, Jack."

"Bye, sweetheart."

The line went dead, and Taylor stood around with the rest of the coven. No way she could go back to bed now. Also, now that she thought on it, why hadn't Mum been in her room? And why was she with Andy in her pjs?

"Well." Alexander put his hands around Bronwyn's shoulders. "We needed some good news."

Everyone at Baile had been edgy and worried since the news about that place in Canada had reached them. Taylor never wanted to see something so horrible again. She hadn't told Mum or Dad what her vision had shown her, but it was some of the reason she had been up so late. The awful images of those people being slaughtered haunted her.

Roderick grunted. "We could all do with a drink."

"Even me?" Taylor perked up.

"Nice try." Dad cupped her nape. "You can have hot chocolate."

Taylor shrugged. It had been worth a go, and hot chocolate was good, especially the way Alexander made it. Almost as good as when Alannah made it.

Bronwyn winked at her. "I'll join you in the chocolate fest."

CHAPTER TWENTY-SEVEN

B y the time Jack had disconnected the call, Emma had their stuff packed and was heading for the door. She palmed her phone and dialed.

Jack slid behind the wheel of their hired car and waited.

Still talking to Sasha, Emma pointed out where he should go. They'd been kicking around Athens for the last day or so, waiting for Sasha to find another lead. He wanted to fall at Taylor's feet in gratitude. Taylor had connected with Mags. The real Mags, and she must have been lucid enough to share her location. He didn't want to get ahead of himself, but hope twisted in his solar plexus. He would get to her in time. He would see her again, hold her again.

"Okay." Emma motioned him take a left. "We're on our way now." She hung up. "Sasha will have a boat waiting for us at Agios Konstantinos. It's the best way to get there."

"How far?" He and Emma had developed their own short-speak.

"Around one twenty kays. Should take two hours."

Not if he had anything to do with it. Jack pressed the accelerator. "We can do better than that."

Emma plugged their destination into the car GPS and then went back to her phone. "God, I could kiss Taylor."

He glanced at her and waited for details.

"She's not only given us the island, but she's given us a viewpoint we can track back to Mags."

Jack voiced what he knew Emma was thinking. "Mags might get moved again."

"Yup." She nodded and pulled a face. "But it's a whole shit ton more information than we had ten minutes ago." She leaned over and checked his speed. "Does this thing go any faster?"

Jack had to grin. "Let's find out."

MAGS'S MOMENT of lucidity was over. Fiona tried to eat as Mags drifted off into whatever screwed up world she spent most of her waking moments in. She tried to force some food past the constant knot in her belly.

For better or worse, Fiona had committed to a course of action, and Rhiannon would be coming for her.

She guided a protein shake up to Mags's mouth and made her take a sip. The blood necklace had been a fucking barbarous thing, but it had kept Mags quiet. She'd hoped by taking it off for a few moments while Rhiannon had been away, that she'd been helping Mags hold on to some sense of herself. Turned out, she'd been right. Mags had held on to enough clarity to send Rhiannon to the wrong place in Canada. But now, as Mags continued to mutter nonsense incessantly, she almost found herself wishing for the drugs again. Mags was trapped in her head, and it didn't look like a nice place to be. After all this time by Rhiannon's side, Fiona was amazed she still had a sliver of empathy left inside herself.

To get themselves out of the villa, Fiona had knocked the housekeeper out and bundled her into a cupboard. She'd lucked out to find a car parked in the driveway. She'd loaded Mags and driven, without any clear idea of where to go from there. They had driven around for a couple of hours, quite a feat on such a small island, but it had given Fiona time to think.

They needed to get off the island and back to Athens. From Athens, she could try to get them back to England. What a fucking laugh. The housekeeper must have been found by now, and Rhiannon's people would be looking for her already.

She'd found a holiday rental unoccupied and broken the lock to get in. The house came with a garage, and she'd made sure to get the car out of sight. From where they squatted in the cellar, small ground level windows provided a view of the harbor. The ferry making its way in and out three or four times mocked her.

How to get on that ferry? There was no going anywhere until they did.

She didn't have the funds to hire a boat. She might not even have the funds for the ferry. All she had was what had been in her handbag at the time she'd snatched it up. Using credit cards was not an option, same with her debit card.

This newer version of herself was a stranger. Old Fiona had never been caught unawares. Old Fiona had plans within plans, contingencies stacked upon contingencies. The situation had dictated she get Mags out and do it immediately, and she'd acted. She should have taken half an hour, ten minutes even, to get them better prepared.

Fortunately, the rental house had nonperishables in the kitchen cupboards. Not much, but enough to keep her and Mags fed for a day or two. If they stayed here much longer, however, she was going to have to find a way to get food. Theft didn't bother her. She'd done it before. The possibility of getting caught by Rhiannon's followers, however, prevented her from sleeping, and tied her stomach in knots.

They'd arrived late at night, and Fiona had no idea how many of Rhiannon's people were on the island. For all she bloody knew, the entire island could be populated by her followers.

Mags's muttering grew louder, and Fiona fed her more protein shake. She never would have thought she'd be grateful that a fitness nut had previously rented the house.

It was empty for now, but at this time of year, it wasn't likely to stay that way for long. Somebody could come along to prepare it for its holiday tenants at any time. Or there was a caretaker out there, soon to pay the house a visit.

Without the blood necklace, Mags had been able to make contact with someone at Baile, and Fiona prayed the cavalry would arrive in time. Even at her most optimistic, however, she had to admit, it wasn't looking good. She'd taken a large, sharp knife from the kitchen and tucked it in her bag. If it came to it, she knew what she had to do.

EMMA STOOD in the ship's main salon and stared at the waves breaking over the prow of their boat. With the captain pushing the boat and maritime law for all he was worth, it would take them just under five hours.

"I'm coming, Mags," she whispered.

Goddess, but she'd failed her witch more times than she could count. If she could go back in time and climb aboard that flight with Jack and Mags from Moscow, she would do it. The rational side of her mind understood that thinking that way was pointless. Even if she could turn back time, it didn't guarantee her desired outcome—Mags, tucked away safe and sound at Baile—but still she tormented herself.

The torment kept her sharp, focused.

Jack lay catnapping on a large, white leather sofa, head propped on a pillow.

She knew better than to assume he was sleeping. The only

person, other than Mags herself, who wanted Mags safe with the same intensity as Emma, was Jack.

He loved her witch. The sort of soul deep connection you read about or watched in movies.

Emma didn't know how the whole Mags, Jack, and her triangle was going to work when they finally got together, but it didn't matter. That was detail and paled in comparison to getting Mags safe.

"Stop it," Jack said without opening his eyes. "I can feel you fretting from over here."

She'd learned early on in their partnership that lying to Jack was pointless. "I just want her safe."

"Yeah." Jack cracked open an eye. "I get it."

And he did. Jack may not be Mags's coimhdeacht, or share the same bond, but he also did a fair amount of self-flagellation.

"I'm tired of all the dead ends, and near misses." She voiced what she would only share with someone who got it as Jack did. "My worst fear is that we get there, and they've moved her again."

"Yeah." Jack groaned and rolled into a sitting position. "Me too."

Emma leaned her head back against the couch to alleviate the ache in her tense neck muscles. "She's fragile."

"But she's strong." Jack gave her a soft shoulder punch. They weren't the kind to hug. "Take it from me. She's more resilient than either of us give her credit for."

The lump in Emma's throat made it hard to speak. "Uh-huh."

"She is." Jack put his head back and they stared at the ceiling together. "We're both the kicking ass and taking names later types."

He had that right, and Emma chuckled.

"So we don't always see that strength comes in different forms." Jack stretched out his legs and crossed them at the ankles. "Mags has a core strength that goes beyond what you or I have. She'll retreat to that place and hang in there."

"Fuck, I hope so." All this time being held by that psychotic fucktard, having who-knows-what inflicted on her.

"We'll get her." Jack nodded.

"We will," Emma said, because neither of them would stop until they did. Even if they had to scoop Mags off the floor and put her back together again.

"And then you and I can start kicking ass and taking names later."

FIONA KEPT her gaze glued to the harbor until watering eyes forced her to blink. Huge, flashy pleasure yachts bobbed at anchor, their flags making a half-hearted attempt to take advantage of the slight breeze off the sea. All those boats, and no way to get on one. Even if she stole one, she wouldn't have a clue how to operate it and get to Athens. If Edana were with her, she would have seduced some person into taking them all the way to the mainland. Then again, if Edana had been with her, she probably wouldn't be here now, doing this stupid thing.

She could always make a run for it on her own. Mags was a liability dragging behind her and slowing her down. Why had she agreed to help her?

Behind her, Mags sat up. It was the first sign of life she'd shown in hours, and it dragged Fiona's attention away from the harbor.

"Emma," Mags said. "I can sense her."

Fiona couldn't place the name. "Emma?"

"My coimhdeacht." Mags smiled. "She's coming."

"Here?"

Mags nodded.

Outside the safe waters of the harbor, the sea met the sky in an unbroken curve. The ferry had come and gone an hour ago. Fiona desperately needed a tendril of hope to cling to. "Are you sure?"

"Oh, yes." Mags labored to her feet, one hand on the wall to maintain her balance. "I can feel her."

"Her?" Fiona was momentarily distracted from the grinding fear. "A female coimhdeacht?"

"Right?" Mags quirked an eyebrow. "As far as I know, first one ever."

Christ! Fiona hoped the bitch could fight, because they were going to need it.

Too many people were roaming the docks between pleasure yachts. People who could belong to Rhiannon. More to pass the time than any real concern, she said, "You look better."

"I feel a bit better." Mags grimaced. "Although, I would love to brush my teeth. My mouth tastes revolting."

"All the sedatives." Fiona cracked their last bottle of water. "They've been keeping you drugged up to the eyeballs since they took you."

Mags accepted the bottle. "I heard Jack."

"Because that's what she wanted you to hear." Fiona went back to her death stare at the harbor. "She got into your mind and convinced you as much."

Mags sipped and swallowed. "I was kind of aware of that."

"Yeah." Fiona hadn't understood how much awareness Mags retained until the news from Canada had reached her. Mags had managed to send Rhiannon and her host of shitheads on a wild-goose chase. "I was hoping that might happen when I took the necklace off when I could."

"Do we have anything to eat?" Mags looked about her with a hopeful expression.

Fiona pointed. "Protein shakes and peanuts, the unsalted kind."

"Ugh." Mags picked up the bag of peanuts. "Who eats them unsalted anyway?"

Fiona agreed, but Mags being more alert had a more important meaning. "You're more yourself."

"It's Emma." Mags opened the bag with about as much enthusiasm as a dog facing kale as his last meal on earth. "I thought it was the air point being active." She palmed a handful of peanuts. "You know, that kept me clear headed?"

Fiona opened one of the protein shakes. Strawberry, according to the label. After downing a mouthful, she was strongly of the opinion that the closest the contents of the bottle had gotten to a strawberry was the one painted on the label. "It wasn't?"

"No." With a pained expression, Mags munched peanuts. "It's something to do with Emma being near me. Somehow, my coimhdeacht stabilizes my blessing."

Fiona shrugged. So much weird and ridiculous had happened, she no longer had the inclination to question. However, Mags appeared as if she could make it without her. She could cut and run, might even have a better chance without Mags. Rhiannon's people would focus on retrieving Mags first. "Listen, keep your eye on the port." She jabbed a thumb at the window. "When your Emma gets here, run for her."

Mags cocked her head and smiled. "Where are you going, Fiona?"

"I'm not sure, to be honest." Mags had an all-seeing, all-knowing look bent on her that made her want to fidget. "But you don't need me anymore."

"Hmm." Mags crunched through another handful of peanuts. "I rather think it's the other way around now. You need me."

Not at all as drugged or doo-lally as they'd all thought Mags to be. "I'm used to surviving on my own."

"Are you, though?" Mags tossed a last handful of nuts into

her mouth and scrunched the bag into a ball. "Seems to me, you're not used to surviving on your own at all."

Fiona wanted to smack the smug off Mags's face. "Bullshit."

"Is it, though?" Mags wrinkled her nose. "You left Baile for Rhiannon, and you've been with her ever since. You let Hannah escape and were demoted to taking care of me." She grabbed a protein shake and cracked it open. "Now, you're hanging by a thread. Rhiannon wants you dead. Roderick would kill you on sight. And you're hiding in a house with me on a foreign island with no way of getting home." She smirked. "And I'm guessing, no money to do so."

Fiona had preferred it when Mags lay there in a drugged-out ball. "What's your point?"

"We need each other." Mags sipped her protein drink and grimaced. "And something better to eat."

CHAPTER TWENTY-EIGHT

S inead felt like a rubbernecker as men, women, and even children flew into action in the gathering dusk. While she and her twin stood in the eye of the hurricane and waited, everyone had more to pack, more to do, more people to gather.

For the most part, as people packed up their lives, they moved with a desperation that spoke of true fear. Some left cabins and locked the door, others left with a trail of discarded belongings strewn behind them, still others darted in and out of their cabins in a flurry of indecision.

And the wolves prowled amongst them directing, chivying, and sometimes bossing.

Sinead couldn't believe she hadn't clocked the difference between the wolves and the rest of the residents before now. The wolf men and women had a predatory way of moving that spoke volumes when you knew what you were looking for. Sara was herding three children into a minivan. That girl was definitely a wolf. She sent a quick prayer to Goddess to keep them all safe.

Noah touched her elbow. "Let's go."

Noah tossed her and Alannah's bags into the back of the silver SUV parked beside them.

Kate sat in the passenger seat beside Zach, Alannah joined Dhara in the third row, and she took a seat beside Noah in the middle row.

Kate and Dhara had packed almost as lightly as them, and Zach and Noah even less.

A woman ran past the front of the SUV with a large, framed picture under one arm and a skillet in her other hand. All these lives would never be the same again.

"Is that everything?" Alannah leaned over and looked at the baggage. A lifetime packed into a few bags and a couple of boxes.

Kate pulled a face. "The most important things are in this vehicle with us."

A bearded man leaned in through Kate's window. "Goddess be with you."

"And you." Kate's voice wobbled, and she squeezed the man's hand where it lay on her open window.

He nodded and darted away.

Kate watched him.

"They'll be fine, Katy." Zach picked up her other hand and kissed Kate's knuckles. "Nobody expected to ever have to use the evacuation plan, but every man, woman, and child in this place had it memorized."

"I hate this." Kate squeezed her eyes shut.

"They'll all be safer when we're gone." Zach put her hand down on her thigh and smiled. "We always knew this could happen."

"Still…"

"I know. Being a leader isn't all perks and gravy." Zach started the SUV and glanced back at them. "All set?"

Shit, but this sucked. Sinead battled her own choked emotions and nodded. "Yup."

Several other SUVs jostled for position as they wove into the forest. Behind them, chaos still reigned as people gave up everything they knew.

Sinead couldn't help but feel responsible. All these people were now running for their lives because of them. She reached behind and took Alannah's hand.

Alannah squeezed back. She understood.

Noah opened his window.

A red SUV with familiar faces drove alongside them. A woman wept silent tears as she stared out the window. Most of these folk had lived in this settlement their entire lives.

She and Alannah had come here to activate the earth point. It had been perilous and frightening, but they'd never thought much beyond the danger to themselves. Now, this entire community was scrambling because of trouble they'd brought right to their doors.

"It's not you." Noah cupped her shoulder. "We were hiding the earth point. We always knew it might come to this."

She appreciated his kindness, but his furry ass had some explaining to do, and she threw him a look to convey as much.

Noah smirked and sat back.

"We need to deviate from plan." Zach glanced at Kate. "We need to get you, Dhara, and the blessed out of the country."

Kate gave him a long look and then nodded. "I'm going with Dhara."

"I never thought you wouldn't." Zach's smile was loaded with so much sadness and acceptance it made Sinead want to comfort him.

"Noah." Suddenly Zach's tone was all business. "I need your senses."

On a nod, Noah stuck his head out the window.

Alannah leaned foward and stared at him. Glancing at Sinead, she frowned. "Is he sniffing the air?"

"Smell," Zach said. "It's our strongest sense. But I'm driving, and I need him to scent what's around us."

Goddess! Sinead nearly laughed at the absurdity. Did she fancy a man who sniffed the air for trouble? Taking a long, slow perusal of his lithe, muscular form, she came to the conclusion that she very much did.

Noah whipped his head back into the vehicle. "We've got unfriendlies ahead."

"I'll text the others." Kate tapped on her phone. "Let them know to take a different route."

The SUV engine roared. Trees whipped past the windows as they jounced through the forest. Rocks and fallen branches scraped the undercarriage, and limbs screeched against the sides. Sinead narrowly avoided banging her head against the window.

"How far?" Zach set his jaw as he drove.

"Maybe three clicks." Noah went back to hanging out the window like the family dog.

Sinead had the distinct feeling she was going to lose her grip on reality soon.

Alannah was way ahead of her, nails digging into Sinead's seat back and eyes brimming with suppressed emotion.

"Direction?" Zach snapped.

Noah popped his head back inside. "North and east."

"Will the others get out?" Kate looked at Zach.

"They have wolves with them too." He took her hand again. "They'll be fine. We have what those dicks are looking for in here with us."

"It'll be okay." Dhara took Alannah's hand. "I know it."

Dhara was the last person in the car who should be handing out reassurance, so Sinead hauled on her grown-woman knickers. "How can we help?"

"Don't kill me before I've had a chance to explain," Noah said.

Well, she could give him the chance, and then all bets were off. Sinead managed a grim sort of smile in his direction.

He winked at her.

Bloody man was irrepressible, and she liked that about him. He kept her hopeful.

Darkness and trees blurred around them as they traveled into the night. She lost track of time and location as Zach and Noah kept up their odd version of blind man's buff. Noah barked updates, and Zach changed direction based on his information.

After a while, the tree coverage grew lighter, and at some point, they cleared the bumpy, unpaved roads and hit smooth tarmac. Judging by the lack of streetlights, they were still on a rural road, but Sinead had no idea where they were. She and Alannah had been hustled into the commune drugged and in the back of a van.

"Where are we?" she asked Dhara.

"Outside Ottawa," Dhara said. "Lanark Highlands."

It still didn't help orient her, but at least she now had a name. "Where are we headed?"

"Toward Toronto," Kate answered. "We'll head for the airport."

"Tonight?" Sinead had a sudden longing for the peace and safety of Baile. If they could get home, they could find a way to deal with Kate and Dhara and activating the earth point. She refused to believe that between Alexander, Roderick, Maeve, and the dead witches, there was nothing that could help them. It might be wishful thinking and her own desperation talking, but she was going with it.

"Not tonight," Noah said. "We need to assume they'll be watching the airports, so we need a plan to get you safely out of here and keep you out of sight. We have a couple of safe places scoped out, and we'll find one of those."

Zach relaxed slightly as they traveled. He glanced at Noah through the rearview mirror. "Anything?"

"We're past them now." Noah drew his head into the car and shut the window. "Let's find somewhere for the night. Get some rest and regroup in the morning."

That sounded like the best idea Sinead had heard in a long time.

As if she agreed, Alannah edged forward and gave her shoulder a brief squeeze. "Everything looks better after a good night's sleep."

Zach relaxed enough to turn the radio on. The wheels swished silkily against the road. Cars grew more numerous around them, and finally, the lights of a small town washed the inside of the car in soft yellow.

They all looked drawn and exhausted.

Pulling into the carpark of a travel hotel, Zach turned to Noah. "Check it out. See if you can get us a couple of rooms for the night."

With a nod, Noah hopped out the SUV and disappeared between the glass automatic front doors of the motel.

Nobody inside the car spoke, and he was back about ten minutes later.

"Done." He handed a key card to Zach. "Two rooms. We'll split up. You with Dhara and Kate, and I'll stay with the twins."

Sinead opened her mouth to protest.

"It's safer that way." Zach beat her to it. "I don't want any crappy surprises tonight."

They all stumbled out of the SUV.

Alannah followed her into a generic hotel room with two queen-size beds.

Noah carried their bags from the car and put them on the bed. "I brought your stuff in. Have you got enough in there to keep you through the night?"

"We have." Alannah managed a wan smile. "What about you?"

He held up a small backpack. "I travel light."

They took turns washing up and getting ready for the night.

Despite her exhaustion, Sinead couldn't sleep.

The murmur of a television, the purr of cars, sounds of doors opening and closing drifted through the hotel around them. In the bed they were sharing, Alannah nodded off just about as soon as her head touched the pillow. And Sinead was left more or less alone in the dark with Noah.

Stretched out on the other bed in a T-shirt and sweatpants, he turned to look at her. "Ask me."

She'd been waiting for answers since the wolves had first entered the dining hall, and now that she had her chance, Sinead didn't know where to start.

Noah's teeth flashed white in the near dark. "Yes, I am a wolf shifter."

"Was it you, the other night in the forest?" Through their drive, she'd pieced that part together.

He nodded. "I was patrolling the borders of the commune land."

"So, you understood everything I said?" Sinead tried to remember everything she'd babbled on about that night. It seemed like weeks ago, and not a handful of nights. Goddess, this was mortifying. She'd sobbed all over that bloody wolf. Sinead could count on one hand the number of people who had seen her that vulnerable.

Chuckling, he turned to one side and propped his head on his arm. "In my defense, I only swung by to check on you. I didn't think you'd sit and talk to a wolf."

As excuses went, that one didn't cut it. She felt raw and exposed. "You should have left."

"I can't do that, sweet thing." His voice roughened. "I need to protect you."

As if she was some helpless damsel. She'd set him right about that. "I can protect myself."

"Never said you couldn't." His eyes glowed in the dim light. "Just that I need to protect you."

She didn't know how she felt about that, and she kept her lip buttoned. On that subject, at least. "So, how did you get to be werewolves?"

"Shifters," he said. "Werewolves are fantasy creatures, and as far as I know, don't exist." He chuckled. "Like zombies."

Now he was going to argue semantics, and she snorted. "Up until yesterday, I would have said the same about wolf shifters."

"Touché." He grinned.

Alannah's rhythmic breathing filled the silent room.

"We're not really sure how we came about," Noah said. "Just that one day, a couple in the commune had a baby that grew up to be able to shift into a wolf. We think the ability to shift has to do with earth magic and how it affected us. That when the earlier witches moved the earth point, it affected the land somehow and pushed the magic into it. We do know that the shifting ability is connected to the land."

"Meaning?"

"It doesn't affect everyone. Not all commune kids can shift, and it only manifests around puberty. Our abilities are strongest when we're on pack land. The land around the commune. It extends for a long way all around the commune, but we can sense when we move away from the earth magic."

He didn't seem any different to her. "So now…"

"I'm unable to shift." He shrugged one shoulder. "I still have heightened senses, but my wolf is quiet."

"Your wolf talks to you?"

Turning to his back, he folded his arms behind his head. "In a way."

"Huh!" Because, fucking hell, what else could she say? She and Alannah had the ability to shape growing things with their earth magic. Bronwyn's herbs, and their kitchen garden grew stronger and faster than normal plants. In theory, all things living on and off the land could be affected. Just because she'd never heard of people being altered, didn't mean it couldn't happen. Hell! Up until a couple of days ago, they didn't think a cardinal point could be moved—never mind moved into a person.

"We protect the commune. Our enhanced abilities make us uniquely suited to do that," he said, those disturbing yellow eyes still locked on her. "And they protect our identity. As far as we know, we're the only ones of our kind."

Sinead wished she could wake Alannah and talk this through with her, but her twin looked as weary as she felt. Since Bronwyn had been catapulted into their lives all those months ago, nothing was as it seemed. Was there a limit to how many times they could stretch and adjust? It was a stupid question, because it didn't matter. The coven was locked in a battle, and it was win or die. "I'm not sure what to make of any of this."

"There's more," Noah said, and his voice deepened.

"Oh, goodie!"

He grinned. "You should also know that shifters have mates."

"Mates? Not as in friends?"

"Not as in friends." He cleared his throat. "We bond with our mates, and it's for life. The mate bond has a specific scent to it that our wolf recognizes and responds to."

"Okay." Instinct warned her she was traipsing through a verbal minefield here, but they may as well get all the surprises and secrets out in the open. "You're telling me this for a reason."

"Don't freak out."

Irritation surged through her. "Have I freaked out so far?"

"Not yet." He cleared his throat.

This was the first time since she'd met him that Noah had demonstrated any discomfort. He'd not even flinched at the drugging and kidnapping. That he was sounding uneasy now didn't bode well for what he was about to verbalize. "And you can't tell someone not to freak out before they know what you're going to say. You could say bloody anything, and I cannot guarantee that the next words out of your mouth won't send me into a screaming bloody frenzy."

"Fair enough." He stared at the ceiling. "We have one bonded mate per lifetime, and we find them by that mate bond scent."

"Uh-huh."

"And you're mine."

That would do it for the screaming bloody frenzy trigger. Sinead gaped at him. "I am most definitely going to freak out now."

CHAPTER TWENTY-NINE

Waiting in the salon, Bronwyn wanted to hop out of her skin. Even her twins could feel the tension in the air, and she rubbed her hand over her belly to soothe them. When they'd last heard, Jack and Emma were on a boat heading for Alonnissos. Since then, radio silence.

Maeve popped her head around the corner. "Any news?"

Bronwyn couldn't stop the face she pulled. She wished she had a different answer. "Not yet."

"I hate this." Sighing, Maeve wandered into the room and threw herself on a squishy sofa. "I wish we knew something. Anything."

"Not anything," Bronwyn snapped, and then winced. "I'm sorry. I didn't mean to take your head off. I don't do waiting well."

Even the panoramic sea view did bugger all to soothe Bronwyn's tension. She was almost too frightened to hope Emma and Jack had Mags and she was safe. Contradictorily, admitting the possibility they wouldn't make it in time felt like tempting fate. And fate was in a particularly bitchy mood right now.

Alexander strolled in, hands in pockets. "Any news?"

"No," Bronwyn and Maeve said together.

"Right." Alexander raised an eyebrow. "All a bit tense, isn't it?"

He ambled over to the huge sea-facing windows and stared out.

Bronwyn wasn't buying his relaxed act for a minute. He'd been antsy all day. They were all on tenterhooks. They wanted to know Mags had been found, wanted to know Sinead and Alannah were safe.

A frowning Roderick entered and opened his mouth.

"No news," Maeve said before he could ask.

Nodding, Roderick joined Alexander at the window.

Tall, and broad-shouldered, they stood with their hands in their pockets, their heads tilted at identical angles. She didn't know how all of Baile hadn't guessed they were father and son before. The genetic stamp was obvious.

Which would make Roderick her twins' grandfather. Somehow the thought made her giggle.

Maeve looked at her for an explanation.

Talking beat waiting and fuming, so she said, "I was just thinking that Roderick is about to be a grandfather."

"Eh?" Roderick whirled and then grinned. "That I am."

He looked downright thrilled about it. That was the thing with the big guy; he constantly surprised a person. You thought he would react predictably, like some medieval throwback with antiquated ideas—and to be fair, he often did—but then he'd go and be sweet and sensitive.

Well, maybe not sensitive.

"No!" the four of them yelled as Niamh and Warren came into the room.

Warren held his hands up in mock surrender.

"I just need to know she's okay." Niamh patted the cat curled in her arms.

That went for everyone in the room.

Andy popped his head around the corner. "I have news."

They all whirled on him. Maeve leaped to her feet, and Bronwyn was right behind her.

"Oh." Andy's face fell. "Not about Mags."

A communal groan followed.

"It's about Hermione." Debra followed him into the salon.

Alexander perked up. He'd always had a soft spot for the former Baile tour guide, now turned accomplice. "Is everything all right?"

"Not really." Debra motioned Taylor into the room. "Taylor has had one of her things." She cleared her throat. "Visions."

"I didn't scry." Taylor glanced at Warren first. "I was more just opening my blessing up, in a general kind of way."

Warren folded his arms and stared at her. "Uh-huh?"

Taylor glared back. "I didn't!"

"Getting off the point," Andy said.

Andy was definitely growing into his role at Baile. Whatever that was. As far as Bronwyn could tell, it was general information, maintenance, and administration. And whatever else Andy took a fancy to undertaking.

"Anyway." Taylor rolled her eyes. "It seems Hermione had a break-in last night."

"Break-in?" Roderick looked to Alexander for clarification.

"Burglary," he said. "Robbery."

A surge of questions came at Andy from all occupants.

He held up his hands. "All we know is that she's had trouble."

"Did you see the burglars?" Warren turned back to Taylor.

She shook her head. "I only saw the police there this morning, and there was a broken window and some stuff."

"Then we called Hermione," Debra said. "And she filled in the details."

"Right" Alexander straightened his shoulders. "I think we should pop past. Have a look. Make sure she's okay."

"Quite right." Roderick stood shoulder to shoulder with him.

"Great idea." Warren joined them.

Bronwyn smelled a couple of plus-six-feet rats in the room, and she glared at them. "You're only going so you won't have to sit here and wait around for news of Mags or the twins."

"So not true."

"I care about…"

"…possible security risk."

Bronwyn held her hands up to stop them. "Just go."

They almost got into a three-man tangle at the doorway.

Taylor shook her head and sneered. "Men!"

———

SINCE WARREN DOVE for the driver's seat, Alexander was forced to take the passenger. A grumbling Roderick clambered into the back.

Bronwyn had called it right. Doing anything was better than waiting for Jack to call. As they left Baile, the wards shimmered.

Just beyond the point where the wards stopped, a man leaped in the road in front of the Landy.

"Bloody hell!" Warren jammed on the brakes.

Unused to such rough treatment, the old Landy juddered and skittered out its back end before groaning to a halt.

Roderick produced a knife at about the same time Alexander found his.

Warren took a handgun from the glove compartment.

The man held his scrawny arms in the air. His tattered old bathrobe fell to midcalf, and a pair of Jesus sandals barely held together over his filthy feet. Fierce eyes glared at them from the small gap between his rowdy beard and tangled mane of hair. "Sinners! Fornicators!"

He capered down the center line and aimed one bony finger at them. "*But the cowardly, the unbelieving, the vile, the murderers, the sexually immoral, those who practice magic arts, the idolaters and*

*all liars—their place will be in the fiery lake of burning sulfur. This is
the second death."*

Roderick muttered, "Revelations twenty-one, eight."

Not believing Roderick knew the bible to that extent,
Alexander stared at him.

"What?" Roderick shrugged. "When you've lived through a
witch hunt, you pick up a thing or two."

Warren leaned closer and peered out the windscreen. "Who
is he?"

"Crackpot." Or that was Alexander's best guess. "They used
to spring up all over the place, but not for years." He had to
think about it. "At least fifty years."

"He's fucking close to Baile." Warren didn't take his gaze off
the man, who now stood stock-still and aimed his face at
the sky.

"Too close." Roderick looked around them. "He's a few paces
this side of the wards."

"He must have come from Greater Littleton." Warren eased
his hold on the gun and sat back.

Alexander recognized the tactic, and it made his nape
prickle. "Rhiannon used crackpots to cause havoc in the past.
They're drawn to her, and she's more than happy to make space
for them."

"I'm getting that hunted feeling again." Warren rubbed his
nape. "And I don't fucking like it." He restarted the Landy.

In front of them, the crackpot pranced and pronked like a
show pony, waggling his shaggy tangled putrid hair as he sang,
"Witches. Witches will burn. Burn in the fiery lake of burning
sulfur."

"Not on my watch." Warren crept forward and eased the
Landy around him.

"She's turning up the heat." Alexander had been around the last
time Rhiannon had decided to attack Baile directly, and she liked to

have a go from all fronts. The police, the taxman, crazies in the village, maybe even the trouble with Hermione wasn't entirely coincidental. Then there was the big shit, like holding Mags and hunting Sinead and Alannah. Not forgetting her globe-trotting and gathering support as she went. She was creating a giant, world-sized fist to crush Baile, and then nothing would stand in her way.

On Rhiannon's last attack on Baile, he'd been on the other side of the wards and firmly on her side. That night had marked his turning point in Rhiannon's war on cré-witches. The horrors he'd witnessed that night had found a spark of conscience in him and ignited his need to change.

"Distraction." Roderick sat back and folded his arms. "She's lighting fires all over the place, keeping us busy putting them out."

"More like a noose." Alexander turned to get a good look at the crazy still yelling after them. "Surrounding us and tightening."

Roderick spoke for them all when he said, "Sod that."

By tacit agreement, they swung past Alexander's former manor house before going to Hermione's.

As the Landy idled outside, they didn't need to speak to know they were all thinking the same thing. The crowd surrounding the manor was twice as large as the last time they'd visited. Through the windows they could see people moving inside the house. New security cameras hung from the trees, and ugly barbed wire fences ringed the once velvety green lawns.

"That's quite an army." Warren snorted derisively. "Bunch of weirdos."

"That won't be all of them." Roderick shook his head. He'd also been there the last time Rhiannon had launched an all-out attack. "She's too clever for that, and she knows what they're facing." He jabbed his thumb at the manor as Warren drove away. "Those are the ones she doesn't mind us seeing. What worries me is who and what we can't see."

Warren glanced at him in the rearview mirror. "Like the ones who massacred those people in Canada?"

"Exactly." Alexander really didn't like where this was heading. "And she has the resources to raise hundreds of groups like those fuckers."

"This is modern-day England." Warren snorted. "I'm bloody sure the authorities will have a lot to stay about armed insurgents roaming the countryside."

They took the corner into Hermione's quiet, residential street.

Alexander pointed at the two men standing in front of a police car. He had no trouble recognizing the bulky DCI Lennox and his slimmer sidekick, Constable Acharya. "You mean like those police?"

The two coppers stopped chatting and watched the Landy approach.

Alexander climbed out first. "DCI Lennox." He held out his hand. "Constable Acharya."

"Lord Donn." Lennox slurred his name like a bad taste in his mouth. "Fancy seeing you here today."

Doors slammed as Warren and Roderick climbed from the Landy behind Alexander.

Alexander sent a quick prayer to Goddess that Roderick kept his gob shut and his wits about him.

Lennox glanced past him at Warren. "I don't believe we've met."

"Warren Masters." Warren shoved his hands in his pockets and gave Lennox a flat look.

"Masters?" Lennox tapped a ballpoint pen on his florid chin. "Warren Masters? Now where have I heard that name before?"

Acharya leaned in. "Known associate of Jack Langham."

"Ah yes!" Lennox clicked his fingers. "Another friend of our missing Mr. Langham." He turned to Alexander with a raised brow. "I'm assuming there's no sign of Mr. Langham yet."

"You assume right." Alexander moved closer to Roderick.

Tension built in Roderick's stiff form like a steam whistle about to go off.

Lennox swung his gaze to Roderick. "And you would be?"

"Wondering what the bloody hell that has to do with you," Roderick snarled.

"My…um…brother." If he admitted to Roderick being his father, Lennox would only get more suspicious. Roderick barely looked over thirty-five. "Roderick Cray."

"Well, look at that." Lennox nudged Acharya. "The very man you were asking about yesterday. Alive and in the flesh."

Hermione's bright red door opened, and she peered out. "Oh hello, Roderick." She smiled at each of them in turn. "Alexander. Warren."

"We came to check on you." Alexander slid into the tense silence. "We heard you had a spot of bother."

Acharya cocked his head. "Where'd you hear that?"

"From me." Hermione bustled forward and hugged Roderick. "I rung them just after I called you lot."

"Friends, I take it." Lennox rocked on the balls of his feet.

"Oh, you know how small villages are." Hermione fluttered over to Warren and tugged him into a hug. "Everyone knows everyone."

Alexander opened his arms to receive his hug. "You and Gemma okay?"

"A bit shaken up, to be honest." Hermione pressed a hand to her chest. "Not the sort of thing you expect to happen in Greater Littleton." She shuddered. "A home invasion."

Warren stepped closer to her. "You and Gemma were in the house at the time?"

Like a shark scenting blood, Roderick went on the alert. "When did this happen?"

"Last night. About three—"

"I'm sure you have lots of questions." Lennox puffed up his chest. "But as this is an open investigation, we'll have to ask you be sparing with the details."

Hermione blinked at him. "But surely—"

"Let's get you a cup of tea." Alexander steered her around the bellicose cop and toward the door. "Is there anything else you need us to do while we're here? Fix a window?"

"Uh…Lord Donn?" Lennox called after him. "You'll be sure to let us know when Mr. Langham joins us again, won't you?"

"Not unless Jack is under arrest he won't," Warren said and gave Lennox a nasty smile. "Or unless you've got probable cause."

Roderick's shoulder brushed Lennox's as he followed. The stare down would have made a braver man than Lennox piss himself.

Before the copper could react, Warren crowded after Roderick and moved them both into the cottage.

"Whew!" Hermione leaned on the door after she'd closed it. "That man does not like you."

Alexander had to laugh. "Minor understatement."

Niamh waited in the kitchen for Warren and the others to get back from Greater Littleton. She was always a bit anxious when he left the safety of the wards, but today was worse than normal.

Alpha crossed her awareness, pressing at her mind for attention. She quested for him and strengthened the link.

Pack was upset. Their churning instincts whirled through her in a maelstrom—aggression, anger, protection. When she pressed Alpha for the reason, he kept showing her wild wolves running through a deeply shaded forest. It didn't look like anywhere she recognized. Alpha showed her a large brown and tan wolf and then an all-black wolf. It didn't make any sense.

Thomas appeared in the kitchen, frowning. "What is it with the wolves?"

"I don't know." Niamh tried to get a clearer picture, but Alpha just kept showing her the same images on a loop. Goddess forgive her, but sometimes she wished animals could speak. "They're really stirred up about something."

"Right." Thomas bunched his fists. "It's making me want to fight something."

At the moment, Thomas probably felt like that without Pack's swirling emotions.

As if he read her thoughts, he gave her a rueful smile. "I take it there's no news."

"Nothing." She wished she could give him something more. "We haven't heard from the twins, and given that they don't know Warren is no longer the leak, that's not really surprising."

He nodded and wandered over to the window and stared into the bailey. "Mags?"

"Nothing yet either."

Thomas's form flickered, and the faint outline of the kitchen sink showed through him. She didn't know how to put this politely. "You look…different."

"I know." He grimaced. "It's the sacred grove. Now that it's fading, I seem to be fading with it."

Niamh's throat dried. They had gotten so used to having Thomas around. It hadn't occurred to any of them that he could just cease to be there. "Are you…leaving?"

"I'm linked to Lavina, and while she's still here…" He shrugged.

Shit! They had to release Lavina from the green with the other witches. "And when we release her?"

"I don't know." He shrugged. Then, his expression grew serious. "But you have to do it, Niamh. Whatever does or does not happen to me when you do, you must give Lavina peace." His jaw tightened. "Whatever the consequences for…others."

Life without him around seemed inconceivable. Thomas was one of them. What would they all do without him? Bloody, sodding hell. What would they tell Alannah if he poofed away forever? "We can't lose you."

"Niamh." His expression softened, and he moved closer to her. "I'm not really here. I died that night."

"Yes, but—"

"As Sinead pointed out, I'm a ghost." He shoved his hands in his pockets. "I'm caught in the wrong place, at the wrong time. I shouldn't be here."

"But Alannah—"

"Is in *her* right place and time." He perched on the table edge. "She is born of this time and belongs to it. We all know I can't offer her much more than a yearning kind of friendship."

Tears pricked the back of Niamh's eyelids. No Thomas to make them laugh with his irreverence. Nobody to needle Roderick, and flirt with all of them. "You can't leave us. We need you."

Thomas shook his head. "No, Niamh, you really don't."

And he vanished.

Panic gripped her. "Thomas!"

"I'm here." He popped back again with his signature roguish grin. "Linked to Lavina, remember?" And then he dematerialized again.

Now she wanted Warren back even more. She needed to share this latest wrinkle with him. Goddess, she longed for his arms around her and for him to tell her everything would be alright.

One of her dogs smelled the Landy before it appeared, and she went to the door. Although, Alannah's fuel of the future didn't need the dog's superior sense of smell to make an olfactory entrance. That stuff stank of pig shit.

Roderick slammed out of the vehicle and stalked toward the kitchen.

He was big, bad, and bloody intimidating with that scowl on his face.

Niamh hopped out of his charge path. "Hi, Roderick."

"Blessed." He gave her a curt nod.

She'd wait and ask Warren how Hermione was.

"Would you bloody well wait!" Alexander yelled after

Roderick as he slammed his door hard enough to shake the old Landy on its axles. Poor old girl deserved more respect than that.

"Niamh." Alexander managed a tight smile before he double-timed it after Roderick, yelling, "You're being a stubborn ass."

Warren climbed out of the driver's side and approached her at a reasonable pace. His joy at seeing her oozed warm and sweet down their bond. The way he found her drop-dead sexy was a knee-wobbler every time.

"Heya." He stopped in front of her and cocked his head.

That irresistible little smirk had her grabbing him and pulling him in for body contact. "Hey yourself."

She took a moment to revel in his big, strong body, drawing in his lovely Warren smell of laundry detergent and hot skin.

Warren rumbled his approval and tightened his hold on her.

"Trouble?" Niamh pressed her face into his neck. Goddess, this man. She was thankful for him in more ways than she could name.

He chuckled. "You could say that. Alexander and Roderick are having a daddy-son spat."

"What happened?" She should let go of him and let him speak. Bugger that! Niamh stayed where she was. "How's Hermione?"

His voice grumbled low through his chest. "Hermione is fine. They had a home invasion last night, but she and Gemma are fine."

Not liking the sound of that one bit, Niamh peered up at him. "Are they safe in that house?"

"We don't know." He shrugged, and his expression darkened. "We tried to talk Hermione into staying here for a day or two, just until we can get to the bottom of it, but she refused."

That didn't sound like Hermione. Since Niamh had known Hermione, she'd been trying to get an all-access pass to Baile. "Refused?"

"She won't be driven out of her house." Warren sighed. "She has a stubborn streak, that one. Roderick managed to get her to promise to let us know if anything else worried her, or anything else bad happened."

"Hmm." Niamh would much rather have Hermione safe where they could keep an eye on her. "And you think it's connected to…her?"

They both knew who *her* meant. Niamh didn't like saying her name, even in her mind.

Warren shifted her to his side and put an arm around her waist. "I don't believe in coincidences. Alexander thinks it's all part of a bigger plan. A sort of concerted attacked from all directions."

"Bugger!" Alexander's theory made too much sense for Niamh to dismiss.

He walked them through the kitchen door. "Everything okay here?"

"Yes. No." She should know better than to lie to her coimhdeacht. It was pointless in any case. The man could just reach into her mind and discover the truth for himself. "Thomas is fading."

"What?" Warren frowned.

"He's getting lighter." She struggled to describe what she'd seen. "More insubstantial. When I asked him about it, he said it was linked to the sacred grove going away. And that the only reason he's still here is because he's tethered to Lavina."

Warren's dismay bled astringent into their bond. He may not have known Thomas for long, but they were brothers—coimhdeacht. His distress transformed into the bitter feel of sadness. "He's not happy without Alannah."

"I know." Niamh tightened her hold on Warren. She didn't know what she'd do if he was suddenly snatched away from her.

"Hey." Warren tilted her chin up. "I'm not going anywhere."

As much as Niamh wanted to draw comfort from his promise, everything around them was shifting and changing so quickly that nothing was for sure anymore. It didn't feel like she could rely on anything or anyone.

"Stop it." Warren pressed a hard kiss to her mouth. "Before Bronwyn arrived, and all this Rhiannon stuff came into the open, you thought you were just a normal girl with some weird ancestry and a handy way with animals. The only thing you could hang your hat on then was death and taxes."

"I know." She clung to his waist as they took the stairs up to the great hall together. "But everything is happening so fast. And people are in real danger. All the time."

"It is not your right to withhold information." Roderick's thundering shout echoed down the stairwell toward them.

Niamh flinched. "Uh-oh."

"I was going to tell you," Alexander shouted back.

"When!"

"When I knew you wouldn't lose your bloody mind and do something sodding stupid."

Roderick growled like a feral wolf.

"I better get in there." Warren sighed. "As unofficial peace-maker, my services are required."

They walked into the great hall.

Roderick stood beneath the stained-glass window, colored light playing across his rigid features, squared off against Alexander about six feet away.

"What does that mean?" Roderick clenched his fists and stepped into Alexander.

"It means"—Alexander pushed his chest out—"that you have a nasty habit of refusing to recognize modern authority. You were as likely to toss that copper out as listen to him. You might even have lost your head and hit him. We cannot risk that."

"Police!" Roderick sneered. "Ridiculous idea."

Alexander stared at him. "My point illustrated."

"You both have a point." Warren released her and stepped closer.

Alexander and Roderick kept staring each other down.

"Alexander did tell you. That time when we took Debra to the village," Warren said.

Roderick growled. "He didn't tell me the extent."

"No, he didn't." Warren's tone was calm and reasonable. "But with all that's been going on, it had to take a backseat."

Roderick glared at Warren. "You knew all of it?"

Warren nodded. "And, for the record, I don't like the police any more than you do."

"Now I am to be treated like a child in my own castle," Roderick thundered. "I have been alive and lived here for longer than the rest of you combined."

"Not me." Alexander sniffed.

"And I am now to be trea—"

"Roderick?" Maeve's sweet voice drifted over from the salon door. She walked toward him.

His attention went her way immediately, and his shoulders lost some tension. "My Maeve?"

"Stop bellowing like an enraged bull." Maeve stopped in front of him and slid her hands around his waist. She dropped her head back and stared up at him with a mischievous smile. "You'll frighten the children."

The effect on Roderick was like a magic wand had been waved. His furious expression vanished to a besotted smirk as he grabbed her hips and drew her closer . "Blessed," he drawled. "I never sound like livestock."

Going on her tiptoes, Maeve kissed him. "Only sometimes."

"He should have told me," Roderick grumbled. "All of it."

Maeve glanced at Alexander over her shoulder. "Yes, he should have. But he had a good reason for picking his time. You know he had no ill intent."

"Are you attempting to placate me?" Roderick nuzzled her

cheek. He was such a big softie for Maeve it made Niamh a bit misty.

Maeve grinned. "Is it working?"

"Always, my Maeve." He picked her up and held her against his chest. Her tiny feet dangled around his knees. "Every. Damn. Time."

CHAPTER THIRTY-ONE

Like a low thrum beneath her skin, Mags felt Emma approaching. She'd lay her life Jack was with Emma, and that caused a flutter near her heart. He would come for her. She knew it, had clung to it through the last terrible weeks of drifting consciousness.

They'd been in this closed restaurant since daybreak, when Mags had made it clear they needed to get closer to the harbor. Emma was coming from the direction of the sea. On a tiny island like Alonnissos, it was just common sense, even if the bond hadn't been tweaking at her from that direction.

Picking at her nails, Fiona paced the floor. "Are you sure she's coming?"

Mags answered, for what, by her count, was the eleventh time. The restaurant smelled of lamb and rosemary and old cooking oil, and her empty tummy grumbled. "I can feel her getting closer. She's coming."

"I never had a coimhdeacht." Fiona pressed her face to the window and aimed one eye to peer between the shutters. "Never understood how it worked."

No, she wouldn't have had a coimhdeacht. Fiona was all

about herself, and her personality would have circumvented the bond.

"They're going to open for the day soon." Fiona went to the other side of the door and peered through those shutters. "We're trapped in here, like rats."

"Emma will be here." And Jack. Jack with the bricklayer shoulders and large capable hands. The man with a deep rumbling voice that could take all her fears and worries away. Jack of the russet eyes and languid, unexpected smile. Without him, her world had bled dry of color, and he was coming for her now.

Fiona wove through the circular tables, their chairs upended on their tops, and stopped at the bar. Then she paced back to the window.

They'd made sure to sneak out of the vacant holiday home under cover of night. Fiona had been vibrating with tension as they left the car in the garage and made their way down the hill toward the harbor on foot.

She'd agreed, however, that Rhiannon's people would be watching for the car, and it made sense to leave it. Someone was about to receive a surprise when they arrived at the holiday house. By that time, Mags would be long gone.

"And she's coming now? Today?" That made twelve.

Mags nodded and poured herself a glass of water. "She is." The heat in the closed space was stifling, but she didn't want to help herself to any of the drinks packing the restaurant coolers. It didn't seem fair to the owners. "And this restaurant doesn't open for lunch."

"How do you know that?" Fiona narrowed her eyes at her.

Mags pointed to the front door. "It says so right there."

Not content to take her word for it, Fiona marched over to the door and flipped the sign so she could read it. The details were written in both English and Greek, clear for anyone. "I still don't like it. Just waiting here like this."

No, Mags wasn't a huge fan of the waiting part either, but Fiona had kept her sane through these weeks with Rhiannon, and now she would return the favor by staying calm as Fiona flew off the rails. She'd thought about reaching Taylor, but now that she was lucid, she was nervous the magical signature could be picked up. They already had a massive target on their backs, no need to add blinking lights and sirens. More to calm Fiona down than anything else, she asked, "What made you join Rhiannon?"

"Eh?" Fiona stopped mid pace and stared at her. "Why do you ask?"

Mags kept it light. She already had her own theories. "You were coven leader. A respected member of the coven. I am wondering why you threw that all away."

Fiona snorted and resumed her pacing. "We were all puppets to Goddess." She stopped and frowned. "At least, that's what I believed at the time."

"And now?"

"We're all puppets to someone." Fiona sneered and went back to the window. "I've just changed mistresses."

"So, why are you here now? With me, like this?" Mags didn't have much clarity from the weeks of her imprisonment, just snatches here and there. Enough to know that Fiona had removed the blood necklace often enough to keep her from losing what remained of her mind. Fiona had taken care of her, and probably saved her life in the process.

"You know why." Fiona sneered. "You made it clear that I had very little choice."

It wasn't an answer, and the evasion annoyed Mags. It would be easier to tolerate Fiona if she didn't insist on snapping like a feral dog. Well, that's what years of being Rhiannon's right hand turned you into. "You know what I'm really asking."

Fiona looked mutinous for a few breaths and then she shrugged. "Because of Edana."

Sensing there was a lot more to the story, and Emma was still a good distance away, Mags waited.

"She killed her, you know." Fiona stared at her hands. "Not just that, but the way she did it. She drained her of blood, taking her to the edge of death time and time again." She screwed her eyes shut. "Until she found something she wanted more." Fiona scowled at her. "You. And then, Rhiannon just tossed Edana away like she was nothing." She shook her head and stared out the shutter gap. Bitter disillusionment leaked from Fiona's taut form. "Like she hadn't served her faithfully for all those years, turned her back on everyone she knew and loved to align herself with Rhiannon."

The way Rhiannon had killed Edana made Mags shudder. She was pure evil, and according to Maeve, Roderick, and Alexander, always had been. "Rhiannon hasn't changed," Mags said, softly, not wanting to rub salt in the wound.

"I know that." Fiona tossed her a glare over her shoulder. "I'm not stupid. I always knew what she was. I've seen things…"

Mags bet Fiona had seen things. Things she hadn't the stomach to question her about.

"I always hated Edana," Fiona said. "She was so bloody stupid and would screw anything that stood still too long."

Mags couldn't prevent the blush heating her cheeks. The Baile coven had always teased her for her prudishness. Goddess, please let Emma hurry. She wanted to be back behind Baile's wards, with her coven sisters, having them tease her again.

"But I loved her." Fiona gave a wry chuckle. Cool blue light from the drink's cooler cast an eerie, pale light over Fiona's contrite expression. "I didn't realize I did until it was too late. She might not have been who I would have chosen as friend, but we were together a long time, Edana and me. The last of our kind. We were a team."

A team that had persecuted her and her coven sisters, but Mags kept that to herself. She touched the bond with Emma and felt it marginally stronger than before. The serene hum from the fridges played counterpoint to Fiona's mounting tension. She just had to keep Fiona from losing her mind for another five minutes or so.

"You could say it's just self-preservation on my part." Fiona growled, as if she was frustrating herself. "If Rhiannon can get rid of Edana as if she's nothing, then I'm no more than that to her."

And that probably came as close to the truth as Fiona could manage. "Emma is getting closer," she said.

Fiona tensed and pressed her eye closer to her gap. "They're here."

"Who?" Mags joined her at the window.

"Rhiannon's people," Fiona muttered as she peeped. "I count four…no, eight of them. We're surrounded."

Mags didn't need to see. She wouldn't know any of their faces anyway. "And those are the ones you know."

"Right." Fiona spun away from the window. "This is never going to work. They'll catch us for sure."

Mags grabbed her shoulders. "Lower your voice. They don't know where we are, and we don't need to send them a sign."

Looking chastened, Fiona ripped out of her light hold. "I could still give you back to them." She sneered. "Save myself."

"No, you couldn't." Mags was done with being threatened and brow beaten. "Your position is as precarious as mine. Rhiannon knows by now who helped me escape. Emma and I are your best chance of getting off this island alive. So, pipe down."

Fiona glared at her, and then her gaze grew speculative. "You said Emma stabilizes you?" She tapped her temple. "You seem all there now."

"Yup." Mags lowered a chair from a table and took a seat. "We all assumed activating the air point would do it. But when I left Moscow, I started to lose my sense of when and where I was again, and Rhiannon was able to get into my mind."

Fiona looked at her doubtfully. "I've never heard of that happening with a coimhdeacht before."

"Yes, but you've also never seen a female coimhdeacht before. Anything is possible now."

With another growl, Fiona went back to her pacing. She stopped close to Mags. "You know I can't come to Baile with you."

"Why not?"

"Alexander." Fiona held out her index finger, and then added her middle finger. "Roderick." Her ring finger came up to join the other two. "Warren." And then with a nasty chuckle. "And your Emma. Not to mention Jack." She shook her head. "They all want me dead."

"It isn't our way to kill," Mags said. She didn't think any of those people Fiona mentioned would throw the accursed woman a welcome party, but they wouldn't kill her. Not without an explanation, at least. "And you don't really have a choice."

With a snarl, Fiona stalked back to the window. "I always have a choice."

"I suppose." Mags would never like Fiona, but the woman had saved her life. "Either way, it's a risk for you, and you may not survive. But I'd rate your odds at Baile as a whole lot better than with Rhiannon."

Fiona couldn't argue with that. She went back to the window.

All her pacing and peering was beginning to wear at Mags's nerves.

"I don't think Emma is coming." Lucky thirteen. "Your blessing is warped. You're mad."

"Emma is coming." Mags stood. "In fact, she's here."

The bond surged through her like a warm, comforting wave

of honey. For the first time in weeks, Mags felt safe. Emma was here, and she was going to get off this island alive. There was still the gauntlet of Rhiannon's people to run, but Emma and Jack would take care of that.

"What?" Fiona stared at her, eyes wide, before she went back to her peephole. Her shoulders tensed, and her voice grew sharper. "There's a massive pleasure yacht entering the harbor." She whistled. "That's a big boat."

Mags joined her by the window and nudged her aside.

A sleek, powerful yacht cruised into the harbor. It was the sort of white-hulled beauty you'd watch on one of those lifestyle type shows that featured the rich and the beautiful. The bond grew even stronger as the yacht's massive engines churned the blue seawater into a breathtaking turquoise. The cruiser turned a one-eighty and began backing into a berth.

Two figures stood at the deck railing, a man and a woman, and Mags's heart pounded. Jack and Emma. Together, and here for her.

"It's them." Now that she could see them, tears flooded her eyes. She wanted to weep her gratitude and her relief, but she didn't have time for that. "They're here."

"What now?" Fiona jammed her hands on her hips and near enough snarled. "We can't just stroll out there and climb aboard."

Mags had to keep Fiona grounded for a few more minutes. "We watch, and we wait."

It seemed to take a thousand years for the yacht to back into a berth. More figures appeared on the deck and threw ropes to people waiting on the dock. Wake churned in the harbor and slapped against the wooden boards of the piers. Berthed boats rocked under the new intruder's turbulence.

Fiona went back to her spy hole.

Not liking her chances of dislodging Fiona, Mags moved to the other window and peeped out.

Jack spoke to Emma.

Emma nodded and she scanned the dock.

Mags wanted to yell that she was here, wave her arms and scream, but she needed to be clever. They were so close, yet so far, and there was no margin for error.

"They've seen them," Fiona hissed. "Rhiannon's people are closing on that fucking boat."

A gangplank extended from the yacht and *thunked* on the dock.

Emma strode lithely down it, with Jack hard on her heels.

They both looked so beautiful and strong and capable. Emma's blond braid caught the bright Mediterranean sun, and she moved like a predator. Behind her, Jack stalked like a dangerous, hunting beast, determination in every overbearing, huge, precious line of him.

Mags concentrated on the bond with Emma. She pushed down it with everything she had.

Jerking to a stop, Emma touched her chest and then looked in her direction. She spoke to Jack and his gaze swung her way.

She wanted to reach out and touch the harsh, strong lines of his beautiful face. Mags's heart thundered against her breastbone. They were so close.

Fiona said something she didn't catch. "What?"

"I asked what the plan was." Fiona crossed her arms and glowered at her. "We're here. They're there, and there's a shit ton of trouble between us."

Three men closed on Jack and Emma from the left. Another two came in from the right.

Fiona had recognized eight. But Mags could only identify the five moving with intent toward Emma and Jack.

Another two men in board shorts crossed the road in front of the restaurant.

"We go." Mags made her decision. "Now."

"Are you mad?' Fiona gaped and then sneered. "Actually, forget I asked."

Mags didn't give a pop what Fiona thought of her. They were in a public harbor. Tourists were everywhere, and the minute Jack or Emma caught sight of her, they would move heaven and earth to get to her.

"Here." Mags tossed a cap from the pegs on the wall beside the door at Fiona. She grabbed a second, ignored the strongly fishy smell, and jammed it on her head. "We have a moment while they're all watching Jack and Emma."

Fiona caught the cap and glared at her. "They'll kill us."

"I'm going now." Mags was done arguing, so she eased open the restaurant door. "You do what you want."

Midday heat and light blasted her as she slid outside to the pavement. Looking left and then right, she crossed the small road separating the restaurant from the harbor.

Emma engaged with the two men from the right. The first dropped like a stone and the second paused and took a step back. With a lightning-fast surge, Emma got chest to chest with the man, and he dropped.

From the left, the other three swarmed.

Jack threw a punch that downed the first man. A second turned and ran, the third met a grimly determined Emma and joined his cohort on the floor.

People noticed the commotion. A woman screamed, and onlookers ran, others grabbed mobile phones and started filming.

The two men in board shorts spun, saw her and Fiona, and started running toward them. A second turned and ran, the third met a grimly determined Emma and joined his cohort on the floor.

"Jack!" she screamed. The time for subterfuge was over. Mags dashed across the road. "Emma!"

Jack made it to her in a flash. Strong arms lifted her off her feet, and they were moving, running down the dock. Around them, people screamed, got in the way, and disappeared. The sound of Jack's footsteps changed as he charged up the gangplank.

"Fucking move!" Emma bellowed, and then Fiona was thrust on the deck beside Jack.

Sirens wailed and lights flashed. Somebody must have called the police.

"Get this boat going!" Emma bellowed.

Beneath Jack, the deck shuddered and vibrated through Mags, and then his voice was in her ear. "Fucking hell, Magdalene. I've got you." His arms tightened until she could barely breathe. "I've got you."

CHAPTER THIRTY-TWO

"I can walk, Jack." Mags wriggled in Jack's arms, but she didn't put too much effort into the endeavor as he carried her into the main salon of the boat. She was finally where she'd dreamed of being through the last nightmarish weeks.

Engines hummed beneath the decks as the boat got underway, and Mags took her first deep breath in what felt like forever. She was with Jack and Emma. She was going home.

Emma followed tight on their heels, and having her so close increased Mags's sense of all right by about a hundred times. "Is she okay?" Emma's face appeared behind Jack's shoulder. "We need to check her that she's all right." She scrutinized Mags. "I can call Sasha, have a doctor meet the boat somewhere."

"I'm fine." Mags struggled to get free and hug Emma. Their bond snapped tight, and she needed the visceral connection with her coimhdeacht.

Concern clouded Emma's gray eyes. She thumped Jack's beefy shoulder. "Put her down."

"I can't." Tension vibrated through Jack's muscles as he held her. "I've finally fucking got her, and I can't let her go."

Emma's gaze gentled, and she patted his shoulder. "Okay. I get it. Let's get her settled in here."

"Where's Fiona?" Mags tried to peer past Emma.

Emma pulled her lips off her teeth in a vicious snarl. "That one is on deck."

"She saved me." She didn't want Fiona dead before she had a chance to tell her story. "She kept me sane, and she helped me escape."

"Which is the only reason she's not swimming with the fishes." With Emma's long, vanilla braid and her strong, tanned arms folded over her chest, she looked like a Viking goddess of war. "We'll talk about her later. First, you."

Jack eased on a sofa and tucked her beneath his chin.

For a moment, Mags lay quiescent in his lap, breathing in the soothing scent of him, letting the heat of his big body warm every part of her down to her soul. The steady *da-dum* of his heart against her ear became her anchor, and she allowed herself to relax. Jack had her. And Jack wouldn't let her go.

Emma dropped to the cushion beside them and ducked her head to stare at Mags. "You're really okay?"

"Feel." Mags pushed down the bond between them. It was there, but muted, like a television set turned to low.

With a grimace, Emma said, "The minute we get to Baile, we are accepting the bond."

"We are." Mags nodded because it sounded good to her as well. She held a hand out to Emma. "Thank you."

Taking her hand, Emma cleared her throat and dropped her gaze. "You don't have to thank me, Mags."

Fiona slid into the salon and stood at the door looking uncertain.

Sitting back and stretching her long legs in front of her, Emma gave her a flat stare. "So, you're Fiona."

"Indeed." Fiona raised her chin and met Emma's scowl with one of her own.

A growl rumbled through Jack. "The Fiona."

"The very same." Emma nodded. "We've been tracking her for years, but this is the first time I've been in the same room with her." She jerked her chin at Fiona. "Proven by the fact the bitch is still breathing."

"Get over yourself." Fiona folded her arms and wandered deeper into the cabin. She glanced at Emma's arm and shook her head. "First time I've seen a female coimhdeacht."

Emma sneered. "Lucky you. For the record, you're not the first evil cunt I've seen."

All-righty then. Time for Mags to take control of the meet and greet before fur started flying. "Fiona was charged with taking care of me while I was held captive."

Jack grunted, and Emma's mouth tightened.

Not a resounding success at peacekeeping, but at least blood wasn't spattering.

"It was a job." Fiona threw out a flippant hand toss. "Much like any other."

Fiona was scared and striking out like a cornered cat.

"You're lying," Mags said. "Nobody told you to take the blood necklace off when we were alone. And nobody told you to keep talking to me and reminding me who I was."

Some of the tension left Jack, but Emma remained wholly unconvinced—if her grim expression was anything to go by, and Mags rather thought it was.

"What's a blood necklace?" Jack glanced at Emma for the answer.

Emma shook her head. "Never heard of it before. Why don't we ask the evil cu—"

"It was a sort of collar, infused with blood magic that kept me confused." Mags really didn't like the c-word.

Leaping to her feet with a snarl, Emma closed on Fiona and fastened a hand around her neck. "You did that to her." Emma's voice was silky smooth and deadly. "You put that fucking abomination on my witch?"

As she clawed at the hand on her throat, Fiona had the good sense to finally look nervous. "I didn't put it on her."

"But you let her wear it." Emma's fingers tightened, her knuckles whitening. "You sat there while that was done to her."

"I didn't have a choice," Fiona sputtered, her face going deep red.

"We all have choices." Emma got right in her face and lowered her voice to almost a whisper. "They might be shitty choices, but we all have choices."

Oh boy. Emotions were running riot. Mags needed them all to wind their necks in. "Em—"

"Emma." Jack's voice cracked through the salon. "Let's not kill her. Yet."

"Why?" Emma batted away Fiona's clawing hands and raised her to her toes by the hold on her throat. "She's served her purpose."

Emma might actually strangle Fiona. And Mags couldn't allow that. Could she? No, she couldn't. She needed to shove down her own murderous impulses as the memories of what had been done to her surfaced.

"Emma." She sat up on Jack's lap. "Please."

With a growl, Emma dropped Fiona.

Fiona crumpled to the floor like a discarded tissue, gasping and hacking for breath.

"I want—" Emma turned away from Fiona, her chest heaving as she fought for control. "No. I need to understand everything that was done to you."

Mags needed to get to her, ease her suffering.

Jack must have sensed Emma was close to the breaking point because he finally opened his arms and let Mags go.

"Emma." Mags wrapped the other woman in a hug. Even taller than her, but lean and whip strong, it felt like holding on to a lioness. "I will tell you everything." She squeezed tighter. "I promise, but maybe not now."

Emma's grip manacled her closer. "I'm so sorry, Mags." Her entire body shook with the effort to contain her emotions. "I'm so sorry."

Tears stung Mags's eyelids, and she felt the wave of grief and remorse through the bond. Dear Goddess, Emma had been blaming herself the entire time. Emma had been lacerating herself with guilt. This strong, powerful warrior would not accept what she perceived as failure in herself. Mags pulled back enough to see her, and then cupped Emma's face.

Emma hid her eyes by staring down.

"We're not doing this." Mags jiggled her head gently. "We're not doing this to ourselves. Do you hear me, Emma?"

Tortured gray eyes met hers. The barest trace of tears shimmered in their depths. But Emma was fighting with everything in her not to cry. "I should have been there," she said. "I knew what a coimhdeacht's job was, and I should have been with my witch."

"Yes, you should have," Fiona chimed in from the floor.

"Shut the fuck up!" Mags swore for what was probably the first time in her life. As much as she was Emma's to protect, Emma was hers. Right now, with Emma vulnerable, she would rip the throat out of anyone who tried to hurt her.

Jack came closer, loomed over Fiona, and jerked his head toward Mags. "What she said."

Fiona crawled away from him and hauled herself into a chair on the far end of the salon.

Honestly, Mags would not be able to keep her in one piece if she kept mouthing off like that. Goddess alone knew what would happen if she tried any of her nonsense with Alexander or Roderick. Or even Warren for that matter. He might not have the history with Fiona that the other two did, but he was carrying his own wagonload of grudges.

Right now, though, Emma was her first priority. "You did what you had to do." She held Emma's gaze. "You did what you thought was right, and you wouldn't be my Emma if you hadn't. And anyway, I had Jack with me when we left Moscow."

Fiona snorted. "Fat good that did."

Moving faster than a man his size should be able to, Jack caged Fiona in her chair. "Try me. Give me one reason, and I'll snap your spine."

"Seriously?" Mags glanced over Emma's shoulder at Fiona. "Would you please stop antagonizing everyone?"

With a shrug, Fiona crossed her arms and looked sulky.

"Neither you nor Jack is responsible for what happened to me." Mags turned her attention back to Emma. "There was a plan, and I was targeted. If it comes to that, I could blame myself for not seeing it before it happened."

"She's got that part right," Fiona said. "Rhiannon had this planned from the get-go. I didn't know why she held back in Moscow, but she must have been waiting to spring her trap. She wanted Mags from the moment she discovered that chink in the wards."

"See." For once, Fiona had said something useful.

"But—"

"I need you to stop." Mags increased her hold on Emma's face. "I need you to stop and move on, because I can't if you can't."

"She's got a point," Jack rumbled and stepped away from Fiona. "We all need to get past this and move on."

After a long moment, Emma nodded and gently disengaged Mags's fingers. "Okay." She took a deep breath. "I'll work on it." She swung around to Fiona. "And working on that one for answers will help me."

Fiona licked her lips and looked around the salon for an escape.

"No luck." Emma grinned, and it made Mags's nape hairs

stand on end. "There's nowhere to go." She jabbed a thumb at the ocean outside the windows. "Unless you're a really great swimmer."

All the fight bled out of Fiona, and she slumped in her chair. "I'll tell you everything I know." She held up a hand. "Although lately, she's been keeping me on the outs, only telling me what I absolutely had to know. She doesn't trust me anymore."

"With good reason," Jack said.

Fiona glared at him but slumped again.

"Are you hungry? Thirsty?" Emma brought all her focused attention back to Mags.

Now that the immediate danger had passed, Mags's body reminded her that it had been surviving on nasty protein shakes for the last twenty-four hours. "I could eat."

"Good." Emma nodded. "I'll get you some food." Then she grimaced. "And I'm going to tell you what Jack is too polite to—you need to get cleaned up as well." With a grin, she took a sniff of Mags. "Because, woman, you stink."

CHAPTER THIRTY-THREE

Mags followed Jack belowdecks to a luxurious cabin outfitted in cream linens and gleaming wood.

"Wow." She turned a full circle and took it all in. She didn't think she'd ever seen anywhere quite as grand. And this from a woman who'd been raised in a castle. The yacht was more like a floating hotel than a boat.

"I know." Jack grimaced. "Emma has friends in wealthy places."

"This is beautiful." She ran her hands over the gleaming wood surfaces, so clean she could see her reflection in them.

Jack cleared his throat. "There's a bathroom through there." He pointed to a door to the right of the oversize bed. "It's fully kitted out with everything you'll need."

"Thank you." Mags wandered to the indicated door and peeked inside. Marble surfaces and brass fixtures caught the sun streaming through large windows. A deep bath sat in an alcove with a perfect view of the sea. "This is wonderful."

Picking up a bag on the double vanity, Jack motioned to her with it. "Emma thought to grab you a few things. Some clothes and such."

"Thank you." That had been very thoughtful of Emma, and Mags certainly didn't relish spending the rest of the trip in the cotton pajamas she had on. They fit okay, if a little big, but she didn't recognize them, so someone must have put them on her. Also, after a day or so spent running and hiding, they were looking a bit grubby. Presented with an option, she couldn't wait to take them off.

"Right then." Jack hovered in the doorway. "If you don't need anything else, I'll…" He jabbed his thumb out the door, and then frowned. "Unless, you're not…you know…and need me to stay. Again. Not that I'm trying to be a pervert or anything—"

"Jack." She put a hand on his forearm to stop him. She'd never seen him so unsettled, and if she didn't know better, awkward. "It's okay. I know what you meant, and I'm fine. It seems that being close to Emma keeps me in my right mind."

He blew out a long breath. "Good. That's good then. So, I'll just…" He whirled and strode out the door.

Alone in the beautiful bathroom, Mags nearly called him back. Blurry, terrifying memories of what had happened to her threatened to sneak up on her and have their playtime in her mind. Details were no less frightening for their lack of clarity.

"You're okay," she whispered to herself. "You survived. Jack and Emma came for you. You're on a ship. On your way home." She braved her reflection in the large mirrors above the vanity. Someone—she hoped Fiona—had braided her long hair down her back before they'd made their escape. Her cheeks were sunken and hollow, and dark smudges beneath her eyes looked like bruises in the pallor of her face. "You do not look your best," she said.

Not that she'd ever been much of a beauty. Niamh was the sexy one, and Alannah and Sinead had the beauty front pretty much tied down. Mags had always been the eccentric, fae-child coven sister.

She traced the harsh line of her clavicles with her forefinger.

She'd lost more weight, and she'd been skinny to start. She looked fragile and fragmented. Or maybe she just felt that way.

She ran water in the bath. A basket of nice smelling things sat on the lip, and she picked lavender bath salts. Lavender was a good smell, relaxing. As she emptied the vial into the bath, the sweet-earthy scent filled the bathroom.

A bar of soap sat in a small soap dish, and she sniffed it. Jasmine. She pushed the soap aside and found a lavender one.

Her magic smelled of jasmine, and she didn't want to think about that right now. She'd been kidnapped and held for her blessing. Her blessing slumbered inside her, quiet and tranquil, but Mags hadn't the courage to go near it. Logically, she understood that her blessing was stable when Emma was about, but the terrifying confusion that had clouded her brain tormented her with what would happen if she used her blessing.

While the bath filled, she loosened her hair and wriggled out of the pajamas. On a neat shelf beside the bath, she found shampoo and conditioner and a comb. Thank Goddess, her hair had been braided, because it would be a snarled nightmare by now if not.

As she lowered herself into the water, it was hot enough to sting her flesh. She needed the heat to seep inside and warm the cold within her. She needed the scald to purify the taint of what they'd done to her from her body.

Her vulnerability, her helplessness washed over her. She'd been entirely at Rhiannon's mercy, unable to think or even speak for herself. They'd reduced her to a mere thing, a tool that served a purpose.

Trembling started from deep within her, radiating through every part of her. The futile sense of violation fastened cruel fingers around her and squeezed. And she was not okay.

She hunched her knees into her chest and tried to fight off the pain, but it came from inside her, from a place she couldn't touch. Pressing her eyes into her knees, she tried to will the terror and anger away. She wanted to kill them, and she wanted to run from them. She wanted to scream and cry until the hurt inside her found a voice and rang through the world.

"Mags." Jack tapped on the bathroom door. "Emma sent me down to check on you. She says you're not doing well."

That damn—no, *fucking* bond. She was definitely taking up swearing.

Jack rapped harder. "Mags?"

"I-I'm f…fine." Not a sane person on the planet would buy that.

And clearly not Jack, because the door opened, and he stepped inside. "Magdalene?"

"Don't call me that!" Her voice ricocheted off the marble tiles. "Don't ever call me that."

He stopped and held his hands out, palms up in a sort of supplication. "Alright…Mags. Is it okay to call you Mags?"

"She called me Magdalene." Sobs shuddered up from her center and constricted in her throat. "She called me that when she was pretending to be you."

Jack's harsh face softened, and his eyes filled with the sort of compassion that would surely break her. "Ah, Mags, my sweet Mags. My beautiful, brave woman." He stepped closer, but slowly and deliberately, as if he were afraid she might bolt any second. "Then I'll never call you that again."

"But it's your name for me." She keened like a lost child, but the pain wouldn't be quiet and wouldn't lie still; it demanded to be heard. Hurt built in her chest and back, and she rocked to alleviate the barrage her skin couldn't accommodate. "You always called me that, and she's made it dirty and awful."

Jack crouched by the side of the bath. "May I touch you?"

She nodded, but she really wasn't sure if she could be touched.

He cupped the back of her head and stroked down her hair

to the waterline. "It's just a name, baby. Just a stupid collection of syllables I put together, so you'd always know it was me."

"She made me think it was you." His touch loosened the knot, and tears streamed from her. Great sobs wracked every part her. "I thought it was you. I wanted it to be you."

"I'm so sorry, baby." His voice shook as if he was struggling to contain his emotion. "I'm so sorry it wasn't me, but I'm here now."

"I wanted it to be you, because then I would know I was safe."

"Christ, Mags." His other hand tightened on the bath lip. "I wish with every part of me that it had been me."

Her voice rose, shrill and uncontrolled. "She used me. She took what wasn't hers, and I couldn't stop her."

"She's a walking dead woman, baby." Jack resumed his long, slow stroking of her hair. "She's so fucking dead when I find her."

And then Mags said the thing that haunted her the most, "And I let her. I let her." She thumped her chest with her fist. "I let her do that to me."

"No." Jack caught her fist and held it.

She tried to fight him, but he was just too strong. Water sloshed over the bath on him, but he didn't move. "No, Mags." He caught her chin and turned her face to him. "Listen to me and listen well. In the days that come, you're going to remember more and more about what happened to you. And you're going to be angry and scared and feel like you will never be free of it." His honey-brown gaze bored into her. "You're going to think about all the things you could have done, could have said to get free. You're going to beat yourself up for all the times you could have gotten away and didn't. All the opportunities you should have taken and didn't." He leaned closer until she could pick out the gold flecks in his irises. "But it's all fucking bullshit. You did nothing wrong. You survived. You did the best you could when the situation presented itself. And. You. Survived."

She had known, at times, what was going on. There had been moments of clarity in the confusion. Maybe if she'd fought harder when they'd first taken her. "But—"

"No. You need to stop that." Jack pressed his forehead against her. "I'm going to tell you something nobody else knows, not even Warren. When I was in prison, I did things—fucking awful things—and fucking awful things were done to me." He retreated enough for their gazes to meet. "And someday I'll give you all the details, but that's not the important bit. The thing about what happened to us," he touched her chest with his forefinger and then his own, "to both of us. The important bit is that when you strip away the human facade, we are all just animals underneath, and we do what we must do to keep breathing in and out. We do that until we can afford to do better. We survive. It's only later that we start to think about all the ways we could have done that better." He wiped her tears away with his thumb. "You survived, baby, and that felt like the hardest part. But this is the hardest part. When the danger fades, and you're not fighting for your life anymore, then your head joins the party and starts in on you about how you could have been a better survivor, like it's some fucking test you need to score top marks on."

The elephant on her chest shifted enough for her to breathe. "Does it get better, Jack?"

"It does, baby." His smile held a wealth of hard-won wisdom. "But perhaps not today." He made a face. "Tomorrow is not looking great either. But it does get better. And you know what?"

"What?"

"Emma and I are going to be right there, holding your hand, through every part of the shittyness." He picked up a bar of soap and lathered it between his palms. "For today, we're going to concentrate on getting you clean and into new clothes." He picked up her arm and spread lather on it. Stretching across her for the other arm, he said, "We're going to make sure you eat and make sure you sleep." He dropped her arm and grabbed a flannel from the basket. Smoothing it over her skin, frowning in concentration, he said, "And you're going to keep breathing in and breathing out. Emma and I are going to keep lying beside you so that if your dreams tear you back into the world, we're there to hold you. We will make snacks, so you don't feel hungry." He sluiced water over her arms with the flannel. "And when you doubt yourself, we're going to keep reminding you that you were worth moving fucking heaven and earth to find, and we're not giving up on you now."

CHAPTER THIRTY-FOUR

"So." Alannah kept her voice down in deference to Dhara and Kate sleeping in the seat behind them. She didn't know that any of them had gotten much sleep the night before, but they were on the move again. "A wolfman?"

Noah was driving this leg with Zach in the front seat. She and Sinead had taken the middle row.

"Don't." Sinead squeezed her eyes together and pressed a finger to her temple. "It's a lot." She threw a look at the front seat. "And keep your voice down."

"Not really possible." Zach glanced over his shoulder and tapped his ear. "Wolf hearing."

With a huff, Sinead folded her arms and glared at him. "This just keeps getting better and better."

"Just wait until the full moon." Noah winked at her through the rearview mirror. "I grow hair on my palms."

Sinead snorted. "I heard there was a completely different reason for that."

"Tell me more, sweet thing." Noah chuckled, and Sinead's cheeks went fiery red.

Alannah had to swallow her giggle. It was funny—in a

buggered-up kind of way. And Noah was charming and so much a match for her bolshie sister. "What does happen on a full moon?"

"He's fucking with you." Zach's deep rumble filled the car. "We're wolf shifters, not werewolves."

It might not be the time or place, but she just had to ask, "Are there werewolves?"

"Not as far as I know." Zach shrugged one shoulder.

Noah peered through the mirror again. "Did she tell you the other part?"

"What other part?" Alannah glared at Sinead. Her twin was developing a nasty habit of keeping stuff from her.

Sinead tucked her chin into her chest and mumbled something.

"What was that?" Alannah gave her a good elbow nudge to let her know they could do this the easy way or the hard way.

Sinead sighed. "Apparently, I'm his mate as well."

"You're his…" And Alannah's sense of the ridiculous got away from her, and she laughed. What a sad pair she and Sinead were. One in love with a ghost and another in love with a wolf.

Nobody in the car shared her levity, and she got it under control. "What does that mean?"

"It means he's bonded to her." Kate's quiet voice came from behind them. "For him, she's it for the rest of his life."

Zach turned and looked at Kate. "The only one."

"Christ!" Kate folded her arms and glared out the window. "That's a lot of pressure to put on a woman. I mean, what if he doesn't do it for you?"

Zach chuckled. "How would you know if you never gave him a chance?"

"He's already had all the chances he's going to get," Kate snapped.

Alannah sensed the conversation careening in another direction altogether, and judging by the tension building in the vehicle, not a happy one.

"It doesn't matter," Sinead said. "I'm going to England, and Noah is staying here."

"No." Noah checked the mirror and indicated a left turn. "If you go to England, I'm coming with you."

Wow! Alannah had to check how Sinead was taking that. Not well if her fish-mouthed gaping was any indication.

"No, you aren't," Sinead snapped. "Your place is here. You belong here." She gathered steam and stuck her chin out. "Besides which, according to you, your…gift…wolf thing…is linked to the land, and if you leave, you can't do… change…anymore."

Noah took the turn and said, "You're my mate. Nothing is more important than you."

"That's bloody ridiculous." Sinead shot forward in her seat. The seatbelt yanked her back, and she gave it an irritated tug. "You only just met me. You can't go following me around the world when you don't even know me."

Alannah was most intrigued by what Sinead didn't say. None of Sinead's objections were around not wanting Noah to come with her, but more about how it wouldn't be good for him.

"He has no choice," Zach said and rolled down the window. He took a sniff of the air. "Uh-oh."

"What?" Noah glanced at him.

"Can't quite catch it, but I don't like what I am getting." Zach shook his head. "Senses are nearly as dead as a human's."

"We're off pack lands," Noah said to them. "We've lost some of our animal enhancement to our senses."

"See!" Sinead poked the back of his seat. "You can't come with me because you won't have your enhancements. You need to stay here."

Kate edged forward and leaned over their seatback. "Is something bothering you?"

"Hmm." Zach threw a half glance over his shoulder. "I've got this itchy feeling that something isn't right."

"Then we should turn around," Kate said. "I've never known one of your itchy feelings to turn out false."

Noah looked at Zach. "Your decision, man."

"Turn around." Zach stared into the darkening evening around them. "And do it fast."

Jamming on the brakes, Noah executed a fancy wheel-squealing, rubber burning turn in the middle of the road.

Alannah clung to the oh-shit handle like her life depended on it. As the world careened around her, she rather thought her life might very well depend on holding on.

The vehicle stopped, and they were facing the opposite direction.

Dhara woke somewhere in the middle of the action-movie maneuver. "What's happening?"

"Zach has a bad—"

Bam!

"Fuck!" Noah punched the accelerator.

The window shattered beside Alannah's head.

Zach lunged back and hauled her and Sinead down. "Keep your heads down." He kept going until he got to Kate and Dhara. "Get your fucking heads down."

"What's happening?" Dhara whispered.

"Gunshots." Zach lay over the two banks of seats now, his one hand on Dhara's head, the other on Kate's.

Bam! Bam! Bam!

More glass shattered. The vehicle lurched wildly forward. Wind rushed through the shattered windows.

Alannah dared not look up. She grabbed Sinead and threw her arms around her, as they huddled together in the seat well. They were thrown this way and that, but she clung to her sister.

"It's okay," Sinead whispered, her nails digging into Alannah's arms. "It's okay, it's okay."

She didn't know how long they drove for. It seemed simultaneously to take hours and be over in seconds.

The car stopped, and Noah yelled, "Is everyone okay?"

Alannah ran her hands over Sinead and then herself. "We're okay." The relief made her sob. "We're fine."

"Zach?" Noah's door creaked open, and then he yanked open the back passenger door. He lunged for Sinead and dragged her out.

"I'm fine." Sinead dusted glass out her hair with hands that shook badly.

Alannah's legs almost gave as she clambered out after Sinead. "Is it safe?"

"For now." Noah finished checking Sinead and glared around them. "I haven't heard any gunfire for a while, and nobody followed us. Zach?"

"All good." Zach unfurled his big body from his sprawl and climbed out the vehicle. "Kate?"

The silence made Alannah look up from dusting glass off herself.

"Katy!" Zach lunged back into the vehicle.

"Zach." Kate's voice held a strange and brittle quality, like it had disconnected from her. "It's Dhara."

"Let me get to her, baby," Zach said.

Alannah could see nothing past Zach from where she stood.

Noah had gone deathly pale and ran to the other side of the vehicle. "Kate, you need to climb out so we can get to her."

"It's Dhara," Kate wailed. "Dhara!"

Noah manhandled Kate out of the vehicle, and Alannah grabbed her. Kate was wild-eyed and ghostly pale. Blood covered her hands and soaked her T-shirt.

Alannah tried to contain her hammering heart and help. "Are you hurt?"

Kate shook her head. Her mouth opened and shut.

Zach edged out of the vehicle, Dhara limp in his arms.

"Zach?" Kate sounded childlike as she looked at him. "Zach?"

He laid Dhara on the ground and dropped to his knees beside her.

Sinead gasped and grabbed her hand in a punishing grip.

In the center of Dhara's forehead was a hole, no larger than a penny.

For an awful moment, Alannah thought she might faint.

"Is that…" Sinead looked to Noah.

Grim-faced, he nodded. "They shot her."

Zach looked up, his fingers still on Dhara's pulse. His stare met Kate's and he shook his head. "I'm so fucking sorry, Katy—"

"No, no, no, no, no." Kate flew at him, nails out like claws. "Don't you dare say it. Don't you fucking dare say it."

"She's dead, Kate." Zach caught her hands and folded them against his chest. He wrapped her close and held her.

Kate fought and shrieked against his hold, but Zach held her, his eyes brimming with more sadness than one man could contain. "She can't be," Kate screamed against Zach's chest. "She's only fifteen. She's not dead. She can't be."

Alannah turned into Noah as he put an arm around her shoulders.

Sinead was already there, her face buried in his chest as she cried.

Beneath her feet earth pulsed, *ba-da-dum*.

Sinead froze and stared at her. She'd felt it too.

"What is that?" Noah whispered.

Like a heartbeat *ba-da-dum*, stronger this time. Small pebbles skittered and danced on the road.

Ba-da-dum.

CHAPTER THIRTY-FIVE

Alexander searched the darkness for what had wrenched him from a deep sleep.

Beside him, his little witch stirred. "Alexander?"

"Listen."

Bronwyn tensed. She felt it too.

The rumble began in his ear, a subliminal roll that built as the seconds ticked by. The sound reverberated through his bones and his blood, and he grabbed Bronwyn and held her close.

A door banged open, and Roderick asked, "What is happening?"

More doors opened. Footfalls slapped down the corridors outside their room.

The sound built to a dull roar. Their bedposts shook the curtains. A glass trundled to the edge of his bedside table, dropped to the floor, and shattered. And still the shaking continued.

Cries of alarm sounded from outside their room.

Their door banged open, and Roderick charged through. "Are you okay?"

"I'm not sure." Alexander wrapped as much of himself as he could around Bronwyn. "What the hell is that?"

"I don't know." Roderick staggered as the floor shook beneath him.

Wind roared through the room, picking up discarded clothing, snatching at bed linen and curtains, howling above the groan.

"We need to get to safety." Alexander scooped Bronwyn into his arms. Magic swelled beneath his skin, pushing at him, filling him to bursting. He wanted to yell to alleviate the pressure. Wind battered him. The earth shook beneath his feet as he staggered forward with Bronwyn.

Roderick fought back to the door. "I'm getting Maeve."

"Do it!" Alexander yelled above the groaning earth and howling wind. Behind them, a window shattered in a spray of glass that peppered his back with tiny stings of flying shards.

Warren shouted from somewhere, "It's an earthquake!"

"No." Bronwyn went stiff in his arms, her eyes glowing with an eerie silver light. "The magic. Goddess," she whispered in a voice that didn't belong to her.

Outside the castle, waves crashed against the cliff, the sibilance adding to the wind and the earth. Taps burst in the bathroom and sprayed water into the air.

Niamh ran down the hallway in her nightie. Her eyes held the same unearthly light as Bronwyn's. "Fire," she sobbed. "It's out of control."

Animals streamed around Niamh, adding their alarmed cries to the uproar.

Wolf howls rode the rising wind. More glass shattered. People screamed.

Around them, Baile groaned and creaked. Ancient wooden beams keened their protest, dust raining down about him as he took the stairs three at a time, Bronwyn held tightly against him.

Lights shattered and sparks lit into flames that burst around them. With a muted *thwump* the tapestries caught fire.

The great hall floor cracked beneath his feet as Alexander ran for the kitchen.

Coven members joined him in the scramble for safety.

With a sharp *crack,* fissures appeared in the pillars of the great hall, snaking up at dizzying speed. The entire fucking castle was coming down on their heads.

Roderick appeared beside him, holding Maeve cradled against him. "Outside." Roderick panted against the strength of the wind pummeling him. "We need to get outside."

Panicked animals tangled underfoot, and he nearly went down hard. Warren's hand beneath his elbow steadied him.

Flames licked the supporting wood beams and lit them in a *whoosh*.

Water poured down the stairs, and when they reached the kitchen, the taps had been ripped off and water was careening into the air, adding to the growing pool on the floor.

Warren leaned through the outside door of the kitchen and grabbed him, pulling him into the bailey. "Is everybody here?"

Voices rose in answer and Alexander mentally ticked off Andy, Debra, Taylor, and Niamh.

Maeve stirred against Roderick and pointed. "Look."

The retaining wall that guarded the cliff to the caverns had collapsed into rubble, but Maeve was pointing at the sky. Green, yellow, red, and blue light boiled out of the cave to meet in the skies above them. The four colors swirled and twined around each other, going faster and faster, thickening and growing in strength.

Mounting pressure pushed at his brain, making his skull scream in protest. His muscles strained and contracted, sinews snapped, his joints popped from their sockets.

Bronwyn, Maeve, Niamh, and Taylor screamed as one, their bodies contorting, their faces a rictus of intense pain.

Above him, in the sky, the four strands of colored light twined into one swirling vortex.

Boom!

Sinead buried her face in Noah's chest. She felt numb as her emotions struggled to catch up with her brain. Dhara had been shot. Dhara was dead.

The earth throbbed beneath her feet, strong enough to make Noah stagger and tighten his grip.

"What's happening?" Alannah's eyes widened in alarm.

From the previously clear sky, lightning cracked around them. Rain hit them in a punishing, stinging deluge. The ground shook. Wind howled, pushing trees this way and that.

Noah dropped to his knees, taking her and Alannah with him.

Earth opened like a glowing wound inside her chest. Her connection to her element shone in a bright beacon of pure green light. Glowing light surrounded her and Alannah, so strong it hurt to look at it.

She lurched for Alannah and clung to her.

Noah wrapped his arms around the two of them.

Wind pushed against them, picking up dust and winding it into a screaming, wailing cone that surrounded their group.

"It's earth," Alannah cried. "It's active."

"Fuck." Noah tensed. "It's so much more than that."

A fireball shot through the night and exploded in the trees around them.

Noah pointed. "Look."

"Dhara?" Kate wrestled out of Zach's hold.

Everything stilled.

Dhara's body rose in the air, pure white light surrounding her. Higher she rose, pillowed on the white light. Her hair streamed around her head, her clothes flapping and battering her still form. She rose above the height of the vehicle—six feet, eight feet, twenty feet, forty feet.

Boom!

An explosion flattened them all to the ground.

Sinead spat dirt as she struggled to her hands and knees.

Around her, the others shook heads and limbs as they tried to get off their bellies.

And Dhara…

She was enshrouded in light. It came from all around her and within her. It beamed from every part of her, so intense Sinead had to shield her eyes from it.

Everything fell silent around them. Earth thrummed low and content within Sinead.

Alannah struggled to her feet, her mouth open, her eyes shimmering with unshed tears.

Dhara drifted slowly back to the earth. Feather light, her body crumpled to the still ground beneath it.

Kate scrabbled toward her and reached her first. "Dhara?"

Dhara lay inert on the ground. The wind died, the rain stopped, and the fire disappeared. In the vegetation all around them, insects buzzed. The moon shone down from a cloudless sky. Nothing was burned, nothing was damaged, and it was as if the last five minutes had never happened.

Sinead shook her head to clear her thoughts.

Dhara's chest rose and fell.

"The bullet wound?" Zach scrabbled closer. He looked up at Kate. "It's gone."

Kate shook her sister gently. "Dhara?"

Dhara's chest rose, once, and then fell. She opened her eyes. Raising one hand, she cupped Kate's cheek. "Blessed."

Everything stopped.

Alexander looked around him, trying to convince his brain that the past few minutes had really happened. The wind was gone. The sea had fallen peaceful. In the clear moonlight, Baile looked as she always had.

Roderick stumbled over. "What…"

The gleaming white light in the sky folded into itself and disappeared.

"Did that just happen?" Warren staggered toward them.

Roderick stared at Baile. "She's fine."

Coughing, Andy helped Debra to her feet. "She's more than fine. She's stronger than ever."

Eyes glazed, Roderick checked his connection with Baile.

"And?" Alexander dusted off Bronwyn and pulled her to standing. He checked every visible inch of her.

"She's…" Roderick frowned. "Present. Really present."

The umber coimhdeacht markings stood out darkly against his arms, almost throbbing with their intensity.

Warren looked at Roderick's markings and then his own. "I can feel her."

"Baile?" Niamh knocked Warren's checking hands away.

"No." Warren checked on Taylor. "Goddess."

"She's here," Taylor whispered. "Goddess is here."

"Eh?" Roderick glanced at her and went back to righting Maeve's hair and clothes.

"Goddess is amongst us." Taylor slapped both hands over her mouth, as if she could hardly believe what had come out of her mouth. "The balance has been established. The two are now on one plane."

Warren crouched beside his daughter. "What are you saying, sweetheart?"

"I'm saying that Goddess is with us." Taylor grimaced and scrunched up her face. "She's a person, just like us."

"Blessed." A tender smile lit Dhara's face as she looked from Kate to Sinead and Alannah. Silvery light surrounded her irises. "My Blessed."

Kate shook her head. "Dhara?"

"Yes, Dhara." The silver light in her eyes dimmed. "But also, not Dhara." Her voice assumed a light, singsong quality. "For the battle to commence, two must be flesh. The balance must be established."

"I don't understand." Tears streamed down Alannah's face.

Gathering Dhara closer, Kate sobbed. "Are you okay, Dhara?"

Dhara shook her head and her eyes cleared. "Kate?"

"What the fuck?" Zach whispered. "She smells different."

Noah sniffed, his movements stiff and clumsy. "I can't really get her smell."

"She's in here." Dhara rubbed her chest.

Kate frowned and wiped her face. "Who, darling?"

"Goddess." Dhara blinked at her. "It's me, but there's also someone else here. I can hear her, sense what she's thinking. It's like she's part of me and separate at the same time."

"I don't understand." Kate sat back and stared at her sister. Then she shook her head. "Is this a dream?'

Zach knelt beside her. "No, Katy. She's as real as you or me."

"Really?" Kate blinked at him, childlike in her desperate need for Dhara to be alive and well.

"See." Zach cupped Dhara's chin and turned her face fully to Kate. "The bullet wound has disappeared."

Sinead could have sworn Dhara got shot, then the world went to shit, then Dhara floated in the air, and now she was lying there saying she was Goddess. Minus any sign she'd been hurt. She rubbed her head. "I'm so bloody confused."

Dhara's eyes flashed with that weird silver light, and her

voice became older and more melodic. "I have chosen this vessel for my rebirth. But she is a child of mine, and I would not remove the Blessed soul that resides within. In time, we will become one, and she will be both Dhara and Goddess."

Sinead wanted to kneel and frown all at the same time.

"Blessed." Dhara/Goddess turned her strange eyes toward her and Alannah. "I am vulnerable in this form. I must be taken to Baile."

Alannah bowed her head. "Yes, Goddess."

Sinead couldn't manage much more than a nod.

"Let's get going," Zach said. "Let's get you to the airport and out of here."

The silver light vanished, and Dhara shook her head. "That is so weird when she does that."

Alannah snort laughed. When they all looked at her, she put both hands over her mouth to try to stop the laugher, but her eyes brimmed. "I'm sorry." She choked. "But I'm having a hysterical reaction."

As if Alannah had freed them all, first Zach, then Kate, and then Sinead all started laughing. It was all too much.

Dhara was also laughing. She stopped and paled. "I think I'm going to pass out now."

And she did.

———

BEAUTIFUL, wondrous earth! It awoke in Rhiannon with a pain that spilled into pleasure. Earth was awake, and she had missed it for all these years. But now, now it was hers to tap and use. All four elements awake and sparking.

She dipped her hands into the dead body in front of her. Some minion whose name she could not remember, and did not care to.

Blood magic savaged her. It almost threw her to her knees

and broke her connection with the blood. It pummeled her from the inside and out, it wrenched her organs and exploded through her blood. So much power available to her now, and as soon as Baile fell, she would not have to use the blood anymore.

Then she felt *her*. Goddess.

"Oh my." She smiled. That was a game changer, and one she had planned for, but still the thrill of it delighted her. "She is amongst us," she said to the crowd gathered before her. And whatever had taken human form could now be killed.

Shoulder to shoulder, they packed into the abandoned soccer stadium. A sea of faces all turned up to her, waiting for her next command.

Raising blood-stained hands to the sky, she shouted, "It is time!"

CHAPTER THIRTY-SIX

Dhara lay at Kate's feet, pale but breathing easily. It was hard to believe the last ten minutes had happened. Hard to credit what had transpired, harder still to accept it.

Sinead knelt beside Kate. Dhara looked so pale and fragile, and horribly young for what she'd just said. But there was one part of her statement Sinead could get behind. "We need to get her to Baile."

"I know." Ashen and staring at her sister, Kate nodded. "I'm just trying to make sense of what happened here." She smoothed Dhara's hair from her forehead. "Our parents died when she was so young. I guess I've raised her, changed her diapers, taught her to use a knife and fork, kept her safe. And now this." She looked shellshocked. "She's Goddess now?"

"No." Alannah looked calm and serene and was doing better keeping it together than the rest of them combined. "Goddess is part of her, but Dhara is still there."

Kate peered into Dhara's face. "Well, shit! What do I do with her now?"

"Come, Katy." Zach raised her to her feet. "We need to get moving. We're sitting ducks here."

"Sinead?" Frowning, Alannah stared at Sinead's hands. "Are you hurt?"

"No." Sinead did a quick mental body scan. She felt fine, exhausted and completely freaked out, but fine. "Why?"

"Your hands." Alannah gaped at Sinead's hands. "They're covered in blood."

Alannah was right. Blood spattered her hands and wrists. Sinead couldn't remember touching anyone, except…

"Fuck!" Zach whirled on Noah. "How bad?"

Noah shook his head. "Not bad."

"Motherfucker!" Zach closed on Noah and pulled the sides of his jacket open.

Sinead's pulse leaped into her throat. She forgot to breathe. The entire front of Noah's shirt was bloodstained. Shaking her head, trying to refute what her eyes were telling her, Sinead took a step closer to Noah. *Mine*! Fierce, primal, elemental, the word pounded through her being.

Noah had taken a bullet. Noah was bleeding. Noah was hurt. But Noah could not, would not…Her mind skewed away from the notion of Noah not being here any longer. She refused to accept even the remotest possibility. Matters remained unsettled between them. They didn't even have a relationship, but he had found her, and she would not let him go.

"He's been hit," Zach said as he lowered Noah to the ground.

Needing to be close to him, Sinead lurched across the distance separating them.

"I'm fine." Noah smiled at her. Blood flecked his lips.

Zach stared at her over Noah's head. "He's not fine." He lifted Noah's shirt and swore again. "He's really not fine."

"A hospital." Sinead couldn't let him die. Not like this, and not now. Not before she had even explored whatever it was that they had between them. "We need to get him to a hospital."

"No." Zach shook his head. "His wolf genetics will lead to questions I can't answer. They can't help him there."

Surely Zach didn't mean to leave him to die. Not while Sinead had a fucking living cell in her system. "Do something."

"I need to get him back to pack land." Zach stood. "The land will help him heal, and his wolf can take over and accelerate the healing."

Sinead stood. "Then that's what we're going to do." Anything to save Noah.

"Nope." Zach stood and hoisted Noah in his arms. "That's what I'm going to do."

"You can't walk there." Sinead would wrestle the big bastard into the car if she had to.

"I'm stronger than you and faster," Zach said. "And I can call for backup before I go."

"No." Sinead wasn't going to take the chance. "We're going to drive you to pack land and see you safe."

"You can't." Zach gestured Dhara. "You heard what she said. Those bastards heading for the community are still out there. Along with whoever shot us. You know what you have to do."

"He is not going to die." The conviction grew in Sinead with every passing moment. "He is not even going to come close to dying."

"You—"

"Zach." Kate touched his arm. "She's his mate."

A muscle jumped in Zach's jaw before he nodded. "Fine. But the minute we cross into pack land, he and I are shifting, and you are going straight for the airport."

They'd fight about that later, but for now, Sinead nodded.

Zach placed Noah in the car and then came back for Dhara. He lay her carefully on the backseat, her head in Kate's lap.

Zach flattened the accelerator as they peeled away down the road. Wind whipped through the shattered windows, whistling and drumming against their ears.

Sinead took Noah's hand. His eyes were closed, and she didn't know if he could hear her. She was operating on instinct.

"I'm here. And if you die on me, I'm going to fucking hunt you down in the afterlife."

She couldn't be sure, but he might have squeezed her hand back.

"You have so much explaining to do." She wiped blood away from his perfectly formed lips with her hand. "And you're not getting away with one kiss and then bye-bye. You owe me, wolfman."

"Sinead." Alannah touched her other hand. "We need to call Baile."

Alannah's suggestion yanked her away from Noah. Sinead couldn't believe her sister had suggested that. "You know why we can't."

Bloody hell, they hadn't even discussed their plan to leave Baile in case Rhiannon was listening. Now, when Noah was down and Dhara so vulnerable, was the very worst time to chance it.

"Things might have changed." Alannah got a stubborn set to her jaw. "They know earth is active by now, and we need their help. We've got a dying man, and a corporeal Goddess. We're driving a car with the windows shot out, and we're surrounded by people who want us dead. We've got a target on our backs, and if there is even the slightest chance they can help us, we need to take it."

She wanted to care about Goddess and earth and the bigger picture, but her attention focused on the man breathing strenuously and leaking too much blood. Their backs were against the wall. If they didn't do something, it was only a matter of time before they were screwed anyway. For Noah, for Dhara, it was worth the risk. She nodded. "Do it."

Alannah grabbed her mobile phone and dialed.

"Alannah?" Alexander answered the call. "Bloody hell, it's good to hear your voice."

"Hi," Alannah said.

"Are you okay?" Alexander's perfectly formed vowels pinged down the line. "We've been worried sick about you two. You can't believe…"

It was hard to hear over the wind in the car and Alannah ducked her head into the seat well. "Is it safe to talk?"

"It's safe, sweetie," Alexander said. "Although, I don't know what the hell you girls did over there, but we've had an interesting hour or so."

"It's too much to explain now," Alannah said. "But we need help."

"Name it."

"We need to get out of here. Sinead and myself and one other."

Kate leaned forward. "Two others. Where my sister goes, I go."

"Mate." Zach's growl made the hair on Sinead's nape rise.

Kate glared at him. "I'll be back, but I can't let her go without me. Goddess or not, she's still only fifteen."

After a long moment, Zach nodded. "Make sure you do."

"We need to come home. As fast as possible," Alannah said.

Sinead couldn't hear what Alexander said next.

"Andy?" Alannah said. "Yes, hi. We're okay." She glanced at Sinead. "We're mostly okay, but we need to come home as quickly as we can. It couldn't be more important."

"No problem," Andy said.

Sinead stopped listening. She didn't know how Andy did what he did, but if he was on this, she had confidence it would happen.

"It's okay." Alannah ended the call. "Andy's got…contacts." Her face gentled as she looked at Noah. "How is he?"

"He's breathing." Sinead kept her palm pressed against the slow beat of Noah's heart. As long as she could feel that, she had hope.

Kate touched her shoulder. "He's a wolf," she said. "They're unbelievably strong, and they heal fast."

"But…" Sinead couldn't speak the rest of her thoughts. Too much blood, too big of a hole in his torso.

"Keep touching him," Kate said. "Even if he's unconscious, he can feel you through the mate bond, and he'll know you're here. It'll give him strength."

In the dim light, the fine, clear lines of Noah's face were made of shadows and peaks. She didn't know what he meant to her, but she knew he couldn't die. She also knew that their paths had just diverged. Before anything, she was cré-witch, a disciple of Goddess. She owed her coven and her Goddess, and she owed Alannah to see her to safety. But still, this man in her arms tugged at parts of her she'd never known existed. "How do I leave him here?"

"Because you have to," Zach said. "Because he would want you to do what you have to do." His gaze met hers through the rearview mirror. "And because you're leaving him with me, and I always take care of my wolves."

Sinead found herself nodding. Zach had a strange way of reassuring her and making her believe him.

Alannah took her free hand. The warm contact gave her another glimmer of hope.

Leaning down, Sinead put her mouth beside Noah's ear. "Are you listening to me, wolfman?" She didn't wait for him to reply. "You don't get to drop the mate bomb on me, and then leave me. You need to hang in there."

Noah moaned and his eyelids flickered.

"If you don't survive, I'll come back here and kick your furry ass, you get me?"

Alannah peered over the seat to Kate and Dhara in the back. "How is she?"

"She looks like she's sleeping," Kate said. "I don't get any of this."

"Trust in Goddess." Alannah's gaze moved from Kate to Sinead. "When it's darkest is when we need to trust the most."

Kate nodded and then snorted. "You mean, trust in Dhara."

Zach drove them onto a highway. Other cars flashed past. The wind grew so loud through the shot-out windows, nobody could hear each other speak. Trying to protect him from the wind, Sinead crouched over Noah.

She'd only just met the man. She was still processing the wolf thing, for fuck's sake. Never mind the mate zinger or the fact that he was pumping blood from a massive hole in his torso.

The roar of the engine and the wind battered her ears. Her heart fisted in her chest. If she were more like Alannah, able to express her emotions, she would cry. But the tears were frozen inside her, encased in fear.

Alannah's phone rang, and she stuck her finger in her ear to answer it.

"Andy?" she yelled. "What?"

Climbing into the seat well, Alannah pressed the phone to her ear. She nodded and cradled the phone to her shoulder.

"He wants to know where we are." Alannah shouted to Zach. "He's arranging a rendezvous point."

Zach thrust back his hand. "Let me talk to him."

"Do you hear that?" Sinead whispered to Noah. "Help is on the way. And as soon as we get to pack land, you're going to morph or transform or shift, or whatever the bloody hell it is that you do, and you're going to get better." She pressed her cheek against his icy one. "I hope you're listening wolfman, because I'm not asking you, I'm telling you."

Cars blurred as they flew by. Zach ducked from lane to lane, never slowing. Sinead lost track of time. She spoke to Noah, clung to Alannah's hand, and prayed. She prayed as she never had. Prayed for her and Alannah, prayed for Kate and Dhara, and prayed for Noah.

Finally, Zach's curt shout carried over the wind and the engine. "Nearly there."

She wanted to weep with relief, but tears were not an option for her.

"Just a few more minutes," she whispered to Noah. "And you'll be fine. We'll all be fine."

Taking an offramp, Zach slowed for a red light before powering straight through. The road twisted through forest, no streetlamps or ambient light breaking the stygian black around them.

Noah's breathing hitched and stopped. Then he let out a long, slow breath.

"Noah?" Sinead pressed her ear to his mouth.

His breathing rasped against her eardrum. Still alive.

Zach decelerated so fast it almost sent her banging into the back of the seat. She held on to Noah as sand and gravel kicked up under the wheels and pinged against the metal exterior of the car.

"Pack land." Zach killed the engine and jumped out.

He ripped open the back door and reached for Noah.

Sinead didn't want to let him go. If she was holding him, she could stop death from taking him.

Kate touched her shoulder. "Zach knows what to do. He's the alpha. He will know what's best for Noah."

Still, Sinead had to fight her protective instincts to loosen her grasp on the man in her arms.

When she did, Zach pulled him from the vehicle.

Sinead cried out at the rough treatment and lunged to protect him.

Zach stripped, throwing clothes in every direction and then he stripped Noah. He bellowed in pain as he shifted from man to wolf in seconds.

The large wolf loomed over the fallen man and growled

Sinead's nape hair stood straight up at the menace in the sound.

"Zach is using his alpha compulsion," Kate said from beside her. "He is forcing Noah to shift."

Zach-wolf growled lower and deeper, his huge teeth closing over Noah's throat.

"Don't." Sinead would rip that wolf limb from limb if he hurt Noah.

Kate caught her arm and held her back. "Let him. Noah's wolf will respond on instinct. Zach needs to activate that instinctive response."

Sinead bared her teeth at the massive beast. "As long as he understands he's going to make a very nice throw rug if he hurts Noah."

A low, dull *thwacka, thwacka, thwacka* came from the left.

Noah's skin shimmered and pulsed, and then came a series of pops, snaps and sickening squelches and Noah shifted to wolf.

Dark patches marred his side, and he whined.

Sinead crouched beside him and stroked him. "You're beautiful." Now the tears wanted to make themselves welcome. "So bloody beautiful, and I need you to do whatever it is you do and be okay."

Noah whined and licked his lips.

Throwing back his wolf head, Zach howled.

The sound drowned out all the night noises, even the growing sound from their left.

An answering howl responded, and then another, and another, until the night was filled with howling wolves.

"Wild wolves," Kate said. "They're coming for him."

Thwacka, thwacka, thwacka. The sound had grown louder now, and lights appeared above the tree line.

Alannah pointed. "I'm guessing that's Andy's cavalry."

Wolves slipped out of the forest. Ignoring the humans and the approaching helicopter, they surrounded Noah and Zach. The wolves wove around Zach and Noah, whining, whimpering, growling.

Air whipped around her head, the sound of propeller blades banging in her ears, as the chopper hovered above them.

Alannah was looking at her phone screen. "It's them," she yelled. "Andy's people."

Stones and dirt stung their skins as the chopper blades stirred up the earth.

"Help me." Alannah grabbed her hand.

Sinead gave her earth on instinct, and Alannah settled the flying dirt around them.

Zach looked up at her, his pale blue eyes boring into her and snarled.

"We need to go." Kate tugged on her arm. "Let the wolves do what they need to do. They know what's best for him. We need to get safe." She squeezed Sinead's arm. "And Noah won't let them help him until he knows you're safe."

Sinead leaned closer to Noah-wolf. "I'm going now because Kate says that's the best thing for you." She stroked his furry head. "But don't you die on me. Promise me."

He nuzzled her hand and gave a weak growl.

"Promise me." She sank her fingers into his ruff. "Promise me you'll live."

From the side, Zach-wolf nudged her and snarled, his eyes luminous.

Somehow, Sinead stumbled out of the way of the landing chopper.

Two men jumped out with a stretcher and loaded up Dhara.

Alannah spoke to them, yelling right beside their ears.

And then Alannah was pulling on her arm, tugging her away from her wolf.

Everything in Sinead rebelled, but Kate's advice made her force herself into the helicopter. As the machine rose in the air with her, Alannah, Kate and Dhara, she peered through the window at the circle of wolves surrounding Noah.

"Trust in Goddess." Alannah folded her into a tight hug. "Trust in Goddess."

CHAPTER THIRTY-SEVEN

"What the hell?" Niamh shook Warren awake.

Outside Baile, Pack howled in a continuous keen that jarred against her ears and vibrated down her connection with them.

"What is it?" Warren came instantly awake.

"The wolves." Niamh touched the aching center of her chest. Wolves poured grief through the bond into her. It felt like she was being split apart from the core. "They're mourning."

Alexander sat and looked up from the opposite sofa. "Mourning what?"

After the call from Alannah, nobody had gone to bed, and they were all gathered in the sitting room. As they held vigil, she must have fallen asleep.

"They feel a wolf's pain." Niamh tried to put into words what was more an outpouring of emotion than anything comprehensive. "They are howling the pain for another wolf."

"What wolf?" Warren tapped into her bond with the wolves. He went still as the feeling hit him, and then wrapped her in his arms. He felt the intense grief the wolves were sending.

On the sofa opposite them, Alexander sat with Bronwyn

sleeping with her head on his lap. Maeve and Roderick were curled around each other in one of the large armchairs. Taylor and Debra slept on another sofa closer to the fireplace. Debra cradled Taylor against her.

The door opened, and Andy strode in. "They have them."

Bronwyn blinked her eyes open and sat up. "The twins?"

"Sasha's people just contacted me." Andy had a mobile in one hand and his laptop in the other. "They confirmed that two minutes ago that they picked up Alannah and Sinead plus another woman and a teen girl from a rural location in Ontario. They're enroute to the airport now. Sinead and Alannah are fine."

<hr>

TIME MELTED FOR SINEAD. She kept her eyes on the tiny huddle of wolves until the chopper took them out of sight.

Alannah held her close, trying to comfort her through a loss she didn't understand.

Sound, noise, light, and shadow all merged into a confusing miasma that she lived through one breath at a time.

The chopper flew for what felt like forever until it finally landed.

More people swarmed around her, guiding her and the others into cars, pressing bottles of water into their hands, asking questions that she was unable to answer.

Alannah handled it all, her hand gripping Sinead's the only anchor that kept Sinead moving forward.

Vehicles moved in convoy through lighted streets and light traffic. Dawn stained the horizon pale gray as they arrived at an airport and drove past a massive lighted terminal building.

More people. More discussions. More nodding and handling of paperwork and passports and stuff.

Then, they were loaded into a compact, sleek jet.

Sinead registered take off by the change in cabin pressure and the inertia pushing her back in her seat.

A man in a neat uniform put a meal on the tray table Alannah had opened for her.

Some part of Sinead's brain registered that she wasn't dealing very well. If it hadn't been for Alannah, she wouldn't have made it through. She needed to get it together. This was bigger than her and some man who had better hair than her.

"You need to eat." Alannah took the cling film off her meal. "And then we all need to sleep."

Sinead's brain stirred into action. "How's Dhara?"

"Still asleep." Alannah put eating utensils in her hands. "Can you believe they have a bedroom on this plane? She's on the bed."

"Good." Sinead poked at her food. "Kate needs to eat as well."

Nodding, Alannah stood. "I'll go and get her. Maybe force a glass of wine down her throat."

"What time is it?" Sinead peered through the windows at the white clouds surrounding the plane.

Alannah shrugged. "All things considered, who the fuck cares."

MAGS HAD ONLY EVER BEEN on small boats. When you compared them to this floating palace—teeny boats. She woke to sun streaming through the windows—forget calling those expanses of gleaming glass portholes—showing off a stream of azure sky and sapphire sea. She didn't know how long she'd slept, but she had a vague memory of a beautiful sunset.

Nestled behind her, Jack's big, hot body cradled her like a nutshell.

After finding her, he'd bathed her, dressed her, tucked her into bed, and stayed with her. Emma had dropped in after her bath and they'd spoken until dinner. Nothing important, just chatting and keeping her fears at bay. After the dinner Emma had insisted on, she'd drifted off to the calming sound of their voices.

She was alive. She was well. And she was on her way back to Baile under the protection of the two people who would fight and die to make her safe.

Jack's arm lay heavy and inert against her waist. His thighs cradled hers and *that* part of him pressed against her bottom.

In her lucid moments of captivity, she'd lain in whatever bed they'd put her in and dreamed of a day when she would be with him again. He was her everything. She'd seen him long before he'd appeared in person, and he was her one. Her person.

She nestled back into his heat.

Jack grumbled against her ear, and his arm tightened around her middle. "Mags?"

"I need…" She wasn't confident with men like Niamh, or sure of her beauty like Alannah and Sinead. She only knew that she and Jack had this time, here and now, and she had no idea what tomorrow would bring. Or the next hour for that matter. They'd waited in Moscow, and come too close to losing each other.

Shifting, Jack raised himself on his elbow beside her. "Sweetheart." His sleep ruffled hair tangled around his head. Those beautiful light brown eyes looked almost green as he gazed at her tenderly. "You've had a bugger of a few weeks."

"I know." She had the vague idea that if a man wanted you, he would kind of take it from here. "But we said, in Moscow." They'd said a lot in Moscow, and she needed to get more specific. "In the bathroom that time, when you stayed with me while I was in the bath." Her face heated under his steady regard. "We said, that if we were ever in this position again."

His expression grew slumberous. "You said that part." Jack didn't seem to be getting the hint.

"Yes, I did. And now we're in a similar position again. So?"

"Mags." He caught one of her flapping hands and pressed a kiss into her palm. "I would like nothing better than to take this where we both want it to go, but you've been through fucking hell. You're vulnerable. Yesterday, you were sobbing—"

"I'm feeling better now." She gave an experimental hip wiggle to illustrate a point. Niamh always said you had to keep it simple with men.

Jack gave a pained chuckle and shifted his hips away from her bottom. "You're not in an emotional state to be making dec—"

She lost patience with him. "You know what makes me angry, Jack?"

His look turned wary. "No, what?"

"People making decisions for me and treating me like a child." She pressed her bottom firmly against his man bits. She knew a few words for that, but they all made her blush. "I'm not a child."

"I know that, Mags." He gripped her hip to keep her still. "I know that very fucking well, but I'm trying to be a decent guy here."

"Well, stop it." Mags turned to her back and wrapped her arms around his neck. "I don't want you deciding whether I'm in my right mind, or emotionally stable." She pressed her fingers into his nape and brought his head closer. "All you get to decide is whether or not you want to do this with me. Yes or no, Jack?" She was so praying for yes.

"Mags." He growled. "You can't even say the words."

Not without blushing. "Yes, I can."

"Then say them." His gaze glinted with challenge, and something far more thrilling. "Tell me what you want me to do."

Just because she didn't swear, didn't mean she didn't know how. "Fuck me, Jack," she whispered.

Jack's eyes widened. "A little more graphic than I was going for, but that'll do."

He slanted his mouth over hers and kissed her.

Mags opened to the touch of his tongue, and a delicious melty feeling spread through her. She kissed him back, chasing the thrilling glide of his tongue against hers, winding her arms tighter around his neck to press him closer.

Groaning, Jack rolled them until she was lying atop him. Teeth clashed, and lips lost contact briefly, before his mouth was back again, and Jack wasn't messing around. He took ownership of her mouth. He broke their kiss and nipped at her bottom lip. "Mags," he grated harshly. "You've got no fucking idea how much I want this. Want you."

She most certainly did, and she slammed her mouth on his to show him.

Jack gripped her hips and positioned her where he wanted her.

Pressed against her, he was hot and hard through the layers of her knickers and his sweatpants. She wriggled, wanting the annoying clothes out of the way.

He grabbed her bottom and moved her against his…cock. Even the word thrilled her. Not as much as the actual cock, but still.

His hands slid beneath her panties and gripped her bare flesh, almost bruising in their grip. And Mags loved it. She kissed him harder.

Her body was burning up. Her skin wanted more friction; her core needed more contact. Her breasts ached for his touch.

Tearing her mouth from his, she sat up. Without hesitation she whipped her T-shirt over her head and threw it across the room.

Jack's gaze fastened on her bare breasts. "Shit." His hands abandoned her bottom to fasten on her breasts.

They were big hands, palming her completely, darker hued than her pale skin.

Mags arched into the contact. It was like there was a direct connection between her breasts and her core. He strummed her nipples with calloused thumbs, and it resonated between her thighs.

Half sitting, he fastened his mouth around one nipple.

The heat of his mouth was scorching, shooting through all her nerve endings. Whimpers, and soft moans and pants were coming out of her mouth as he lavished attention on first one breast then the other.

She wanted him to keep doing that forever and she wanted more, so much more. "Jack."

"What, sweetheart?" Color flushed his cheekbones, and his breathing was as ragged as hers. "Tell me what you want."

"More. Do More." She ground down on his cock.

He dragged one big hand to her panties and stopped at the edge. "More here?"

"Yes." She would beg if that's what he wanted, but she wanted to feel his touch there, between her thighs were she was so hot and so achy and so needy.

His gaze glittered dangerously as he slid his forefinger beneath the top of her panties an inch. "Say it."

"Touch me." That one finger, so near and yet not nearly close enough. "Touch me there."

"Where?" He slid the rest of his fingers into the top of her panties and waited.

She undulated against his hand. "There. Touch me there."

"Your pussy?"

"Yes." She lifted slightly to give him access.

Jack slid his hand between her thighs, his big fingers parting her folds. "Fuck, you're wet."

"Yes." And getting wetter. "For you, Jack."

He found her clitoris and stroked, slow and sure.

Mags pressed into his touch, increasing the pressure.

He slid a finger inside her, his thumb playing across her clitoris.

Mags said something, moaned things, actual words or not, she couldn't tell. Her entire attention was focused on where he was touching her, stroking her, building the pressure.

Jack's hand left her, and she cried out a protest.

Then he shifted beneath her, tugging down his track pants and baring himself.

Mags gasped. She hadn't thought they were quite that big. Fascinated, she wrapped a hand around him.

On a hiss, Jack jerked his hips into her hold. "Like that." He cradled his big hand over hers and moved her over him. "Like that, sweetheart."

He was hotter than she'd imagined, the skin velvety over a hard core.

Mags thrilled in the power she had over him. She couldn't take her eyes off the way he looked in their hands, the way his big body writhed and thrust to increase the motion.

And suddenly, it wasn't enough. "I want you inside me," she said.

Jack grabbed her hip with one hand and his shaft with the other. He positioned the tip at her entrance and slowly entered her.

He was big, and she'd never done this before, and Mags's body tensed at the new intrusion. But she was ready for him, and she slid down on him a tiny bit.

Jack grit his teeth, his jaw tight, the tendons in his neck tense.

He brought his thumb back and stroked her clitoris.

Mags relaxed more and let him deeper inside her.

It wasn't entirely comfortable, but her body knew what it wanted, and she slid farther down on him.

"Slowly," he rasped. "I'm not going anywhere."

The pleasure from his thumb eased her further, and she took him deeper still.

Carefully, inch by inch, he went, until he was fully seated inside her.

She rocked her hips on him experimentally and gasped at the new sensation, a fullness that felt so good and so right. Mags did it again.

"Jesus." Jack's grip on her hip tightened. "I'm not sure how—" On a groan, he thrust up into her.

Pleasure built from where he stroked her, and she moved with him. The pressure increased, building from deep, deep within her, and she forgot the stretch or any discomfort, and just let it take over. Mags's orgasm curled up from her toes and took every muscle with it, in a spasm and release that sent her flying.

Jack took hold of both her hips and controlled their joining. He moved faster now, thrusting harder and deeper.

A new sort of pleasure started up from where they were joined. He hit a sweet spot inside her, and she chased that new sensation with every grind and jolt of her hips.

When she came again, Jack was right behind her. His fingers digging into her hips, his hips jerking.

Mags dropped to his chest, still joined to him.

He folded her in his arms and held her close to his heartbeat, the skin hot and damp where they touched.

"Mags." He tensed slightly. "No condom, sweetheart."

"We don't need one." She pressed her face into his neck and inhaled his sweaty, musky sex smell. She could get so used to that smell. "Goddess handles that with her witches."

He stroked her spine. "Right."

And then she giggled. "And there is still the matter of those four children."

Jack's chest rumbled beneath her ear as he hugged her tighter. "Yes, there is that."

CHAPTER THIRTY-EIGHT

Alannah hid her concern about Sinead behind being busy and useful. It's what she did best, after all. She managed to bully her sister into eating and drinking, and even closing her eyes for a bit during the flight.

In the back, Kate had fallen asleep next to Dhara on the large bed. Dhara, who was now glowing with a faint pearlescent light to her skin.

Ah well. Alannah tucked that little fact away with all the other stuff that had her brain in a scramble.

Wing lights winked and penetrated the dark surrounding the plane. She made herself a gin and tonic and sat by one of the windows and stared at the flashing wingtip.

Earth was active, she felt it thrumming through her entire being, but she and Sinead hadn't even had a moment to celebrate the success of their mission. Truth be told, neither of them felt much like celebrating. Activating earth had come at a cost for both of them, and Goddess alone knew how much it was going to demand from Dhara and Kate in the future. And all those people scrambling for their lives in Ottawa. Alannah prayed they all found safety.

As relieved as she was that Dhara hadn't had to die to activate earth, the situation had just gotten so much more complicated.

Dhara and Goddess were now one being, and a vulnerable fifteen-year-old being at that.

She added more gin to her tonic and took a healthy sip.

Sinead whimpered in her sleep before settling down again.

She studied Sinead's features, so nearly the same as hers, as her sister slept. Sinead's nose turned up a little more on the end, and her eyes were slightly larger. Alannah had a pale beauty spot near her left eye, but they were only details the two of them really noticed. They'd never really spoken of falling in love and having partners. They'd always had each other, and she supposed, there had been this tacit idea that whoever else came into their lives, they would always be twins first and partners to another second.

At least, she'd always had that notion.

Her glass seemed to have emptied itself, so she poured another. She'd never been much of a drinker, but the situation kind of called for it.

They were going home. Home to Baile. And for her, home to Thomas. The gin eased some of the tension from her shoulders, and she took another hefty sip. Alannah couldn't say how or when he'd become more than a charming, amusing companion. He had made her laugh, always popped into being beside her, and woven himself into her days seamlessly. To be quite honest, she hadn't really registered how important he had become to her until people around them started taking notice.

At least, she now had Sinead's blessing.

Alannah snorted into her drink. As if that made a bugger of a difference to what she and Thomas faced. She owed Sinead at least part of an apology. Much of her anger at her twin had been directed at the situation, and her own frustration with it. She didn't want a relationship with a spirit. Spirits couldn't hold you, kiss you, make love to you.

The attendant made his way down the dimly lit cabin toward her. "We'll be landing in just under an hour," he whispered.

"Thank you." Alannah smiled and finished her drink.

Onwards.

She got up and woke first Sinead and then Kate.

The attendant brought them some pastries and coffee, which nobody touched.

Sinead glanced at Dhara and did a comic double-take. Sidling close to Alannah, she whispered, "Is she glowing?"

"Yup."

"Buggering hell."

"Quite."

As Kate didn't comment on the glow, neither Alannah nor Sinead said a word about it. All three of them went about getting ready for landing, which, considering they had only a few bags between them, took all of four minutes.

Kate pulled a croissant into tiny pieces and scattered them across the tray. She jerked her head at Dhara. "She's still…asleep."

"Right." Alannah did her best to sound reassuring. "I'm sure she'll wake when the time is right."

Sinead nodded enthusiastically. "Absolutely. I mean, a lot has happened. Perfectly natural she'd be exhausted."

Kate's eyes narrowed, and she looked from one to the other before chuckling softly. "You both suck at lying."

"Right." Sinead sighed. "Truth is, we don't know any more than you do."

"True." Kate grimaced and sipped her coffee. "Let's agree to stick to the truth with each other." She drained her cup and placed it back on the tray. "I kind of think the time for platitudes and half-truths went winging past on a flying pig a few hours ago."

Sinead laughed, and some of the tension in the cabin eased.

The attendant returned and cleared their trays. "The captain asked me to let you know that transport is waiting for you when we land." He made quick work of the crumbs around Kate. "She said to let you know that all precautions have been taken and to be prepared for a swift extraction."

"Sounds nasty," Sinead murmured.

Kate gestured Dhara. "What about my sister?"

"Preparations have been made," the attendant said. "A team is waiting to load her onto the transport as she currently is."

"Good." Kate nodded and stared at Dhara. "Goddess alone knows—" She snorted a laugh. "I have to stop saying that, because apparently Goddess is on the plane with us and currently unconscious."

"Dhara knows just doesn't have the same ring to it," Sinead said.

The fasten seat belts light blinked on, and the cabin pressure changed as the plane descended.

Out the window, the plane broke through the clouds, and a blanket of lights spread over the land they were hurtling toward.

Sinead looked at Dhara. "I can't wait to hear what Roderick has to say about this."

And Alannah laughed. She really couldn't help it.

True to the attendant's warning, the plane landed, and the doors opened. Men and women in combat fatigues eased into the plane with a stretcher and scooped Dhara onto it. Other men and women hustled her, Sinead, and Kate into a waiting van. Their bags were loaded, doors were slammed shut and the convoy moved forward.

It was full night outside, and their procession moved fast, barely stopping other than when it was absolutely necessary.

An armed guard sat beside the driver, constantly scanning outside their van.

Another peered out the back window, weapon at the ready.

Three sedans drove in front of them and another three behind.

Alannah felt like a bloody queen. One with a broken crown.

Given recent events, it was no surprise that she, Sinead, and Kate remained as tense as their guards. Their convoy hit the highway and picked up speed, moving silently and swiftly over the miles separating them from home.

Occasionally the guard in the passenger seat would murmur something through an earpiece.

"What's with you and Zach?" Sinead broke the silence and stared at Kate.

Kate started slightly and her face went carefully blank. "What do you mean?"

"You know what I mean." Sinead fixed her with a no-crap stare.

"It's…screwed up." Kate looked mutinous.

Sinead snorted. "That part we got already."

Kate stared out her window, streetlamps painting her face yellow as they zipped past. "I'm his mate," she said and shrugged. "According to him, anyway."

"And you?" Sinead was never one to let a secret go unpried. Then again, they had nothing better to do as the miles stretched out between them and Baile.

"I don't know." Kate rubbed her chest. "I mean, this is the first time I've been apart from him since we were kids. I miss him."

Sinead touched her own chest and nodded. "I know."

"But he's the pack leader," Kate said. "And I had my responsibilities, and neither of us are good at taking orders. We're much better at giving them."

"What will you do?" Alannah joined the conversation.

"First, I need to see Dhara settled and okay." Kate looked into the back of the van where Dhara lay on her stretcher. "And then…I don't know. My people are scattered, and they're not safe like that."

"Baile has room to spare," Sinead said.

Kate nodded, as if she was considering it. "For now, I just want to see Dhara safe and behind those wards of yours. After that…I'll have some decisions to make."

Sinead nodded. "Well, you're not alone. We're all in this thing together."

"Apparently so," Kate said.

Alannah put into words what had been becoming clearer since Niamh had come back from South Africa. "This fight against Rhiannon is happening all over the world. In separate pockets. We need to find a way to work together."

Sinead growled. "We're buggered if we don't."

They lapsed into silence.

Familiar landmarks appeared outside the vehicle.

"Look." Sinead pointed.

Up in the distance, perched on her hill and barely visible, Baile had just come into view.

Tears sprang into Alannah's eyes. They were almost home. Somehow, the difficulties and terrors of the last few days seemed more manageable, and like there would be answers to their questions.

"Wow." Kate leaned forward. "It's so much bigger than I thought it was."

"It's the finest castle of her age in England." Dampness glistened in Sinead's eyes. "War hasn't touched her, and she's not been disturbed by time. She's perfect."

As they traveled closer, rectangles of light blinked from the stone walls.

Alannah played a game with herself, imagining who was behind those windows. Perhaps Mags, making one of her crazy skirts, or Alexander and Roderick arguing, or Maeve taking the piss out of Roderick. She pushed away any thoughts of Thomas. They were still too raw.

The Greater Littleton sign flashed past the window.

Alannah felt some of the pressure in her chest ease, as the ache in her heart increased.

"This place is adorable." Kate pressed against her window and stared at Greater Littleton as they wove through the town.

The station, the Hag's Head, the Copper Cauldron, the Toil & Trouble Hardware Shop, the Speckled Grimoire Book Shoppe.

"Neat." Kate chuckled. "All the names are witchy."

"We've been hiding in plain sight," Sinead said.

Then they were circling the village green, the truncated rectangular plinth where Roderick and Maeve had stood still squatting proud in the center. There were a lot of people around for late night in Greater Littleton. More than Alannah had ever seen before.

Their car cleared the village and climbed the hill toward Baile.

Now the details of the castle became clearer and sharper.

As they crossed the wards, Alannah shivered. Earth pulsed stronger than ever beneath her skin. She glanced at Sinead. "Do you feel it?"

"Yup." Sinead grinned at her. "I can feel the wards as well."

Alannah quested out and touched them. Where they had once been faint silvery power lines, they now beamed like runway lights through her mind. "We're safe," she said to Kate. "We've just crossed the wards."

Sinead winced. "But that thing is still in there. The anomaly. We need to remove it."

And there is was, a stain on the glimmering purity of the wards.

"Yes, we do." Alannah took grim satisfaction in the prospect of removing any trace of Rhiannon from Baile forever.

"Baile," Dhara whispered from the back. "I am returned to you."

Kate spun and stared at Dhara.

Dhara tried to sit up and got caught against the restraints. She frowned down at them, and they unclipped and dropped to the side of the stretcher.

The guard sitting beside Dhara jumped.

Dhara smiled at him. "Be calm," she said. "Here, I am my most powerful. Here lies the source of my strength."

Apparently, Goddess was in charge of the Dhara body right now.

The vehicle darkened as they passed under the gatehouse. Tires scrunched against the stones and sand of the bailey, and the convoy stopped.

Alannah scrabbled to open her door. She missed the handle and it opened for her, courtesy of the passenger guard. She almost fell out of the car in her eagerness.

The kitchen door banged open, and Roderick's massive shoulders blocked the light for a moment before he sprinted out.

Sinead scrambled toward him, and he snatched her into his arms and hugged her off her feet. "Blessed."

Laughing, Sinead said, "You'll crush me."

Roderick placed her on her feet, and then Alannah was being yanked into his arms. The familiar size and comfort of Roderick made her cry freely now. He surrounded her in home and safety and everything familiar and good.

Then more people appeared in front of her, laughing, hugging, crying, and all talking at once.

She and Sinead were passed from one person to another in a dizzying tangle.

Roderick caught sight of Dhara and Kate first. He froze and stared.

The pearlescent light surrounding Goddess beamed bright and pure.

"My Lady." Roderick dropped to his knees. "You are amongst us."

One by one, the people around Alannah stopped moving and also went to their knees.

Kate looked uncomfortable.

Goddess smiled and held out her hands. "It is time for me to take my place in the world." Then the light blinked out, and Dhara gave a short, awkward wave. "Hi. I'm Dhara, and this is my sister, Kate."

CHAPTER THIRTY-NINE

"She has the right to know," Maeve insisted. She really didn't feel right about not telling Alannah, but Roderick was being stubborn. What a surprise!

Roderick threw one arm up. "What does Alannah have the right to know? We don't know anything for sure."

"Don't give me that." He drove her mad sometimes. "You know that if there's even a chance of Thomas…" She couldn't say it. "The worst happening, she has the right to know."

"Would it change anything?" He raised an inflexible eyebrow at her. "Even if she knew, it's not going to stop Thomas from going wherever Lavina will go."

They'd gone for a walk in the forest to have this argument. A gloomy, chilly day reflected her mood. Autumn was coming, and with it, Samhain. Normally, the coven celebrated with great feasts and bonfires. When the veil between this realm and the sacred grove was thinnest, she had even been able to call forth spirits of past witches. But with the sacred grove disappearing, she didn't have a clue what would happen on Samhain.

"I just wish there was another way. A way that would guarantee he stayed." But even as she said it, she knew she was clutching at straws. The witches on the green deserved to be released, and Goddess had tasked her with doing so. All four elements were active now, and it meant she could cast in four and release them. The problem being, with the sacred grove, and Goddess now Dhara, and Thomas himself making noises about the only tether holding him to this place was Lavina, they could lose him.

Maeve was so sad for Alannah she wanted to cry, and she was determined not to let Alannah get blindsided by this. "If it was you, I would want to know."

Roderick's grim expression softened, and he cupped her shoulders. "Would you, my Maeve? Even if you knew there was nothing you could do about it?"

"Yes." Because maybe then she could fight against it or brace herself. Then again, if Roderick were gone, nothing could prepare her for his loss. "It's not fair."

"Blessed." Dhara stepped out from behind a tree. In jeans and a graphic T-shirt, she looked like any other teen, except for her glowing silvery eyes. "The balance must be set right."

Maeve was torn between kneeling and snapping. This whole Dhara/Goddess thing was going to take a lot of getting used to.

Roderick, who seemed to be handling it better than her, bowed. "Is there nothing that can be done, my lady?"

"The wrong has already been done, Roderick." Goddess stepped closer to him and touched his shoulder. "It is that wrong which must now be righted." She looked at Maeve with her strange, ancient eyes. "Thomas is out of his time, and his place, Blessed. And as much as I would spare the Blessed Alannah, the damage which will be wrought, if he stays, it will be so much worse." She took Maeve's face in hers. "Would you trust me, Blessed? Would you trust that I will take care of those I call my own?"

Put like that, there was not much she could say.

Goddess's lips twitched. "There is always more you can say, Maeve. However, it will not change what must be done."

Afternoon shadows shifted, and Thomas materialized beside a large oak.

Great! Now they had a bloody gathering. The very thing they'd been trying to prevent by taking this conversation for a walk.

"Do I get a vote?" Thomas's mouth twisted into a wry grin. The trees behind him were dimly visible through his flickering form. He was growing more insubstantial.

Roderick swore and clenched his fists.

The pain he felt about Thomas fading seeped into the bond, and Maeve felt how much this was costing him too. Thomas had been his brother in arms, his companion, and his friend. They had fought together the night Thomas had died, and when she and Roderick had entered this new time, Thomas had been an anchor. Roderick had been hiding from her how much this was tearing him apart.

Maeve took his hand and threaded her fingers through his.

"Of course," Roderick said and then checked himself and looked at Goddess. "By your leave, my lady?"

Goddess nodded and motioned Thomas to continue.

"Do it," Thomas said. He touched his chest. "This is tearing Lavina apart, and it's worse now that Goddess is amongst us, and all four elements are active. Do it soon."

Roderick nodded and resolve bled down the bond, coppery and sharp. "Tonight."

"Tonight." Thomas inclined his head. Then he looked up at Maeve, and his eyes were so somber she wanted to cry even more. "And don't tell her," he said. "I don't want her hurting herself trying to change the inevitable. It will be harder for both of us if she knows."

And Maeve was beaten. She would fight Roderick, even argue with Goddess, but Thomas had given his life for the coven all those years ago, and he had a right to decide the manner of his fate. "Okay," she whispered, the guilt over betraying Alannah burning through her.

Thomas disappeared again.

Maeve asked Goddess, "Do you know what will happen?"

Goddess's expression grew sorrowful. "It must be done before Samhain. Or the lost ones will never be able to return."

"Samhain." Roderick frowned, and a surge of realization shot down the bond. "Of course."

"What?" Maeve tried to pry the answer out through their bond.

"All the different attacks, all the gathering forces." Roderick growled and shook his head. "I should have realized before. It's all been building."

Maeve wasn't entirely following. "To Samhain?'

"Yes." He tugged her against his chest. "At least we now know when Rhiannon's attack is planned."

It made sense. Samhain brought tremendous power with it—if a person knew how to tap those powers. More ancient than all of them, Rhiannon would know. "Are you sure?"

Roderick rested his chin on her head. "Aye, Blessed, she will harness the power of Samhain."

"Is that true?" Maeve turned to Goddess for extra confirmation.

Dhara's eyes had lost the silver light as she blinked at the spot where Thomas had vanished. "Was that guy, like, a ghost or something?"

⁂

ALANNAH STOOD on the battlements and watched as Maeve and Roderick walked hand in hand back to the castle. They'd been in the forest, and the dejected slump of Maeve's shoulders augured badly for the conversation they'd just had.

Thomas hadn't been near her since their return, but she sensed him around her.

"I know you're there," she said.

Wind whistled lightly through the stone crevices around her.

The others had told her about the sacred grove and the old witches' spirits moving on, but it was the loaded silence that followed the conversation they'd had in the salon last night that spoke louder.

She knew. "I can feel you getting weaker." Like a part of her was being leached from her being. "You're bonded to Lavina, and she has to move on."

Wind chilled the tears on her cheeks.

The gray autumn day reflected her mood. Even the colors on the changing trees seemed muted and dull. "You have to go with her," she said. "I suppose some part of me has always known that."

Movement flickered near the tower wall, but it shifted back into shadows.

"You weren't supposed to be in this time." Her chest constricted around the growing ache. "We were never supposed to meet." And then she spoke the taboo between them. "Never supposed to fall in love." She wrapped her arms around her as if she could contain the pain inside. "And I do love you, Thomas. I can't stop it any more than I can stop what happens next."

"Alannah?" Sinead called up the staircase.

She wiped her face with her sleeve. There would be time for tears. After. She turned and ducked to clear the top of the small arched doorway that led back inside.

As soft as a leaf falling, she heard him. "And I love you. Be happy, my love."

MAEVE'S GUILT nearly choked her as she followed Roderick through the secret passageway from the caverns to the village.

Following, Alexander and Bronwyn held hands. They would need a witch from every element to make this work. Mags was missing, but Dhara could call air.

Alannah and Sinead walked behind them.

With every step, Maeve wanted to turn and warn her, but she had given Thomas her word.

Roderick took her hand and squeezed. They had to release the witches and do it now. Samhain was only a few weeks away.

Taylor had insisted on coming, and she followed the twins with Niamh and Warren. Behind them, came Andy and Debra.

Last, but hardly least, came Kate and Dhara.

All too soon, the tunnel ended in the crypt below the village church. Motioning them to wait, Roderick ascended the staircase to the graveyard first.

He disappeared from view for a moment, and then came back. "All is well," he called down.

Maeve followed him up the mossy, damp stairs and breathed the fresh air of the still night.

The green was empty, with a few stray bits of litter from the crowds who occupied it during the day.

Andy had done one of his computer things, and the police had cleared the green that night, but he'd warned them that a stray person could still be hanging around.

It couldn't be helped. The witches who had sacrificed everything for the future deserved to be freed.

A dog barked in the village, and a lone car drove the road circling the green and turned off. Dim strains of televisions drifted over from the houses.

The wards kissed her awareness as she moved deeper into the green and crossed them behind Roderick.

Alexander, Roderick, and Warren spread out in a protective arc in front of them.

Dhara appeared at her elbow. "You need to do it now."

Nodding, Maeve drew fire and opened her magic to the lost souls.

One by one they appeared, as she had last seen them all those hundreds of years ago.

Colleen stood swaying with her arms raised. Blood streamed down her arms. She said something that none of them could hear and then crumpled to the ground.

Beside her, Lavina took the knife and slashed her wrists. She raised her arms, calling east and air as she had that long ago night. Lavina kept her arms raised until the wounds to her wrists became too much, and she dropped to the ground as well.

The scene played out, like it had that night, as one witch from each element called her cardinal point and then fell.

One by one around the circle, until they were all lying on the ground like broken dolls.

Maeve felt again her terror and confusion of that night, the dawning horror of what they'd planned.

And then it started again with Colleen back on her feet, with her hands raised.

Maeve watched it play out once more before she stepped into the center of the ghostly witches. Roderick stood beside her. That night, he had almost not made it in time. She had been distraught that she would lose him, and then, at the last moment, he had burst onto the green and held her close as the magic took them into stasis. Lavina had sensed Thomas die that night, and in her ghostly existence, she was condemned to that agony time and time again.

Maeve turned to Alannah and Sinead and nodded. It was time.

Taking Alannah's hand, Sinead stepped forward. "From the north, we call earth." Green light sparked between their clasped hands and grew into a glowing nimbus.

It spread over them into a radiant sphere around them.

Dhara was next, and she nodded her reassurance to Kate before she stepped closer to the spirit witches. "From the east, I call air." Yellow light surrounded her and twirled lazily in the air above her.

The trapped witches slowed in their grisly pantomime. Colleen stopped altogether, and as Dhara called air, so did Lavina.

Niamh crossed and stood opposite Sinead and Alannah. Raising her hands, she said, "From the south, I call fire."

Red light sprang from her and danced around her.

And finally, Bronwyn, stood opposite Dhara. "From the west, I call water."

Now, it was her turn, and Maeve looked to Roderick.

He nodded. This had to be done.

Maeve raised her arms. "Goddess, hear our prayer."

White light flickered into life from within Goddess and lit her like a softly glowing torch. "I hear your prayer, my Blessed."

"We cast in four, this our spell." Maeve pulled earth, air, fire, and then water toward her.

Four columns of light shot clear of their calling witches and surrounded her hands.

Bronwyn, Alannah and Sinead, and Niamh stepped clear.

Maeve wove the elemental powers around each other. "Goddess start again the march of time. Take these Blessed from this place and return them to whence they must bide."

Goddess's light grew brighter.

Shadowy male figures flickered into life behind the witches. The phantom coimhdeacht, the spirits of the men who had died beside their witches on that horrible night.

Maeve lowered her arms and directed the woven thread into the center of the dead witches. "By air, by earth, by fire, and by water, we cleanse this land. We purify this place, and we end this living death."

Magic crept through the ground, spreading like a stain. Each light located and filled the witch of its element.

"Goddess, release these, your Blessed." Maeve spoke the final line of the incantation. "So mote it be."

The living witches echoed her softly. "So mote it be."

Goddess stepped closer. Her white light had grown brighter until it was hard to keep looking at her. She stepped into the center of the clearing. "Your service here is ended." White light shot from her into the ground. Like a wave, it rolled over the ground and submerged the other light streams as it went.

The light hit Lavina and lit up her face. She turned to Maeve and smiled. "Blessed be."

And then she was gone.

The spirit witches blinked out as the light hit them. The light kept moving, past the circle of living witches until it reached the spirit coimhdeacht and it swept them with it.

Thomas went last, his gaze locked on Alannah. His voice echoed softly. "Live on and to your fullest."

He was gone.

Alannah stared at the place where Thomas had disappeared for the last time until her vision grew blurry. *Live on and to your fullest.* Screw him for that. How the fuck was she supposed to do that now that he was gone?

"Alannah." Sinead put an arm around her shoulders. "Come, we need to get back to Baile."

Back to Baile? For what? She wanted to fade into the ether with the other spirits who had been liberated.

Her feet moved independently of her mind as Sinead led her back behind the wards and down into the crypts again.

"I wanted to tell you." Maeve's tear-streaked face appeared in her line of vision. "But Thomas asked me not to. He said it was better this way."

Better for who, she wanted to shout. But none of this was Maeve's fault.

Poor Maeve, so guilt-stricken about something she didn't need to be.

Her voice sounded strangely normal as she said, "It doesn't matter. He wanted to go."

An irrational anger inside her wanted to ask why he hadn't wanted to stay. To stay for her. With her. But she knew the answer. Thomas could not stay. None of the spirits that had been trapped here had belonged here.

"Alannah?" Roderick touched her hand.

She turned to look at him. Her neck muscles felt stiff and awkward.

Roderick opened her hand and pressed something into it. "He wanted me to give you this."

She stared at the flat metal disc in her palm without registering it.

"It's his family crest," Roderick said. "He had it on a medallion he used to wear around his neck." He cleared his throat. "When he was still living. I found it in the barracks this morning."

She traced the image of a large bird with her thumb.

"Come." Sinead moved her forward again.

Her legs felt like jelly, but Sinead's arm around her kept her upright. Closing her fingers around the medallion, she clung to it so hard it dug into her palm.

Goddess walked just ahead of her.

"Why?" She didn't realize she'd yelled the word until everyone stopped and stared at her.

Goddess turned and looked at her. A sad, sweet smile spread slowly over her face. "I am sorry for your pain, Blessed."

Alannah didn't want her to be sorry; she wanted her to take

it away. She wanted Goddess to bring Thomas back, make him alive again. "Why did you make me love him if you were always going to take him away?"

Protectively, Kate moved closer to Dhara.

"It was not his time, Blessed," Goddess said, her eyes glowing. "There was nothing but pain for him here."

And now there was nothing but pain for her.

Somehow she was walking again.

The passage ascended into the caverns. She hadn't really looked at the caverns when they were going to the village. She had known what would happen, had even been so bloody stupid as to believe she was prepared for it, resolved. They'd said their private goodbye on the battlements.

Now she looked at the caverns.

All four elements glowed from the embedded crystals in the walls. Green, red, yellow, and blue, they twinkled and gleamed within their intricate patterns. At another time, she would have marveled at the beauty of it.

Tonight, it felt like a betrayal. Each one of those patterns represented a past witch, told the story of her life and her magic. And woven in there somewhere, was Lavina's story, and with hers, Thomas's.

He had barely even said goodbye. Was that for his sake or hers? She didn't know, and it didn't really matter.

Fresh sea breeze met them at the opening to the caverns and she breathed it deep.

Sinead held her elbow as they climbed the stairs to the bailey.

In the bailey, Roderick had stopped and was looking around him keenly. "They're gone," he said. "All of them."

Warren nodded as if he felt it too. "The old coimhdeacht."

"Come, darling." Sinead kept her walking. "Let's get you inside." Sinead knew that she would want privacy before she broke down.

A shadow flit over her, and a soft brush of air passed so close to her head that she stopped. The shrill whistle of a raptor made her look up.

Moonlight catching on its white and tan plumage, a kestrel circled above her.

As she looked up at it, the kestrel called one more time and then flew up to settle on the ledge of her bedroom window.

Niamh stopped and stared up at the kestrel, before she turned to Alannah. "It's here for you," she said. "It's here to watch over you."

CHAPTER FORTY

"It's there again."

Alannah turned to find Sinead glaring at the light-brown bird perched on their window ledge. It had been four days since Thomas had left, and the bird arrived every morning and sat outside her window.

Niamh told her it was female, and the same bird that had perched on Thomas's arm when he'd first discovered that animals could touch his spectral form.

Torn between shooing it and finding it comforting, Alannah joined her sister at the window. "Should we open the window?"

"We're not Niamh." Sinead snorted then cocked her head and studied the bird. "Unless you've morphed into Snow White, and I can expect all sorts of woodland creatures to pay us a visit."

Alannah managed a smile for Sinead's benefit. Her twin was doing her best, but she was hurting too. Moving slowly, she edged forward and opened the window.

The kestrel cocked her head and studied the open window. She ruffled her wings and hopped closer.

"Should we give her a name?" Sinead watched the bird.

The kestrel looked right back at her through the opened window.

"Niamh will kill us if we do," Alannah said, and then on a surge of rebellion, "How about Kai?"

"Kai the Kestrel." Sinead narrowed her eyes as she stirred it around her brainbox. "I like it."

Kai craned her neck closer to the open window, and Alannah held her breath.

"You know what?" Sinead was studying her now. Or rather her throat.

Self-consciously, Alannah touched her chest. "What?"

"The medallion." Sinead touched the metal disc Alannah had taken to wearing. "There's a bird on it too."

"Right." Alannah tipped up the medallion and studied it. "I haven't really looked at it."

Sinead leaned closer and examined Thomas's medallion. "And it looks a lot like Kai."

"Huh." As much as she would like to believe Kai was connected to Thomas in some wonderful way, she was all out of the moonbeams and mysticism type of magic.

"We should research Thomas's family. Andy has all the records and those tricksy little internet fingers of his. He could see if the crest on the medallion matches Kai. Maybe there really is a connection to Thomas."

Her resistance to the idea surprised her. "No." Feeling depleted of moonbeams and mysticism was different to finding proof it didn't exist in any form. "Let's just leave it as a possibility."

Sinead gave her a sad smile and nodded. "Possibilities it is then." She flung an arm around Alannah's shoulders. "We're a sad pair, aren't we?"

"It's a bit pathetic really." Alannah leaned into Sinead's comfort. At least they still had each other. "I loved him, but it's not like we were ever a real relationship."

"You were real." Sinead leaned her head against hers. "You don't have to press sweaty bits together to be real." She sighed. "Noah kissed me once."

Sinead had been holding out on her. "He did?"

"Uh-huh." Sinead made a face. "It was a really good kiss."

"Good or fantastic?" Concentrating on someone else's drama did help.

Sinead blushed. "Fucking fantastic. I nearly jumped him in the middle of the forest."

"You should have jumped him." They'd both run out of time.

Sinead huffed. "I absolutely should have."

Kai took off from the window ledge, and they watched until she flew out of sight.

As much as she would like to stay in their suite and wallow, Alannah wasn't really the type. She preferred to stay busy. "Let's go and fix those wards."

Sinead nodded. "Let's do it. And then you can bake enough to feed a small army."

"I'm not sure I'm up for that yet." Thomas had always hung about her in the kitchen, chatting, flirting, making her laugh.

"Sorry." Sinead grimaced. "It will get better, Alannah. There will come a day when you're not so sad."

She nodded because Sinead expected it. "I know. And the same for you. But until that day, let's make those wards safe."

Baile was quiet as they walked downstairs and crossed the great hall. Andy's office door was open, and Debra sat by the window working on a laptop. She glanced up and waved.

In the kitchen, Niamh and Warren were taking advantage of the empty room, and he had her on the kitchen table as he kissed the crap out of her.

Sinead absolutely should have jumped Noah in the forest.

Warren must have heard something because he leaped away from Niamh as if she'd caught fire.

"Carry on." Sinead waved at him. "Don't let us stop you."

Blushing, Niamh climbed off the table. "Not the best place for it anyway."

"Right." Alannah ignored the pinch of envy. Even if Thomas had been here, they couldn't have had what Niamh and Warren did.

"Your kestrel went hunting," Niamh said. "She'll be back."

Footsteps clattered down the stairs from the great hall and Taylor trotted into the kitchen. She ran to the door and peered out. "Is she here yet?"

"She?" Sinead glanced at Alannah. They had heard about Mags being kidnapped by Rhiannon and were now waiting along with the rest of Baile for her return. Even Sasha couldn't give them a clear update, as the ship's captain had gone radio silent for security reasons.

Sinead hung over Taylor's shoulder and stared at the empty bailey. "Is it Mags?"

"No." Taylor deflated a bit. "But there is someone coming, and she's connected to Niamh."

Niamh looked startled. "Me?"

"Uh-huh." Taylor nodded and looked proud of herself. "And she's not alone. She's bringing another coimhdeacht." She gave her father a naughty look. "And he is such a snack."

Warren jabbed a finger at her. "Oy! Settle down, you."

"Hotter than Roderick." Taylor giggled and backed away from Warren. "Even hotter than Alexander."

"That's it." Warren lunged for Taylor and tossed her over his shoulder. "You're going to your room. For the rest of your life." He pretended to reconsider. "Well, at least until you've lost all your teeth."

Alannah joined in the laughter. It was good to be home, even if it felt empty and cold without Thomas.

Niamh joined Sinead at the door. "Someone's coming for me?" She called over her shoulder to a still giggling Taylor. "Are you sure?"

"Niamh!" Taylor rolled her eyes. "I am always sure about these things."

"I'll let Roderick know," Warren said. Then he snorted. "Although he probably already does. He has a sense for coimhdeacht heading this way."

Sinead walked to the other end of the kitchen and motioned Alannah to join her. "We'll see everyone later," she called over her shoulder. "We're going to have a look at those wards."

They headed for the kitchen garden, taking the back passages though the storage areas and the old laundry, where the stench of Alannah's fuel of the future hung heavy in the air. She really needed to make it smell decent if it was ever going to be a thing.

They let themselves out into a chilly, overcast day.

The gardens had fared well in their absence, although she wasn't sure what she'd expected to happen in a few weeks. It felt like they'd been gone so much longer.

Sinead led the way to the far end of the kitchen gardens and into the orchards. Apples were ripening on the large, ancient trees, and they would need to pick them soon. She'd always loved the process of picking and preserving the harvest. It made her feel in tune with the life rhythm of the land.

Crouching beside Sinead, she dug her fingers in the earth, touching her twin's.

Earth leaped in response to their call, sure and steady and strong as an earthquake. It was thrilling to finally feel the full extent of their power.

They took a moment to feel the land, the plodding aware-ness of the large trees, the languid slowing down of the grasses and shrubs as they prepared for winter. Insects skittered around their awareness, an integral part of the earth they served.

Alannah took the lead and guided their blessing to the wards.

With earth active, they could see the wards clearly, like an intricate spiderweb of white light. After finding the flaw, they paused and studied it. With their newly heightened magic, the blood magic made her belly heave. Last time they'd been this close, they'd been viciously repelled.

Sinead strengthened the connection to earth and called more power into their blessing. "Let's take out the rubbish," she murmured.

They encircled the flaw with their blessing.

Blood magic struck out, hitting their magic like someone pounding into them with a shovel.

Sinead called even more earth. Trees stirred above them, bushes rustled, and long grasses bent in their direction.

Seen clearly for the first time, the flaw in the wards was like a creeper plant. Its tentacles grew from a central point and seeped into the gleaming light of the wards, turning them dull and lifeless on contact.

Alannah struck. She grabbed the thing like a weed and tugged.

It lashed back and she had to grit her teeth against the force. The pain in her head grew, and Sinead screwed her eyes shut.

Alannah drew more from the well of power Sinead had gathered.

Her vision blackened, and she had to close her eyes as well. Tightening her grip, she pulled harder.

The flaw shifted an infinitesimal amount.

"Keep going," Sinead rasped as she pulled even more earth.

Tiny fissures spread from where their hands were buried in the soil, zigzagging through the loosely packed ground.

Alannah took a breath and heaved on the nasty interloper. She kept the pressure going.

Blood leaked out of Sinead's nose, but her fierce gaze told Alannah not to stop.

The flaw gave with a creak and an ear-exploding *boom*. Once free of the wards, it withered like a dead plant and disintegrated into dust.

Alannah then began the delicate work of taking the minute filaments that made up the wards and weaving them back together again. When she was done, she waited to see if her repair would take. Power pulsed through the wards, passing seamlessly over the repair. They had done it.

Dropping on her back, Sinead released earth. "Take that, you bitch!"

THE RECOIL THREW Rhiannon across her sitting room. She slammed into the wall, and a bone in her shoulder crunched on impact. For a moment, the world wavered in front of her eyes, and she thought she might pass out.

So, they'd repaired the wards.

She licked blood off her split lip. From the moment she'd felt earth activate, she'd known it was only a matter of time.

A minion scuttled closer. "Mistress, are you all right?"

"Get away from me." She kicked the woman back. "I'm fine."

And she was fine. All four elements were active, and there was so much magic, beautiful, glorious magic. Just there for the asking. Just there, waiting for her, until Samhain.

Her annoyance at being bested by those stupid earth witches faded. It was too late in any case. Those wards couldn't help them anymore.

"Come, my little toy," she whispered. "Do what I have created you to do."

CHAPTER FORTY-ONE

Niamh was beginning to think Taylor had gotten it wrong, and nobody was coming. She'd been hanging around the bailey for most of the day.

"Niamh." Taylor rounded the side of the castle. "We have time to make another TikTok."

Dear Goddess, she was deeply regretting agreeing to do these bloody things. Still, her followers were now well into the hundreds of thousands and each new TikTok got more views than the last. She left the commenting and whatnot to Taylor.

And speaking of dear Goddess, Dhara wandered out of the kitchen. "You guys are on TikTok?"

Most of the time, she looked so much like a normal teen that it was hard to reconcile her with Goddess. But Niamh had also seen her eyes go silver and seen the way she'd released the trapped witches on the green.

"It was Taylor's idea," she said. "We think it's going to help me build a platform for my blessing."

Dhara nodded and approached shyly.

It must be difficult for her to have had her life upended in this way.

"You're a guardian, right?" Dhara also had a source of knowledge that could only have come from Goddess. "That must be so cool."

"Right!?" Taylor widened her eyes at Dhara. "We made the best TikTok the other day with one of the wolves. People lost their minds over it." Her cheeks flushed with excitement, and she spoke faster. "There was this one guy, who was like there's no way that can be real. And then all these other people jumped on his ass and shouted him down. It was the best."

Dhara peered over Taylor's shoulder at her phone. "What are you gonna do today?"

"I don't know." Taylor peeked at her. "I thought maybe something with the dogs."

"Yeah." Dhara nodded enthusiastically. "People love dogs. Or cats."

"Cats!" Taylor looked impressed. "We haven't done a cat TikTok."

Niamh was beginning to feel like the odd man out.

Taylor looked up at her. "Can you call one of your cats, Niamh? Maybe that Scottish wildcat thingie."

Niamh repressed the urge to point out that she didn't call her cats like they were good little soldiers but dropped it. One step at a time. Sunning itself on the far side of Baile, the wildcat definitely didn't want to be bothered, so she quested out to a village tabby who had taken to hanging around. "There's a cat on his way."

"Good." Taylor's fingers flew over her phone as she did… something. "Because we don't have much time before your visitor gets here, and we really need to post something today." She looked to Dhara for support. "You have to keep your content fresh, or you start bleeding followers."

The cat sashayed closer, curious to see what was going on.

For the next fifteen minutes, Niamh did as she was told. She'd learned not to argue with Taylor when it came to making

TikToks. She was getting better at it too, but she was still relieved when Taylor pressed the load button on her phone victoriously. "Done! And perfect timing as well. Here she comes."

Goddess raised her head, her eyes gleaming silver, and she smiled beatifically. "Ah! My new Blessed, and she brings with her a Beloved."

Niamh saw nobody, and she squinted in the direction the girls were staring.

A silver sedan began the ascent from the village to Baile.

Roderick and Warren came striding from the practice yards. From the healer's hall, Bronwyn led Alexander into the bailey. Andy and Debra came through the kitchen and joined them. All of them stood and watched the car creep up the road.

"Where are the twins?" Bronwyn looked around them.

Roderick glanced at her and then went back to watching the car. "They're resting after repairing the wards."

"Good." Alexander nodded and slid an arm around Bronwyn's shoulders.

"What's going on?" Kate joined them.

"A new coimhdeacht," Roderick said.

"And a new witch." Maeve nudged him in the gut. "Let's not forget about a new witch."

Roderick winked at her.

"Did someone say something about a new witch arriving?" Hannah, with Charlie on her hip, wandered over from the healer's hall. She was spending more and more time in there.

As it followed the winding road, the sedan disappeared from view.

"I hope those nutters don't give them any trouble," Alexander said. "Do you think we should go and see if they need help?"

Warren answered. "Nope! Let's see if this new bloke has got

the stuff. If he is who we think he is, a couple of religious nutters won't stop him."

Niamh tried to think who it could be. The only other witches she knew…no! Well, she had invited them, but she hadn't thought at the time…and with Ulwazi dying.

"You think it could be them?" Warren slid an arm around her waist and pulled her against his warm bulk.

She really hoped so.

The car reappeared around the bend and headed their way. It cleared the gatehouse and rolled slowly into the bailey.

Nofoto peered through the windscreen, caught sight of Niamh, and grinned and waved.

"It is them. It's Nofoto."

The passenger door opened before the car had properly stopped, and Nofoto leaped out. Bundled up in a coat and hat, she threw her arms wide and grinned. "We are here."

"And I'm so glad you are." Niamh grabbed her into a huge hug. Their experiences in that cave had bound them together across the distance. "Let me introduce you."

A tall man unfolded from the driver's seat. And Taylor was quite correct, the man was a snack. Actually, he was a buffet meal for twelve. Tall, dark, stacked and with a face carved from granite. His dark gaze moved over the bailey, assessing.

Warren slid an arm around her waist and murmured, "Steady on."

"Mandla." Nofoto gestured imperiously at the big man. "Come and meet everybody."

Mandla raised a dark brow, and face impassive, sauntered closer.

Nofoto wriggled beneath his arm and got her arm around his waist. "He is my protector."

On Mandla's dark skin, the coimhdeacht markings were a darker brown, but just as visible. Unlike Nofoto, he was not all wrapped up but wearing a button down with the sleeves rolled up to the elbows and a pair of jeans.

"Mandla." Roderick held out his hand. "Welcome, brother. You are one of us."

Mandla took Roderick's hand and shook it. He stopped and studied the markings on Roderick's arm. "We have the same marks."

"I have them too." Warren held out his arm for Mandla. "Which means, for better or worse, you're one of us."

"See." Nofoto beamed up at him as she patted Mandla's huge chest. "I told you we would be welcome."

Mandla gave her an inscrutable look.

"And this is Niamh." Nofoto gestured to her.

Introductions were made in the bailey before Alexander invited the guests into the kitchen. He put the kettle on for tea, and they all took a seat at the table.

Niamh wished Alannah had done some baking, and then felt horrible for being so selfish. Alannah needed time and love from them, not endless demands to fill their bellies. She turned back to Nofoto. "How's your mother?"

While Mandla loomed near the window, Nofoto had taken a seat at the table. "She's fine." Nofoto smiled. "Busy now that she has taken over from my grandmother."

Nofoto's grandmother, Ulwazi, had died the night Niamh activated fire. She couldn't help thinking that Ulwazi would still be alive if she hadn't intruded herself into their lives.

Warren reached beneath the table and put a comforting hand on her thigh. He carried his own guilt about that night.

"Actually." Nofoto looked at Mandla before she spoke again. "She's only okay."

Niamh did not like the sound of that.

Neither did Roderick, as he got super focused and leaned his elbows on the table. "There's trouble?"

"Yes." Nofoto grimaced and pulled the hat off her head.

Mandla moved closer to her.

"There has been some trouble in South Africa. My mother has had to take our people and leave Johannesburg." She glanced at Mandla. "They have gone to the rural areas."

Faces around the table turned grim. Nobody really wanted to be the one to guess at the reason.

"Rhiannon." Alexander broke the stalemate.

"Her people." Nofoto gripped her hands together on the table. "There have been a number of incidents involving my mother's people. South Africa has a lot of crime, so it took us a while to identify that we were being targeted."

Every way they turned, that bitch was already there. "Is everyone okay?"

"So far." Nofoto shrugged. "But after my mother was run off the road last week, we decided to make ourselves scarce."

Kate and Dhara looked at each other, and then Kate spoke. "We had similar trouble in Canada." She looked at Nofoto. "I'm going to need to go back and help find all my people."

"Sasha is reporting attacks against his group," Andy said. "They've also warned their people to be careful and are talking of going underground."

"Because I have Mandla, we decided I would be the best person to come here and see if you could help," Nofoto said.

Roderick looked at Mandla and then Nofoto. "And how did your bond happen?"

"After Niamh activated fire, I came into my powers." Nofoto smiled and unbuttoned her coat. "It surprised the hell out of me at first."

Mandla grunted.

"So, you're a fire witch?" It didn't matter, but Niamh was glad she had a coven sister sharing her element.

Nofoto slipped out of her coat and winked at Niamh. "I am."

"In the years since Goddess has been dormant, many blessings have changed and adapted." Dhara's eyes had gone slightly silver. "In different places in the world, they have developed different skills to suit the needs of where they live."

They had Dhara, and then Goddess, and now apparently the two of them at the same time. This was going to take a lot of getting used to.

"What is your blessing?" Maeve leaned forward, her face eager.

"Well…it seems that I can affect the weather." Nofoto cleared her throat and looked wary. "You never said anything about having a weather blessing."

"Weather witch?" Aghast, Roderick studied her. "I haven't seen one of those since the coven numbered in the hundreds, and then it was a type of side blessing. Normally a sensitivity around weather that a warden could have."

Nofoto laughed, and it was a happy sound that made Niamh smile. "Oh, I can do a little more than that."

Mandla huffed and shook his head.

"How exciting!" Maeve's eyes twinkled. "I'd love to see you in action."

"What more can you do?" Alexander cocked his head and looked intrigued.

"I can make it rain." Nofoto shrugged. "Call up a storm, make it go away."

"Cool." Taylor stared at Nofoto with admiration. "Could you create a hurricane, or a tornado?"

"No." Mandla gave Nofoto a hard look. "Don't even think about it."

She waved him off. "Theoretically, I suppose I could, but that kind of thing could be fairly devastating."

"That might be useful." Alexander brought the teapot to the table. "There's a battle coming, and who knows what Rhiannon is bringing our way?"

Roderick stilled and looked toward the gardens. "But at least the wards are now safe."

"Oh!" Taylor perked up suddenly and a delighted smile spread over her face. "Mags is home."

Tires scrunched on the gravel of the bailey.

The Chronicles Conclude in *Joined In Spirit.*
The Cré-witch Chronicles is a complete five-book series consisting of ***Born In Water, Purged In Fire, Raised In Air, Cradled In Earth,*** and ***Joined In Spirit.*** Read the prequel and origin story , ***Cast In Stone***, to discover Maeve and Roderick's story.

Joined In Spirit #5 Cré-witch Chronicles

A Deadly Twist
A Blood Witch Rising
And a final battle in which winner takes all.

All four cardinal points are now active, but the increase in power for the cré-witch coven means a corresponding boost for their enemy, who is deadlier and more determined than ever to steal it all for herself. And with a fledgling Goddess vulnerable to attack, the witches must rally to protect her, all while grappling with a rule change to the laws of magic that bears far-reaching consequences.

Mags is once more safe at home, but what should be a joyous occasion quickly disintegrates into tragedy as Rhiannon strikes at the very heart of the coven. As the coven reels, her hostile forces surround Baile.

Around the world, allies are being hounded and killed. Only one coven member can rise to meet Rhiannon's challenge, and in this final game, it's winner take all as the Cré-witch Chronicles conclude.

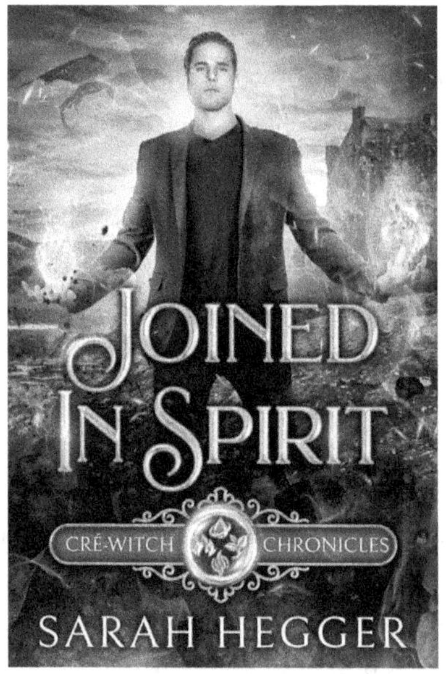

Get Joined In Spirit

For first dibs on news, deals, and giveaways, and so much more, join the @Home Collective

Or if Facebook is more your thing, join the Sarah Hegger Collective

Anything and everything you need to know on my website http://sarahhegger.com

ABOUT THE AUTHOR

Born British and raised in South Africa, Sarah Hegger suffers from an incurable case of wanderlust. Her match? A hot Canadian engineer, whose marriage proposal she accepted six short weeks after they first met. Together they've made homes in seven different cities across three different continents (and back again once or twice). If only it made her multilingual, but the best she can manage is idiosyncratic English, fluent Afrikaans, conversant Russian, pigeon Portuguese, even worse Zulu and enough French to get herself into trouble. Mimicking her globe trotting adventures, Sarah's career path began as a gainfully employed actress, drifted into public relations, settled a moment in advertising, and eventually took root in the fertile soil of her first love, writing. She also moonlights as a wife and mother. She currently lives in Ottawa, Canada, filling her empty nest with fur babies. Part footloose buccaneer, part quixotic observer of life, Sarah's restless heart is most content when reading or writing books.

Hegger's utterly delightful first Ghost Falls contemporary is what other romance novels want to grow up to be." – Publisher's Weekly, Best Books of 2017

"The very talented Hegger kicks off an enjoyable new series set in the small Utah town of Ghost Falls. This charming and fun-filled book has everything from passion and humor to betrayal and revenge." –
Jill M Smith, RT Books Reviews 2017 – Contemporary Love and Laughter Nominee

Becoming Bella
"Hegger excels at depicting familial relationships and friendships of all kinds, including purely platonic friendships between women and men. Tears, laughter, and a dollop of suspense make a memorable story that readers will want to revisit time and again."
Publisher's Weekly, Starred Review

"…you have a terrific new romance that Hegger fans are going to love. Don't miss out!"
Jill M. Smith – RT Book Reviews

Blatantly Blythe
"Ms. Hegger has delivered another captivating read for this series in this book that was packed with emotion…" Bec, Bookmagic Review, Harlequin Junkie, HJ Recommends.

Nobody's Fool
"Hegger offers a breath of fresh air in the romance genre." –
Terri Dukes, RT Book Reviews

Nobody's Princess
"Hegger continues to live up to her rapidly growing reputation

for breathing fresh air into the romance genre." – Terri Dukes, RT Book Reviews

"I have read the entire Willow Park Series. I have loved each of the books … Nobody's Princess is my favorite of all time." Harlequin Junkie, Top Pick

My Lady Faye

Conquering William

Defying Roger

Henry's Honor

Love & War Series

The Marriage Parley

The Betrothal Melee

Western Historical Romance

The Soiled Dove Series

Sugar Ellie

Standalone

The Bride Gift

Bad Wolfe On The Rise

Wild Honey